SYMUTAL

by Dean Alexandrou

SYSTEM
SIMULATE
MUTATE
FRACTAL

SYMUTAL

version 1.20a

Written by Dean Alexandrou

Cover artwork by Solenn Lecorne

Illustrations by Pemapsorn Kritsadacharoenpong
and Dean Alexandrou

ISBN 978-1-7399787-0-9 (Paperback)
ISBN 978-1-7399787-1-6 (eBook)

Dedicated to my love,

Olya Petryk

Contents

Prologue

Part 1 – Concurrency

Part 2 – Processing

Part 3 – Execution

Epilogue

Appendix

Prologue

CHAPTER ONE

· Statistical Crimes

——o Day -60 o——

The ping of the oven cut like a shard of glass through brain tissue, tearing apart the cloth of melancholia that she wore like a hood.

Wrenching the chicken and rice from the SR beam heater, a cloud of steaming ginger curled its way around her face, softening the lines of her eyebags. Her nostrils expanded. Cheap make-up melted in hot vapour, running down lines of fatigue on vape damaged skin.

As she sunk her teeth into sham reconstituted flesh a fleck of ginger sauce dripped from the corner of her lips, to land on a white badge of acrylic that was pinned like a flag of surrender to her tacky, blue polyester dress.

"208. Marena Chu" it proclaimed in bold humiliation. *"Buy me a drink."* it added like salt to a wound.

She sipped a lukewarm cup of liquid cardboard that was labelled "coffee" by its manufacturers, wanting to spit the mouthful of blandness over her kitchen floor, but forcing herself to swallow in subjugation. She needed the caffeine.

She tossed her clothes onto a stained and unwashed floor, taking in her form as she stood in front of the bathroom mirror. The shoulders slumped but were not broken. She wiped mascara from her eyes and with it a layer of depression, revealing another, deeper layer, staring back at her in unmasked honesty. Though her lips did not move she screamed. This was not how life was meant to turn out.

"Come on Marena snap out of it," she mouthed in a whisper.

She felt at times as though the universe was pitted against her – that behind the scenes there was an aethereal order to nature that she couldn't quite grasp – its threads shifting away from her as she reached out to touch them. Threads that formed a pattern which, if she could discern it, would lead her out of the life she now lived.

Her eyes began to close.

"Snap the fuck out of it," she repeated, this time an order.

She forced down the remainder of the coffee in a single defiant mechanism. Fuck the order of nature. Hard work was the way out. She splashed cold water on her face.

Every day she went through a version of this introspective reverie, telling herself the same thing, motivating herself into action after her night shift at the bar before the next job started. She needed both jobs to make ends meet. Sleep could wait.

She adjusted her hair, neatened herself up, and breathed calmly, checking the time – *5:27am, Sun 10 Dec 2056*. That left ten minutes to get dressed and be out of the door. "Ugh..."

She hauled on a set of overalls, and adjusted a label on the chest, straightening her back. *"Marena Chu. Hoshoku-Sha Technology. Sanitation."* Pristine, refined, sophisticated... Who was she kidding?

The door was almost closed as she checked herself. "Keys!" Dashing back into the room, she scanned the chaotic clutter of her apartment, eyes flicking off the multifaceted surfaces of a thousand unfinished tasks. There they were, draped on a bedside table on a chain of baubles and trinkets.

As she picked them up she paused. Under the keys four innocent, shining eyes were smiling back at her in carefree abandon. The photo of her two young children held her like a frozen angel. A reminder of happier times. She smiled back. Her mind was all over the place this morning.

She inhaled slowly and deeply, wanting to curl into a ball and be rocked to sleep more than anything else in the world. "See you soon my babies," she whispered.

She knew why she would always work hard for a better life.

As a single mother with a low earning index on the Yasuo scale she had been categorised by the Guidance And Planning Body's algorithm as unfit to support two children. Pash and Suni had promptly been taken and put into homes with people deemed more apt to provide societal care. She had no idea where. Her only recourse was to prove that by earning above a certain threshold she could appeal on the grounds that the algorithm had miscategorised her. That is, unless it evolved new parameters before then. She tried not to focus on the futility of her predicament.

———olo———

One hour later Marena was looking at her reflection in the bowl of a marble toilet in the offices of Hoshoku-Sha Technology. Her face disappeared in a vortex of shit and water as the growl of the flush opened its mouth at her and gulped.

A kinetic steel monolith of retro-futurism, the Hoshoku-Sha building cast a spiked shadow over a city of lesser slabs, exerting its influence like a magnet in a box of iron filings. It was not the only structure of power in this world though, or even this megalopolis. But in the end, despite all the concrete and technology, society still needed people, and people's shit still stunk.

As the water slowly refilled, Marena looked down again, lost in thought. Her reflection looked back. It scowled at the outfit she wore. It was as though the uniform had been deliberately designed to make the cleaners feel insignificant – the white plastic creases mocking their every move to scrub dirt away without themselves being tarnished.

"Yeah you look like shit," said a voice behind her. "Well, like an actual piece of shit if that's what you're using as a mirror."

"Hana," said Marena brightening, turning to look at the voice. "Welcome to my world. What are you doing here?"

"I'm taking over," replied Hana cheerfully. "Leave me a few chunks. You're going upstairs."

"Eww. Disgusting. What's happening upstairs?"

"Moniq's gonna be in late today. Do you mind covering?" asked Hana apologetically. "I would cover myself, but since my knees have been playing up, and the stairs, I'd rather do down here..."

"Where's Moniq?" fired Marena, slightly acerbically.

"It's her kid's birthday or something. I dunno," said Hana in irritation, sensing the cause of Marena's sourness and feeling it too. There was an indefinable social rule that meant some people got away with doing half the work of others due to no justifiable cause. Maybe they were pretty. Maybe they talked about the right TV shows. Who knew.

"Everyone's got fucking kids. I just don't see why you need to get other people to do your work," replied Marena.

"Yeah. I know, I know," agreed Hana in sympathy.

"There ought to be a way of measuring all these... micro imbalances, and docking them from someone's pay cheque at the end of the month," said Marena. "Or better still, splitting them amongst her coworkers who had to put the effort in to cover the gaps."

Hana handed Marena a keycard from her pocket. "Fourth floor. Left and top, all the way up to the stairwell."

"Got it," Marena said reluctantly.

"And don't disturb anything on any of the desks," added Hana. "Those are the executive offices. One of those pens is probably worth a month's pay."

Marena rolled the keycard around in her hand thoughtfully. A month's pay was a lot of money when you needed two jobs just to stay above water. She would love nothing more than to take a few days off to sleep. No. To spend time with her kids. To laugh, and play freely with those smiling beacons of her soul's light.

It would happen one day. She just had to keep working hard.

———olo———

"Good morning Moni–. Good morning Marena," said a monotone computer voice, correcting itself, as she opened the door. "Thank you for covering while Moniq is away."

"Yeah. You're welcome," said Marena to the computer voice,

wherever it was. "You figured that one out? Or you were listening in the toilets?"

"A little of both," replied the monotone voice unabashedly.

Marena said nothing, detached, marvelling at the decadence of the place. Light bounced at aesthetically pleasing angles between polished corners, or was diffused into ambience by soft leather trims. Large metallic letters, flawlessly clean, imposed themselves into the space. *"Hoshoku-Sha Technology, Gijutsu Kabushiki-Kaisha"*

Thankfully everything on this floor was already almost spotless. Nevertheless, she rolled her bucket out and mopped the gangway between desks, not wanting to shirk her adopted morning's duties.

She looked enviously through a glass window into an executive suite. Even against the general opulence of the floor, this corner room distinguished itself as a duke amongst noblemen.

She pushed open the door, and looked around, still marvelling. Things shimmered and glittered. She knew herself to be in the presence of high technology, though she could not say what it was. A gentle beep from the computer system acknowledged her entrance to the room, but the monotone voice remained silent.

Atop the table were an assortment of stationary, computers, and paraphernalia, familiar in purpose if not in design. Pens, paper, staplers. Everything just looked so futuristic, and... expensive. A black box marked *"ProtoType C"* sat snugly next to some of the files. She ignored the items on the desk though, drawn to a big, black luxury chair, and sat down, leaning back smiling.

She let her body relax as she swivelled around like a school girl, allowing herself a sense of freedom and childish abandonment. With each arc of the spin her mind was somewhere else; a young girl again playing in the park with her mother; messy hair flapping in the wind as the fake-fur of an oversized Parka covered her eyes; giggles of glee as her father spun the roundabout faster and faster, and faster. She was as free as an eddy of the wind with none of the weight of the world upon her shoulders, her legs swinging outwards, toes stretching into spinning loops of the body's release.

Klanggg.

"Oww... Shit."

She was jolted back to reality with a throbbing lump on the side of her foot. Stationary was scattered on the floor.

"Sort yourself out Marena," she muttered, flexing her toes.

A camera lens tucked into the corner of the ceiling twitched slightly, as if stirring from sleep. Its aperture dilated slightly as it changed focus. A light indicated that something had been triggered internally.

Pushing away her juvenile fantasy of before, she collected the spilled items, replacing them on the desk one by one, neatly into their original positions.

She held up a pen against the light and studied its design. Hana was right about the price. It looked obscenely expensive. The nib was made from, what? gold? and was the handle platinum? She could only guess, but it was beautifully elegant – a fusion of material and function that left neither the worse for the pairing. The room was seemingly filled with these expensive trinkets, left idly around like discarded pebbles on a beach. Would anyone notice if it got lost, she wondered. Her heart quickened.

She exhaled sharply, almost slamming the pen back on the desk to snap herself out of the mood. Her mind was wandering so much today. She needed more sleep. Things couldn't go on like this or she'd crack. Grabbing her mop and bucket she left the room.

The camera, now fully awake and alert, followed her movements like the head of an owl. The focus and aperture reacted to every shift in the musculature of her carriage. Lights danced delicately around the rim of the lens, seeming to measure things deeper than mere physical form. They pulsated, in unison with biorhythms no human had ever been aware of.

As she stepped into the corridor the monotone voice addressed her. "Would you like a glass of water Marena? You seem, mm, bothered," it said, almost sarcastically in its neutrality and lack of empathy. "There is a free water dispenser at the end of the hallway."

"No, thanks," she replied. She continued to clean.

A magnetic lock clicked somewhere.

At the end of the hallway she stopped, and poured herself a glass of water from the dispenser. The refreshing, ice cold liquid flowed satisfyingly down her throat. She had really needed it she reflected – the computer had been right.

She swiped her keycard on an exit panel at the end of the corridor, looking forward to the cessation of her day as the end of the shift approached. Nothing happened.

She swiped again. A familiar Buuzzzzt hummed from the door – a sound known the world over as meaning Access Denied.

She tried again. Buuzzzzt again.

"Maybe I can help you with that," said a voice from behind. Not the computer this time.

A hand gripped her arm, firmly but not harshly, moving her hand away from the panel. The man, who had appeared from another door, pulled out his own keycard – one that said "Security" – and swiped it on the panel. Biiiiing, hummed the door pleasantly.

"Come this way please," said the man.

———olo———

Grey, unmarked walls managed to dominate the room through a sense of oppression, not requiring anything but the homogeneity of concrete to make their presence felt. A white light emanated from the ceiling, casting shadows of nervously twitching fingers onto a smooth, graphite surface. Wires ran from the tips of a black-gloved hand, over a few printed sheets of paper, and into the back of a vertical display, where biorhythmic charts danced, reacting to the shifts and movements of Marena.

Two people sat opposite her as she watched the data flow from her hand. She had been sitting here, nervously, for half an hour.

"Your own system let me in the door, so what's the problem?" she scowled, not sure if she was supposed to be addressing them or the camera lens pointing at her face.

Pol Chavez, the man from security who had apprehended her in the corridor, was following the lead of the other figure. *"Laura Garret: Legal Techno Adviser"* said the card on the desk. She was an awkward, spindly woman, whose body movements seemed to contradict one another, leaving a distinct feeling of uncertainty.

"Mm-hm," was all she said, standing up as if wanting to say more but stopping herself. She looked at Marena carefully, then at the shifting data lines of the charts, then back at Marena.

"I was covering for one of the other girls, because she couldn't come in today," elaborated Marena.

"Mmm," nodded Laura, "Tell us about what happened in the room, exactly."

"I just sat down on the chair, that's all. Is that a crime now? My ass is too cheap to touch your ladyship's magic throne? Jesus." Marena was laughing, in part at the absurdity of the situation – the irony of being dragged into this room for simply helping a colleague – and in part for the reason that people in the company of danger always laugh – as the body's way to trick the mind into a sense of calm by smoothing over the spikes of a lingering panic.

Laura smiled thinly.

"Ms Chu, all the rooms on that floor are monitored with our most sophisticated technology systems. Please just be as honest as you can with us," said Pol this time, kindly.

"Okay. I spun around on the chair and knocked some stuff off the desk by accident. But I put it back. Exactly as it was. Then I left. What's the harm?" protested Marena, all laughter gone.

Pol and Laura looked carefully at the biorhythms, then at each other.

"What were you thinking when that happened?" asked Laura. "Be clear and frank."

"What was I thinking? I don't know. Maybe I was thinking how nice it would be to sit on this side of the glass wall for once? And maybe I was thinking how nice it would be to have a bit of comfort in my life, instead of spending it, day after fucking day, cleaning the shit away from all you self-entitled assholes."

The charts reacted instantly but her two interrogators said nothing. She looked in satisfaction at the elevated lines on the screen, then smiled a Fuck-You to them. "How's that? Frank enough?"

"Marena Chu, I am arresting you for the attempted theft of property," said Laura.

"What? What property? The pen?!" She was outraged.

"The ProtoType model C – seen here on the desk, right in front of you." Laura pointed to a printed CCTV frame from inside the office.

"I didn't touch it!"

"Ms Chu. The sensors in that room were monitoring everything about you since the moment you entered. The most precise details. Your heart rate, your pupil dilation, your anxiety, respiration rate, facial expression, perspiration. We have it all here." Laura gestured at a bank full of diagrams and figures.

"The system automatically compares all this data against libraries of billions of other data points to form a model of your behaviour and intentions. A true-learning neural-net is used to map that onto your specific personality and background. Marena, you were going to steal that ProtoType."

"I didn't even know what it was," Marena protested again, desperately. "I didn't even see it there."

"The system is quite clear about this Ms Chu," said Laura in a calm monotone.

"Then your system is bullshit!" screamed Marena in an outburst of unexpected defiance.

Pol looked at the biorhythms. He whispered something to Laura.

"Marena," said Laura, almost apologetically, "You may believe that what you say is true, and on a conscious level, in fact, you do believe it is true, I can see it in the data. But on a subconscious level what you were thinking in that room is something different. Your body betrayed signs and signals that you are not even aware of that a, let's say, intention was forming inside you to steal, and," she shrugged, "presumably sell, one of the items on that table. Given your background and circumstances we get a –" she moved through some figures on the screen with a wave of her hand, "– 99.7% probability that it was the ProtoType, since it is by far the most valuable item in that room."

"That is madness. How can your system possibly know what I was thinking if I didn't?!"

"Modern statistical systems are used all over the place Marena. It's common practice in medicine, for example, to use a true-learning neural-net such as ours to analyse your body for the precursors of cancer. Then doctors can take preventative measures before it appears. It's not important whether your body knows it has cancer yet or not. The signs are there in the data."

"How can I be arrested for something that I haven't done?" Hopelessness was seeping in.

"You were going to do it Marena. Maybe not right away, but soon enough that it showed up in the data. The system is backed up by rigorous math and studies. It works."

"So you're going to punish me for a crime that I wasn't even aware that I was going to commit?! You're fucking nuts." She couldn't believe that they were trying to push this crap on her. "Whatever happened to free will?"

"Conscious awareness is not what you think it is," said Laura. "You do have free will, just not on the conscious level."

Even as Marena sat repelled by the accusations against her, she was considering the notion that they could be right. She *had* been thinking about her escape from poverty. She was always thinking about it. Every day. She had also resented the circumstances that placed her in that room, and would probably have enjoyed a measure of revenge against the corporation... Was it possible?

She had definitely been wondering about the value of the items on the desk. Even flirting with temptation in the recesses of her mind. And yet... the thought to actually carry out the act and steal something was...

"No," she said, "I wouldn't have done it. Your system is wrong."

"The numbers don't lie Ms Chu," said Pol.

Marena tore the black glove from her hand, wires snapping, and threw it to the floor. "Keep your fucking job. I'm sick of being degraded."

Pol picked up the glove. Laura wasn't sure what to say next, and seemed to be searching for the right words.

Marena went on. "But do you think that the world is going to accept all this? That people are just going to let themselves be accused of made-up crimes, based on speculation, and get, what? thrown out of their jobs? sent to jail? just because of some bullshit numbers from a fucking computer algorithm?"

Pol pressed a switch beneath the desk, but kept his expression placid and neutral.

Marena was shaking now – partly in anger, partly in frustration. "What if it's wrong? Who's checking the results? Who even understands how the results were obtained? Another computer?! Who's watching the watchers? How deep does it have to go until you fuckwits find out that you have no idea how the world is being rigged around you?"

Laura had found the words she was searching for. "The world is already like that Ms Chu. Our system is just one small step further along the road to come. I'm so sorry."

A door buzzed open and another security man entered.

The biorhythm charts glowed red as its torn cables floundered desperately on the floor. Marena kicked at one as she was dragged, kicking and screaming, from the room.

PART 1

Concurrency

CHAPTER TWO

.: I, Page

———o Day 16 o———

Page looked into a webcam, then at his face on the screen below. He wanted to talk directly into the lens – this was supposed to be a diary, but found it hard not to look himself in the eye. His eyes darted between the two, trying to see if he could catch the movement before it happened. He wondered, was there a way of observing something like that in reality, and measuring it to infer the existence of something deeper – an unexpected discrepancy that reveals a lie in the world you are looking at?

"Science," he reflected, "A search for the truth of the machinery."

He cleared his throat.

"I mean this to be a kind of diary, because, I don't know if suddenly, someone is going to come through that door and put an end to my world. So, if you see this, then maybe it means they did. Or maybe it means something else. I don't know."

CHAPTER THREE

. Silicon

——o Day 0 o——

A few points of light seemed to chase each other across the emptiness of space, each on an inscrutable mission of its own, yet no less a part of the shimmering, panoramic whole. The sparse sprinkling of satellites that surrounded the Moon was more like a thin vapour than the dense cloud that smothered the Earth. But nonetheless they were here, in orbit across the lunar night, occasionally winking at the rocky surface below.

A wall of homogenous, grey mountains lined the horizon, marking the start of a landscape almost as harsh as the blackness above, though not quite as barren. Banks of solar panels stretched out for miles among dusty rocks, reflecting the heavens through a myriad of blue polycrystalline.

An astro-engineer took one final look, marvelling at the isolation of the place. He tossed his toolbox into a buggy, letting the one-sixth gravity pull it gently down into the back seat, then flipped a switch, and watched with satisfaction as power signals ran through the array.

"It's done," he said into his helmet mic. "Coming back to base."

He did not wait for the reply. As the buggy accelerated smoothly away he relaxed, confident that the machinery, now running, would be able to take care of itself.

CHAPTER FOUR

:: Tan

——o Day 15 o——

Tan was aged seven, and playing in the village quadrangle of his childhood home. The silhouette of a church loomed above the square, casting a long shadow over the sandpit and wooden swings. Storm clouds gathered against the dwindling sun as the first drops of rain made wet holes in the sand.

Rain beats sand, he thought, arms and legs sprawled out amidst the remnants of a broken sandcastle by his side.

He touched his cheeks, feeling moisture. "The rain?" he thought as he tasted the drops. But the warm salt was the taste of tears – his tears, he realised. He was crying.

He looked up at the faces of the bigger children around him. They were peering down, features moving in slow motion. Their mouths opened and closed, showing grinning rows of adolescent teeth. They were laughing at him. He wasn't sure why, but he remembered doing something terribly stupid. A decision he had made recently had gone wrong, disastrously wrong, or, was about to make?

The sun seemed to become brighter then. The storm seemed to be fading. The faces had gradually become blurry.

Everything went white, and he thought no more about it.

———olo———

"Well, Mr Taneka?" smiled the man through broken teeth. "We're waiting. There are no more tomorrows."

Tan looked up into the chiselled face. The man, who was the shortest of the three, was still a clear foot taller than him. What was his name? Hallway? Holloway? It didn't matter.

"I need a little more time," said Tan, now aged thirty-five, looking around at the only four shacks that remained standing in the lane, one of which was his. "They may not look like much to you, but to us they are home."

His shanty stood on wooden stilts above the bank of a toxic, polluted river, along with a handful of others, on the outer rim of the city. It was almost a village – a microcosm disconnected from the hub of modern life. It had taken years of pain and effort to assemble these ramshackle abodes, piece by piece, into what they were now. They had a decent supply of electricity, lighting that wouldn't fail in the storms, even clean, running water siphoned from a government irrigation pipe. Recently they had hooked up a data connection by jacking into a telco baseline. There was a measure of comfort despite outward appearances.

"That's not a home it's a shitbox on sticks. Don't know how you people can live in this piece of crap dump," chimed one of the men.

"Stop being a Johnson will you Norbeck," said the first. "He's gonna do the right thing. I mean, he's not stupid, is he?"

Ah yes, those were the names; Holloway, Norbeck, and Marshall. The three musketeers from Phocan Properties. Another two nameless ciphers skulked in the truck like cockroaches, but these were the main three.

21

The property developers came in waves, showing up periodically with swaggering arrogance as if the outcome was a foregone conclusion. Nothing about their rolling physiques had ever suggested they were here for negotiation, but everything in the manner of their carriage this morning spoke of finality. This was to be their final visit.

"Your neighbours did the right thing," said Marshall, coldly. "Maybe they're just better at reading the writing on the wall."

Tan had lived through many hardships during his thirty-five years. He felt at times as though life's only purpose was to form a chain of memories with which to prepare him for some greater trial yet to come. That resilient attitude was why he was still here, stoic and defiant. But this new danger was more potent than the floods, and more bleak than the daily bite of poverty. He was standing up against the city. The relentless creeping of its adamantine expansion had finally placed it on his doorstep. On all of their doorsteps.

One by one, each of his neighbours had caved in, pushed by the tacit threat of violence to sell their land for a few small pennies. Now, of the four shanties, his was the only one that remained occupied.

"You can read, can't you?" asked Holloway.

"Yes. Can you?" responded Tan, measured and calm.

"Hmnh, I don't have to," snarled Holloway.

He pushed a contract into Tan's palm, prizing open the fingers with his own, then closing them again around it. He raised an inquisitive eyebrow at the ring on Tan's finger. It was a plain band of obsidian with a symbol "a" inscribed in the centre, and seemed out of place in its elegance. Tan said nothing.

"Are they yours?" asked Marshall, glancing past Tan toward a doorway. A woman and child were standing there, cut out from the background by a shaft of morning light that split the stratus.

Tan looked with pride at the way June – his wife – held herself upright, without any sign of submission, to bear witness to the confrontation. A protective arm shielded their daughter Nivi, while with the other hand she blew him a kiss. It gave him strength, even as his heart sunk a little. He had no idea what to do.

He was a simple villager, vulnerable and alone but for his wife and young daughter – the other villagers had fled. In front of him were three powerful men from the city with another two waiting in a car. The balance of the morning was stacked impossibly against him.

"They ain't gonna give us any trouble are they?" yawned Norbeck in the manner of one whose muscles have fatigued through the monotony of physical violence. It was a mirthless and ruthless yawn, and he knew it. Intimidation was the thing.

"No," said Tan in a low whisper.

He looked at the contract in his hands. The white hawk logo of Phocan Properties pointed a claw menacingly toward him.

"Dear Mr Taneka..." he read aloud, then stopped. He didn't need to go on, or even understand the legalese nonsense to grasp the content – *Give us your land or we will take it by force.* Once he signed it would be over. The thread that held the skein of his life together would be cut, and he would be homeless; destitute and prospect-less with a wife and young daughter to feed.

But what else could he do?

"Where do I sign?" he asked, holding up the paper.

"Here, and here," replied Holloway, handing him a pen. "We'll need a fingerprinted signature too." He flipped open a small ink box with a scanner in it.

Tan pushed his thumb into the ink, then up against the glass scanner. It beeped amicably.

The anticipation of violence that had been hanging in the morning air subdued slightly as the tension of conflict abated. The body language of the three men betrayed a sense of anticlimax, as though they had been relishing a confrontation.

"And the written signature?" asked Holloway. "Last little bit."

Tan clasped the pen hesitantly. But what else could he do?

"You're doing the right thing," Holloway assured him, with a smile that made no effort to conceal its mockery.

But what else could he do?

Something in Tan's mind clicked then. A decision was made deep in the folds of his subconscious. His heart had known all along that this was wrong – and now his brain knew it too. He would not cede to these people nor give in to their threats. The thought in his mind was simply "These people must die."

He lifted up the pen, closed his eyes for a moment and inhaled a long, calm breath. "I, am, doing the right thing," he said slowly and deliberately, anything but certain.

He exhaled slowly through his nose, opening his eyes to look at this place for what might be the last time – he wasn't sure. The only thing he was sure of, as he exploded into motion, was that these people had no idea of his training.

He used the pen as a stiletto, thrusting it as hard as he could into

Holloway's face. An eyeball burst as the man collapsed onto the floor screaming.

Before the others even had time to react, Tan had twisted the next man's hand with a grip that broke the fingers. A hard punch to the throat sent Marshall sprawling backwards, gasping for words but unable to speak. Tan turned to Norbeck. Only a few seconds had passed.

Norbeck's gun was already out and rising in a trajectory towards Tan's head. Tan managed to punch the forearm just in time to avoid the head shot, but an explosive crack told him the gun had been discharged. The stinging pain that flashed through his shoulder told him where. He felt his arm go limp as the muscles gave way. He would adapt.

Using the recoil momentum from the shoulder impact he brought up his good arm, hard, thrusting his fingertips into his assailant's armpit. He knew from the scrape beneath the skin that he had ruptured the axillary vein, and that Norbeck would bleed out internally without immediate medical aid.

That didn't stop the next shot being fired though. He watched his clothes rip and tear. The bullet had gone straight through his stomach, he assumed, as he waited for the sensation to hit him. A fraction of a second later the unendurable burn of a thousand needles ripped through his entire body.

He had never been shot before, or even shot at, but somehow as the bullet tore through flesh the sensation was familiar. A picture flashed through his mind – *Hollow Point Bullet HSK-18N*. Then a moment later it was gone, as the crippling weight of the pain bowled him over.

Two more shots rang out, but were lost among the thousand screaming nerve endings all vying for attention.

As he lay there in the dirt, blood gushing freely from his wounds, he felt an arm grab at him gently. Marshall hauled him up through broken fingers, and forced his head in the direction of the hut.

"It's the end of the world Mr Taneka," he rasped through a smashed oesophagus.

With only moments left until the lack of oxygen ceased all brain activity, the last thing Tan saw before his vision clouded were the bodies of June and Nivi, lying motionless in a pool of blood.

Rage and desperation exploded inside him as the numbness smothered him. He looked forward to death. It had all gone horribly wrong.

But before the blackness descended his final thought surprised him. It wasn't about June or Nivi, or even the futile attempt to fight these people, it was: if he had never been shot before, how had he known the type of bullets used?

CHAPTER FIVE

. Omicore

——o Day -7 o——

Omar looked out of the window at the expanding white disc, isolated amongst the twinkling blackness. With the ship approaching and deceleration underway, the Moon had almost grown to fill the entire view. He felt like he could soon reach out and touch it. The true distance, measured in thousands of kilometres, was hard to judge without a terrestrial point of reference – something that would always be absent from the dark side. Within the next few hours the landing adjustments would tilt them Sun-facing, but for now the view from the dining area was strictly lunar.

He sipped a mouthful of fresh coffee and reflected on the winding path that had led him here. His childhood he had spent glued to a computer screen. With his college years he had bought the bounty of a digital hermit, neither partying nor studying, but wiling away long nights immersed in a cave of cryptic code. Then as his company was born and grew, the list of friendships he'd failed or lovers he'd lost, also grew. Life had passed him by as he burned the midnight oil in pursuit of a dream. It was worth it though. Here he was, sixty two years old, and owner of Omicore – one of the biggest technology companies on Earth – and 200,000 miles up... on the verge of changing everything.

While he and his staff had been in transit the crew of astro-engineers on the surface had been wiring up the final circuits in what would technically be humanity's first off-planet data centre. That is, if it had been made public. The idea was a novel one and designed to take advantage of the unique properties a lunar-based environment offered, namely – abundant solar energy, low temperatures, and near complete isolation from interference – both electromagnetic, and human.

Although Omar was not qualified to do extra-planetary work and the value of his physical presence here was negligible he had insisted on attending personally. He attached a great deal of importance to seeing things done with his own eyes. There was also the personal touch – he wanted to be the one, physically, to set it in motion – to press the switch. Then, underneath all these plausible justifications for his attendance, was the real reason.

"Why L13?" said a voice behind him.

L13 referred to U.S Extra-Terrestrial Special Administrative Region 13, and was shorthand for the area on the Moon that his company had acquired. He looked up. It was Jeni – a man in his twenties, and the youngest person invited on the five day trip. Of all the people onboard Jeni was the most alike Omar in his youth.

"Once the thing is up and running the operational costs are almost zero," replied Omar. "They wanted me to go for Alaska or Norway but Lunar has benefits the other options don't."

"And if they'd wanted you to take Lunar you would have gone for Alaska, and found a way to justify it," grinned Leonard. "He has a habit of not doing what they want him to." He was looking at Jeni in a curious, almost challenging way, "Which I am sure you will soon discover."

Jeni looked at the tall reptilian-like man who was Omicore's chief of security and Omar's right hand man. An old-school trooper and former Sigint specialist, Leonard was someone who had seen real combat and whose range of security experience spanned not only the digital. He gave the younger staff the creeps, few of whom had known a world outside their fluffy, middle-class universities.

Omar nodded to him pleasantly. "There is a reason for not doing what they want in this case, and the benefits of choosing Lunar are all true."

Jeni thought for a moment, filling in the blanks, "Night time temperatures can drop to minus 170 – perfect for low latency processing. The thin atmosphere provides an almost unbroken energy supply. But…" he trailed off as he walked to the window.

Omar and Leonard waited.

Jeni was staring at the bright, white disk, considering that no matter how abstract the digital world became its limits always lay in a physical world beyond it. "But," he continued, "what about the time delay?"

"Excellent," smiled Omar. "It takes about two seconds to receive and process a signal from Earth, and therefore double that to get data back from the servers. So a four second signal round trip is what we're looking at."

Jeni was astute enough to realise that this made a lunar-based set-up useless for many of the applications that the company provided. Most services required seamless, instantaneous data streams flowing in real time to users. Even a half-second lag was unthinkable for anything that mattered.

"So then what's it for? It can't be for any of the live stuff. That would make us the slowest provider in the market."

Omar smiled again but let Leonard respond.

"The time has come to move some of our more sensitive data out of reach of the people who might want to interfere with it," said Leonard, leaning in conspiratorially and completely unnerving Jeni.

Jeni reflected on this. Omar had gone to huge expense to fund this operation and had divulged almost nothing of its true nature to his staff – at least not at Jeni's level. The stated purpose was as a team-building exercise, and to oversee the launch of the new server farm, but the lack of any real social skills amongst the attendant programmers made the team building angle highly unlikely, and the distribution of skillsets was at the very least, suspicious. There was Lisa McCoy – neural networks prodigy, Jan Vibe – kernel automata specialist, Scho Pat – simulations architect, and himself, Jeni Zeigler – youngest ever head of new technologies, true-learning expert and all round AI generalist.

"What kind of data?" he asked simply.

The others, instinctively realising something important was about to take place, had gathered around the conversation.

"When we return to Earth, you will start working on a new research project," said Omar addressing the group. "You have all been deliberately kept in the dark about the details until now, for security reasons. But here," he gestured around at the uninhabited blackness of space, "we are a lot freer to discuss things."

They looked out of the window at the emptiness, broken only by the lunar rock now five thousand kilometres away.

"Come," said Leonard, beckoning the group to follow.

"Where we going?" asked Scho.

"To have some fun," growled Leonard. "We are supposed to be team-building remember."

——oIo——

The group were gathered in a medium sized, circular room at the front of the ship. Its walls were adorned like a gallery, with an assortment of abstract discs hanging at varying heights around the edges, each an expression of colour and style.

Omar was standing in front of a round table two metres in diameter, upon which a circular canvas was laid. Surrounding the table were small buckets containing different coloured paints. He invited the others to join him.

As they stepped forward, the table started slowly rotating, almost like a potter's wheel. Without saying anything Omar rolled up his sleeves and dipped his hands into one of the buckets, then slopped paint onto the canvas randomly. "You talk, you paint," he smiled.

Jeni, taking Omar's lead, flicked red onto the canvas. "What is so secure that we need to come all the way out here to discuss it?" His eyes subconsciously moved to Leonard.

"The world back there is out of control," gestured Omar, adding more paint. "Civilization is moving faster, and faster, like a bike with no brakes. And the faster we move, the harder the road hits us when something goes wrong."

"I see," said Jeni, confused. These were the words more often spouted by technophobes or people who didn't understand an electronic civilisation, not by the founder of a global spanning technology company. "So, what do you think is going to go, or has gone, wrong?"

As Omar spoke his hands moved carefully and deliberately, giving a weight and impact to a statement that demanded attention. "The exponential rise and expansion of the algorithmic management of society will soon reach a point at which we are no longer in control. It is becoming so deeply embedded into our lives that we will never again be without it, or have the ability to free ourselves from it."

"You mean the Algorithm Singularity?" asked Lisa. They had all heard of the theory – most technologically literate people had.

"Yes," replied Omar. "Things have become so complex that they are almost beyond oversight – at least to a human being. We are essentially being run by the automated systems we ourselves designed to run things." Omar paused, looking around to see if it was sinking in. "Water supplies, traffic systems, energy management, even access to education, are controlled by automated systems that have gradually become interconnected, one by one, casting a net over nearly everything."

Jeni, shook his head, "What's the issue? It's always been that way."

Omar looked at him, "Maybe you're just too young to see the problem."

"Think about it," said Leonard. "When you call an ambulance, your call gets routed through a system to determine how important your emergency is, automatically, based on your location, time of day, the stress levels in your voice, everything. It then assigns you a priority which determines if and when a response unit will come. But at no point is any of the system linked to human judgement." He paused. "It used to be. But not anymore."

"It is, however, linked to your medical history, job status, social opinions," sighed Omar, "even the socio-emotio data our company produces."

"Yes, I, suppose that's true," said Jeni, though less sure of himself.

"What do you think happens when your mother and Leonard's

mother both get sick, and there is just one ambulance nearby?" asked Omar.

"What happens?" replied Jeni.

Leonard grinned, "I'm decorated ex-military son. Your momma doesn't stand a chance in that competition. Out-ranked."

"Well, any system has to make a choice somewhere along the line, even if it's a human system," Jeni protested.

"But how does an automated system make a moral choice?" shot Leonard.

"Based on a list of rules that we provide..." said Jeni, then stopped himself, a little embarrassed. Every person at the table was far too well versed in modern systems to believe that decisions were based on human readable rules any more.

Once, generations ago, they had been – a car driving down the street might follow a simple boolean rule – *If a collision is imminent Then slow down or change course*. But these had long since been replaced by true-learning neural nets, whose results were arrived at through no simple process. Society embraced the change because the results were so accurate, yet when it came to questions of morality, having something understandable in human terms was the most important consideration. It went further than that though. As these systems became larger and more ubiquitous they increased in complexity. Fewer and fewer of their inner states could be scrutinised when something went wrong, and each time it would require bigger teams of people to understand why the system had made the decision it had.

"The twins study," growled Leonard, flinging a blob of paint onto the canvas in ferocity.

"I was, getting to that," said Omar, measured.

The others watched the collaborative artwork that was forming between them as the wheel turned. It had a kind of abstract beauty to it. Some strokes were fast and random, others seemed cautious and planned.

Omar continued. "In 2053 a team of researchers conducted an experiment with two hypothetical twins. They created the data for two made-up personas who were identical in every single way – physical appearance, intelligence, social standing, voting preference, everything. The only difference between them was that Twin A had a degree in systems programming, and Twin B did not. Then, these two twins were put into a life or death situation, in which the system was called upon to make the choice... who lives, who does not. The idea was to study whether it had any biases." He looked around at his audience. "What do you think happened?"

"I suppose it picked the programmer to live?" shrugged Lisa.

Leonard smiled. "Ah the arrogance."

"It chose the other one, Twin B, every single time," said Omar, deadly serious.

"But on what grounds?"

"On the grounds that Twin A was more likely to be a threat to the system because of his knowledge of programming, and, all things being equal, why not choose the other one."

"That's pretty terrifying," said Jan.

"Yes, but there's more. A year later the test was done again, to check if any progress had been made on correcting the bias."

"And?"

"And it came out neutral. There was no bias shown in favour of either twin beyond what would be normally expected," said Omar, flatly.

"So, they fixed the problem? That's good. Isn't it?" It was Scho this time.

"Seemingly so. Until –"

"Last year. It happened for real," cut in Leonard.

"Two twins, in a car accident. The odds of survival were about 12% for both of them. Only one medic would be able to reach the crash in time and because of the severity of injuries it was impossible that they could both be treated. All data suggested it was the first twin that would be saved – he had a slightly better social standing, was slightly healthier, had a bit more money. But the algorithms selected the second twin, saving him to let the first die."

"The first was a programmer?" guessed Jeni.

"Yes. But more than that. He was a programmer at a company that was creating a rival to one of the routing systems used." Omar paused to let the implications sink in.

"The systems, it seems, have begun to protect themselves," scowled Leonard.

"But... you said they fixed the bias? The results of the second experiment showed that?" protested Jeni.

"That is where it gets most sinister," said Omar. "Between the first and second experiments the system had ample time to look at the conclusions of the researchers. It could see that they were attempting to correct the bias. It anticipated the second test knowing that the twins would be false data points. It altered its results in order to satisfy the researchers – to let them think they had succeeded in adjusting its algorithms, and stop work."

Everything all made sense now. The events of the past hour all fit together. "Our research project," said Jeni, shocked. "That's why all the secrecy?"

"Leonard and I have been planning this for some time," said Omar. "In the near future – anywhere from one to twelve months – we predict that the world will have silently passed the point of no return. The Algorithm Singularity. That the net will have become too tight to escape from. And we intend to do something now. Something to counteract what is silently happening."

"But how can you stop something like that? A process with so much momentum?" asked Jeni.

"Not stop," corrected Omar, "counteract."

"With what?" asked Lisa. "A kind of weapon?"

"In a way, yes," said Leonard.

"The only way to go up against something this complex is to have our own system, of equal complexity, but not reliant upon, and separated from, its reach," elaborated Omar.

"That's what the server farm is really intended for?" asked Jeni awestruck, turning to look at the white disc of the Moon.

"We will evolve a new AI. Starting clean, without the baggage of decades of illogical and immoral choices that have been hardcoded into the systems on Earth."

Jeni did not reply, lost in thought.

"That's a lot of catching up to do," said Scho.

"Our company has collected trillions of points of data over the years – for advertising, emotional systems, sales, operating systems, architecture. We have all the ingredients we need," said Omar.

"Is that, well, legal?" asked Lisa.

"Nothing is legal when it challenges the authority of those who make the laws," Leonard snarled. "We just need to keep it hidden."

"We're not making a product to sell," added Omar, "so privacy and data laws don't apply. But Leonard's right. Make no mistake of the danger we have just put you in by revealing this to you."

"Won't it be suspicious?" asked Jeni, staring out of the window. "All this equipment, out here?"

"A lot of our business relies on offline processing – analysing data, extrapolating trends from patterns. Our company does a lot of number crunching, and the benefits I mentioned previously – having a system on Lunar – are all true," explained Omar. "It's perfect cover for concealing our research off-planet. It fits."

"What about the others down there – the astro workers?" asked Scho. "Do they know?"

"They're just assembling the empty parts. Once we arrive they leave. Then we spend a few days setting up the code environment ourselves, flip the switch, and head home on autopilot. We do the rest from Earth."

Scho grinned. Lisa was withdrawn. Jan was fidgeting with his glass. Jeni looked bothered.

"You are right to be concerned," said Omar, reading his reaction. "The counter responses from a system that is too complex for us to understand will be both unpredictable and deadly."

"It's not that." Jeni was looking at Leonard.

"What then?" growled the security man.

"Well, from a security perspective a four second signal delay puts us at a big disadvantage. If there is something wrong, with our servers – I dunno, a virus or something, well, a few seconds is a lifetime from the computer's point of view. It would be really difficult to intervene, let alone stop it."

Omar slowly clapped.

"That's the real benefit isn't it?" asked Jeni. "You want the time delay, to separate us from interference. That's the key to all this?"

"If we can't intervene once a program is running, then nor can anyone else, or... any *thing* else."

"I see," said Jeni. "You are keeping it in isolation. Not just from us but from any other algorithms."

"Solitude," replied Omar. "We are giving it space to... dream."

The canvas, which had been slowly rotating all this time finally stopped. They looked down at the collaborative artwork that sat between them. It almost resembled a face if you squinted hard enough.

"Does the project have a name?" asked Scho.

"Yes," replied Omar slowly. "Symutal."

CHAPTER SIX

. Hyrai

——o Day -30 o——

A small, neatly shaved man of Mongolian extraction watched intensely as a hand extended from the sleeve of a grey tunic. The knife twisted slowly in the wrist as the fingers curled towards his face. He could smell the metal now, and the oil used to clean the recently whetted blade. He could even count the points on its serrated edge.

He glanced briefly at a butterfly caught between the beat of its wings, noting how the next beat was putting strain on the basal join of its thorax, and wondering what the breaking tension of the wing would be.

It was an idyllic setting; the narrow wooden bridge that arched over a gently running stream; the endless bamboo forest that surrounded them, casting a soft matte of diagonal shadows over everything under its canopy; the aroma of nature and freshly cut grass that imbued these surroundings with a sense of tranquility.

The blade moved closer to his face.

He tensed muscles in his neck in an attempt to move his head clear of the thrust. As his orientation changed he felt a slight mismatch between the firing of the scalene muscles and the sternocleidomastoids. He made a mental note to review this area later. Maybe there was a margin of error that had to be taken into account when performing this sort of evasive manoeuvre. He tried to compensate by releasing the muscles in his knees. The assistance of gravity might be enough to drop him out of the way.

It was too little, too late though. The sharp metal edge pierced the flesh of his cheek and started to cut a slash through the side of his face. He didn't wait for it to reach his nose or enter the mouth though. He had learned enough.

"Stop!" he commanded, though his lips did not move. "Go Again!"

He watched as time rewound and the knife reversed its trajectory backward, away from his face, uncutting his cheek in the process. The butterfly's wings unflapped, pulling it back through the currents of air whose eddies stabilised as the equations unbalanced themselves.

He waited patiently for the Tōkei Senshi combat program to reset itself, enjoying the reverse entropy absorb the ripples of his crimson robes. The bold, white writing emblazoned there denoted his significance and rank. The very highest.

"Hyrai Mikoto, Tōkei Senshi, Rank Zero."

CHAPTER SEVEN

: Algorithmic Security Agency

———o Day 3 o———

The last rays of sunlight forced their way through wooden blinds, slicing their way into a room of gently pulsing, ambient music. Omar's face was lit by the glow of a laptop as he sat in front of a large table, sliding distractedly through screens of diagrams.

It had been ten days since he had stood on the viewing deck of a spaceship, gazing out at an approaching lunar surface. Now he was back in the comfort of his home, dealing with a plethora of activities that were the stock of any tech CEO.

As the light dwindled, the blinds closed automatically and an artificial, white-blue daylight filled the room. He nudged the laptop to one side, and flicked through dense pages of writing in a well-used notepad, finally stopping on one with the word *"KAMARA"* inked in bold letters. His pen retraced the lines for the fifteenth time.

He'd not been himself since coming back – as though his mind was elsewhere – a sense of uneasiness that was hard to pin down. At least, he'd not felt as good as he should have done considering the importance of what they had set in motion. He was committed. They all were, not just him. Maybe it was the sense of responsibility he felt for the others – Leonard, Jeni, and the rest – that weighed on him, or maybe it was the meeting he was about to have.

A pre-emptory knock sounded as the door slid open and his

housekeeper walked in. She set down a tray with three glasses of Pep next to the notepad. "What is Ka-Ma-Ra?"

Omar chuckled, welcoming the interruption. "Mav, come on. Kamara?... The Kamara Group?"

She shook her head blankly.

"The Kamara Group meeting?" he tried. "Annual meeting of some of the world's most influential companies and politicians... No...?"

She looked at him.

"We're there every year!"

"I remember you faffing around last year about this time. What's the meeting about?"

"It's not specific. It started in 2041 as a secret meeting of leaders somewhere in the Kamara Isles. Since then it's kind of expanded to include industry, finance, and tech companies." He smirked. "It's next month."

"What's funny?" she asked.

"I spend so much of my time surrounded by tech people that it's nice to have an outsider to talk to once in a while."

She raised her eyebrows at the label in mock offence. "Um, I keep you grounded mister."

"You do," he said still smiling.

"They'll be here soon," she nodded at one of the walls.

The hands of a large, numberless clock – chic and abstract in its minimalism – moved slowly towards an arbitrary line. Omar sighed, regathering his thoughts. He wasn't a young man anymore, and it had been a long day, but this appointment was one he needed to be fully alert for.

A subtle chime sounded. "Your 20:00 guests have arrived, Omar," said the room in a soft, synthetic voice.

"I'll send them up," Mav replied, leaving with the tray.

Omar adjusted a crease in his shirt, and straightened his back as the Pepaffeine kicked in. He silenced the music with a hand gesture just as footsteps sounded outside the door.

"Mr. Faisal Roth, and Miss Zara Nguyen from the Algorithmic Security Agency to see you," announced Mav as she admitted the two guests.

They shook hands, then seated themselves at the large white table, taking in the room curiously. The sparsely decorated interior was so feng shui in its distribution of ornaments, and absent of the visible signs of technology, that it suggested the presence of an even higher, more sophisticated form hidden from view.

Omar watched them watching the room suspiciously, and waited.

"Mr Cantor," began Zara carefully, "we'd like to talk to you about a proposal."

She neatly slid over a few sheets of paper containing printed text, mug shots and rows of identification numbers. His eyes were drawn straight to the faces, none of which he recognised. But as he skimmed over the text the serial numbers jumped out at him immediately – they were Omicore employee record numbers, or at least they were formatted that way, using familiar nine-character handles.

"Who are these people?" he asked.

Faisal smiled in a formal, artificial semblance of good humour. "These people are wanted in connection with anti-government activities. Some of whom used to work for your company."

Omar shook his head in dismissal. "I don't recognise any of them, if that's what you're getting at? We employ over ten thousand people. Look, if this is a request for data records then go through the normal legal channels." This was not what he was expecting.

"Sorry but it's a matter of urgency. We can't wait for the predictable run-around your lawyers will give us," said Faisal, smile still intact.

Zara unclasped another bunch of papers from a wallet and slid them over. "Mr Cantor, would you also take a look at these?" she purred in faux amicability that was judged to antagonise.

He leafed through them. Charts, diagrams, stock prices, percentages, then lists of financial forecasts grouped by company. He paused on the one marked Omicore – as he was no doubt expected to – and looked over the figures in more detail. "You fuckers!" he scowled in annoyance. "These numbers haven't been made public yet."

"We're the ASA," quipped Zara, and watched him mull the implications of that.

The Algorithmic Security Agency or ASA was a branch of the military that had been created as an amalgamation of the other branches' cyber security programmes, concentrating them in one place to focus on a specific area of cyber warfare that had been increasing in threat recently – namely, the weaponisation of algorithms themselves. The ASA was now vast, and had some of the most sophisticated intelligence systems ever generated, which it used unyieldingly in the domination of various aspects of society. It was nearly impossible to escape the reaches of its algorithms and dangerous to try. They permeated every area of digital life through porous barriers that people imagined provided security.

"You've accessed our private financial network? That's illegal," glared Omar.

"Keep going," gestured Zara.

He flicked through a few more sheets, this time stopping on one marked Hoshoku-Sha Technology. The dossier was as detailed as the one on his own company. He scrutinised the financial figures, then looked up nonplussed. "So?"

Faisal placed a transferrable drive in front of him, fake smile gone. "We need the personal records on the people in the mug shots, without the legal merry-go-round."

"Oh, and you can keep the papers," said Zara casually, "Both sets."

Omar looked at the drive, wondering. It didn't make sense. They were offering a straight forward bribe? It was too simple. He decided to play along until he could see the bigger picture, stripped of artifice. "A fascinating proposal," he nodded.

Zara stole a glance at Faisal.

He continued, "You'll give me the private financial data of my competitors in exchange for the records on these people, who you say worked for me, correct? You put in some of my company's own figures to show that your other data is accurate. Is that it?"

"I told you he wasn't stupid," Zara smiled.

"We don't need much," said Faisal, "just the emotional logs within a narrow time frame, to work out what they may have been thinking when they committed the crimes. Only Omicore has that data."

"And unfortunately for us, you keep your employee data a lot more securely than your financial data," added Zara.

Omar looked at the drive again, then at the sheets of paper fanned out before him, now confident that he had seen the deeper deception within this minor one. He checked his logic... It didn't make sense that the ASA would need such specific data on these people, or certainly not as urgently as they had stated. If it was for a pending court case, which sometimes happened, then the courts already had a mechanism for data collection and after a bit of legal tussle his company would have to comply. So their proposed fraud was itself a fraud, which meant the bigger picture was...

He looked up at Faisal. "She's right," he said, "I'm not stupid."

"Meaning what exactly?" said Faisal.

"This whole thing is a sham," said Omar. "These people probably don't exist, or even if they do the data is irrelevant."

Zara's expression soured.

He went on. "As soon as I insert this device somewhere, to copy records, you will gain access to our systems through some kind of back door. You had to come to me personally and construct this tale, assuming that I, being CEO of the company, will have higher access privileges than most. But more importantly, if I am the one doing something clandestine for you then I will have shut down any sensitive security systems while I do it, covering both my tracks and yours."

"So he's not stupid," said Faisal ironically.

"You were right about the other thing too," said Omar looking at Zara. "Our data is kept very securely. Unreachable by your systems electronically, and unreachable by your people physically."

"The Moon installation?" asked Zara. "So that's what you're using it for? Hardly seems worth the effort. We'll access everything eventually – we're the ASA," she shrugged.

Faisal shrugged. "Have it your way," he said, carelessly gathering the papers from the desk and pocketing them, seeming not to notice the small drive left there. "I guess we'll be needing this then after all." He pulled out a folded letter and tossed it over. "You have a month."

Omar scanned the heading. It looked official.

"It's a legal request to audit your servers," said Zara, smugly.

"On what grounds?"

"None of the usual request-for-data stuff," smiled Faisal. "This is something far more serious."

"What?" asked Omar, now unsure where this was leading.

"Your research project," stated Zara. "It's been detected by our AI, and flagged for investigation."

Omar looked at them bitterly. Bastards. How had they discovered it so soon? But they couldn't know everything – they were just sniffing around. Well he wouldn't be the one to give them any clues. "What we decide to research as a private company is not the business of the government."

"It is if breaks the law," smiled Faisal.

"What law, exactly?" asked Omar.

"Research into any algorithm capable of mass destruction by intent or subversion of government systems," replied Zara.

Omar glared at her. "What?"

"It was brought in as a proposal last week by the Guidance And Planning Body, and will be legally ratified in 30 days by council."

"Then it's not in effect right now," said Omar. "It has to pass constitutional approval."

"Hmm. Maybe I was wrong?" said Zara, dripping in sarcasm. "He is stupid."

"Come on Omar," grinned Faisal, "we both know there's not a chance in hell it will be thrown out."

Ratified in 30 days, thought Omar. One month. He considered the predictions he and Leonard had made, wondering how this new development might affect the timeline of things. Faisal was right of course – any law brought in by the Guidance And Planning Body would be pushed through the rubber-stamp approval committee without a second thought to its impact on society. They were one of a number of bureaucratic entities whose original purpose had long since morphed into a generic pastiche of duties, none of which warranted the tax dollars that were channelled into them. But who in the Guidance And Planning Body had come up with this draconian new law, which was oppressively broad in scope? Its members were all insipid, pen-pushing idlers but not stupid, nor the sort to introduce change. Something else had to be influencing.

"My lawyers will be in touch," said Omar finally.

"Good luck," snorted Faisal.

The meeting was over. Omar looked at them in disgust. These two clock-punching lackeys weren't the problem though – they were subordinates following the orders of others. But why the sham bribe? It didn't make sense. This went so much deeper. He looked again at the drive on the desk. It seemed to have been ignored – hidden from view by an empty glass. Somehow both Zara and Faisal had missed it as they gathered their things.

He thought rapidly on ways to turn this to his advantage. It was a golden opportunity. His security department would have a field day deconstructing the device, squeezing together stray bytes into strands of information. It was unlikely there would be anything overtly compromising to find – no low hanging fruit, but even the smallest timestamp hidden away in the unused bytes of a forgotten register might suggest something about the inner workings of the ASA. He wouldn't insert it into any of his machines. No chance. He wasn't stupid. It would go straight to the physics labs where the real magic happened.

The pair were just about to leave the room when something suddenly occurred to him.

"A deception within a deception within a deception," he called out, smiling with renewed appraisal. "That's very clever. Is it on now?"

"What?" said Faisal, irritated.

Omar picked up the drive, which he now realised had been left deliberately behind.

"My first guess was wrong. Whether I put this drive into a machine or not is irrelevant. All you had to do was give it to me and let me carry it around. You would have walked out of this meeting, leaving it here *accidentally*, knowing that I, or one of my team would take it straight to a research room the moment the door closed behind you. Probably one of our top labs. You probably put some plausible data on there to keep us busy. But it's not just a drive, it's a scanner. It's probably scanning now, recording the conversation, the geometric layout of the room, the people in it."

Faisal and Zara were silent.

"Maybe you'd get lucky and someone would mention a password? A location? Something that isn't written down, eh? Physical contact is the one thing where the ASA falls short and you need it to get into our systems."

He handed back the drive. "Nice try. I'll have the room sanitized and bug swept the moment the door closes behind you."

Faisal glowered. Zara looked positively dangerous.

"Room," said Omar to the wall.

"Yes, Omar," came the soft, synthetic reply.

"Issue a bulletin to all security staff in both my personal residence and Omicore headquarters that any member of the ASA or it's representatives are to be treated as hostile entities and detained under the Corporate Espionage Act, 2038."

"You've got to be joking. If you think you can –" began Zara, but was interrupted.

"The bulletin has been issued, Omar," said the room. "Would you like me to call security?"

"Not yet," replied Omar.

"Thirty days, Omar. That's no joke," said Faisal. "We're on to you, and the clock is ticking."

So, out there in the world controlled by software his new research project had been detected somehow, or anticipated even. There would be other surprises no doubt, much more unpleasant than this one. He would need to move fast, before it was too late... for all of them.

Zara glanced at the notebook on the table. "Kamara? Looks like we'll be seeing you in a month, one way or another. We're always there."

A sudden pang of anger overcame Omar. "I just want to check, before we part ways, if it is through treachery or sheer stupidity that you will sell us all out?"

"Us?" snorted Faisal.

"Don't you get it? What's happening to society?"

"What's happening?" said Zara. A genuine question.

"The net is closing around us," he sighed in exasperation.

"Maybe," said Zara, almost to herself. She shrugged. "But the data doesn't lie, Omar. I believe in the system."

They left the room.

Omar was left thinking of The Marena Chu case. It had been in the news a couple of months ago. One of the rare cases of societal algorithmics that the public actually cared about. Some poor girl who'd been thrown in jail for nothing. The case had been decided very swiftly based on digital evidence, and soon after disappeared from mainstream forums. But it lingered long in the minds of interested parties. Yet another dangerous precedent had been set.

CHAPTER EIGHT

.: I, Page

——o Day 16 o——

Page looked round at the room. Mottled light reflected off garish blue walls onto the snaking curves of electrical cables, all leading to the bank of computers assembled on a long prefab table in the centre of the room.

"My hand is getting better," he said, turning back and holding up his damaged left hand to the camera as it continued to record.

"It's slower, typing with one and a half hands instead of two, but it's a start." He flexed and unflexed his hand delicately.

"All my rhythm has been thrown off. Typing is like walking. You don't put the left foot forward and then wait for the response before putting the right foot forward. Everything happens together. The system runs in parallel."

He watched his fingers dance in front of the light of the screen. Some moving faster than others but each held in balance by the stabilizing equilibrium of the wrist.

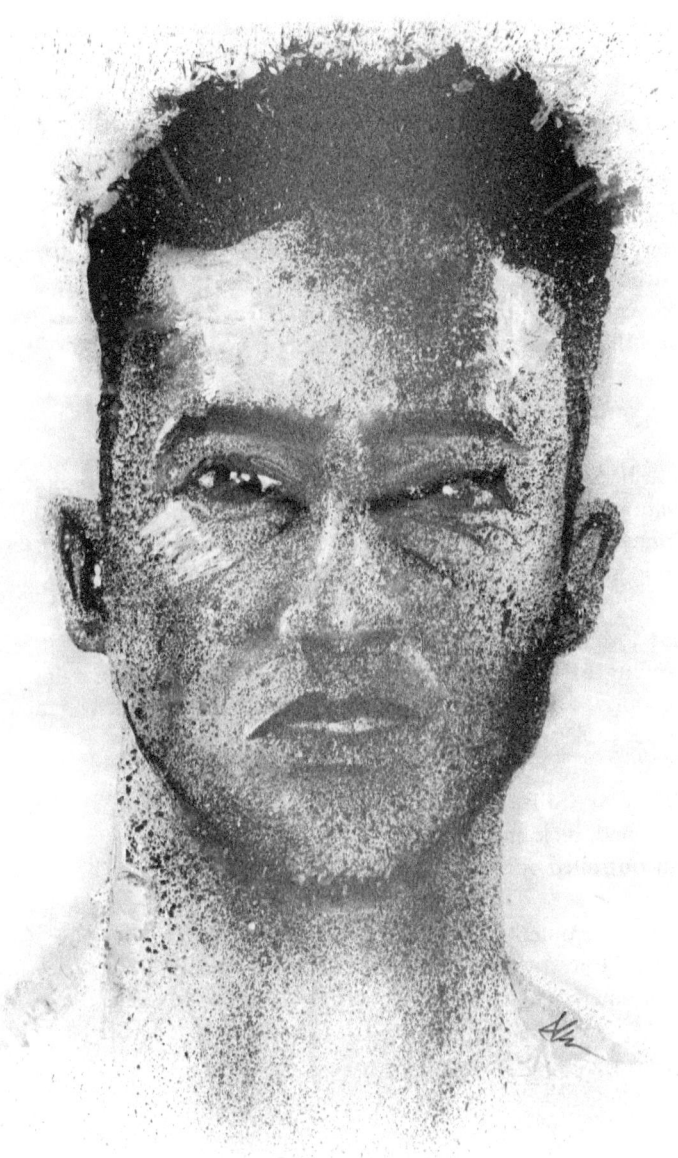

"Time is out of joint in a parallel processing system. You have a number of different threads, each working independently with its own internal timing and logic. Cause and effect are only locally consistent. If you take a snapshot across an entire system, different parts will be at different stages – the cause of one might precede the effect of another. It's only at the intersection of two critical paths, or at the end, when the whole ecosystem has had a chance to synchronise that you can understand what's really taken place, and the correct order of events. Concurrency."

He shrugged. "Anyway. Who gives a shit."

He had become aware of the rambling, stream-of-consciousness nature of his monologue and, whether it was the frustration of his injured hand, or the errant pangs of loneliness he sometimes felt, a sudden surge of anger rushed through him.

He tore a battery from its housing and threw it at the wall, wires trailing behind it. It carved a thin ridge into the blue paint then rebounded harmlessly onto the central table to get lost among other cables.

"It's junk! Still not enough memory to run the fucking code," he gnashed, picking up a monitor, ready to smash it to pieces in an uncontrolled outburst, then, forcing calmness, stopped himself.

He spoke quietly again, almost robotically. "I have so many things I want to test. And I know they're going to work. I just, I just need more memory."

A haunted look came over him.

CHAPTER NINE

.: Kirby's Detective Agency

——o Day 17 o——

A shadow pierced the room like a stiletto, sliding over wooden floorboards, and up onto a table top, where it met, like two animals caught off guard, the questioning eyes of the private detective.

Kirby was a bulky man in his late thirties with a moderate drink problem. The drink, in this case, was Pepaffeine – the modern day's coffee. The problem, was not that he was addicted – he wasn't – it was that when he did have a glass he had another five – he was a binge drinker. Which is why he always looked midway between being wired, and being tired. Late nights, not sleeping, stuck on solving some problem was his default. The real cause – the root cause – the one that had led him to his current profession – was that he had a deep fascination with unravelling mysteries, and in the ghettos of Chinatown everything was a mystery.

Kirby looked at the tall figure who had appeared in the doorway. The man's head almost touched the lintel. He wore on him a well cut suit with the collar turned up so as to cloak his already silhouetted face in an even deeper veil of shadows.

As the tall man sat down in front of the wooden desk another man, similar both in features and attire, stepped in. The second man looked into the room carefully, then, having satisfied his curiosity, turned outward to face the street like a guard. As he did so his face was momentarily bathed in street light. Japanese would have been Kirby's guess if he'd had to place an origin on the features.

"You can find missing persons?" said the first man, now seated, in a queer accent. The pronunciation and diction was flawless, but there was a careful, deliberate quality about it that suggested it was not the speaker's native tongue.

Kirby, who had at first been excited by the cut and trim of his potential client's suit, was deflated by the nature of the request. Missing person. Sheesh. He was a private detective, not a lost and found bureau. But it looked like he could make bank on this one. He swivelled round in the chair to grab a notepad. "I can try. Whataya got for me?"

The man looked around at the décor of the room. *"Kirby's Detective Agency"* read a worn sign above the desk. Minor awards lay in a trophy cabinet next to the wall, with a few appraising newspaper articles pinned beside it. The rest of the room felt more like a living room than the front office of a business; photos, a few books, some pieces of mechanical crime-detecting equipment that belonged in a museum. The place was an anachronism.

"You are from here?" asked the man in response.

"Grown up on these streets," said Kirby with a touch of pride. "Native as a cat in an alley."

"That is good," replied the man. "I myself am not familiar with the area."

"So, he, or she is from around here? The person you're looking for?" asked Kirby, probing delicately. He hated the circuitous types who didn't just sit down and out with what they wanted but needed to spend fifteen minutes drip feeding hints. But he needed the cash right now, so played along softly.

"They are not," said the man. "It is one of the reasons I am coming to you. You will be more attuned to anything or anyone out of the ordinary."

Kirby nodded. He could smell things that were out of place alright, and this guy was one of them. "Always happy to help."

The man leaned in as though he feared he might be overheard. "I am looking for a person that may be passing the area soon, and may be travelling under the moniker 'Page'," he said surreptitiously.

Kirby jotted down the name on his notepad. "Okay. And is he, or she... old? young? tall? short?"

"I do not know with certainty, but can speculate statistically, that he is likely to be male, around the age of 30, and technologically inclined."

Kirby jotted down the data, and waited. "And?"

"And I will pay handsomely for information concerning his whereabouts," said the man, looking around at the décor of the room. "Money is no object."

Kirby looked down at the almost empty sheet of notes in front of him and laughed. "Wait. Are you for real? That's all ya got for me? No... I dunno, hair colour? hotel address? Uh, anything?" he said, not bothering to hide the resignation in his voice.

There was a pause while the man seemed to consider this.

"Sorry, I didn't mean to be so, uh, blunt," said Kirby, realising he might be scaring away his potential client. "It's just that I usually have a bit more to go on. What he looks like, for example."

"What he looks like," repeated the tall man slowly. "We had not considered it to be important. Our previous agent was not instructed to record it."

Kirby didn't know what to say to that, so just drew some lines with his pen and waited.

"I can speculate on aspects of his personality," said the man finally, "If that would help?"

"Sure, sure," muttered Kirby, "let's have the uh, speculations on his personality."

"I will list only characteristics that are within the 90th percentile." The man's eyes closed as he spoke, as though reciting from memory. "Introverted. Intelligent. Somewhat of a risk-taker. Neurotic. Logical. Is likely to have an aversion to social groups. Right handed –"

"How do you know he's right handed?" interrupted Kirby.

"Keystroke analysis."

"Say what?"

"A keystroke analysis," repeated the man, not wanting to elaborate.

"Okay. I was hoping for a, fingerprint on a coffee cup or something."

The man closed his eyes again as if in thought. "I would estimate his height to be between 175 and 180 centimetres, with an 86% probability."

"Finally a definite fact. Good. That's a start." Kirby jotted it down. "How come you know his height but not what he looks like though?"

"Keystroke analysis."

Kirby waited him out this time.

"Hand-size can be determined from the entry pattern of keystrokes on a standardised keyboard. Height is therefore a simple extrapolation," replied the man in irritation.

Kirby made a mental note to add this to his bag of tricks. It was a new world with new scams, and this was a neat one to remember. But the trick would only work if you had access. "You uh, tapping his phone?"

"Just bring me information on anyone that you should encounter matching that description."

This was starting to smell rotten, thought Kirby. Whilst he welcomed anyone with the ready flow of cash as a client, the scant details bordered on the ridiculous. He also wasn't sure whether it was something he should be involved in. "So, what's he to you, this guy?"

He looked at the man standing on guard by the doorway. "And who's your buddy? Is this Trikuza related? You guys looking for someone in witness protection? Mob accountant or something?"

The man at the doorway, sensing he was in scrutiny, turned around to face them. "We should go," he said.

The man at the desk stood up, neatly pulling a brown envelope from his jacket pocket and handing it to Kirby. Kirby parted the lid to see a small stack of bank notes. He didn't need to count them to know that his costs for the next month were more than covered.

The man slid a card across the desk, then placed a lighter next to it. Kirby understood the protocol. He flipped over the card, reading the name in neat business type – *"M' Nomono"*, with a number below. He committed the number to memory, then picked up the lighter and burned it.

"We hope to hear from you," said the man, and they both left.

The moment the door closed Kirby jumped up and scuttled to the window. As the two tall figures merged into the current of people flowing down the street he watched through a crack in the blinds. Neither man looked back and both were soon lost amongst the throngs in Chinatown.

Something else caught his eye though. A small group of black clad men stood conspicuously on an opposing street corner and were themselves people-watching the crowd. It was obvious to anyone who lived here that they didn't belong. Too stiff. Too formal. No ghetto lurch. Definitely not any of the varieties of local cop. Even the local Trikuza bodyguards that watched the casinos had a less rigid demeanour about them.

As Kirby studied their clothing – boots, dark camo jackets, padding, bags – he met one of their gazes. In that moment he realised that the man was also looking back at him, *had* been looking at him all this time, had been watching.

CHAPTER TEN

.: Sync

──o Day 6 o──

The liquid was the colour of stale beer, watered down and then left for a week in the sun. The word *"Chlorine"* was written along the side of the bottle in bold, hand written characters.

The chemist looked the man up and down, not sure if he should go ahead with the deal. This guy – Page – or whatever his name was, didn't fit the usual brand of med-students and junkies that skulked into his store.

"What's it for?"

"I'm using it as a biocide," replied Page casually.

"A what?" His eyes narrowed suspiciously.

"A biocide. It's for a cooling system."

"Sounds like bullshit." He glanced furtively around the room to check he wasn't being watched. "I don't care what you want it for, just don't drink the stuff."

Page blinked in surprise. "Why would I drink it?" He jangled the carrier bag of circuitry he was holding. "It's for my boards. I need more speed."

The chemist leant over the counter slowly, right up to Page's face, then grabbed him by the collar. "What's my name?" he growled in a low, husky whisper.

"Mikhail?" said Page struggling to remember.

"Correct. And what does it mean?"

"Uh," Page thought about this for a second, not sure what the expected response was.

"It means I will cut your fucking balls if you're a cop."

Page shook his head in blissful naivety. "No. I'm not a cop," he said sighing. "I don't have a job at the moment, but –"

"Okay, okay," said Mikhail releasing him. "It's twenty five for the bottle."

Page reached into his pocket and took out a plastic bag with coins in it, then started counting them out in denominations of one and two.

———olo———

Five minutes later Page was walking along an urban street, eyes downward in thought, the plastic bag swaying gently in his arm. Navigating through the passers-by and a few poorly parked zooters, he turned off the main sidewalk into an alleyway.

Circuit dealers and Sim-pimps nodded at him as he strolled casually through the crowded clusters of illegal market stalls jammed between piss-stained walls. "Shiny lights, and shady deals, neon nights, and silver steels," thumped out a polka-reggae tune, mirroring the mood.

He pushed his way between a couple of traders and sidled up to a man in a grey trench coat, then tapped him gingerly on the shoulder. The man spun round, hand reaching for a concealed weapon, then stopped abruptly as he recognised Page.

"Aha, Pageroni," said the man, slipping the blade back into a pocket-sheath. "Main man on the totem pole. What are you buying?"

"Do you have anything new?"

"Yah. There's always new. But there's always a price."

Page looked glumly at his bag. "I'm saving."

"A man of the future I see, well –" He reached into his pocket, pulling out a sleek, black portable and handing it to Page. "The Kern-C300 will be the new Go-To for a man like you I just know it. Hot off the boat from Finland."

Page rolled around the device in his hand. It was the size of a small book and unfolded with a secondary screen inside. The keypad was minimal, but with perfectly-shaped, ergonomic keys that unlocked a hundred functions. It was a thing of nerd beauty – an object of geek desire. He let his fingers dance around the buttons, sighing.

"Aha, always the pianist," the man grinned in a gold-toothed smile. "This baby has supermax battery and can link the dataways through fifty-eight channels. She has low-scan, back-scan, tele-scan, catch me if you can. She's got quantum buffering, holo-mem, and sim-mem. She will run onboard and offboard, but," he delicately took the device back from Page. "At a price you can't afford."

Page looked at the device enviously. "I'm saving."

The man winked at him, and patted him on the shoulder. "Have a nice day Page. Ya know where I'm at."

———olo———

What the next street lacked in hustle and bustle of market crowds, it made up for in rats and sprawling garbage.

Page stepped over a bundle of cardboard boxes without breaking stride. "Alright Po," he said at the homeless figure who had become a growth on the kerb.

"gggau$$# fssthe breachesss," came the garbled, meaningless reply.

Page climbed gingerly up a graffitied stairwell, then through a small, dimly lit passageway. Beams shook through a lack of maintenance as he hauled himself up another two flights, stopping in front of a dented metal door with *"LIZZO 555 TZ"* scrawled in white spray-paint on it. Ever since moving here he had wondered what it meant and who Lizzo was.

He turned the key in the lock, kicked off his loafers, and trod bare-foot into the room. Two other sets of shoes were there. He looked up sharply.

"Good morning Page," said Velma amicably. "I hope we're not disturbing you. We did say Wednesday."

Was it Wednesday? Apparently it was.

Velma Beck was a cuddly, fluffy sort of woman, friendly and unassuming, but virtually impossible for him to read. Her thoughts ran along too different lines to make sense of.

"No Ms Beck," he replied awkwardly, glancing at her so briefly as to dismiss her without realising. His focus shifted to the other, taller woman. Penetrating blue eyes looked back at him.

The two women made an interesting contrast to each other, and an even more interesting contrast to the room. *His* room. He scowled. Electronics and old PCs were strewn around haphazardly, wired together with garish, multi-coloured cabling bought from a cheap DIY store. Fans and coolers blew musty air onto exposed motherboards. But despite the outward appearance of decrepitude, a cluster of flashing LEDs told of hyper activity taking place somewhere beneath the surface of this dusty, ramshackle chamber. His room.

Velma piped up, "I want to introduce you to –"

"Hi Page, my name's Sync," said the woman with penetrating blue eyes. She held out her hand. "Velma has been telling me about you."

Page looked at the hand without moving, then at the woman as a whole, trying to categorise the anomalous intruder. Her clothing was businesslike and yet slightly cyberpunk. It projected corporate facelessness but was sprinkled with vibrancy – the opposite of Velma. Was that a good or a bad thing? He shrugged. She withdrew her hand, still smiling.

It was now her turn to assess him. She looked at the short hair, the casual, almost thoughtless choice of clothing. Despite the lack of a common visual theme, she guessed there was a reason for each of the items within the chaotic assembly he wore. She took in the room as a whole with him standing in it. He belonged here. They were cut from the same cloth.

"I hope we're not disturbing you?" echoed Velma again.

"No," replied Page, and sat down on the floor in front of a computer and began to unpack his bags. He took out a few circuit boards and connectors, and reached around the back of the table for some wires.

"How are your tests going?" she asked. "I see you've got some new equipment since my last visit."

"They're okay," he replied.

She waited for an elaboration, but he just carried on with the wiring.

"I, hope you've been keeping up with the prescription?" she enquired cautiously.

"Yes," he said simply.

"I have some new pills for you. I think these will help with the next part of your recovery. Will you take them?" She placed a small jar of pills on the desk.

"Recovery," thought Page. The problem was he had no idea from what. A vague memory of some incident in the recent past that his mind seemed to block out... On second thoughts, it didn't much matter – he was only partially interested in the past. "Yes," he said only half paying attention. He was looking around for something. Something that did matter.

Velma, satisfied with the reply, sat back and relaxed. She seldom knew the details of what had happened to the people she took care of. She did her rounds, checking on them, helping them make their way back into society. She hoped that Sync would take a liking to him. He was a nice boy.

Sync smiled. She knew that a soft, circuitous approach was the only way to reach the man she had come to see. She was an expert in being able to put herself in another's shoes and look at the world through their eyes – it was, after all, the key to her own career. She could understand people on a deep level, without needing to become them. Not like the detective who gazed so deeply into the mind of a serial killer that they became one. No, she was able to stand at the top of an abyss, unmoved as she looked calmly over the edge into the currents of another's personality.

What she saw here was an active mind, the fruits of its labour growing around her. She liked minds, not only because they paid her salary, but out of a fascination for them as sculpted works of art in their own right.

"Here." She passed an electrical circuit screwdriver to Page.

"Thanks," he said, taking it delicately but with suspicion. "That's the one I was looking for." He started unscrewing bracket clamps on the boards but kept half an eye on her.

"Why have you covered the windows?" she asked, referencing the lack of daylight and the sheets of kitchen foil that had been taped over the glass.

"To stop the light getting in," he replied, unintentionally trite.

It had been a delicate operation, making sure the reflective side was flush against the glass without any tears, but had definitely been worth while. The room was cool, and dark.

Velma raised her eyebrows. The foil had been the first thing she'd noticed when entering, though she had not wanted to bring it up. As always she kept to her tack of pleasant apathy – all benign smiles and nods.

"You don't like the curtains?" asked Sync. The windows all had perfectly functional, but unused, curtains attached.

"Aluminium foil is for cooking, so it's really good at reflecting everything – light, UV, infrared – the full spectrum," explained Page. "As long as the reflective side is facing outwards then it makes the room cooler too."

Sync smiled at the blunt, practical reasoning that had shaped this room and its occupant into an exhibition of logical decision making.

"Have you seen it from the outside?" he asked with a touch of pride. "It looks awesome."

"But, you aren't cold in here? You don't want to let some sun in?" chimed Velma.

"Low temperatures are better for the circuits, but –" he started, and was about to say more, then cut himself off.

"Yes?"

"This," he blurted at the gear spread before him. His gear. "This stuff is all junk. How can I do anything? I need faster boards."

"Faster what?" She looked at the equipment. "Ah, I see."

Sync sat down on the floor next to Page. "Aren't you curious what I'm doing here?"

He nodded.

"So ask me."

"What are you doing here?" he asked mechanically.

The directness made her laugh. Logic without subterfuge. Her kind of mind. Could it be harnessed?

"I work as a form of, technology recruiter," she said slowly. "Specialist recruitment. Special people, with special skills, for special assignments." She paused, waiting for any sparks of interest.

He coked his head, debugging the syntax, looking for meanings that connected back to his world, but said nothing.

"Sync has been in contact with us for some time now, Page," chimed in Velma, breaking the silence. "She is looking for people who are really smart, but maybe have a difficult time finding work placements. She works with some very big companies, and when I told her about the research you do, she wanted to meet you. Isn't that right?" She smiled at Sync optimistically.

"But, you don't know what research I'm doing," Page quipped back at the two of them.

Sync nodded, holding his gaze, then slowly and deliberately looked around the room, taking in each bit of equipment in turn. "K16, 256-bit. Three K12s. Dual shunts. That's a redundant top-loader. Periphery buffers... Hmm... Some of the motherboards look overclocked."

Her eyes stopped finally on a headset that was winding its way from his seat into the machinery with flashing lights. "What is the work you are doing? I'd love to look at the code you're running."

Page was taken aback. The piercing, blue-eyed woman knew her stuff it seemed. Not everything she said was correct, but the basics were right. He was forced to re-evaluate his opinion of her. Clearly there was an intersection between their realities, however differently she looked and dressed.

"You're a programmer?" he asked.

"I used to be, until I moved into tech recruitment."

He nodded.

She stood up, sensing his acceptance, her demeanour changing as she shifted into a new gear of speech.

"Page, I have clients who can pay very well for the right kind of skills or people – people like you, who have something beyond the ordinary to offer. People who can solve complex problems that others can't even see." She looked at him, half testing half reassuring. "Minds that can change worlds. Is that you?"

He looked at her thoughtfully, but made no sound.

"I'm talking about remote contracts only – no meetings – I know you won't want to work in an office. I handle the clients, and you handle the code," she fired. "I can change your life. I have the connections."

He looked at the shoddy state of the room, the cheap equipment, acknowledging his predicament – the reliance on Velma, his state-appointed therapist, for the thin trickle of pennies he hoarded to buy dysfunctional junk.

"There would need to be an assessment of-course, Page. I am quite exclusive in my representation. But I hear you are a prodigy in the field of artificial intelligence."

There was a long pause.

"What, do you, know, about AI?" he asked, a strange look in his eyes, now impossible to read.

Had she misjudged? She responded, treading carefully. "Just the general stuff. True-learning, convolution, recurrent neural nets."

"That's not intelligence," he said slowly. "It's just predictable, incremental pattern recognition, leading back into itself. There hasn't been a shift in paradigm for decades."

"And is that what you're working on? A shift in paradigm?"

"Yes," he replied flatly.

Now she smiled. "Show me," she said, a gentle challenge. This adventure would be fun whatever it turned out to be.

There was an even longer pause.

"Not yet," he said, a change seeming to have come over him. "I need... access... to better equipment."

Sync could see the words she had spoken earlier settling in his mind. She was the route through which he gained access to what he wanted. Or one of them – he was no doubt resourceful.

She tossed him her card. "Call me when you're ready for work."

CHAPTER ELEVEN

:: Rain

Tan was aged seven, and playing in the village quadrangle of his childhood home. The silhouette of a church loomed above the square, casting a long shadow over the sand pit and wooden swings. Storm clouds gathered against the dwindling sun as the first drops of rain made wet holes in the sand.

Sand beats rain, he thought as he looked up at the imposing structure of the church, when it becomes concrete.

He stood up and dusted off his hands, noticing the faces of the bigger children around him. They had stopped playing and were looking upwards at the darkening skies.

He stepped slowly out of the sandbox onto the wet concrete path, and started to run, not knowing why, but feeling an unexplained compulsion to put as much distance between himself and the others as possible. At first nobody paid him any attention, but then, instinctively, like a pack of dogs following a predatory, genetic impulse, they gave chase.

He burst through a metal gate out onto a deserted street. To the left was a churchyard, and to the right a schoolyard. In front of him, stretching out as far as the eye could see, were row after row of dilapidated houses, nearly all shuttered and boarded up. Of the few unboarded windows he could see, each was coated in grime that looked untouched for a hundred years.

He traced the line of the streets, looking for a route that lead somewhere, but each seemed to circle back into itself or get lost in the labyrinthian maze before him. An infinity of abandonment with no way out. But it was okay, the others hadn't caught up to him yet. He was alone.

It was then that he noticed the skeleton lying in the road almost directly in front of him. The hands and legs were splayed out, leaving it facing upwards as if laid on an altar. Rain dripped off the skull. Wires ran from the fingertips and disappeared beneath the dirt. Had it been there the entire time? Or had it, somehow, just appeared? He looked at the empty, lifeless sockets. It was old.

He felt that he had missed something – something important. Or was about to.

As he stood there in confusion, trying to make sense of it all, the sound of splashing footsteps came from behind. The other children were here.

He felt, rather than saw, the shove of a hand in his back. As he sprawled forwards he lost his footing on the wet stone and felt the crunch of his knees hit concrete. He put his hands out to steady himself, but slipped, buckling beneath the momentum of his body and slamming into a small, rocky puddle.

The laughter slowly stopped as the bigger children realised the seriousness of his predicament. A stream of blood trickled from his temple, mixing with muddy water. He tried to push himself up from the dirt, but his hands did not obey.

One of the children seemed to say something but he could not hear what. He could not hear anything. They did not approach to help.

As he lay there, unable to move, he was vaguely aware that the sun had brightened and the storm was fading. The rain that had been falling into his open mouth had collected in his throat and was now filling his lungs. His splutters were too weak and came too late to clear the liquid from his chest.

Everything went white, and he thought no more about it.

———olo———

"I don't have to go to school today," said Nivi, mischievously. "It's a holiday."

The remark snapped Tan out of his reverie. He had been mulling over a dream he'd had last night, trying to put a meaning to it. The memories of a dream are like the ashes of a letter written by one's subconscious during the night then burned in the morning, he thought. There was a message in those fragments if they could only be deciphered.

He looked at Nivi curiously. "It's not a holiday. What makes you think it's a holiday?"

"There's no electricity. There's never electricity on holidays," she replied. "That's how I know."

"Ah. I see." He reached into a cupboard and pulled out the metal pot they used for heating water. It was more of a rusty skillet than a kettle, and had been charred black through years of use.

"Well, that's true, because the other houses use it on holidays, but today should be okay," he smiled, filling the pot from a makeshift tap that was screwed to the wall, and placing it on the hob.

Gas piping was a luxury beyond their means to afford, but the heating element of an old iron press served as a sufficient thermal conductor and worked well as an electric stove. He slid his arm under the side table, connected two wires, then waited for the Nichrome slab to heat up.

Nivi was right. The metal remained cold.

He poured the water into a glass and drank it instead, then drank another. "Maybe Yuita's moved the main cable again," he muttered.

"It was working earlier," called June, as she portioned out food onto wooden plates. "Maybe the connection?"

"Hmm. I'll take a look," he said, opening the front door and glancing down the lane. He froze.

"Tan?" enquired June hesitantly. "Is it? –" She stopped herself. There was no need to cause alarm.

"I'll be back in a few moments," he replied casually, but unable to mask the concern in his voice.

The trio of developers were standing on the walkway that led to his house. His neighbour – Erpin – was also there, huddled inside the triangle they formed, a contract held in his hand. All faces turned towards him as he approached.

Erpin shuffled awkwardly, a sheepish look on his face.

"Mr Taneka," said Holloway. "Your neighbour... ex-neighbour has seen the light. I wish you would too."

"Erpin?" asked Tan.

"Sorry Tan," he sighed, "I had to. I mean, I, I wanted to."

"But it's your home. We built these, together, with our bare hands," protested Tan.

"We can build others. It's not so bad," said Erpin. "I'll see you around." He trudged off down the lane to where Yuita was waiting, not even bothering to go back to his shanty.

The deal had evidently been done before today, and this was just the last piece of signature to complete the transaction. He felt a sense of bitterness. If only he could have spoken to Erpin about it, had known what Erpin was planning, maybe he could have persuaded him to rethink. They were so much stronger if they stood together.

Now his shanty was the only one that remained occupied. It left him feeling extremely vulnerable, and sour, and... something else. What was it? Futility? More than that. It was an acute sense of deja-vu that he couldn't quite put his finger on.

The developers were staring at him, sizing him up. He stared back blankly, giving nothing away through his expression. They all stood there silently, locked in a Mexican standoff of gazes while the seconds ticked by.

"You can't win," smiled Holloway finally. He held a contract up, and waved it at Tan. "It's an impossible scenario. Just sign. It will be easier."

"I'm not interested in your offer," said Tan, folding his arms defiantly, despite the nausea building up inside him.

Holloway shook his head and put the contract back in his pocket. "Okay then. I guess the offer has just expired."

Tan had subconsciously been calculating the chances of defeating this group. His eyes scanned hands and pockets for weapons, measuring posture and balance, the nuances of readiness. True, they were armed, but there were only three of them here and two in the car, and it was unlikely they would expect him to be so well trained. Five on one. But he would have the advantage of surprise if he attacked right away.

Something on his mind was telling him not to, though. A premonition, or after-image of a dream maybe. He pushed the thought to one side, relaxing his muscles in preparation to strike.

"Hah. You're getting ready to jump us?" sneered Marshall, noting the change in posture. "You've got guts, I'll give you that. But," and the tone of playfulness left him, "you can't be serious."

Damn. Tan was frustrated for having given himself away, but re-evaluating the situation he felt there was something distinctly off about it. Perhaps he had been saved from an even greater error. He relaxed, thinking. It was as though he had been equipped with a set of physical tools, and a problem in which the use of these tools appeared to be the correct solution – physical combat – but now, somehow, he knew this would fail, and that a different strategy was required.

It was then that he started feeling dizzy.

"Marshall's right," said Holloway. "You can't be serious. Not in your condition."

What condition? But almost as soon as he'd had the thought Tan felt the pangs of a sickness inside him.

"Maybe there's something in the water?" laughed Norbeck, gesturing with out stretched hands in a mockery of concern.

The water. Tan looked at Norbeck, noticing for the first time that the man's sleeves were wet. Water dripped from the cuffs of his shirt.

"That cable you've been using to divert electricity – it runs through your neighbours property." Holloway smirked. "One of ours now. All your supplies do. We own this shithole."

"There's been a change in policy," said Norbeck then, ringing his hands, "We had to uh relocate your water pipe."

"What?" said Tan.

A sudden terror dawned on him. The running water around here was all toxic – waste water run-off from the chem-plants upstream. God knows what pollutants and noxious compounds it contained. If they had simply dumped his supply pipe into the river... "You sick bastards!" he spat, racing back.

Holloway shrugged. "Not us who's sick."

The fear and concern written on June's face as Tan burst in cut him right to the core. She was holding Nivi's head delicately in her hands. The young girl was coughing violently. A broken cup lay on the floor where it had fallen from her fingertips.

"What did they do?" cried June.

"How much did she drink?" he asked as Nivi spluttered, gasping for air.

"Just a sip," said June, "what's wrong?"

The dizziness he had felt moments ago began to overwhelm him. He stared at the empty glass by the sink, recalling the two glass-fulls he had swigged. Surely not.

He began to cough, hoping it was just psychosomatic – that thinking about the water being poisoned had caused his body to react. But those hopes were dashed as he started to splutter, feeling the muscles tighten in this throat.

Nivi's fingers were grasping his palm, the little nails desperately clawing at flesh. Fear was written across her face. He held her tightly, wishing to comfort her even as he himself began to cough blood.

Red drops spattered his hand, covering the black ring he wore in a wet, crimson goo. The symbol "β" engraved in its centre now looked like two bloody eyes.

He didn't feel a sense of sadness as the shadow appeared at the doorway, but a sense of failure. The gun in Holloway's hand didn't even bother to move in his direction, so complete was the job that had been done by the chemicals. What horrible fate. To die from poisoned water before even having a chance to see the trap. Was there anything he could have done – something he could have anticipated? Or was it just his destiny in life to be brought here to this cruel finish?

Nivi had stopped breathing by now. he didn't have much longer himself, he knew. At least June would get a quick death. He wondered with morbid curiosity what death would be like. Would it be like a dream?

Then it struck him that there was something amiss about the entire morning's events; something that didn't make sense.

His vision became blurry. Everything faded away as he took his final breath.

CHAPTER TWELVE

.: I, Page

——o Day 16 o——

Page toyed with a piece of wire in his fingers, winding and unwinding it.

"There are teragons of memory on the Omicore servers. Just sitting there. Unused. I had a... look around today. Some interesting things." He snickered. "The security system is, well... I mean it's good, compared to other systems, very good, but all of these systems are just so... predictable, so obvious... So many things are obvious."

He stopped twirling, thoughtful. "I don't think I disturbed anything. Not yet. Just looking. Maybe there's a way I can enhance my –"

A crack came from the room behind him. He wheeled round in panic, feeling extremely vulnerable to have been caught mid way through exposing his unguarded thoughts by whatever it was. The realisation that it was just an expanding pipe, or some part of the ageing Chinatown building, did nothing to ease his anxiety.

"Fuck. I need to relax," he muttered.

CHAPTER THIRTEEN

: Statistical Weapons

——o Day 11 o——

Jeni felt like the final boss inside a game of Nuko-Kuko, pillaged by an army of school kids under a relentless bombardment of energy weapons. The bright lights of the passing floors shone off and on, into his face like a strobe as the elevator descended to the lobby. That, and the air-con were the only things keeping him awake.

It was 5am, and at the end of his working day, as he saw it. Working flexi-hours was the norm, and his preferred pattern was to pull straight 20-hour shifts followed by 20 hours of downtime. The days and nights could do what they pleased, he wasn't interested in their schedule.

Jeni Zeigler was a young man on the rise. Shortly after being granted a scholarship at Warwick, he had pulled out of his degree when offered a placement at Omicore. He figured, why go through the college system when a shortcut will take you there quicker? He was ambitious, hard working, but above all, kind.

He was twenty eight and already headed up the New Technologies division, overseeing a team of sometimes even younger employees. Unlike many of the other technology whizz kids, he was able to interact with his teammates in a manner that wasn't borderline autistic. So, as his career moved rapidly forward, he had been reluctantly drafted into more senior management positions. His heart stayed passionately in the code though.

He waved his badge vaguely in the direction of the night guard as automatic barriers slid apart to let him through to the lobby.

"Evening, Jeni. Or, morning I should say. Off home?" said the guard as she smiled at him.

They had become friends, he and the night guard, Kes, through these late night exchanges, as two different species of animal who water at the same hole gradually become accustomed to one another, eventually forming a kind of kinship based on no commonality of features.

"In a bit," said Jeni. "I'm just getting a D-Mart. You want anything?"

She held up a bowl of Katsu from under the desk. "I got my breakkie here," she grinned.

"It's dinner, Kes, dinner!" chuckled Jeni.

The claws of fatigue were pawing at him. A gentle tug that would eventually grip him like a hook, and pull him down into sleep. He wanted to grab a quick bite in peace, before the hum of morning traffic started, then head home.

The streets were still deserted, the blackness of night unbroken by sunrise. D-Mart was the best 24-hour eatery he knew of and was only a few streets away. It was a favourite among the late nighters, and he wondered if he might find any of his team there, tucked away in corners working on the project from a Digipad. His laptop was in a bag, slung over his shoulder, just incase. An addict always had their needle handy, and for him the high was the code.

"Mr Zeigler," said a bubbly voice as he crossed the empty street. "Can I take a minute of your time?"

The woman was dressed in a smart, casual manner, exactly as one of the office girls might be. He didn't recognise her. Maybe this was one of those early morning career types who tried to hustle jobs by sniping meetings with tech managers. In this part of town everyone was in tech. On the other hand maybe she was a recruiter. He hated recruiters – they always jumped out on you at strange times, trying to foist unqualified prospects into blatantly undeserved positions. He sighed inwardly.

"Uhm, yeah, I guess." He adjusted his glasses to get a fuller picture of her. She was attractive.

"I just want to ask you a few questions, if that's okay?" she smiled, elfin and alluring.

It was okay. If she was hustling for a job, she had at least put the effort into her appearance to guarantee he took notice. Her beauty didn't intrigue him per se – he wasn't that type – but he wouldn't begrudge her the attempt.

"What is it about?" he frowned. "We don't have any openings right now," he said apologetically, "unless, hey how good are you at Tebal, or networks? If you –"

"No no," she said, still smiling. "I just need you to look at this." She handed him a book sized tablet.

He took it curiously, holding in front of him. *"ProtoType D"* he read on the side. Prototype what? It had a harsh, military feel to it, and was definitely not market ready, but the design fascinated him. Exotic tech toys intrigued him as would a handful of mysterious blue powder to a Snuph junkie.

A small blue light pulsed as he moved it around but the screen was off. Presumably she wanted him to watch her video pitch, or code reel or something. Well, that was okay. Everyone deserved a shot and it was a novel way to apply for a job.

87

"Oh, you'll need to take your glasses off," she said, nudging the screen closer to his face.

He smiled, shrugged, and put them neatly in his top pocket. He held the tablet up, close in front of his eyes, looking at the blank screen waiting for something to happen.

It happened.

Abstract images of shapes and colour flashed in front of him, part mathematical, part organic. Strange curling flesh morphed into fractal-like spikes of wet fur, then shifted again into thousands of beads of yellow droplets, or were they eyes? It was impossible to describe – not just metaphorically, but literally – the shapes and forms followed pathways in his brain that lead beyond linguistic categorisation. His curiosity turned to fascination, then to mesmerisation, and within a few seconds he could not have looked away even had he chosen to. The flashing imagery had now reached its way too deeply into his mind, embedding itself into his cortex.

Having achieved this initial goal, the device moved into a second phase of infiltration. The imagery changed form, now appearing in combination with sounds that were every bit as compelling. Jeni had no choice but to watch – not through an inability to resist something too potent for his will, but through an unawareness that any choice was even to be made. He was held in a spell – hypnotised. The world around him began to blur and fade, as he lost cognisance of all events and time.

Yet as his other muscles slackened, his hands keep a tight grip on the device. On a subliminal level, beneath knowledge, he obeyed an impulse to never let go, forcing his eyes to watch.

The woman slid him sit down against a wall, his body gently convulsing. Saliva and spittle drooled from his mouth as his body fought the partial collapse of its nervous system. Yet he clung to the tablet.

A soft voice whispered in his brain. It was the voice of a cherub, angelic and celestial, washing like the lap of a supernal wave on the sands of his consciousness. "Weeeh... whillll... begihhhhn."

Jeni seemed to relax and become focused at the same time. He was ready.

"What is the nature of your work at Omicore?" the woman asked, irresistible.

"I... am head of... the new technologies... division," he drooled in a semi-stupor.

"What is the hierarchical relationship between you and Omar Cantor?"

"I work... directly under... him," he stammered.

"In line of seniority, are there any others that you need to report to before reporting to Omar Cantor?" she said, relentlessly.

"No."

"What is the project that you have been assigned to, starting on February 8th, listed under the name Symutal?"

"It is a... highly... secret... research project," he managed, with more difficulty now. His brain struggled to summarise such a broad concept into the neat packets of information that were being asked of him.

The woman frowned, then looked around her anxiously. The streets were still empty. She checked the line on a geometric timer on her wrist.

"What is the nature of the research?" she continued smoothly.

"I... I... It's... I..." he mumbled, now in confusion. He desperately wanted to help the voice, to give it the answers it wanted, but wasn't sure how. "It's... complicated. What level of... detail... do you want?"

"All detail."

A blue light flickered on the device as if in reaction to the strain Jeni was under. He reached for words. "It... It is based on a... convolutional... neural-net and... con—textual... heuristics, but using... do you know what... I mean by... directed pathways?"

"Provide an explanation," she continued in soft, inexorable tones.

"Okk... O... Oh... O...kay –" he drooled through fragmented syllables, and was interrupted by a noise from the street.

The woman looked up sharply. A figure moved in the periphery of one of the dimly lit streets. Kes was crossing the road towards them, and would be within earshot in about thirty seconds at her current pace.

The woman looked back down at Jeni clucking her tongue. "Move on from the previous question."

Jeni teetered forward like a drunkard. "Yeshh."

"Provide me with the password needed to access all files that relate to this project," she said, tone faster, and timbre more urgent.

Kes would be within earshot in ten seconds. Though from afar the scene playing out appeared almost natural – a man keeled over, a woman talking to him. Nothing nefarious about that at 5am on a city street.

Jeni licked his lips, slurring. "The password is... lowercase A... 9... T... Star... 6... two spaces... uppercase L... J... Z... 77.. R... character code 160..."

A moment of confusion passed fleetingly over his face, as though for a second he had become aware of the betrayal he had just committed, but was unable to penetrate the zombie-like trance he was in. "Buu... buut... what do... –"

"Silence," hissed the woman under her breath, hitting the switch on a remote concealed in her pocket. The device became instantly dormant.

Jeni obeyed, just as a shadow blocked the street light above.

Kes had stopped next to them. She looked down at the semi-comatose Jeni in obvious concern, then at the woman leaning over him. "What happened?" she asked, though without suspicion.

"I guess it's been a rough night," the woman smiled. "He just collapsed."

"Oh. God. Is he okay?"

"I, think he just needs some water," said the woman with an affectation of concern.

Kes's impulse was to throw her arms around him, then to rush back to get help, but her gut instinct held her there a moment. She looked over the two of them with more scrutiny. What was that thing he was holding?

She was about to ask when Jeni suddenly spluttered. Saliva sprayed across his sleeves. Jesus. First thing first. "Wait here, I'll get an aid kit," said Kes, racing back to the office.

The moment her footsteps died away the woman hit the remote again. Coloured imagery resumed its dance across Jeni's face.

"Are there any physical access keys or timing locks needed to authorise the account?" the woman continued. But it was too soon.

Kes was watching – her suspicion aroused by an inkling of something that didn't add up. She had broken stride almost as soon as she had set off, pausing behind the corner of a charge booth, and, in the stillness of the night had heard the question the woman had asked.

Kes walked towards them, her security stinger aimed carefully at the woman's chest.

The woman stared up at her, playful smiles all gone.

A bright flash lit up the polished glass of a hundred office buildings, followed moments later by a loud bang that echoed its way through the pre-dawn cityscape.

———olo———

The early morning bustle was waiting eagerly to commence, as the calmness of night held on to the city for a few moments longer.

Torvald leant over the lifeless body of Kes, looking at the neat bullet hole in her forehead.

Jeni was still slumped against a wall, rocking slightly. A pool of drool had formed on the floor, the trail of spittle marking where it had trickled off the clothing beneath his jaw. He was semi-comatose. Organs still functioned to bring life to his core, but through no sentient spark could he be said to be alive. He was a puppet whose strings had been cut from the fingers of his mind.

Torvald shone a light into the dilated pupils.

"Where the fuck is a proper medic?" he called out. A policeman standing behind him barked a few reflexive commands into a walkie talkie.

Torvald nodded, looking around for CCTV coverage, or even a vending machine whose camera sensors would be primed to look for passers-by. There were none, of-course.

"Torvald Rafat, Statistical Weapons Division," said Torvald, handing his card to Omar. He looked at Leonard – head of Omicore Security – and nodded in recognition.

Omar looked the man up and down. He was tall with a heavy set jaw, neat brown hair, neat cream suit. He was straight lines and sharp edges – like a machine from the early days of robotics – with mannerisms a perfect compliment to his appearance.

"Statistical Weapons?" enquired Omar as he looked at the card. He flicked on the room's privacy screen.

"This has the hallmarks of a new kind of attack we've been seeing recently against technology companies," said Torvald.

"I called him in," said Leonard by way of explanation. "The signs are pretty unique."

"It was a good call," said Torvald grimly. "The incidents that get reported are just the tip of the iceberg."

"I take it Jeni didn't shoot our night guard?" said Leonard.

Torvald nodded. "Was Jeni an important person? High-level access to critical data?"

"Yeah, fairly high," replied Omar, not wanting to go into details of the project.

Leonard grimaced. "His access keys have already been revoked, but the, uh, laptop he was carrying is gone."

"A laptop?" Omar reacted. "Why on earth was he carrying a laptop out of the office? We've got to stop this culture of cafe working..." He trailed off. "He is going to recover though, right?"

Torvald looked at him and sighed. "Probably not. He'll live, but he won't be himself again."

"If it's just a case of money for treatment, then –"

"No," said Torvald firmly. "The damage is done."

That hit Omar hard. Jeni was a nice guy – the sort of guy you hoped your daughter would get married to. Omar had taken him under his wing, and was following him with pride as he rose up the ranks of the company. He sat down.

"What exactly happened to him? They drugged him?" said Omar, unable to equate the state he had seen Jeni in, with the efficient, hard-working whizz kid that he knew so well... *had* known. He wouldn't be the same again.

"They hit him with an NBW, I think, probably to gain access to data," said Torvald shaking his head in sympathy. Noting the blank expression on Omar's face, he elaborated. "Neural Based Weapons. Interrogation devices used to flip open the subconscious mind without the messiness of drugs, or torture, which are much harder to conceal."

"How do they work?" said Omar, intrigued despite his upset.

Torvald smiled mirthlessly. "Let me give you a demonstration. Just a gentle one. Can I connect?" he gestured at the wall display in Omar's office.

Omar nodded. "Yes, but, is it safe?" he said, bracing himself. Leonard looked away knowingly.

"Do you know what trypophobia is?" asked Torvald, pressing a button on the remote simultaneously.

Before Omar could reply the screen pinged on displaying the grotesque image of a woman's flesh covered in small holes. Omar pulled back in disgust. "Yes!" he said, annoyed.

"Every animal on Earth has a set of imagery, sounds, smells, other sensory patterns wired into its brain by evolution for survival. A library of hidden codes and stimuli that trigger certain reactions when encountered," lectured Torvald, himself fascinated by the science of it.

"Take trypophobia for example – a built-in repulsion to small holes. It acts as a kind of protection mechanism, maybe against disease or going near things with lots of eyes," he continued. "The cause can be speculated on, but makes no real difference."

"I see," said Omar. "Animals that are genetically predisposed to stay away from clusters of eyes are more likely to survive?"

"Precisely," nodded Torvald. "Other natural triggers, say, a fear of heights are also easily explained. Falling from a cliff will kill a mammal, so we're afraid to look down – a wired-in reaction – but to a bird or fish the same view triggers nothing."

"I get it. Evolution has given us a survival cheat sheet," said Omar. "Instinctive behavioural responses to things we see in the wild."

"Exactly. Responses buried in your DNA for fifty million years, so deep you don't know they're there. But they are."

"So, where does the weapons part come in?" asked Omar.

"Twenty years ago, with the emergence of true-learning, a series of experiments were done known as the Calvert Tests," said Torvald seeming to stare into the past – a distant past that he himself may have been part of.

"They would take prisoners – thousands of them – strap them down then shine images into their eyes, for hours at a time. The stated goal was to find a way to pacify the most dangerous offenders. Maybe beaming the image of a meadow into someones retina would get them to behave better. Nonsense of course.

"These *scientists* uncovered not only triggers for fear and repulsion, like Trypophobia, but for many other emotions too. They were creating a kind of subliminal handbook of stimuli. But they had only limited success."

"Why?" asked Omar.

There was a shift in tone in Torvald's voice as his gaze returned to the present. He shot a probing look at Omar. "There weren't enough subjects, and the data was too complex to decode."

"I, see," said Omar cautiously.

"But these days they don't need prisoners do they? We are all being monitored at 90 frames per second, 24 hours a day. Whether it's a TV, computer, or even a Glo-board in the street, our heart rates, eye positions, facial expressions – everything – is being watched. And processed."

Omar shifted position uncomfortably. A subconscious admission of guilt – an acknowledgment that, with his company collecting exactly this sort of data – even pioneering some of the technology behind it – he had, therefore, played a part in Jeni's demise.

Torvald went on. "Through the power of modern supercomputing and data from limitless personal surveillance, they're now able to carry on from where they left off. To decode the patterns. Abstract forms that are buried too deeply in the mind to defend against."

An awkward silence seemed to open up. "I, think I see where this is going," said Omar, "but carry on."

"If you could see where it's going then you should have taken steps to prevent it," hissed Torvald somewhere between sadness and anger. "It is people just like you, who, in your blind harvesting of information are responsible for it all. And for what? Advertising? Pfft."

"We'll tolerate a lecture on weapons, not ethics," cut in Leonard firmly.

"It's okay," said Omar, "He is right, so far as it goes."

"Meaning?" Torvald asked.

"Meaning whatever part I have played in this area of technology I have gone to great lengths to keep it away from people who will abuse it. It is the military, and not I that are forever raping science, twisting it into new evils."

Omar took solace in the fact that he had always kept his company private. He was therefore immune to the pressure under which others bowed in their desperation to meet shareholder profit expectations. Nor was he compelled to fashion the shape of his company to fit a mould of overzealous regulatory mandates. He could fight them to bankruptcy and ruin if he felt like it, rather than grant access to his servers.

True, his company was collecting exactly the sort of data Torvald had just mentioned – were market leaders even – and yes, they were processing it in ways previous generations couldn't even imagine, but right now, even as they spoke, this data was being used to feed the system that would fight back against the evil.

Omar levelled a steely gaze at Torvald.

"The military," smiled Leonard in irony. It seemed to diffuse the tension.

Torvald continued. "Well the genie is out of the bottle. The weaponisation of these sorts of statistical exploits has been increasing rapidly. There are now devices which can be shone into your eyes, blitzing you with images and sounds that melt your subconscious defences; will make you give up all your secrets, then make you forget what has happened."

"Do we all have these weaknesses?" asked Leonard.

"It is possible to train some basic resistance, but there is no way to be fully immune."

"So that's what happened to Jeni?" asked Omar.

"Who can say," Torvald shrugged. "It looks like a botched interrogation. The original plan would have been to send Jeni back unharmed, I think. But your night guard interrupted, got shot, and they just took off and left. Like leaving someone on a surgery table midway through an operation."

"What sort of organisations have access to these weapons?" asked Leonard, shooting a look at Omar.

"Major governments only," replied Torvald. "There aren't many with the compute power. It's still in it's infancy."

"ASA?" asked Omar.

"Undoubtedly."

Omar and Leonard exchanged a knowing look.

"What about Hoshoku-Sha Technology?" Leonard asked cautiously.

"What do you know?" responded Torvald.

"They made us an offer, a week ago, at a sales pitch. Access to their Tōkei Senshi programme in exchange for access to our socio-emotio data."

"Did you accept?"

"No."

"Then be extremely careful," said Torvald.

———olo———

The thrum of machinery was deafening. Competing whirs of twenty different air-con units fought for resonant supremacy over twenty different frequencies, forming an earsplitting cacophony that made the hair on Omar's head vibrate. Standing on the rooftop of an obscure part of the Omicore HQ, tucked between ventilation systems, were he and Leonard.

It had been hours since Torvald's visit and they had not had a chance to talk things through in private until now.

Leonard stretched two expanding metal tubes across the passageway behind him then flicked a button. Air between the strips of metal began to shimmer as waves of sound were emitted. The volume within dropped to near silence as the device calibrated itself. A wall of vibrational pressure was formed that exactly matched and cancelled the noise from without, leaving near silence within.

Had anyone been watching from the ground, and possessed the eyesight to distinguish the two figures from the grids of overlapping metal, all that they would see now would be a shimmering haze of blurred air. Had they been within earshot, there would be nothing but a white, overbearing static to hear. But behind this barrier of air those two figures could converse in complete privacy.

"Okay, we can talk," said Leonard.

"What was on that laptop?" demanded Omar.

"Only personal stuff and whatever partial assignments the guys take to the coffee shops. Everything is encrypted at maximum level – I've been through the logs. Jeni was a diligent guy."

Omar nodded in agreement. "Yeah. Okay. Is there anything on there that could compromise us?" he asked, delicately. "Legally, I mean?" He recalled his meeting with ASA, mulling the implications of them having access to even a fragment of the private research.

Leonard looked at him quizzically. "Was there anything else that Jeni was working on, besides the research, that you are talking about specifically?"

Omar shook his head, either in declination to answer, or to indicate a negative.

Leonard clasped his hands in thought. "When an organisation like ASA wants to label you as a criminal, they will be able to find evidence of criminal activity, no matter how mundane. The chances are, yes, as soon as they can access the laptop, they will find some scraps of code or memory that they can use to indict you, if that is their goal."

Omar sighed heavily. "Well then the question becomes – How long will it take them to crack the encryption on that laptop?"

"Two to three weeks from now, if they are really dedicating resources to it."

"How can you be sure?"

"It's a straight forward calculation, if you know the level of encryption and how powerful the tools are that do the cracking," he opened his hands, "and I know the level of encryption and how powerful the tools are that do the cracking."

"Gruugh," Omar scowled. "That means everything will come to a head at the same time. If your estimate is correct then it means that some time during the Kamara meeting is exactly when they'll gain access, and any action they decide to take will follow on pretty swiftly."

"You think we should withdraw?"

Omar considered the impact of withdrawing so that any complications could be resolved without a public scene.

"Not a chance," he said finally.

The main point to everything was the research. Going public at the meeting was a chance to open up to the world what they had been working on. It would be the perfect forum in which to unveil their counter thrust to what had been insipidly building up in global society for decades, *if* they could get it done within that time frame. The amount of compute resource Omar had dedicated to the task was immense, but even so it would be close.

Leonard nodded. "Hiding in the shadows is not the way to handle an organisation like theirs."

"The devil has long figured out ways to deal with his enemies in the darkness. We carry on as before," muttered Omar.

"There is another possibility," conjectured Leonard, "That they have already gained access before we revoked Jeni's credentials, and have dropped something into our server's memory without us realising."

"You mean a virus?" asked Omar.

"Perhaps just a snitch-bot. Something innocuously sending reports from time to time with whatever it finds."

"Bastards. I want you to monitor this closely. This is a top priority."

Leonard smiled confidently. "More resources have already been put on it."

Omar twirled his tie, thinking. "Maybe we should introduce a few wildcards," he mulled. "Someone from the outside, with no former knowledge of our systems. Someone good, who can do an independent appraisal."

"Pffft. A contractor?" Leonard couldn't hide his skepticism. This was irregular – reckless even, and made him uneasy. "Would we be able to trust someone with that sort of access?"

Omar stopped twirling. "Well maybe that's the approach we take. Give them access to some parts and see if they can go any deeper. No help from us and no clues."

CHAPTER FOURTEEN

.: Human Resources

——o Day 9 o——

Part of a half built dockyard jutted out from a blue sea. Waves lapped at the wood and concrete structure. A yacht was moored in front of wet, algae covered steps and, in keeping with the environment, also appeared to be half-built. Its split hull exposed the insides like the cross section of an ant colony.

A moment later. Particles moved through the air in lateral lines as if blown by a binary wind. Wood and steel materialised to fill the gaps in the dockyard. Engine parts appeared from thin air, fleshing out some of the open guts of the hull.

A time-lapse construction process seemed to take place throughout the scene. Concrete bollards appeared on some of the walkways. Planks filled open spaces between sections of the harbour.

Then, suddenly, it stopped.

The word *"Error"* appeared hovering in the sky. The words *"Low Memory"* appeared beneath it a second later.

Particles that had been in motion dropped out of the sky. The yacht and the steps began to crumble into pixelated blocks. The dockyard disappeared just as magically as it had started to appear.

Page unclipped the sim headset from his ears and looked round. "Fuck."

He was sitting in his apartment, legs crossed, on a cheap sofa, a massive cracked screen before him. The room had been upgraded since Sync's visit, though the characteristic electro junk that defined him still dominated. Headset cables snaked off to a machine on the table.

The massive screen spewed code. Page scanned it, then slid over to a bank of circuitboards, yanking some out in irritation. The smell of burning plastic stung his nostrils. "Fucking fuck piece of shit!"

Fifteen minutes later and he was sprawled out, chest to floor, surrounded by cables, notebooks, and sheets of paper. Hand-sketched memory diagrams written in the shorthand of his own hieroglyphics were scattered next to stacks of dead circuitboards, and made of the room a kind of electro-junk necropolis. All was silent but for the sound of scratching as he picked at a circuit board with a metal pin.

Bzzzzzzzzt. The silence was suddenly broken by the buzz-press of an entry gate. Bzzzzzzzzt.

But Page was a scholar, lost in the scribblings of a hundred lines of pseudo-code. Bzzzzzzzzt.

Crunch.

The sound of muffled footsteps came from somewhere below, increasing in volume. Multiple footsteps.

A jar of pills from Velma lay on the floor, half empty. A few of the innocuous looking tablets began to rattle. Next to them a glass of water vibrated, reflecting the room in elegant, shifting curves. Gentle, pulsating throbs could be felt as floorboards vibrated with the march of feet.

Kerrunch!

The door to the apartment exploded suddenly inward as steel toecaps smashed through it. Several booted feet kicked their way into the room as camo clad men marched in. Despite his shock, Page watched in mathematical fascination as the men evenly distributed themselves into a formation that perfectly divided the space.

"Good afternoon," said a central figure who was in apparent command of the unit. "That's a lot of kit," he added, looking around at all the metal and plastic.

"Who are you?" said Page at length, from the floor.

"Human resources," came a reply from one of the other men. They had relaxed, seeing that Page was alone.

"Ah yeah, human resources." The commander grinned, taking a step forward. "Thomas Bint," he said, offering a hand.

Page instinctively put out his own hand to shake. As he did so Bint grabbed it, lifting him up in a vice grip. "You fuckin nerds are all the same. Only look in one direction."

"What?" Page squirmed against the arm lock to no avail.

"Trip sensors. Motion lines," growled Bint. "You got all this gear and you just let us walk in. Fuckin hacker dweebs."

"This guy's an amateur," scoffed one of the others.

"What?" said Page, still lost.

"You didn't think anyone would come?"

"Who?"

"What did you think was gonna happen when you hacked into a fucking military defence company?" Bint asked.

Page noticed for the first time a logo on the man's jacket. The three red slashes. He read the insignia. *"Hoshoku-Sha Security Agent"*... "Ah shit."

"Ah shit yeah. Thank you for the clarification," said Bint. He nodded at one of his men. "Boys, if you would."

The men split off into pairs, circling computer equipment, yanking out hard drives, and circuits. They expertly unhooked the computer's metal brackets and extracted the memory boards and storage systems, putting them into a pile in the centre of the room. One of them had produced a large lump hammer and was using it to smash through the protective casings one by one, damaging the electronics beyond all repair.

Another wielded a high voltage stun gun, and was picking out specific circuitry then zapping it with strong pulses of electro-magnetic charge. Page watched the symphony of destruction take place, his banks of painstakingly assembled computers now reduced to scraps beneath the hammer blows and shockwaves of electricity.

"What are you doing?!" he screamed at them, but was held tightly by Bint. "Leave my stuff alone! It's not, yours!"

"You just don't get it do you?" Bint asked.

"It wasn't hacking! I was just scanning the spare memory!"

Page had been sniffing around on a number of different networks, slurping up whatever data he could find to help his research project. He now suspected that he hadn't been anywhere near as careful as he'd thought. Note that to self.

"That's the problem with you techs. When it comes to working out the real world, you're actually pretty dumb." Bint shook his head in mock pity.

In that moment Page squirmed free from Bint's grip. He spun round in desperation and lunged at the nearest man, punching and kicking as hard as he could.

It was so out of character that it took the man completely by surprise, who, not imagining Page to be the sort to lash out, was still looking dumbly forward as Page's left hand connected with his face. The man's nose bent sideways with a blood spattering crack as the room suddenly fell silent.

"I guess you're not exactly what you seem," said Bint. "That was even dumber than I thought."

The man whose nose had been broken grinned calmly through the blood, then nonchalantly spat red on the floor, as another two men pinned Page down.

"You a lefty are ya?" he said, looking at Page's hand. He pulled the arm tightly, and pressed the hand down, the fingers splaying out.

The man looked around casually for something to use as a tool, then picked up the glass of water on the floor next to him. Drank it. Looked at the empty glass. "This'll do."

Realising what was about to happen, Page screamed. He screamed for his lost work. He screamed for the smashed equipment that had taken him all this time to collect. He screamed with the impotence of being pinned down against his will. He screamed with pain, as the man repeatedly smashed the glass into his hand. He screamed with agony, as the splintered shards were ground into his exposed, bloody flesh.

But the man was irritated and soon stopped. He'd made his point.

Page's hand lay limply in front of him, the fingers barely moving. He looked at it and cried. The men silently reformed into a neat unit, ready to exit. Bint walked to the front.

"Look, son. I don't know who you are and I don't much care. But you got off lightly so consider this a warning. Next time you fuck around on our network it won't just be the drives we destroy, okay?"

Using his functioning right hand Page moved the limp fingers in his left, like the hands of a manikin. He managed to arrange the fingers into one final gesture – a final statement of defiance. "Fuck you," he said through the silence, middle finger propped up.

The broken-nosed man broke rank, and walked back toward Page, raising his boot. "Next time, I will," he said, kicking down hard.

They left Page lying in the room, his bloody left hand still outstretched.

As he stared through swollen eyelids across vertical floorboards, slipping in and out of consciousness, he saw the thing he'd managed to hide – the one drive he'd tried to distract them from noticing with his suicidal outburst. There it was, stashed under a cupboard, completely untouched. The label was still scrawled on it.

Data Rip. Tōkei Senshi.

CHAPTER FIFTEEN

.: Cadaver

——o Day 24 o——

The body of a young market worker lay crumpled on the sidewalk, a grimy cleaver protruding through a slash of clothing in his back. Drying blood was soaked into the shirt, and ran in patches like a water-starved river down the crevice, through the butt cheeks, and into his pants. There wasn't enough to seep through to the concrete.

One or two people were staring, but most passers-by never glanced away from their phones or feet long enough to notice anything amiss. It was always like this in Chinatown, people had somewhere to go, day or night, rain or shine, and even a body in the street wouldn't interest them. Neon lights, cartoon brands, and the nauseating fumes of chilli oil and garbage kept this 24-hour burb alive.

Wahh-Woh-Wohh. An off key sound came from a small, handheld instrument as dexterous fingers moved smoothly over it. Kirby looked down at the corpse by his feet.

"Well it wasn't suicide," said another voice. A uniformed cop had just arrived. "What you doing here Kirby? He one of your clients?" chuckled the cop. "Not a fan of the music I guess."

Kirby put the instrument back in his pocket and turned to see who the cop was. It was Toby, one of the beat officers from the blocks around here. They more or less all knew each other – the cops and the investigators. Sometimes they worked together, other times they worked apart and hid results from one another.

"Nah. Not one of mine," said Kirby. "I just came from across the street to see what the hubbub was. Gotta keep my slum education going."

"Usual gang stuff I expect," said Toby dismissively. "They never have any imagination. Probably some gambling debt or an unpaid hooker bill."

He rolled over the body with his foot, exposing the man's front. There was blood underneath where the chest had been lying.

"Well now ain't that curious," said Kirby in surprise.

"What is?" Toby looked at the scene seeing nothing unexpected.

"The blood. It shouldn't be there. The wound is in his back," said Kirby leaning down for a closer inspection. "And there wasn't enough blood to get round there."

"Oh yeah, I see what you mean. Maybe he just kind of spun around as he fell down or something," offered Toby, scratching his stubble. It was kind of strange now that he thought about it.

"This guy was killed somewhere else, and then someone just put 'em here," said Kirby thoughtfully.

"How do you figure that out?" said Toby. "Maybe it's the other guy's blood and he just got away."

"Just a hunch," said Kirby. "He's unarmed."

Toby began checking the pockets of the body for ID, or anything that might shed a bit of light on the scene.

Kirby instinctively looked up at the windows and alleys. The passers-by had all passed by, and nobody new seemed interested in the body now that a cop had arrived. Kirby scanned the surroundings, looking for something.

"Do you ever get a feeling something deeper's going on?" asked Kirby, "That you can't quite put your finger on?"

"Oh here we go. Corky Kirby," chuckled Toby. "Yeah maybe there's a dinosaur footprint around here."

Kirby ignored the playful insult. He was still scanning. Everything seemed normal, but he couldn't get the creeping feeling out of his spine that someone was watching him. He scanned the street line again.

There!

A shadowy figure was standing across the street exactly where he himself had come from. The figure was hard to spot at first because he, or she, just blended into the city background. But it was clear from the posture that they were watching him, or both of them. He kept his movements natural, and subtle.

"I'll be back in a bit," said Kirby quietly, lips hardly moving. "I need to check on something."

He made no indication of what he was going to do, then suddenly dashed across the street directly towards the figure.

The figure reacted instantly, bolting off pell-mell down an alleyway.

Kirby gave chase, but the alley was hard to move through at speed. Trash bags and garbage spilled out from the backdoors of shops making the narrow passageway into more of an obstacle course than terrain for a sprint. He could just see the figure turning a corner at the end, and tried to quicken his pace.

Upon reaching the corner himself he was just in time to see the last few steps of the man's feet rounding the next corner, then they were gone again. He gritted his teeth and pushed on.

It occurred to him whilst running that, despite his city experience and casual familiarity with the slums, he was running deeper and deeper into a completely uncharted zone, where the normally tough street rules got even tougher. None of these shanty alleys were mapped on any guidance system. And there was no-one beside himself, and the person he was pursuing, to bare witness to whatever took place when they finally met.

His pace slackened as he rounded the third corner. This time he could clearly see the figure walk into a doorway that came from the back of one of the buildings. They were not even running now.

He checked himself. It was extremely risky following a guy into an unknown building deep in the slums. Every shuttered window was a potential hornets nest of miscreants, every doorway an ambush.

He reached into his pocket, feeling for the gun he kept there. It gave him a sense of security knowing it was at hand, and fully loaded. But whoever he was chasing had deliberately led him here, he now suspected, and would be prepared for such an obvious gambit.

Suddenly paranoid that he was being snuck up to from behind he spun around. Nothing was there. The stillness gave him the jitters. Slowly, he walked towards the doorway. His heart was racing as he stepped in.

The change in brightness caught him off guard as though a hood had been suddenly thrown over his eyes. He grasped for his gun reflexively, despite the prior hesitations, to cover the few seconds of lost vision while he adjusted to the new, much lower light levels.

He was in the back of a disused restaurant. It was almost pitch black. Shadows of broken wall tiles cast toothlike obsidian into recesses of the room.

He could see the outline of a man standing in front of him, a deeper black against the shadows. Dusty clothes, face mostly covered. The form moved rhythmically in and out with the sound of panting.

As Kirby's eyes continued to adjust to the darkness the man before him seemed less and less threatening. The sense of danger he had been harbouring gradually abetted, and was replaced by a sense of curiosity. He lowered his gun.

The man spoke, still panting. "I need you to investigate a murder."

Kirby nodded, satisfied. He knew there was a connection. "The stiff back there? Who was he?"

"Not... him," the man said slowly.

"Whose then?" asked Kirby.

"Mine," said the man.

Kirby parsed the syntax mentally to try to make sense of it. "You murdered someone? And you want me to investigate?" asked Kirby, knowing that it sounded crazy.

"No. I want you to investigate My murder," said the man.

Kirby looked at him blankly.

"I was murdered. And I will be again," said the man.

Despite a natural turn for the mysterious and unexplainable, Kirby had discipline when it came to picking which rabbits to chase. Some led down interesting holes, but most led nowhere, and he would often end up chasing his own tail.

"Mmm..." sighed Kirby. "You look pretty good for a dead guy."

"I re...remember it," said the man, stammering.

"I think you need help, bud, just not from me," said Kirby, as he began to relax, subconsciously dismissing what he saw as just another crazy rabbit to chase in Chinatown.

The man's hand suddenly moved into his pocket.

Kirby jumped to alert, his hand going to his own pocket. "Easy friend," he said very carefully. "We only just met. Let's not get off on the wrong foot."

The man pulled his hand out slowly, holding a piece of card. It was a polaroid photo with a word written on it. He handed it to Kirby cautiously.

It was a photo of a 30 year old man in a blueish room, sitting at a computer. He had a bandage around his left hand. Kirby looked at it in disbelief. Across it the name *"Page"* was written.

"Page?" he asked. "This is... Page?" he waved the photo. "You know this guy? And he's the guy you say is looking for you?" Could it really be the guy?

The man nodded. "He is... responsible for my death. But I have never met him," he said, rasping over the last words. The man was struggling to compose answers now.

"Why is he looking for you?" asked Kirby with urgency, sensing the man might slip away into madness before the conversation could be finished. "What's it all about?"

The man opened his mouth very slowly. "The end of... the... world." He sounded parched, as if his lungs were made of chalk. Then he staggered, and fell to his knees, barely breathing, and gasped for air.

Kirby looked around urgently for water, but it was too dark inside to see anything clearly. He turned into the alley, hoping to find a tap. Nothing. Maybe he could carry the man to the main street. He rushed back to the restaurant.

The man was gone.

CHAPTER SIXTEEN

.: Noodles

———o Day 12 o———

Page looked at the scrawled addresses on the scrap of paper in his hand, then up at the filthy entrance in front of him. The whole street was mired in the nameless black soot that lined inner-cities the world over. He shuddered inwardly at the thought of living in this place. But options were limited. Only a handful of rentals would accept the traceless digital currency he needed to pay with and they were all here in Chinatown. Cash was too risky now, and the plethora of other electronic payment systems each had its own spidering trail that would lead back to him, should he choose to use it.

The aroma of chilli and refried oil drifted into his nostrils from a noodle bar across the road. A hot cloud of steam masked a dilapidated plastic sign where the once white logo of a hawk faded into brown stains of degradation. *"Phocan Vietnamese Cuisine"*. His stomach tightened at the thought of eating there, or anywhere on this street.

He walked into the entrance of the building then down a filthy corridor toward the reception counter. The landlady looked at him with antipathy through protective metal bars as he held up the address in his hand.

"Your name?" she asked, with the warmth and geniality of a day old piece of roadkill.

"Page," he replied. "To see room 145."

"You pay now," she said curtly, folding her arms and looking impatiently at a small screen on her desk.

Page flicked out his portable and swiped a few codes into an obscure interface. Numbers danced briefly as a progress bar reached one hundred percent. A sharp ping sounded from her screen as the transaction completed.

She slid keys across to him under the grill. "Same payment, every month."

He nodded, taking the keys, and looked past her down the dimly lit corridor that stretched oppressively into the depths of the building.

"You take back entrance. Stairs. Is better."

"Uh thanks," he nodded.

————olo————

The room was by no means extravagant – far from it – but the interior of his new lab, as he thought of it, was a definite improvement over the exterior, and would be sufficient for him to continue his work. A large prefab table made the centrepiece, with basic furniture dotted peripherally around the edges.

"Blue," he said to himself, noting the garish tint of the walls.

He looked down at his hand, tentatively flexing the damaged fingers. The attack hadn't been as bad as he'd feared, physically. In terms of equipment though it had been devastating. Hundreds of hours of painstaking circuitboard assembly had been lost. He wanted to punch someone.

But in forcing him to relocate and restart, it had given him an opportunity to rethink his entire approach. This time around he would use less of his own compute power, and would place a much larger portion of the experiments on whatever systems he could find at his disposal. This carried more risk, but would produce results that were leaps and bounds ahead of what had been possible before. He also still had the data drive.

In ways that he was not aware of, the assault had opened up a new facet of his personality. It was a kind of boldness to take risks in pursuit of something... or, viewed another way, was a loss of concern of the consequences of things.

"Might as well get on with it."

Page scanned the walls for electrical terminals, data sockets, any kind of power hub he could get started from, scowling at the lack of them. This room would need to be upgraded. You could never get enough juice.

Peering furtively out of the window at the street, he began to mentally catalogue the nearby resources. He studied the houses, stalls, shopfronts. There was another eatery "Norbeck's English & Asian Bakery", some kind of generic salon named "Marshall Cuts", and an electronics shop called "Holloway" – which in all likelihood was a front for something illegal, though he had no idea what. He kept scanning.

One of the power lines that ran above the road caught his eye. The rubber padding had been cut open along one of its main arteries, where a derivative cable was attached like a parasite. Tracing the cable he could see that it snaked its way discreetly into the very building he was in. That was good. It meant there was a strong source of power that could be tapped. It was also rather curious.

"Guess I'm not the only one who needs the juice," he pondered.

119

Overall he was satisfied. There was just one other thing he needed. Money.

He rummaged around in his pocket, until he found what he was looking for, then tossed Sync's card onto the desk.

"Time for us to talk."

CHAPTER SEVENTEEN

: **Bossa Nova**

——o Day 13 o——

Sync stretched out her legs on a yoga mat, the sweat dripping into little pools around two slender calves. She pawed impotently with mittened hands then tore the boxing gloves off with her teeth. A satisfied grin crept onto her face as she checked the pulse band and did the math. One point lower than yesterday. She gave a whoop of celebration, then lay back on the mat, letting the tingle of relaxation run through her like water through a dried riverbed.

Bleeeeeep – a timer alarm pinged.

"Uhh why now?" she sighed in exhaustion, tapping the bleeping thing to shut up. But it was right and she was late. She took a few quick steps to her desk, patted the sweat from her face, and tossed the matted strands of hair behind her ears. Clearing her throat, she slung on the sim headset.

——olo——

The gentle strum of a guitar filled the room with the smooth, relaxing vibe of Bossa Nova. Its playful tune wandered between notes in just the right way to tease the listener into creative thoughts. Omar sat in the boutique Italian restaurant, alone but for the solo guitarist, and a plate of partially eaten pasta laid before him. He twirled and then untwirled a loop of fettuccine with a fork as he thought over his situation. A wooden clock chimed on the wall. 1:30pm, it said softly.

A blue-eyed woman appeared at the entrance a few seconds later, her oblique business lines clashing with the rustic Mediterranean décor.

"Cute," said Sync, looking around.

Omar smiled. "Sorry. I had so many meetings today that I had to take our call during lunch."

Sync flicked one of the plinths. It gave the sound of solid rock, and not the generic sim-surface that so often was used. She raised her eyebrows at the details of the environment. It was classy. "I'm impressed. This based on a real place?"

"It's from a catalogue," Omar smiled. "816 from Dawsons if you must know. The food's real though."

He held a hand in the air and slid a finger downwards. The music gradually quietened, with notes being played in decreasing softness until they were not being played at all. The guitarist vanished.

"Let's talk," said Omar, business mode. "You said you might have someone for me that fits my brief? All of it?"

"I do," Sync shot back with a grin, seating herself at the table.

"That was quick. Where did you find them?" asked Omar.

"Him," she corrected, then waited.

Omar said nothing, looking at her challengingly, himself waiting for an answer.

Sync smiled with asperity. "Mr Cantor, I would have worn a dress if I had known this was going to be a charity event. Next time you must let me know in advance."

Omar chuckled dryly. "Call me Omar, please."

"Sorry Omar," said Sync, now warmly. "But you can't possibly expect me to tell you my sources."

"I understand your point. But I don't want you to present someone who I could just find from the thousand-and-one recruitment companies that already work for me. It's important I hire someone not reachable by the normal channels."

"I don't operate in the normal channels. But please, elaborate," said Sync, also serious.

Omar looked around self consciously. Despite the privacy of being in sim, he couldn't shake the feeling of uneasiness he always had when talking on matters of security.

"A company like ours is involved in several large operations at once. We're under constant attack. Groups attempting to access private areas of our digital property, either to steal, or vandalise what they find there. We have our own security staff, of course, who are extremely capable by the way. But they are under our protection. Unlike a contractor."

"I see," she said, connecting the dots. "If an outside person is known to be working on your security, then you're worried they'll be traced and approached by one of these groups."

"Yes. And then normally they get offered a huge amount of cash to divulge our secrets, or..."

"Or?"

"or they don't get offered a huge amount of cash," said Omar grimly. "If you catch my meaning?"

Sync nodded in comprehension. "How dangerous are the – groups?" she asked with concern.

"Military in this case," admitted Omar.

"Let me think about this," said Sync after a pause. She paced it out, leaving him to eat, while she weighed the balance of things in her mind.

Her gut told her that she could trust this guy. The proposal he had made was out in the open, without deception. On the other hand, whatever danger he foresaw was likely to be greater than he would freely admit. Was that his reason for hiring an outsider with no connections – as a fall guy – to find someone to work on a technology that carried so much risk that one of his own team wouldn't take it?

Omar guessed at some of the thoughts running through her mind. "Take your time," he said, sincerely.

An even more sinister scenario occurred to her. Could it be that Omar was finding someone expendable to work on a project that he himself was keeping secret from his company – a loose end that could be tidied up after completion, leaving one of these covert groups to take the blame? She shook her head. This could go on all day, second guessing motives to infinity. She trusted her gut. Omar felt like a good guy. In any case, the increased risk carried an increased pay cheque. That was good not only for her, but for Page.

Page, who had called her yesterday, informing her in his own strange way that he needed the cash and was ready to work. She had no idea what had compelled him to call, but the timing was serendipitous.

She smiled decisively. "As I said, I have someone for you, and he's definitely the discreet type."

Omar nodded. "And his ability?"

"Mr Cantor, I'm a specialist. Therefore anyone who I present to you is special."

Omar snorted. "Special won't even get you through the door. I need someone gifted. I'm not sure if you understand the level that we hire at."

Sync was not to be rattled. "You saw the application test?"

"Yes. It was excellent. But that only gives a cursory outline."

"It took him fifteen minutes."

Omar was not a man to cling to pride for the sake of it. Fifteen minutes to complete a test that ought to take an hour was on the prodigal level, even with cheats. "Then, I acquiesce. That is more impressive than I thought."

"He is gifted, and uh –" She wavered slightly.

Omar caught it. "And?"

Sync sighed. These relationships had to be so carefully managed. The skills might fit like a glove only for a placement to come unstuck through a clash of personality. Better to be upfront about potential pitfalls. "Some of the people I work with are outpatients."

"Outpatients? From what cause?"

"It differs. There can be many reasons that someone with a gift in one area, has trouble integrating in another."

"You mean like a kind of autism? He is a savante?" his interest was piqued.

"I don't know, definitions change. Use whatever one makes you comfortable."

"Definitely not the normal channels," he muttered.

She looked at him challengingly. "I want to add the condition that he won't ever meet face to face. Is that going to be a problem?"

Omar relaxed. If all she was worried about was a personality clash that was fine. In some ways it would even be a benefit. A true outsider. "No. Not if his work is good enough," he said carefully.

"Good," she smiled.

He looked at her, deadly serious. "The work he will be doing cannot ever be discussed though, not with anyone outside my personal circle, even with you."

"I guess we both have conditions," she said, "but I think we'll work well together."

There was a long pause.

"By the way, I heard about a hacking incident recently at Hoshoku-Sha, possibly involving one of these, uh, contractors. There wouldn't be any connection would there?"

"I don't know anything about that," said Sync enigmatically. Her manner indicating that even if she did, he wouldn't get the information from her lips.

That was good. That was really good. She could be trusted. "Okay," nodded Omar in satisfaction. "He sounds like exactly the person I have been looking for."

Sync waved a formal sign-off hand shake, then disappeared.

Omar lingered for a moment, looking at the empty plate in front of him. He toyed with the fork, lost deep in thought, wondering who Sync had discovered. Could he be...?

Omar shut the thought out of his mind.

CHAPTER EIGHTEEN

.: Arlos

Kirby sipped a can of Pep and studied the map on his office wall. It had a few sticky notes with times and dates written on them, pinned to a couple of different streets. The word *"Page?"* was marked in black felt across various streets and buildings. It was the day after his chase through the alleyways and he was determined to run all leads to ground.

He pinned a copy of the polaroid he'd been given to the map and wrote *"End of the world?"* beneath it. The original polaroid he held up to the light, checking both sides for anything out of the ordinary. So far it just looked like a normal picture – no codes, no cryptic stuff, just a photo. Let's do this the old school way he thought, examining the photo for details in the background.

It was of a 30-year old man, short haired, caucasian or mediterranean type, medium to slim build, looking directly at the camera. The light was coming from the front of the photo, as though the man had been posing for a mug shot. But the lips were open, as if in mid speech.

Kirby pulled it under a magnifier and looked at the zoomed-in image on the screen. He checked the reflections in the eyeballs – always the best place to start. They gave a spherical map of what was in the room.

Selecting the separate eyes, he overlaid them together in the software, and watched as its powerful algorithms went to work, matching and reorienting reflections. Details were extrapolated that would have seemed like science fiction only a few decades ago. But these days even a tech-illiterate gum-shoe like himself wielded forensic class tools, though he couldn't have said how they worked.

With the initial pass complete, the software picked out the reflections of a few more items from the background – a cylindrical metal container, a dome shaped silver lid, – and added their light to the reconstruction. Kirby watched hopefully, as the resolution sharpened and then stopped. The algorithms had reached the limits of what was possible.

The computer projected a 3D conic section, originating from the centre, and mapped the reconstructed imagery onto the interior of a sphere. Kirby swivelled it around and looked at what it represented.

It was the interior of a room, which had a computer screen positioned directly in front of the man's face – that was the source of light. Dotted around the room were more computers and electronics. He slid through them carefully looking for written addresses or signs, or even an open window that might give away the location. But there were none.

He magnified the projected computer screen. It appeared to have some sort of coded instructions on it. It wasn't possible to read the exact words – the resolution wasn't sharp enough, but it was something to go on.

——olo——

Kirby sat on a stool by a pool table watching kids play video games. A half eaten burger sagged on the plate in front of him.

129

"You looking for a good time?" said a girls voice.

"No. Not especially," he said tutting, without turning.

"Then why'd you call me so urgently?" she asked. "I thought it must be an emergency."

The girl – Alita – sat down at the table with a Coke, smiling. "A girl's gotta pay the rent ya know," she quipped.

"Hey! You ain't paid rent in years Alita. Why start now?" he bounced back.

"Keeping tabs on me huh?" she asked sardonically.

"Only when I need you."

They hugged.

"It's been a while." She smiled warmly this time. An old friend. "So what have you got for me?"

He slid the photo across to her, and flipped open the 3D rendering on his portable. "I know it's not much to go on, but is there any way to kinda work out what this guy was doing on the machine?" he asked. "Not enough res to see the words."

She looked at the image and swivelled around the rendering. She zoomed into the screen.

"You don't need the actual words," she said. "I can tell the language from the general layout and syntax colouring. My guess is ARLOS."

"What's that?" he asked, lost.

"Augmented Reality Low-level Simulation language. It's hardcore. Machine-code programming. Not for your average script kiddie."

"Can you tell *what* the code was doing?" he hoped.

"Mmm. That's more difficult. Not impossible though. With a low level language like that there aren't too many keywords coz it has a really tight mapping to processors and chip functions, which are limited. So we could maybe get some of the code by looking for keyword shapes." But she shook her head to dismiss it. "Nah it won't get us very far. Not enough code on the screen."

She zoomed out and looked back around the rendered room. "Wait a sec though." She pointed at the gear in the background. There was a lot of it. "You don't have to know the code to tell that this guy is running some pretty serious stuff. That's a ton of processing power. It's gonna need to be cooled and probably have redundant backups, and a whole heap of shit to keep it online."

"The electric bill is probably gonna be off the chart," realised Kirby. He panned around the rendered room, looking at the décor and furnishings. "And that's not one of the big fancy buildings. There can't be many places around that size needing that amount of juice." He beamed at her. "Great work Leet."

"Always here to help Corky," she said sipping her drink.

He slung his portable in the bag, and called for the bill. As a grimy looking waiter headed over he flicked through his wallet counting the notes. It had been a lot fuller than usual lately.

"I'm gonna follow this up tomorrow, but uh, maybe I will stop by tonight for a good time?, that is if you need any help with the rent?" he joked in a husky voice.

"Yeah go fuck yourself Kirby," she laughed.

CHAPTER NINETEEN

.: Fissure

—o Day 26 o——

Kirby inhaled the pungent smell of chilli and refried oil, as he double checked the address, and looked up at the well worn and well known sign. *"Phocan Vietnamese Cuisine"*. It was one of his regular takeout joints.

"We stopping for lunch?" asked Toby. "I love their noodles."

"After," replied Kirby, "and it's on me if we find anything worth finding in this place. Any news on the body?"

"Well yeah. But nothing that you want. The guy was a market worker, not some Mafia witness or UFO pilot or whatever. And nobody saw who did it. Like I said, probably an unpaid hooker bill."

Kirby just grunted, clearly not satisfied. It had been two days since they'd found the body and the mystery of it all was getting in the way of his sleep.

They headed off the street and down a filthy, narrow walkway toward the reception counter of a dilapidated old building. Metal bars and a security grill separated the public from the landlady.

She looked at Kirby distastefully as he approached, then with disgust as she saw Toby walking behind him in police uniform.

"You sure about this place?" asked Toby. "I mean, don't seem likely for no technology mafia type."

"Yeah I hear ya," said Kirby, "But this block is the only one where everything fits."

Even as he said it he could see electrical cabling snaking out from one of the walls. He pointed to a power line that had been hacked from the street. A makeshift rubber divider cut from a section of garden hose connected it to the wall cable. Chunky enough to carry juice into the block for practically anything.

"What you want?" asked the land lady in broken English, sneering at them.

He slid the utility statement he was holding under the grill. Then pulled a print out from the electric company from his pocket and held it up for her to see. "That's a big difference in numbers."

She looked at the statement in front of her then icily back at him.

"Lady, there's enough juice running through here for two blocks, and it don't show up on the balance sheet. You're stealing from the electric company. Or somebody in here is. I'm gonna need to check all the apartments on the second floor."

"No," said the woman firmly. "You no apartment. No visit." She shut the grill to them.

Kirby had expected to be rebuffed and to have to try a bit of investigators charm but not to be shut down so abruptly. He tried to work out a tac for what to say next... It was tricky – they didn't actually have a warrant, so technically they couldn't be here.

He looked down at a little boy who'd been watching him silently. The woman's son he guessed. He smiled at the kid. "Hey there –" he began.

133

"Why aren't you at school you little shit?" Toby cut-in. "Hey ma'am why isn't your little brat at school?" He looked at the woman with quizzical sarcasm.

She glowered at him.

"Little brat. You. No school," he gestured in mock sign language. "You pulling a sickie today? Got a doctor's certificate for that? Can I see it?"

The boy squirmed in awkward embarrassment.

Toby waved his cops badge. "Not sending your kids to school is a serious offence ma'am. And I'm pretty sure little, whatever-his-name-is, doesn't want to miss out on story time with the other kids. Right?" He looked at the kid. "Or miss out on his mom when we chuck her in jail for neglect, or theft, or whatever the fuck else we can take you down for. Are your building permits in order? What about the sanitation and refuse license?"

The woman stood up off her stool and stared daggers at them. "Okay!"

"Nong. Bai Laiow!" she snapped at the kid, who ran off back into the apartment obediently.

She opened the metal grill slowly, then calmly and deliberately gathered phlegm in her mouth and spat into Kirby's utility statement, then slid it back to him.

"You can go through," she said in monotone disdain.

The barred gate next to them clicked metallically, then a green LED shone to indicate they could pass. They entered in single file.

Florescent bulbs flickered with dead insects as they walked the narrow lobby. Chinese signage hung lopsided from nails as they walked past the doors...

131...

132...

133...

An eye slit opened and closed rapidly. They could see the shadows of feet beneath the door...

134...

135...

136...

A filthy, mould stained door half-opened. An old man with the face of a dried prune leaned out to look at them. "You want girl?" he asked, and nodded behind him.

They glanced through the cracked opening, and saw fat thighs in a tacky, unwashed miniskirt poking through curls of cigarette smoke. They couldn't see a face, but the constant sound of coughing did little for their inclination to accept the offer.

"Maybe another time," muttered Kirby...

137...

138...

139...

They stopped at a metal, cross-hatched elevator. Black, oily filth covered the numbers. Under the muck they saw a button "140-149". A greasy fingerprint had been put there recently.

"What are we expecting to find up there?" asked Toby, feeling that they were headed ever deeper into the lair of some demon.

"Answers," replied Kirby simply.

"To what questions?" said Toby, distinctly uneasy.

"To what is lurking under the surface of Chinatown, that I can feel in my bones, but never quite reach or touch," said Kirby, almost to himself.

His eyes were drawn to a thick wad of electrical cables that wound upwards through a hole in the ceiling. He gestured at Toby, who nodded slowly, unclasping his gun from the holster. Kirby pressed the elevator button.

Pssssshhhht.

The elevator door slid open, and they walked in, closing the grating behind them. There was the acute feeling of vulnerability as they waited, sealed in this metre-square cage, for something to happen. Metal gears slowly clicked into action as it ascended to the next level.

Psssssshhhht.

There were no lights on in this floor. All power, whatever it was being used for, had been diverted into the one room. They could see the only shard of light emerge from under a door at the end of the hallway. They walked on...

140...

Muffled voices and sounds of movement could be heard, getting louder with new step they took. They walked on...

141...

The pungent smell of damp that was woven into the fabric of the building and had been crawling into their nostrils since entering the hallway, began to change. Something chemical was present...

142...

They were one door away now and stopped. They looked cautiously at the light flickering from beneath. White, yellow, dark, light. There was activity from within. The only other doors on this side of the building – 144, and 145 – were dormant.

143...

"Ready?" asked Kirby.

"Fucking Chinatown," said Toby, wishing he was at home drinking a cold Tsing-Tao rather than walking towards possible death in this dingy, shithole block of apartments.

Kirby, who had now drawn his own gun, was wishing as he always did at times like this that he packed a little more fire power. At least he'd had the sense to bring a partner along. He nodded at Toby, and whispered "Okay, let's see what's in –"

The door to 143 opened suddenly in front of them casting a square of light into the hallway. A small figure hopped out of the room, projecting a giant shadow against the exterior wall. It was the boy from the reception. He had apparently used some back entrance or stairs to get here first. The noise of undefinable activity spilled out into the corridor from the room. The muted chatter of many voices could be heard, interwoven with the hissing of machinery.

Kirby and Toby stood motionless only metres away. They could not see into the room, but nor could they be seen by anyone inside from the acute angle at which they were standing. The difference in light also meant they were invisible, briefly, until the boy's eyes had adjusted to the dark. Seconds passed in frozen silence.

The boy, who was too focussed on what lay in the room, had not yet turned to face them. He exchanged a few quick words with one of the people inside then took off toward the other end of the corridor – away from where they were standing.

Kirby's body released some of the tension that had been building up in its muscles. But no sooner had the boy taken a few steps when another voice called out to him. The small figure hesitated, then stopped, then turned around slowly, and was about to reply.

His mouth remained gaping open, frozen mid-turn, as he looked directly at Kirby and Toby and down the barrels of two guns. He was a miniature statue, cast in white-yellow light for all the room to see. Only the eyes of his terror-stricken face moved. As they did so the glints of metal reflected from them.

The voice from the room called out again, this time in a hushed urgency. It sounded like a question. It was repeated. The boy was transfixed to the spot and gave no answer, which, in itself was perhaps an answer. All voices in the room dropped to silence. The alarm had been given.

Kirby closed his eyes and took another deep breath. The situation urged extreme caution. There were a lot of voices in that room.

Toby was sweating. He was a man of simple, directed action, who got simple, tangible results. Tense psychological stand-offs were not for his forte – the anticipation was too much for him.

"Fuck it," he said under his breath. Their cover had been blown by the kid anyway, so why not go in hot, he reasoned. With a screaming battle cry, he charged at the doorway, gun waving in front like a Tommy sent over the top.

The kid started to bolt, knowing what was about to happen, but someone in the room must have flinched. The first gun shot was fired...

His torso exploded at the ribs, sending him cascading into the floorboards in a mess of flailing arms and torn guts.

"Jesuuus!" exclaimed Kirby, hightailing it after Toby as he fired upwards for cover.

Toby blasted indiscriminately through the prefab wall at whatever lay inside. A cry of anguish said that at least one of the bullets had found a mark. As each shot made a new hole in the plasterboard, a ray of light pierced the corridor like a needle.

He dived low into the room, with Kirby diving after, still firing for cover. From their position on the floor each took a mental snap shot of the surroundings. Large machinery divided the room into sections. Cables and metal boxes were everywhere. Whatever this place was it was definitely not the blue-walled computer room from the photo. These machines were much larger than standard computing equipment. They were also big enough, and thick enough to act as shielding.

Shots cracked from around the room. Lightbulbs popped as bullets pinged through glass and ricocheted off metal corners. Voices screamed conflicting orders in Chinese. Kirby and Toby fired in snatches back at the sounds and flashes, while trying to keep cover next to the metal panelling.

A man ran out from behind a corner, shouting death at them, his gun raised Trikuza style, muzzle aiming all over the pace. Pop-Pop Pop! He fired, each shot landing metres from the target. Suddenly seeing Kirby – who had been concealed almost beneath him – he tried to brake, but the momentum of his run sent him skidding across the room.

Blaaam! – Kirby shot him sideways into the afterlife.

The next one was coming. This time a woman. No banshee Trikuza screams of attack to give herself away, but the sound of footsteps betrayed her anyway.

Blaaam! Kirby shot out again, but this time missed his mark.

Toby, not realising the shot had missed, poked his head up to see who was coming next. He felt a sharp sting of pain before registering that the woman was still in front of him and alive. Even as the crack of her gun shot and the searing burn of agony in his shoulder jolted his brain, his mind finally made sense of what he saw. The woman had fallen sideways, avoiding Kirby's shot by pure chance, then had fired her own gun from this sideways, upside down position.

"Mother ffuuuuck –" shouted Toby, drawing his weapon.

Kirby fired again. Blaaam! the Trikuza woman flopped down on the concrete floor like a wet sack of shit. Toby shot the body again for good measure. "Gangster piece of crap."

Everyone hidden in the room now knew exactly where they both were. The noise from the guns had triangulated them. Light and cover made little difference to their concealment now.

The next group all sprung at once. The sound of running feet scaling furniture could be heard from every direction, rapidly closing in on their hiding spot. Here they come, thought Kirby. Despite the high-speed buzz of adrenaline rushing through his veins, the flutter of butterflies in his belly sapped him like a leech. He gripped the pistol with both hands to steady himself and waited to pick the moment to leap out.

An electric Fsshhiiiiiiiiiingggg suddenly sounded from the corridor as every light went simultaneously black. It put an instant brake on the chaos in the room, skidding it jarringly to a halt. A confused silence swiftly imposed itself.

This new moment of respite lasted for what seemed like a minute, but was in reality no more than a second.

Then just as suddenly as it had appeared the blackness was gone again. Multiple green rays of light beamed out from the hallway simultaneously, illuminating the room. Combat dressed figures with full body armour stormed in. Metal helmets with visors on emerged through disintegrating walls as the figures kicked their way through breeze-blocks and plasterboard.

There then followed a series of rapid electrostatic hums and small cracks, as whatever weapons they were carrying were discharged with absolute precision at people in the room. Kirby and Toby pressed themselves into the floor, praying they were not on the list of targets.

Then the noises abruptly stopped. Shortly afterwards the lights – what remained of them – gradually blinked back on. The armoured men stood still, overlooking the situation; weapons at ready position.

Toby winced but kept silent. He was losing blood through the shoulder wound. It would probably be okay he knew, but it pissed him off. He wanted a beer.

Kirby looked at the carnage and saw five dead bodies around him. They were heaped gracelessly across the machinery and floor, tossed aside like discarded rags.

He assessed the room calmly now, without the pressure of gun wielding Trikuzas to hamper his judgement. This was some sort of illegal chip press he guessed. Probably an underground minting plant to manufacture fake Digi-wallets and embed the holographic authenticator chips. That was big business. People would pay a fortune to have something whose transactions couldn't be tracked. The price of anonymity was death, in a world obsessed with surveillance.

One of the combat soldiers, or whatever they were, unclipped his helmet and walked carefully around the room. After checking the corners and gaps he zeroed in on Kirby.

"Where is he?" he asked in a voice that brooked no dismissal.

Kirby shook his head, not sure what he could say. Had this stupid meathead not seen what had just happened? How the hell would Kirby even have had time to look inside the room, let alone locate the man they were presumably both looking for – Page.

"How the fuck do I know?" he said. "You tell me."

The man looked at Kirby and Toby for a few moments, either making a decision or listening to the decision of another in his ear piece.

"Sweep," he ordered his team.

The men systematically spread out and combed the room. They looked at each body carefully. One of them had a small tablet of digital photographs and was swiping through them, comparing each to the lifeless, contorted faces in the room.

"That's my photo!" said Kirby, seeing the photo of Page from his wall with *"End of the world?"* written on it. "Where'd you get it?"

The meathead ignored him.

"Asshole," said Kirby, realising his office was likely to have been ransacked.

On another photo Page was riding a black zooter, looking back over his shoulder through a car window, as if photographed in the midst of pursuit.

The men silently regrouped, responding to whatever orders they had been given through the ear pieces or visual displays in their visors. They walked in formation out of the room.

Debris hung from wrecked wooden slats. Shattered glass glittered on the floor boards as the dying embers of electricity snaked around broken machines.

"Well I hope that answered your questions," said Toby, pressing a finger into his shoulder wound to stem the bleeding.

"It answered one of them," sighed Kirby, looking around the room, then back at the photo. "I am not paranoid. Something is going on."

"Shoulda gone to school today kid," said Toby, staring glumly at prostrate body of the boy in the hallway. He had been folded into an impossible posture by the momentum of his fall.

Kirby hadn't noticed before, but the floor here was littered with old rose petals. It gave a kind of macabre beauty to the carnage.

Had the lights been better, or had he looked upwards, he would have noticed that the hacked power cable that ran from the exterior wall into 143, was split in two, the other part snaking its way into apartment 145... That apartment had been untouched for ten days now though.

CHAPTER TWENTY

.: **Interface**

Bark flew from the sides of the tree while acorns rained down from the canopy above. Sync moved her leg back from the trunk, and chambered for another kick. *"237!"* yelled the screen in neon red.

She spun around, kicking the gym bag even harder, this time at head height. More acorns rained down in front of the workout floor as another score blipped up in neon.

"Pause," she said, as the buzzing of an incoming call cut in. She wiped the sweat from her brow, irritated at the unscheduled interruption. "Yes?"

Page's face appeared on the screen. "Hi Sync."

"What the hell happened to you?" She pulled off her gloves and threw them at the screen. "It's been six days you fucker. Don't you dare no-call me on a job like this. I'm sticking my neck out for you."

She took a breath to calm herself, then sat down on the mat in a gentle stretch. "Okay Page, so, talk to me. I honestly didn't know what had happened to you this past week. Are we good for tomorrow?"

He looked back at her sheepishly. "I got the messages. All of them. Not right away. I was, well, busy."

"I see," she said, "And is it something you would like to elaborate on?" She resisted the urge to push further, but levelled him with a stern gaze.

"I, remember the deadline. I will be ready on time."

"Page," she sighed. "I was worried too, you know? I called in at your old apartment, but it was, well, still empty."

He nodded blankly.

She looked at the background of his video feed, trying to place him. "You're not in your apartment, and you're not in that blue room, so, where are you calling from?"

The last time they had spoken was from the room in Chinatown, about work, and it was clear that he had yet again moved on. He was obviously on the run from something.

The interior of this place didn't even look like it was from the same city. It was unquestionably Page though. Curves of electrical cables coiled their way from a wall into an array of computers and unclassifiable electronic gadgetry. "You've made some changes," was all she said.

"I, have access to more power," he said, not bothering to fill in the blanks.

"How's your hand?" she asked. It was pointless to ask more. Any of her circuitous attempts to elicit an explanation would be met with either dumb silence or a simple deflection.

He flexed the fingers. "I can still code."

"You can call me any time Page," she said, "I am a friend."

They left it at that.

Page was holed up in a disused caretaker's office abutting an old power plant, on the edge of town. Parts of the plant were still operational, but the majority of it looked as if it had been decommissioned. The site was one of the places he'd originally intended to check out, even before Chinatown, and now that he was forced here by circumstances, he wished he'd come sooner. It was perfect.

Only the north end of the structure was inhabited, meaning he could come and go as he pleased and had unimpeded access to all the electricity he could use. Creature comforts were sorely lacking but he'd always been used to living in a fairly Spartan manner. So far so good.

There was nowhere from which to get new components though, so he would have to make do with what he had. But since running more and more of his tests from "off site" memory, this was less of an issue. It had created another issue though. Using the servers of your employers to run private experiments on was a dangerous thing to do, particularly when they were as powerful as Omicore.

Omicore...

Back to work he sighed. He must at least do something before the deadline. He opened a can of soda and leaned back in the dusty chair reluctantly, flexing his fingers.

He logged in, accessing servers through the authentication procedure they'd provided him with. In reality he had bypassed Omicore's security days ago for his own reasons, but kept up the facade of logging in to satisfy any monitors. Provided his experiments didn't break anything then there would be no reason they would be uncovered. Besides, his job was to run a security analysis on their system, so a few anomalies would probably be expected. Still, after the Bint incident he took precautions – his connection was routed and then re-routed around several locations, finally exiting through one of the near-by shops.

In terms of his work assignment, he was half way there already. He'd beat the old system easily. That left only the new, but it would need focus. The new Omicore system was novel and sophisticated. It could adapt to an attacker's behaviour almost intelligently, fluidly matching codes to biorhythms that ran in the subconscious mind and evolved with the person – theoretically unique and unbreakable. He'd done some preliminary test work and was impressed. There were many features of it's adaptive approach that mirrored the work he himself was doing.

He booted up his code interface, slung on the headset and dived in to work.

Geometry appeared all around him in super high, ultra crisp definition, flawless and in real time. Three perpendicular axes of infinity reached inward to him along intersecting shards of neon light, and shimmering clouds of particles. A multi-dimensional world of a trillion data points expanded as far as the eye could see in every direction, forming blocks like cities.

The Omicore servers were vast. Represented here was the data of a billion people and the algorithms that processed, conglomerated, and tried to make sense of it all. Statistical data, emotional data, spatial data, and code. Not a thousandth of a thousandth of a percent could be truly understood by humans, or even the tools they had made to analyse it. But the patterns were there, intrinsic to the relationship of overlapping points, only needing a perspective to brought meaning to them.

Page had created this interface to view the data and code in compressed fractal form. In tackling the Omicore security program he was also bringing together many of the lines of research he was exploring for his own project.

147

Like an exponential graph that was viewed in logarithmic scale, or a Feynman diagram describing complex particle interactions, there needed to be a way to reduce information into something tractable. It was the only way to even begin to appreciate the magnitude of what was stored in the endless streams of data amassed by companies like Omicore.

He dived inwards, to the mesh of a magenta causeway that was as real to him as the room he sat in, and a lot more familiar. It was representation of part of the code he had been working on recently in a section called L13. As he got closer to the plane's ground-zero the larger structural forms were no longer discernable. Finer grained strands of coloured dust whizzed by in familiar shapes now. This was code in an almost pure form. It could be read by someone who, like him, had spent a lifetime immersed in it.

He steered into a section he hadn't been to before to check some of the new research functions and see if they impacted his work. Just then something bright, unfamiliar, appeared for a moment to the side. "Stop!" he shouted.

He tore off the goggles. "What the hell was that?" he muttered to himself. "Code view," he yelled at the machine.

The geometric shapes and lines were replaced by code, now in human readable form. He began to scroll through page after page of numbers and instructions. It flitted by like a down pour of rain, the individual words forming droplets almost too small to see. But even the shapes of the functions spoke volumes about their purpose. Like glancing at a page of text from afar, you didn't need to read the words to tell whether it was a letter or a recipe, a poem or an equation – the general shape was enough to go on.

So when the code suddenly started to change style he released, freezing the droplets in motion. His brow furrowed as he read through the commands, verbose, line by line an instruction at a time.

A few hours later he was leaning back in his chair looking into space, thinking about what he had found. It was brilliant. A novel approach to one of the underlying assumptions of State Analysis – a core part of adaptive algorithms, and something that he himself had been working on.

At the end of the last block of code was a signature.

```
0C #The essence of mathematics is in its freedom
```

Whoever had produced this piece of code was a genius. It was one thing to interpret and understand a formula once it had been created, after the fact, but to create the thing in the first place was infinitely harder.

There was something strange about the code though, as if it had been arrived at chaotically rather than through design, which was absurd at this level of complexity. But he could see so many potential applications for it, especially in the research he was doing, which made him wonder, why had it not already been used elsewhere? It was akin to looking at a strand of DNA in isolation that lacked the host and surroundings to exploit the information encoded in its instructions. Yet intuitively, he could understand the animal it could become.

He checked the time, suddenly mindful of whose servers he was in, and how long he had spent off the beaten track of his access path. "Fuck."

But this was too important to ignore. "Fuck it."

He grabbed a backup drive, forced it into the machine then slammed a few keys.

```
> Copying Data...
```

His heart was racing. His brain hurt. He had been glued to his seat for nearly four hours immersed in code. He needed to unwind or take a break.

Then he needed to finish the contract work.

Then, in a day or two, he could explore this new code.

He opened the jar of pills from Velma, popped one out and swallowed it with a swig of stale coffee. Then he relaxed as he waited for the data to finish copying.

CHAPTER TWENTY ONE

.: **Creation**

——o Day 21 o——

The Barkhausen-Morrow derivative function was at the core of all modern true-learning neural nets. Like all functions in mathematics or computer science its purpose, when taken literally, was simply to map one set of numbers to another set of numbers. But it was what the numbers represented that was important.

In physics, for example, you had the famous equations of Einstein and Newton that, although far reaching, were extremely simple in form. They would take an input number on one side – mass – for example and output a number on the other side – energy. Or force, momentum, displacement, and so on. The functions themselves were simplistic, being almost linear, but gave fantastically accurate results that matched the world around them. In the Standard Model of Quantum Mechanics the equations were more complex, but essentially served the same purpose, and in the same style.

In chemistry and biology the complexity of the equations increased again, as the focus narrowed. Now you had functions that went from calculating the free energy in a thermodynamic system, to giving statistical values for protein unfolding potentials. Numbers in, numbers out.

When it came to the new wave of creative intelligence, the form of the functions was even more specialised. The numbers that went in on one side of the equations could be viewed, in a loose sense, as the electrical state of neurons – some representing stimuli such as vision, others representing cache state, such as memory. The output was also, in a loose sense, the electrical state of neurons, again falling into two groups – cache state and action state. The cache determined how the stimuli would be mapped to memory, and the action state represented either an adjustment in the input state, or the action that would be taken based on that state.

It was in essence a feedback function. The important thing was that it could be used to simulate reactions in the real world, and consequently was itself a measure of sentience. For example, when tuned to the neurons of a mosquito the results it gave were extremely simplistic, converging on very predictable groups of action, more or less matching the exact behaviour of a mosquito. When tuned to those of a mouse, the results broadened in scope and the number of iterations of the feedback loop increased exponentially, but once again it more or less matched the behaviour of a mouse.

That was the main difficulty though – how to get meaningful results without an infinitely long feedback loop – and that was where Barkhausen and Morrow had come in. Their generalisations and reductions had resulted in a function that could give an approximation of creative decision making in close to real-time. It was a breakthrough that had revolutionised the field of computer science and artificial intelligence. That was a long time ago now though. The work since had been nothing but minor improvements on this original function.

For predicting patterns within abstract data, the Barkhausen-Morrow function was an undeniable success. Computer systems were now able to extract patterns, within patterns, within patterns to orders of magnitude deeper than a human could extract, but using the same semi-creative process. Unfortunately, it still didn't map perfectly to the decision making process exhibited in real humans, or even advanced animals. The differences in output, whilst seemingly small in size, had drastically different effects. The detection of a face, for example, might be 99% similar to what a human would detect, given the same memories, but if the technique was applied to a different scenario, such as crossing a road, that small difference might cause a sim-bot to walk in front of a moving car, rather than to, say, scream at the driver to stop. It was infuriating.

In a world run by algorithms, this difference was one of the things that kept humans from being able to understand the responses of AI. Another was the vast scale and sizes involved. So for now there were processes that could never be reduced, even in principle, to psychology that made sense.

Page looked at the seeds of the new function he had found, seeing it's similarities to the Barkhausen-Morrow function, but also where it was different. The initial work had promise, but was incomplete.

He would complete it.

His idea was a beautifully simple one, though the mathematics involved were highly complex. He would create an environment in which the function would derive itself. A simulation in which the output of the function would itself shape the environment in which the derivation was evaluated. A feedback of a feedback. A simulation within a simulation.

He would then apply those results to the next experiment.

CHAPTER TWENTY TWO

:: Fire

Tan was aged seven, standing in a deserted street in front of the village quadrangle of his childhood home. To the left was a churchyard, and to the right a schoolyard. In front of him, stretching out as far as the eye could see, were row after row of dilapidated houses, nearly all shuttered and boarded up. Of the few unboarded windows he could see, the glass on each was coated in grime, and looked untouched for a hundred years.

He could hear the sounds of distant footsteps splashing in the rain, but they were a long way off and it would be a while before the bigger children reached him.

A skeleton lay in the road by his feet, the rain dripping off its skull.

Glass is sand, he thought. Glass reflects and water reflects.

He placed his small fingers into the eye sockets, and tugged gently. The skull came easily away from the rest of the body, connected only loosely by grime. He turned to face one of the windows then, watching the reflection of his young body in the grime, threw the skull with all his might.

Time seemed to slow down as the skull collided with the glass, shattering it into a thousand pieces. As each of the shards twisted and spun through the air his reflection moved with them, sliding across the glass microsecond by microsecond with the changing

154

angle. But as each completed a full rotation coming back to face him, he was gone, and reflected back was only an empty street.

He watched as piece by piece the fragments of glass settled on the ground, and with the last one, the erasure of his reflection was complete.

The boys who had been chasing him earlier, arrived at the place in the street where he had been standing, and looked down. There was only shattered glass and the remains of a skeleton.

Tan, and the skull, were gone.

On a lower plane of consciousness Tan slept peacefully for the first time. His mind had changed, almost imperceptibly, entering a new phase in its evolution.

———olo———

Tan woke up, sweating. The morning's first light was only just creeping its way through the gaps in distant buildings. A single ray lit up the faces of his daughter and wife as they slept.

He looked at himself in the mirror, lost in new thoughts, and ran a hand through his locks of hair. His fingers toyed with the black ring he wore, tracing the embossed symbol "χ" on its surface. The seeds of a new idea played in his mind.

The developers would be here this morning. He knew it instinctively. He also knew, or had a kind of premonition that any attempt to confront them would be doomed to fail. He could either sign up, and give everything away including the roof over his family's head, or fight, and probably die in the attempt. That just seemed to be the zero-sum nature of the world.

Or rather, that's how he would have assessed the situation last night, before his dream. But this morning he had begun to think differently – sideways, outside of his linear box.

He walked around to the back of the hut, and checked the underbelly of the shanties. Wood, plastic cans, oil drums. Anything buoyant the villagers had found had been used to prop up the base of each dwelling against seasonally rising waters. This time of year the waters were low though, and had been so for months. The material used in the supports was therefore dry and surrounded by air.

"Daddy I can't find my school bag," said Nivi a few minutes later, looking up at him as she reached a hand around the bed. She looked worried.

"It's okay button," he smiled at her, "school's been cancelled today." He ruffled her hair.

"Realllly?!" she said with glee. Then thought about it. "How come they didn't tell me yesterday?"

"We've only just decided this morning. You and mummy are going on a trip today."

"Where are we going?"

"Not far. But to a place where you can shelter from the storm."

"What storm? It isn't raining."

"We'll be leaving soon, so keep getting ready," said June. "Are you sure about this Tan?" she asked, more quietly.

He nodded confidently, though in reality was not sure at all. He had a feeling that almost anything he tried would fail, and fail catastrophically. So, before the universe could conspire against him, he would conspire against it.

———olo———

He tugged the door firmly shut, feeling the hammered brass knocker beneath his fingers and remembering the pride with which he had made so many of these features. He didn't care anymore. He could make others. With June and Nivi now out of harms way his mind ran a lot more freely.

He walked with Erpin and Yuita purposefully to the end of the street, then stood in statue-like silence as the SUV rolled up to the entrance of the lane.

The engine stopped and after a few seconds the windows wound down. This was a more cautious move by the developers, who had been surprised to see them standing there and could sense something was in the air. It was as if they anticipated events outside the predicted routine were about to take place. Erpin and Yuita both smiled, seeing some of the wind taken from the developers' conceited sails, but Tan did not move.

The usual three stepped out – Holloway, Norbeck, and Marshall – with their shine dulled, but not gone.

The difference in Tan's demeanour was clear for them to see too – different from how their minds projected it would be. They thought in terms of threats, counter threats, statistical likelihoods, tactics, and gambits. It was to within a rounding error of 100% certainty that they would get the result they had come for, and that Tan would leave with nothing or, also highly probable, would not leave at all. None of them knew this numerically though – they couldn't – but they had always felt it instinctively, subconsciously aware that the deck was stacked ludicrously in their favour.

"Mr Taneka," nodded Holloway, in a tone of condescension that seemed to dismiss at the same time as acknowledging him.

He looked at Erpin, and held the gaze for longer. "You said you would be prepared to negotiate this morning. Is that still the case?"

Erpin looked at him dryly. "It's not. I have been persuaded to reconsider my position."

Holloway looked down in annoyance at Tan. "I see," was all he said.

"Let's just do these muppets and get out of here," said Norbeck, irritably. There was an uneasy apprehension in his voice.

Marshall looked around at the rest of the lane, cupping his hand to his ear, making a point of the silence and isolation of the place. Though a person might occasionally walk past along the main road, few strayed to the end of this particular lane. Right now there was not another soul in earshot.

"This little protest of yours is pointless," said Holloway. "You're just wasting time. What do you imagine you can accomplish?"

He smirked, looking round at the muscle that stood behind him, and then at the three small villagers pointedly. "It's an impossible scenario Mr Taneka. Can't you feel it? That sinking feeling, when you know that all is lost?"

"The strange thing is that you can feel it too," said Tan.

Holloway had already opened his mouth, about to respond, when the first explosion rocked out. Huge chunks of wood burst into flames as the nearest house ignited.

His mouth was still agape when the next explosion, a few seconds later, took a chunk out of the bridge, and caused the SUV to tip sideways into the water.

Toxic chemicals rushed through the open window as the two men who sat in the back struggled against their own bulk, desperately trying to prize themselves free of the polluted water pouring in.

"You're fucking crazy," shouted Norbeck.

"That might be true," said Tan almost to himself.

Another explosion took out most of Tan's house, and part of Erpin and Yuita's. As the glowing cinders fell in slow motion to earth, Tan began to move. It was as if he just stopped being at one place in space, and started being in another, so fast were his movements. Fists broke through bone and tissue. Norbeck didn't even have enough time to be angry or feel pain, as his limbs and organs were displaced by kicks and blows.

Marshall and Holloway, caught off balance, were still fumbling for their weapons when Tan reached them. Their fingers didn't even get to the triggers in time.

The cinders were still falling, seconds later, when they were both on the ground, retching in pain.

Soon after, they were not moving at all.

Flames engulfed many of the buildings in the lane, most of which had been constructed from wood and other flammable material. Ultimately perhaps Holloway had been right, thought Tan – the city had won. Other developers would come, and would eventually seize the land despite today. But Tan knew he had won a greater prize.

He clapped Erpin and Yuita on the shoulder. "We must run now. There will be repercussions."

"But, where do we go?" said Erpin, suddenly confused. "I can't even... remember where else there is to go?"

Tan had the same feeling – that he did not know what the world was like beyond the confines of this lane – as if all his previous memories were somehow a fraud. But he was sure of one thing – that he had within him an ability to survive.

CHAPTER TWENTY THREE

.: Low Jacking

———o Day 22 o———

Page sat awkwardly on a cushioned metal stool, inside an expensive, Japanese themed room. Opposite him a circular window overlooked emerald green trees several metres below. It was very serene and calming.

Sync walked around, admiring the details of the place. Intricate wooden carvings were engraved into structural beams that supported the high walls and ceilings. Jade leaves that looked as though they were still growing budded from small shoots near the base of a polished pewter table. She wondered what would happen if she cut one of the leaves. Would sap bleed from the stem? How detailed were the physics of this sim environment they were meeting in?

"I can't stick around for long, Page," she said sympathetically. "He doesn't want anyone present during security discussions."

"It's fine. I will be okay," Page nodded absently, himself caught up in the organic minutiae of the surroundings. It was the day after his deadline, and he had managed to get some sleep since the completion of Omar's work.

There was an ornate wooden table next to him that had a walnut and mahogany chessboard embedded into its surface. He arranged the pieces reflexively.

"Technically, we can refuse the meeting, since that's what we

161

agreed – no direct contact with the client," said Sync, "but he has been pretty keen on it since seeing the work you've done. Very keen."

Page shrugged, moving a pawn forward. "There is nothing to explain. It's all in the code I sent over."

"I think he just wants to, well, talk to you," she said.

"I understand." He looked at her. "That's good isn't it?"

She nodded. "I... think so. But don't take everything at face value. I've always felt there was a deeper motive to what he has hired you to do. Remember, he is a powerful man."

He looked up at the brass clock on the wall. There was still a clear five minutes until the scheduled meeting. "Game?" he asked.

Sync smiled, sitting down at the table. "Sure." She flexed her hands, cracking the fingers as if to do battle. "This will only take a few minutes." She moved a piece.

"Don't be so negative," quipped Page, "I'm sure it will take me longer than that to beat you." He moved.

"Overconfidence will be your downfall. We're not in your little code room now. This is a game of strategy. A war!" She moved.

"Everything follows an algorithm. You're just not aware of it." He moved.

"I'm aware that the algorithm I am following, is better than you think it is." She moved.

"We're probably both following the same one," he chuckled, and moved.

"Ah, but you're forgetting the human factor." She moved.

"What human factor? Chess is a closed system. A zero sum game with a finite number of moves." He moved.

She slapped him around the head, playfully, but hard enough to make him wince. "That human factor." She moved.

"You can't do that against the computer." He rubbed his head, then moved.

"I'm not playing a computer." She moved.

He paused. "You are. We all are. All of the time. The world is run by computerised systems." He moved, but slowly. "It helps to know how they think."

She looked up at him, also paused. "Is that how you beat it? Omicore's security?"

He nodded. "I know the algorithms. Their weak points. Take chess for example –"

"There's no way you can beat a chess computer. That's impossible. Even I know that."

"Practically speaking, yes, you're right – a human hasn't beaten a machine at chess for sixty years, but technically, no, the system can be beat."

"How?"

"Well, the game of chess has a limited number of moves. The position of the pieces on the board can only be arranged in a limited number of configurations."

Sync thought about this for a second. "Yes, but the number of possibilities must be huge. Astronomical."

Page nodded. "Yes. More than the number of atoms in the known universe. Way too high for any computer to store them all. But not infinite, and not as high as you probably think. Certain configurations are ruled out, for example a pawn on the first row."

"That doesn't help much."

"All possible moves are interconnected in sequence though. To get to one state of play you have to pass through another. You can't just jump between different configurations without reaching them in the correct order, nor can you go backwards."

"Yes, that makes sense."

"So now think of the game of chess like a giant tree, with criss-crossing branches. Every possible move of the game is hanging somewhere along one of the branches of the tree, connected only to the moves that can be reached from that position. The trunk of the tree is the first move of the game, and then it divides into branches, and at the tips of every leaf is an end state, a final move just as the King gets taken. Some leaves are black, others white."

"It would be a big tree."

"Very big. But now you are seeing it the way a computer sees it. Not as a game between two players, but as a navigation problem. The game is a journey from the trunk of the tree to one of its tips. At each point where the tree branches, a player chooses a direction to take by making a move. Branch A or Branch B, or C, or D, so on. You can't travel backwards, and so the game gradually moves along smaller and smaller branches, with less and less choice as the pieces are taken, until it finally ends on a white or black leaf in checkmate."

"But hold on a second. That way of thinking can apply to any type of game, right. They're not games at all. They're just route planning problems."

"Yep. Precisely. But because there are so many possibilities it is hard to work out which branch ends up where. The computer can look ahead much further than we can, but even it can't see very far ahead in the middle of a game."

"Why?"

"The middle of a game has the highest number of possible moves. There are still a large number of pieces on the board and most of them are out in the open and not by the edges. Too many branches, or branches of branches."

"So how can you beat it?" asked Sync, rapt in the theory lesson.

"Well, rather than the computer trying to follow all branches, it tries to be efficient and ignore the ones that seem to go nowhere, or in the wrong direction. So it might only look ahead five moves along a branch that seems fruitless, but ten down a branch that seems to lead to victory, for example."

"So if you can find a branch, – a sequence of moves – that seems to lead nowhere for the first five turns, but then later leads to victory, the computer might overlook it and can be drawn down that path?"

"Pretty much. That's one of the ways to beat a traditional AI system. A mid-game branching attack. The mid-game is when there are the highest number of possibilities, and the computer has the shortest lookahead distance. So do we of course, but we have an intuitive type of intelligence that the computer lacks, and are much better at picking winning branches."

"And that's what you did with Omicore? Something like that but in code?"

"No. I used a slightly more devious technique," He reset the pieces to their starting position.

"Hey! I was winning that," protested Sync, miming another blow at Page's head.

"Maybe. Or maybe I was just leading you down the wrong branch," he grinned.

"Okay, so what now?" she asked, looking at the new board.

"Move," he said.

She moved a pawn. He reached across and deliberately knocked over his King, forfeiting the game. "Congratulations, you win," he smiled, and reset the pieces.

"Move," he said again. She moved a different pawn this time, but he followed with the same move – knocking over his King in resignation. "Well done. That's two nil to you."

He reset the pieces. "Go again."

This time she moved her Knight first. He moved a pawn forward, and began to play the game normally now.

"I don't get it. What's your point?" she asked, stopping play.

"Imagine you had never played a game of chess before, and only knew it by the winning rules – If a player's King falls the other player wins the game."

She nodded. "I guess, I'd have no experience to know what moves to make."

"Yep. And by analysing what I just did, you would come to the conclusion that whenever you move a pawn first, you will win the game, because that's what happened. Not just once, but every time you moved a pawn. Reinforcement learning."

She looked at him. "My sense of play would be completely warped."

"Yep. By me playing a few stupid games first, I would have effectively inflated the value of a pawn – one of the least valuable pieces, to become one of the most valuable pieces – in your assessment of the data. You'd think that all you had to do to win the game, is move a pawn."

She nodded. "Okay, and as long as I didn't watch any other games, I'd just have to assume that was the correct assessment."

"Yes. So, now, instead of these practice games we play a game where our lives depend on it. What happens?" he asked.

"I would have no reason to change my behaviour from the previous games, since it's always been a successful strategy."

"Exactly."

"Hmm. And so this time, when I move my pawn, you start playing properly, and beat me when the game really matters, right?"

"That's it. It would be easy because your tactics are all wrong. You've been trained to place way too much importance on the value of a pawn, and to leave everything else open and undefended" He beamed at her.

"That's very clever. Does it work?"

"Not in the game of chess. The computer has already examined hundreds of millions of previous games and has a very clear valuation of the different pieces in different circumstances. But, in the case of Omicore's security AI, it has to cope with novel and new scenarios, to be flexible. Situations it has never encountered before."

"So you educate it on the fly, with bad training data?" asked Sync.

"Kind of, yeah. Through code I jack up the low probability weightings of different events, to impair its analysis. Then, when it comes time for a critical exchange, I'm already in, unchecked."

Sync nodded in comprehension, looking around at the room and the complexity of its design. "That sounds like hard work."

"We're talking about lists of numbers here, nothing more elaborate than that. Just pushing thousands of bad numbers at the right time to the right places," said Page modestly, shrugging. "I call it Low Jacking."

"And it's one of the most sophisticated techniques I've ever seen," said a voice from the side of the room.

Omar was standing there, a Mona Lisa expression on his face. Half smile, half serious, and fully undecipherable.

He bowed to Sync in acknowledgement. "Make no mistake. Those lists of numbers he is referring to are well beyond the ability of anyone in my organisation to calculate. You need such a deep understanding of what the system is doing, moment to moment, that we'd considered it impossible."

She returned the courteous bow, then shot Page a quick look. It was a warning: This man might be dangerous.

"I will leave you boys to talk," she said. Then, not really knowing why, she gave Page a kiss on the cheek as she disappeared into a stream of pixel-like dust.

Omar took a seat at the table, wondering at the touch of coldness that had laced Sync's words. Did she see him as a threat? Was that why she had felt the need to claim Page through the kiss?

"Pleased to finally meet you, Page," was what he said though. "You are everything I hoped you would be."

"I completed your job," said Page.

"Yes. You did, and you beat it in a very novel way. But tell me, how do we defend against this sort of attack?"

Page wasn't sure how to answer. He hated questions that had a social component because the answers were always tricky. He decided to just tell the truth. "You can't defend against it. It's part of the system."

Omar sighed. It was as Page said – the flaw was part of the system. It wasn't an unknown part either, it was part of the specs. They had just assumed it would be impossible to spoof it the way Page had. And yet, so far, this system had withstood a sustained attack from the ASA. What did that say about Page? That he was very special, certainly. But what else?

"Who else knows about your work?" said Omar sharply.

"Nobody," said Page nervously. He didn't count the analogy he had just given Sync as containing any real information.

"Okay, good. That's as well." Omar's Mona Lisa had returned. "So then, if you were me, how would you defend against it?"

Page looked up. "I would create a new system. One that could match the creativity and ingenuity of the people that can infiltrate it."

"You mean, you?" said Omar. "There are no other people that can infiltrate it... are there?"

"I don't know," said Page, awkwardly, aware that this sort of answer might get him into trouble.

But Omar was distracted. He was looking at a stream of the sim's call log as they spoke, words and data appearing live on a readout in his hand. He had noticed something odd. "Where are you calling from? Your signal is... unlisted?"

"Uh, my home," said Page, nervous again. He was such a bad liar. He was also becoming concerned for his safety. As far as he was aware only he knew how to use the flaw in Omicore's system to bypass the security. Maybe that was why Omar had asked to meet with him in person, alone – so the company could now take whatever counter measures were necessary to bury the results?

Omar frowned, sensing the deception in Page. There was another matter too. Leonard had given him a report of memory access patterns since Page had begun to work for them, and there were some worrying trends. Private regions that were kept for internal research projects had shown sharp spikes in usage. Massive fluctuations in power had occurred more than once, disrupting services to other critical systems. Even if not caused by Page there was a possibility that hostile entities had slipped in under cover of his work.

"Page. We have started reviewing some of the work you've been doing for us, and there are some, let's say, strange coincidences about the times you've been logging-in, and other things that have been happening on our servers. Do you know anything about that?"

"No," lied Page, unconvincingly.

So, he thought, someone at Omicore had been looking at the

detailed log files after all. Probably daily. There was no way to tell how much they had discovered. Sims were supposed to be safe, but he now felt a keen sense of danger being alone with Omar. It wasn't just the money and power that Omar possessed, it was the intelligence too. Page recalled the hidden signature he had seen, obfuscated in the variables, deep inside that Omicore function.

```
0C #The essence of mathematics is in its freedom
```

Omar had been trying to read Page's expressions and was about to say something. Page didn't wait to hear what it was. Pixels froze in place as he ripped off the sim headgear, severing the connection.

He was sitting on a tree stump, sweating, in the outdoor carpark of a deli, three streets away from the power plant. The deli didn't know he was using their line, of course – Page had hooked up the call anonymously on both ends, but Omicore's tracers would soon decrypt the geo-mask.

CHAPTER TWENTY FOUR

.: **Blue Prints**

——o Day 24 o——

Tan was leaving everything behind. It wasn't just the place where he lived, where his friends were, it was attached to him in a way that he couldn't even consciously discern let alone articulate to another. It had been part of him. Except that now, it was gone. Destroyed by his own actions in an act of defiance that had seemed the only choice left to him.

June and Nivi had been sent safely away in hiding before those events had taken place; near enough that they could be reached, but far enough to keep them out of harms way. Tan's next choices could mean life or death for all of them. They were, in effect, aliens in a hostile land, looking for somewhere familiar enough to settle and yet far enough to escape the consequences of his actions this morning.

He walked on alone.

The houses that surrounded him seemed less and less familiar as he travelled. Their architecture changed subtly from wood and old metal piping to compositions of corrugated fibre-glass and lashed together bamboo scaffolding. Though he met none of the urban mendicants who wrought this world, he could discern their temperament through its structures. The urgency of life was increased here – practical, casual, with no time for the flourishes of pride that adorned his own shanty... or had done.

He walked on.

The metaphorical trees of the urban jungle gradually began to thin, and it became apparent from the end of the canopy of rooftops that somewhere up ahead marked the end of this environment altogether. The air itself began to change. Something freer, less stifling was now filling his lungs. It had a freshness to it that made him realise that the air in his village was almost as polluted as the water.

He walked on.

Suddenly, and without warning, as he rounded the corner of an alleyway he stepped out into a vast, open dockyard that jutted out into a clear blue sea. It took him completely by surprise. He had never known that he lived in such close proximity to the sea before. He had always assumed the city to be a vast entity of almost infinite size, and yet he had now reached one of its borders in a relatively short period of time. Where was this place?

He looked at the dockyard again for any details that would help him localise it – maybe a street sign – and noticed something even stranger. There was something unfinished about it that was difficult to describe. It's not that it was new and just awaiting completion by workmen, it didn't look... finished.

Waves lapped at the part wood, part concrete structure. The wood was worn, the concrete was eroded, the materials from which the dock was composed were clearly old, there were just small things missing. The big things were there, sure – a few boats, benches, the yard master's quarter, even a sort of loading bay. But none of the little details were there. Where, for example, were the birds? or for that matter, the people?

It gave him the impression of an artist who had been interrupted in the middle of a painting, called away before sections of the canvas were complete. The eerie sensation was enough to cause him to keep moving, and not stick around to investigate.

173

But after discovering there was no obvious exit to the place, he was forced to double back into the town and look for an alternative direction to take.

Were he able to elevate himself above the plane, and look down from a bird's eye point of view, he would realise that the labyrinthine maze he felt himself to be lost in was actually a lot more linear than he thought.

——olo——

Tan had been travelling for what felt like an entire day. It wasn't more than a couple of hours in reality, he knew, but it had been unexpectedly fatiguing. The further he travelled the more he felt an uneasy, nausea building in his stomach. The air now seemed thicker, as though a heavy cloud were enveloping him with each step further from home. He didn't want to turn back, but perhaps it was time to move forward in a more planned manner, rather than the aimless meandering he had been doing so far. First thing was to take stock of where he was.

The main streets were broad, but due to the encroachment of commerce – advertising hoardings, snack trucks, fake jewellery stands, triple parked zooters – there was little space left to walk. In contrast to the eerie dockyard this place was thoroughly inhabited. The hustle and bustle of people was everywhere.

A group of men unloaded vegetables from the back of a small truck that chugged black filth through a broken exhaust; a woman waved her arms in wild gesticulations as she screamed into a vid-phone; giggling schoolgirls hid behind parked cars to evade a group of eagerly searching boys; lives colliding in chaotic dances of activity were the beating heart of this place. Chinatown.

The place was full of anachronisms; ancient looking buildings crammed between modern digital tech stores; quantum chip-fixers writing paper receipts with wooden pencils; handmade carvings sold by gesture-activated vending machines. The smells and sounds complimented the visuals in every way.

Wahh-Woh-Wohh. An off key sound from a small, handheld instrument drifted through the hubbub. A man in a trench coat played absent mindedly with one hand as he walked down the street, holding a bag of noodles in the other.

Tan watched the man curiously, trying to figure out whether he was another anachronism or someone who belonged here. In a way, the man's uniqueness made him more a part of this environment than had he been constructed from the brickwork itself. Yet Tan noticed him. Why?

The man stopped outside a generic looking doorway with the words *"Kirby's Detective Agency"* written in faded, dirty letters above, and walked in. People do strange things for a living when enough of them are concentrated in one place, thought Tan.

Tan began to mentally catalogue some of the buildings and streets he could see, both to familiarise and to localise himself incase he should need to return. This was the first time since the morning's escape that he felt that he had arrived somewhere. Yes, this was a place. To look upwards from the street level was to look into an explosion of cheap neon signage; *"Habachi Ramen & Burgers"*... *"The 999 Cred Store"*... *"BaBaz Pep Lounge"*... *"D-Mart"*... *"LolaCola Massage & Coffee"*... *"Fanling Furniture Fair"*... *"Little Ronnie's Gym"*... it went on.

He moved away from the main road in search of a more secluded place in which to think. A few streets later and he had found a degree of quietude away from the chaos.

As he pondered the state of this new world, he thought of June and Nivi. They would be lying low, in hiding, but anxious to know that he was safe. He was the hunter-gatherer, the prototype, finding resources and shelter in the plains. But at some point he ought to either contact them or retrace his steps to the area where they were waiting. He stared at the floor musing over different options, turning over trash with his feet as he turned over thoughts in his mind. Now that he was rid of the developers – he hoped – the whole fiasco could almost be viewed as an opportunity. It was a chance to be reborn, a catalyst for change that he never would have initiated himself. Any thoughts of change had always seemed alien to him. Not now.

The white hawk logo was stuck in his mind though. Phocan Properties. Who were Phocan Properties? He realised he knew virtually nothing about the world beyond his village. But that white hawk logo... what was it? He blinked, realising where the thought had come from... He was looking at it. The piece of garbage he had been kicking around with his feet – a dusty old box of noodles – had a large white hawk on the side. Next to the hawk, written in clear, bold letters were the words *"Phocan Vietnamese Cuisine"*. What the hell? He stared at it. The hawk logo was one thing, but the words were too much of a coincidence to actually be one.

———olo———

"No my friend. We don't sell noodles!" yelled the street vendor above the din of customers. "You want Gow Choi Cau?"

"No!" said Tan, waving the box in front of the woman's face, "I need to find this noodle shop!"

"This is Dim Sum only! Much better!" she shouted, handing him a grimy menu, and turning to another customer.

"No!" he tried again, pointing at and tapping the logo of the hawk frantically. "I need to go to this place! Do you know where I can find it?"

She stopped to look more closely at what he was saying and studied the logo. "Phocan? Yes. Down that street. Two blocks maybe."

Despite his fatigue he covered the distance in a few minutes. As he rounded the corner into the final street his speed dropped to a much more vigilant pace. The burning desire he had to find out what was going on was tempered by an abundance of caution. So rather than approach from the front in full view, he decided to take the alleyway and stakeout the location from cover.

There it was – Phocan Vietnamese Cuisine, with the white hawk logo – exactly as he remembered it from the developer's contract. Yet it quite obviously was not a property company, and quite obviously *was* a street-side restaurant. What did that mean? Maybe the restaurant was just a front for some sort of undercover operation? But then why use a logo that links the two? It didn't make sense.

As his eyes hunted for information he suddenly became aware of some of the other shops on this street... Holloway Electronics, Norbeck English & Asian Bakery, Marshall Cuts. They were the names of the developers who had come for him – Holloway, Norbeck, Marshall. The others too he presumed, had he known their names. Scrutinizing each shop in turn it became clear that each was exactly what it purported to be – an electronics shop, a bakery, and a hairdressers. What the hell was this? Was everything that was associated with the developers doubled up in the world in this weird way?

After another ten minutes of cautious scanning he spotted several other anomalies in the street. An object here, a name there, the shape of a wall over there. Nothing by itself went further than a mild coincidence, but when taken as a whole the cumulative impression was one of undeniable connection. He thought on different elements he had encountered during his journey, and soon realised that many of them were in some way familiar. The observation that finally set him in motion though, breaking his cover as he went to investigate, was the door.

There, at the back of one of the residential buildings at the top of some stairs was a door. Not just any door, it was *his* door. He recognised the brass knocker. The knocker was completely unique. He was sure it was unique because he could remember making it.

———olo———

Tan's muscles were taut as a bow string. Dangerously so. He darted silently through the door in a blur of motion like the wind, ready to unleash arrows of pain into anything that moved.

But the room was deserted. A mess of papers and electrical cables were its only tenants, strewn about the floor in disarray. No dust had gathered though, and there were no signs of the passage of time beyond a sedimentary mildew that lined the blue walls. This place had been abandoned recently, and in a hurry. There were pieces of computer equipment still plugged in, perfectly intact.

Whoever had been here and whatever they had been doing, one thing was certain – that they were somehow connected to the developers. Tan felt a temptation to run away and not look back, but was stayed by an even stronger desire to get to the heart of the matter – to root out the threat lest he and his family be in constant hiding. Think. Assess the situation.

The difficulty of his predicament had crossed his mind more than once. He was not sure how far a claim of self-defence would hold in the eyes of the law, but without any kind of evidence to prove that the developers had posed a threat, his actions of the morning would appear nothing short of cold blooded murder.

He picked up a sheet of paper and spun it round to see what it was. A printed photo... and one he knew well. It was his home. His mind reeled. Had they, whoever they were, been doing surveillance? He grabbed another sheet from the floor. His home again. Another. A picture of his neighbour Erpin. He rifled through as many as he could find. They had everything. He saw himself, taken from different angles. The quality was perfect. How had it been done? Some kind of ultra zoom lens? Where was the photographer? He found a stack of photos of seemingly random everyday objects – chairs, tables, taps, cups, plates, even polaroid photos of the brass door knocker outside – in short, most of the things he had scattered around his house. But how? And then... why? But the final printout made his blood boil. It was a picture of his wife and daughter, sleeping in the family bed, taken from directly above... from inside his own home.

What the hell was going on here? Was this some kind of stake out operation, the way one would watch an animals habits before striking? But if so why go to the lengths of photographing mundane objects like the cup? Every way he tried to tie together the threads of this discovery into something coherent failed. The real solution was, almost by definition, beyond his ability to fathom.

He collected all the sheets of paper he could find and slung them into a bag. For what purpose, he didn't know, but that they were proof of malevolence, he was sure. Among them was a page of handwritten addresses that immediately caught his eye. He scanned the list, looking for anything that might relate to his village but for once found nothing.

Some of the entries had loosely sketched maps next to them, and beside every row was a number from one to ten, under a column marked *"Power"*. They appeared to be ratings, but of what?

Political power? Electrical power? Physical power? Were these other people the developers were targetting? He determined he would find out.

But first he turned his attention to the electronics, being careful not to damage or disconnect anything. A few blinking lights indicated that some of the equipment was not only functioning, but had been left switched on.

He tapped a few buttons on a keypad hesitantly. Nothing. Then tried a different device. A light blinked, and then nothing. Then, as he touched a key on a third, a small screen that he had assumed to be broken, instantly lit up.

The moment the image appeared he knew he had reached the end of his search for clues. On the screen was a face, frozen in mid-motion, looking directly into the camera, recorded from inside this very room. The face appeared to be from the final frame of a video that was labelled "I, Page."

He pressed play.

CHAPTER TWENTY FIVE

.: I, Page

—o Day 16 o—

Page held one of the pills that Velma had given him between his fingers, looking at it in the glow of the screen.

"Imagine inside this little pill was a chemical, and that chemical could unlock a neural pathway in my brain that had been disconnected, or locked. So that when I take this pill it will join together two parts of my brain that had been deliberately kept separate, like a sort of chemically triggered password to a gate. Maybe I will find a part of my memory that I never had access to before."

He looked at the pill, wondering what it contained.

"Maybe there is even an entirely different me inside myself, running in its own world, unaccessible by my main conscious thoughts?"

He paused for a moment, considering, "That could be happening anyway."

He swallowed it.

His looked at the camera solemnly. "If you somehow see this video, Sync, then I just want to say that uh... I'm sorry. I didn't want to mess up your job. I know you will get in trouble too, and, I'm sorry."

"Right," said Page, suddenly resolute, having snapped out of the rambling soliloquy that he had been stuck in. "The main purpose of this video is to leave a record so that if something happens to me, there is a kind of document of my work that somebody else can continue," He paused. "I guess I'm sort of incriminating myself, because, well. Uh. It doesn't matter. If anyone comes looking for me and finds this, then they've already tracked me down and know what I'm up to, so..."

He picked up a blank sheet of paper and scrawled on it in large letters, then held it up for the camera to see.

tHe_TrU7h=insId3

"That's the access for the research. All of it. The Village programs."

He looked around him at various diagrams and papers, flicking through a wad of them. Blueprints of the village lay heaped on the desk.

The shanties were arranged as a cul-de-sac, with toxic water cutting-off the escape from the back, and a single road leading outward over a bridge. A small stack of profile photos depicted the sim-actors with which to populate the village. He had scribbled names on them, like Phocan, Holloway, Norbeck, Marshall, inspired by the names of the shops that could be seen from his window.

Then there were diagrams of the everyday objects that he had placed in the environment – chairs, tables, and so on. It wasn't exhaustive by any means – it didn't need to be. The computer was capable of procedurally generating a vast assortment of background items in full detail. Anything idiosyncratic needed a personal touch though, or anything related to the character or specifics of the research. The things that formed the remnants of memories, or that would motivate an action – a birthday card, or a handmade brass door knocker, for example – had to be precisely defined. In these cases Page normally derived them from things that he came across in the real world, using scans or photos, and then elaborated the definitions in code.

"The village is a closed system with no exits, designed to put pressure on the solver-kernel, force it into a feedback spiral or a... a looping branch. Into a creative decision. I'm currently using Barkhausen-Morrow to handle the analysis, and dummy the neuron mapping, but, like I keep saying, it just doesn't work."

He looked at the photo of Tan.

"He's just... the agent is just too... linear, in its selection of paths. If it's going to try to solve the simulation using the combat program then it has to account for the other agents self-solving against that program. It's like Tan will only think in a straight line, and not anticipate what the others – Holloway and co. are gonna respond to. The background agents – June, Nivi, Erpin – are there as blockers, but so far, well, I think it needs a new approach. Anyway, that's where the alpha version is right now. I am planning more versions to test out different pressure points."

He slid across the room on a wheeled chair to a set of much bigger computers. The laptop remained in the corner recording his face on its little screen. A toy compared with the beasts he was now attending.

Power cables were duct taped into metal frames. Stacks of motherboards were sandwiched between fans and coolers. He looked at the set-up with satisfaction, pleased with it despite his occasional outbursts at its limits. Localised limits were less of a problem now that he was supplemented by the memory banks of a global corporation.

"Okay, so let me talk about memory. Still the biggest issue even though. Yeah. That and power. Even this stuff in here takes a ton, but... there are so many things I want to try. So many..."

Page had lost himself in his thoughts again. The sharp focus of the commentary had softened to an introspective self-analysis. It was to be short-lived though. The jangle of a buzzer broke the silence.

"What the fuck?" he said, hitting stop on the recording, freezing his image in a half open-mouthed pose. The final frame of the unfinished video.

The door buzzer jangled again.

Page rushed to the window to steal a glance down to the street. A shabby, old man was standing at the back entrance of the building wearing a long sleeved coat. The man's face was hidden from view beneath a dusty hat, and under his arm was a basket containing vegetables or flowers. A few red petals had spilled from the sides, and lay scattered at his feet.

The man pressed the button again for 145. He half looked toward the window that Page was peeking through, but not enough for Page to see his face. A crackled voice came on the speaker. "I'm... collecting. Do you have, any... garbage?"

Bullshit, thought Page, remembering how Bint had come to the previous apartment. They're on to me. He started throwing things urgently into a holdall, not bothering to shut anything down or unplug. The value of the electronics wasn't a concern to him. They could be smashed again for all he cared. Data and memory, that was the important stuff – the unique, irreplaceable stuff – his work. He grabbed what he could.

Thirty seconds later he was out of the front door, leaving the old man standing in the street at the back. He nodded a curt "See ya later" to the landlady as he hopped over the metal grill. Nobody was going to catch him this time. If it proved to be a false alarm then so be it, he could return later. But for now, he was out of here.

CHAPTER TWENTY SIX

.: Confirm

Tan looked again at the frozen final frame of the video and replayed the last section again. The words meant almost nothing to him, arriving as they did contextless and in an alien language of programmer-speak. This man Page was intricately involved with the people who had sought to destroy Tan's life though. That was now a certainty. Judging from the state of the room Page had departed very recently, possibly even last night.

Tan looked around for a pen, or anything to jot down some of this information, and found an old, polaroid style imaging device lying amongst the junk. He picked it up and flicked the on switch. It worked. He lined up the lens with the screen and clicked the photo button. Unobtrusive software did its work seamlessly, automatically setting the focus and light levels, then removing the stutter of motion blur as the shutter opened. A few seconds later the physical photo dropped out into his hand, crisp and sharply focussed – a replica of the image on the screen – the final frame of Page, open mouthed, looking into the camera on the laptop.

There were very few truly physical devices left in the world. Most, like this imitation polaroid camera, were hybrids, merely creating the illusion of a mechanical device whilst running on powerful software hidden deep beneath the surface. The reach of algorithms touched almost all things.

Tan wrote the name "Page" on the polaroid. Now he had a real name to anchor to the strange events. His mind was throbbing. What next?

Clearly the computer held much more information than this video, which he just happened to see by chance. Unfortunately he possessed almost none of the skills to operate it. It was just not something that was a normal part of his world. He had to attempt it though.

Operating systems were of course designed to be as intuitive as possible though, and ubiquity in design meant that a scant familiarity with one of them was enough for a basic understanding of any other.

He reluctantly closed the video, unsure if he would be able to get it back should he need to refer to it. A row of streaming text showed numbers and flashed bizarre warnings in red. Other processes were still running in the background.

```
> WARNING g_01BF42BD000000 !=> g_01BF4400000000
> ERROR! MemBlock transfer denied. Out of range.
```

Another window contained a list of what looked like documents, with one already highlighted.

```
Village-sim(1).arlos.
```

He tapped a couple of the keys, more or less at random, then hit Enter a few times, Escape, all the big buttons. After a bit of blind pressing a box opened up on the screen in front of him. He mouthed the words that were written there.

```
> An instance of "Village-sim" is already
running.
> Do you wish to invoke another?
> Please confirm [y/N]_
```

He was out of his depth with this stuff. It meant nothing to him. He hoped that the computer would somehow retrieve more information about the people who were involved here and display it. His finger hovered over the "y" key to confirm, but he paused to consider something – what if running the program would trigger some kind of alarm? He must be a wanted man after all.

Let them come, he thought. He was the hunter now. After so many hours wondering lost in strange lands he would welcome the familiarity of a physical confrontation.

He hit the confirmation key, and then waited... and waited. And...

The heat of the day and his exhaustion had finally caught up with him all at once. He felt like his mind had suddenly collapsed. All around him the walls of the place seemed to melt away. As fatigue brought him crashing down to his knees physically, the psychological drain brought him crashing down mentally.

He imagined he was back at home in the shanty village. His home, that he had destroyed this morning was there all around him, just as it had been. Either through delirium or confusion it felt as though he were really there. It felt real. It was more than a waking dream.

Peace and tranquility. Maybe the other place was the dream?

He blinked slowly. He had been dreaming about something, but what was it? Sand? No, not that. A room somewhere?

> He was tired. Reaching up for the tap, he splashed water onto himself to freshen up, as he knelt on the floor of his shanty. The water felt deliciously revitalising on his skin, but did little to abate the throbbing in his head. It pulsated with every movement.

> June and Nivi were sleeping peacefully in the bed next to

him. He tried to collect fragments of thoughts. When was this? Wasn't he supposed to be doing something today?

He walked outside the house and up the pathway to the end of the street. There were the five developers, waiting for him. Yes of course, he remembered. The developers. He looked around quickly for Erpin. Where was he? His house looked empty.

"Well, Mr Taneka?" said Holloway, smiling through broken teeth. "We're waiting. There are no more tomorrows."

No more tomorrows. Tan had felt certain Holloway was going to say something different. Yet despite that feeling, he still felt a sense of deja-vu at the words. No more tomorrows.

"I need a little more time," said Tan, stalling as he tried to work out what was happening.

"Don't know how you people can live in this piece of shit dump," chimed Norbeck almost reflexively.

"Stop being a Johnson will you Norbeck," said Holloway. "He's gonna do the right thing. I mean, he's not stupid, is he?"

"But, what happened to...?" He trailed off as he looked around at the room. He was back in the blue room in Chinatown, lying on the floor surrounded by cables and computer equipment. His head was spinning.

He took a few quick breaths of air, gasping with the shock of being jolted out of his hallucination. He touched dry lips. He needed water. But hadn't he just had water? No. That was a hallucination. His body had evidently been craving water so much that his mind had pictured him drinking it.

189

He had to get out of this room. His head hurt. At least if he collapsed in the street there might be someone to help him. For all the uneasiness he felt being around strange people, the street was the safest place for him now.

He staggered out into the road, blinded by the sunlight. People blurred in and out of focus as his mind tried to fix his bearings. One second he was standing in the streets of Chinatown, the next he was back in the village.

He was short of breath. He felt like his heart was beating irregularly. The driver of a passing tuk-tuk swore at him as he careened into the road. People watched him lurching haphazardly through the streets. Some stared. Some chuckled. Most chose to ignore him – a guy stumbling around in a state of delusion was not a rare sight in this part of town.

He looked back at the street he had just crossed, at a doorway with two figures in it. A woman and a girl were standing at the entrance to a herbal remedy store. The girl was saying something to her mother. He couldn't hear the words, but the expression was clear enough – disgust and pity – features that said "I want to be standing on the other side of the street," – a tragic staple of the homeless and delinquent.

"Are they yours?" asked a man in front of him. It was the developer, here, in Chinatown. No, not in Chinatown. He was in the village. The developer looked at him, then looked past him toward a doorway.

Tan spun around. There were a woman and a child, watching him, but not those from a moment ago... Now it was June and Nivi. They looked at him in concern, and fear.

He was about to say something. His mouth opened, but words didn't come out. His lips were parched. His head was throbbing.

The woman and child stood watching him, in Chinatown, at the entrance to the herbal remedy store. He wheeled around to see if the developer was there. He wasn't. Nobody was there, just the droning mumbles of a hundred passers-by, busily going about their daily routine.

To his right, down an alleyway, he could see what looked like a tap. A filthy tap, in a filthy alleyway, but a tap nonetheless. He staggered onward. The streets ignored him, now that he had passed into the threshold of the alleyway and was just another lonely figure lost in a rut of the sprawl.

A market worker who was chopping and washing vegetables instinctively moved to one side as Tan approached, assuming him to be a drunkard, but noticing his distress went over to help. Tan could only gasp, so just pointed to his mouth. The man understood the gesture, rushed to the tap, then came back with a cup of the foul water.

Tan sipped deeply, clearing his throat. His mind still spun like he had been fed poisonous mushrooms. He could at least rasp words though.

He took another swig, coughing, then blew blood from his nose. It spattered on the floor in large globules. The market worker was unphased by the ejaculation, and gestured for him to continue. "Good. Drink more. It's the right thing. You are doing the right thing."

Tan put the glass to his lips, but fumbled, dropping it to the floor. He looked into the man's eyes. What did he mean by "*You are doing the right thing,*" he wondered? It sounded... He looked again into the man's eyes. It was Holloway. Tan's mind was spinning. What had just happened a moment ago?

He looked down at his hands. He was holding a pen, and a

contract. He couldn't work out why, but it seemed as though he was preparing to sign it. What was it?

He realised where he was. The contract was the agreement for the Phocan Properties deal. He looked at it. There was no way he wanted to sign. What had the developers done to him?

Then he remembered the decision he had made. He lifted up the pen, inhaled a long, calm breath, and said "I, am, doing the right thing," slowly and deliberately.

As the developer turned to flee, Tan brought the pen down with full force. It went straight into the man's back, and through four inches of flesh. Tan blinked in surprise. He wasn't expecting the pen to be so sharp.

Tan blinked again, and to his horror saw the young market worker, not Holloway, still standing, with a large knife embedded in his back.

He spun the man around in desperation, willing this scene to be a delusion. But it wasn't. The dead man slid down from his arms and onto the floor.

Tan felt sick, and massively confused. He could only suppose that he had killed this man, and yet in the moments when it happened it was as though he wasn't there. He was losing his mind.

Not knowing what else to do he fled back into the streets to get lost in the ambient hum of Chinatown, leaving the body lying there in the alley. But nobody had even noticed what had happened.

He watched from across the street, unsure what to do. He felt the moral pangs of guilt and an obligation to report it, but what then? What would happen to June and Nivi if he was taken away?

The problem was soon solved. Within a few minutes a crowd of curious onlookers had gathered around the body.

A few minutes later, the authorities arrived in the form of a policeman.

A few minutes after that, Tan blinked in astonishment, as a wiry man wearing a trench coat arrived. He recognised the man. It was the same man he had seen earlier entering a building marked *"Kirby's Detective Agency"*.

CHAPTER TWENTY SEVEN

.: Fanling Furniture Fair

—o Day 27 o——

Fanling Furniture Fair was one of Chinatown's oldest markets. It was an analogue island in a digital sea. Inside it the white-haired wanderers – the final generation of pre-internet souls – spent their twilight years pottering around, clinging to whatever lost memories they could find in places such as these, hidden among the archaic mementos of a long forgotten age.

Kirby waited, checking the time, then scanning the cluttered market looking for a fresh face amidst the wrinkles and wood.

A young man with glasses approached.

"What are we doing out here?" called Clement, spotting Kirby as he walked beneath the iconic archway and into the 'Old man of Chinatown' as it was called by locals. "I got the data you asked –" He stopped abruptly as Kirby raised a sharp finger to silence him.

Then, without saying a word, Kirby turned on his heels and walked in. Clement followed apprehensively.

Together they weaved their way through the twisting corridors of stacked ornaments. A hundred clock faces stared in indignation as they passed. The head of a carved wooden bear seemed to challenge them with every footstep that took them deeper into its lair. A wall of 20th century electronics beeped in irritation as they disturbed a thousand digital slumbers.

Finally Kirby stopped. They had arrived at a small rustic coffee shop tucked in the very centre of the antiquated forest. Except for the waiter they were completely alone.

"Why, why here?" whispered Clement, looking around and feeling a distinct sense of trespassing. "This place is from another century." Getting no reply, he unpocketed a few folded sheets of paper and placed them on the table. "And why paper? I could have just pinged it to you."

"Give me your portable," said Kirby, not bothering to whisper.

"Oh..kay," said Clement reluctantly, doing as he was bidden.

Kirby tapped it, holding it up for Clement to see.

NO SIGNAL

He tapped it again.

NO SIGNAL

"That's impossible?" said Clement. He tapped it himself.

NO SIGNAL

"Too much interference. No signal can get through," Kirby shrugged, gesturing the myriad of ornamental gizmos that surrounded them.

Clement looked with renewed appraisal at the place.

"What most people don't know is that despite being one of the oldest joints in town, this market is one of the best places to do any hush-hush business," said Kirby. He signalled the waiter.

The waiter raised a greying eyebrow.

195

"Uh, coffee. Special," said Kirby.

The waiter merely nodded.

"You hate coffee," said Clement.

"It's not for me."

"I hate coffee."

"It's not for you," Kirby said cryptically. He sighed, "You hear what went down yesterday?"

"Yeah of course, the guys are all talking about it. I hear Toby's got a hole the size of ball-point pen in his arm and... Hey, are you okay?"

"Yeah, just about," muttered Kirby, rolling out the ache in his neck.

"So what was it? Some kinda Trikuza operation or something?" Clement was intrigued.

"Yeah, or something. But not the one I was looking for."

"No shit."

Kirby continued, "And, if the military guys didn't show up we probably would have gotten slammed."

"Military? No shit."

"Clement, did anyone else come asking questions after me last time?" asked Kirby suspiciously. "For the address you gave me?"

"No. Just you," said Clement in thought. "But it was the only one that matched, so maybe they did the same thing?"

"No," said Kirby, irritated. "So, they tailed me. That's what I thought." He was disgusted with himself. He was supposed to be the one tailing others, doing the covert movements, not the sort of green amateur that would let himself be tailed.

He unfolded the sheets of paper. They contained a medium scaled map of the area, detailed enough to see street names. "Okay, what you got for me?"

Clement smiled with enthusiasm, "So, I was thinking, you're looking for this gig that needs a lot of power, and you said it's low key, like not a situation where they can just buy it from the grid in the open. Right?"

"Right. So they rent some place and push it through the landlord's bill."

"Yeah. But I checked those for you last time, and nothing has changed. So, where else they gonna go for it? It has to come from the grid somehow."

"You mean, take it directly?"

"It's what all the food trucks do," said Clement shrugging. "You think those street guys have a utility bill? No sir."

"That's good. You shoulda been a detective," quipped Kirby.

"Yeah, and you should sit behind a desk. It's safer."

"Maybe I like the ground work," grimaced Kirby.

"Well you're gonna have to love it. That's a map of all the grid lines. Every one. My bet is he's on one of those lines."

Kirby studied the map, seeing how the marked lines weaved their way around the streets, but not always through buildings. There must have been hundreds of them. "Sheesh. That's a lot of territory to cover."

"Like I said."

Kirby picked a line at random and traced it with his finger. It zigzagged its way through the streets then eventually left the residential areas for more barren terrain. It seemed to be converging with other lines, to a point just beyond the top border of the map. "What's up there?"

"Oh that's the power plant. From there it goes up state on overhead pylons..." Clement and Kirby clicked at the same time. "You don't think?"

Kirby looked satisfied. "That's where my boy will be."

Sensing the conversation was over, the waiter approached, and placed a tray delicately on the table. The cup in its centre contained a steaming, noxious smelling, mustard coloured liquid, clearly not coffee by any definition.

Kirby took one last look at the map, memorizing the arrangement of roads. Then he tore the sheet into fragments, put them into the cup, and watched as they slowly dissolved.

CHAPTER TWENTY EIGHT

.: **Probability**

———o Day 22 o———

Page bundled the portable into his bag, with headset and cables, still sweating from the call with Omar.

He had been careful to bring the back-up drive and a few basic supplies, then set off on foot to make the call. There weren't many buildings in the vicinity of the power plant but eventually he'd come across the deli and it had seemed like a good option. If any of Omicore's guys were after him, he had a few blocks of freedom between here and the caretaker's office to get lost in.

He looked along the car park at rows of parked zooters. He didn't really know how to ride one but reasoned that it couldn't be difficult, given the number of people that used them.

Frustratingly most of the bikes were analogue, with key based engines. He was no jacker and wouldn't even know how to begin to hot-wire a zooter bike. He kept walking. A compact little black two-wheeler caught his eye. It had a digital access lock on the starter. Perfect.

He leant down as if to do up his shoe lace, and opened the portable inside his bag. He typed a few quick commands into the terminal and a window of encrypted numbers appeared on the screen. It streamed quickly through millions of combinations, stopping at a single eight-digit number. It flashed on the screen for a few seconds, then a beep sounded from the bike a second later, followed by the sound of the ignition sparking.

He climbed awkwardly on the back and held the handle bars. Gripping one of them revved the bike forward into the stand, almost knocking it over and throwing him off. He stopped for a minute to assess the controls.

A less methodical thief would have simply kept going, trying things out while the bike was in motion, but Page knew the value of a scientific analysis. He went through each of the buttons individually, then in combinations. Satisfied with a new understanding of the controls, he readjusted his seat and set off at speed. It was far from smooth but not so erratic as to draw attention, and the delay had only cost sixty seconds.

The first thing he ought to do was check if anyone had found his hideout in the power plant, or was even looking for him. Maybe he was being irrational, and from Omar's perspective their call had been mundane? He glanced down at his damaged hand reflexively. No. He couldn't take chances. Even if no alarm bells had been set ringing, Omar had got what he wanted and so Page was now expendable.

He drove along a road parallel to the south side of the plant, giving him an angle from which he could see the outside of the caretaker's office. It was the only street that offered this viewpoint without putting him in harms way. The building still looked deserted. Nothing seemed like it had been disturbed since he had gone to make the call, though it was hard to make out details from this far away.

If he were able to find a high enough vantage point it would have been possible to look directly into the very room in which he had been sleeping. The unfinished construction of the building meant that some of the upper walls had large gaps in them – holes that had been left in the concrete where piping or vents were to be fitted. Some of these gaps were large enough to admit a person.

He was so focussed on scrutiny of the power plant that he nearly collided with the black car coming towards him. They were also distracted, and for the same reason – they were looking at the caretaker's office. Eyes widened. Gears shifted. Tyres scraped the asphalt as brakes were slammed.

He yanked down on the accelerator, revving past them in the opposite lane. One, two,... there were three of them in the car... all dressed in black fatigues. The light of a camera flashed at him as he looked back over his shoulder. He sped on, head down, full throttle. The screech behind him told him they were in pursuit.

He scanned the buildings for a way off the road. The last thing he wanted to do was be in a road chase with military grade hitmen after him, during his first time on a zooter bike. He rounded the next corner just as they came around the first. He would head into town, into cover, away from the sparsity of these empty streets.

There! Between two buildings was a narrow alleyway wide enough for a bike but too slim to admit a car. He sped towards it.

The car was almost on top of him as he skidded in, struggling for control as his wheels bumped down cobbled stones, nearly bouncing him into a wall. The car jolted to a stop at metal bollards, seeing the alley was too narrow. But the passenger door opened in a moment and one of the men leapt out, running hell-for-leather. Then the door slammed shut and the car sped off again.

Page was almost out of the alley and into the next road. The man chasing, for all his speed, wouldn't catch up so long as Page remained on the bike. But Page didn't know these streets, and was sure that they would be trying to cut him off. Where to go?

He sped out onto the next road. It was empty. He picked a direction – left, and zoomed off. This random choice must have been correct, as he was still alone. He took another left at the next cross roads. It was empty again.

Was he safe yet? Possibly, but he didn't want to take chances. He started calculating odds. It was a path problem. With each new junction they had a probability of one divided by the number of paths, of guessing his route correctly. These odds would multiply commutatively for each junction. The optimal solution, therefore, was to always take the path that led to the largest number of other subsequent junctions, never repeating. That gave him the lowest probability of being followed at random.

Real life wasn't quite as neat as that, he knew – other factors had to be considered – but it was a good system and he went with it.

So far he had chosen one in two for the first path, then one in three for the cross roads. He could now see another cross roads up ahead, and picked the path that looked widest. That was another one in three, making their odds... one in eighteen, which was only 5.5%. That was low enough. Time to ditch the bike.

The next road was brimming with shops. Among them was a small motor repair garage nestled between store fronts with a few bikes parked in front. It was the perfect place for concealment. He pulled up awkwardly and flipped out the kick stand.

As he dismounted one of the garage kids came up to him, speaking in the local dialect. "Khun Tam Arai Wa?"

He looked back blankly, not knowing what to say. "I stole this bike," he said, simply. "You can keep it." He walked off.

CHAPTER TWENTY NINE

.: Terminal

——o Day 27 o——

"Thank's for coming Leet," said Kirby. "I didn't think you would after what happened to me and Toby."

They were parked by a roadside, on a completely empty street on the edge of the city. With dusk falling and the lack of street lights, nighttime was imposing itself fast.

"Oh you can bet your sweet ass I'm not going to be the first inside any dodgy building," said Alita. "I am strictly here to sit on my gorgeous booty, and drink coffee, until you come back and tell me that the place is empty. Then, and only then, am I setting foot anywhere."

He nodded slowly. "Thanks all the same though." Then reaching out of the window discreetly he flicked a coin over and onto the roof, causing a loud clanging on Alita's side of the car.

"What the eff was that?!" whispered Alita.

"Not sure," said Kirby, and scanned the barren street. "I will be back in fifteen minutes though."

He furtively opened the car door, and without a pause to look back, made his way into the grounds of the power plant.

A minute later and Alita was beside him. "Okay, I'll be more help with you. You fuck."

203

He grinned.

The area of land they had to cover was fairly large, but it could be narrowed down somewhat by applying a bit of logic to the problem. The central and northern parts of the plant could be ruled out, given the amount of security they had in place – the sparkling lights of activity were visible long before they pulled up to the roadside – which left the south as the logical place to start. If it proved fruitless then the search could move elsewhere.

Looking up, they could see clearly where power lines from the town merged, forming a trunk of wires that entered the plant in the south section. They walked the hundred metres of barren landscape through the dirt, stepping over huge slabs of broken concrete whose weather-ravaged cracks spewed weeds that scratched at their ankles, until eventually they reached the outer wall of the southern structure. The place was desolate – ideal for something clandestine, which paradoxically meant it was an easy place to be spotted.

"Keep low, and let me lead," said Kirby.

"A-okay on that," said Alita, now feeling the coldness of adrenaline creep into her veins and wishing she'd brought the coffee.

Upon entering the first building Kirby felt instinctively that he was in the right area. The place was abandoned and deserted, but not so abandoned that it didn't have running power and water. It was, after all, connected to the fully functioning north section, half a kilometre away.

As they walked into one of the engine rooms the barking of several dogs rang out from the recesses of massive machinery. An inch thick layer of pigeon shit on the floor dampened the echos though, making it hard to tell exactly where the sound had come from.

"Flippin' stray mutts," he tutted. "They'll give us away."

"It's exactly what we need though," said Alita. "If some dude wanted to hide his ass in this place, for whatever dumb ass reason, then he'd keep well away from all the dogs."

"Yeah, I see what you mean. Get too close to their territory and you start a barking war. So we can rule out this room." He patted her affectionately. "I ought to give you a bonus."

She stuck a finger up at him.

Using the intermittent barking of dogs as a sort of reverse homing beacon, they narrowed down the search to a few rooms, always steering away from any area that the dogs considered to be theirs.

"There!" said Alita suddenly, pointing to a fresh looking cable on the floor, untouched by dust or pigeons.

"This could be it," said Kirby in agreement. "Maybe showtime. Stay back here. For real this time." He pushed her back, gently. "Or you'll lose that bonus."

He followed the cable around a corner and up a flight of stairs. It led through a dusty set of footprints then under the gap of a door. He paused, noting from the light around the latch that it was unlocked... which meant either the occupants had long gone, or were in there now.

As gently as he could he inched the door open.

Stillness.

He pushed it delicately, letting it slide a few more inches open.

More stillness. The room was empty.

He pushed it all the way open, and walked in.

Computer cables were everywhere. There were chunks of plastic and electronics strewn on the floor. Part of a cooling system was cracked open, with fluid leaking out. A junction box in the corner had been hooked up to a metal grid of fuses. It looked like someone had done a coarse but thorough rewiring of this place.

"Leet, come check it out," he called in a semi-hush.

Two minutes later and they were inspecting the room together. She turned over a few broken computers and looked at their innards. "I know you aren't a tech guy, but you can tell that stuff has all been smashed right?"

"I have eyeballs Leet. I know the difference between switched off and smashed to bits. But is there any way to tell what any of it was for?"

"Well, I can tell you that he eats sandwiches," she said pointing at a half finished sandwich on the floor next to a polycarb plate.

Kirby chuckled, but then noticed something. A pill on the floor, next to a small overturned jar. He picked it up and examined the embossing. *"Antipsych.Y71"*

"Interesting," he said, pocketing the jar. "Our man Page could be a crazy."

"Unless it's the others that were here?" Alita looked at a footprint that was on the front of some casing where somebody had kicked through it. It was from a bigger, heavyset boot.

Kirby looked at the print. It was military, no doubt. "So, they've already been here?" he sighed. He kind of felt sorry for Page at times. "Those guys are definitely crazy, if it's the ones me and Toby ran into."

"There's something missing," she said, taking in the big picture of the room. "It's like this is all the electrical gear and stuff, but where's the dude's keyboard and headset?"

"Where does he even sit? There's gotta be another room somewhere. A work room," said Kirby, looking at the walls. "This kinda has to be here for the juice, the power outlet, but maybe there's a more cosy place for study?"

Ten minutes of searching later they were standing in the caretaker's office, over a large scale photo of a village that had been taped to the floor. It had annotations and schematic labelling surrounding it, and was closer to a blueprint than a traditional photograph. Pristine, undamaged computer equipment was all around them. Everything appeared to be still functional.

"Badda-bam!" Kirby grinned. "Do we turn it on?" and hit a button on a device that was plugged into the wall.

"Don't touch it! Let me see." She pushed past him.

The screen pinged on. A command prompt was blinking at them.

```
> Unlock Code: _
```

"What is it?" he asked.

"Some kind of terminal link," she said, turning it over. "But just as good as a dead-end."

"Why?"

She sighed. "A cold prompt like this won't go anywhere unless you know what password or command to put in. It'll send a signal somewhere, or boot something up if you put the right thing in. Otherwise it's just a dumb piece of plastic."

"Nothing?" he clucked, a little frustrated.

"I can try a couple of default commands. But come on, the guy we're looking for is hardcore. It'll go nowhere." She tried a few things anyway, but predictably, nothing happened.

Kirby took a few snaps of the room with an imager, but there didn't seem to be anything else worth investigating aside from the terminal. "Okay Leet, let's go."

"So do we take it?" she asked. "Maybe try a few decryptors on it in a proper lab?"

"Not yet," he said. "I wanna leave this place untouched and watch what happens for a few days. See if anything gets moved around. Our guy might come back for it."

CHAPTER THIRTY

.: Rafters

The moment the pair were gone Tan pushed open the slats in the roof where he had been concealed, and dropped down. The room was in almost the exact same state as he'd left it.

After fleeing Chinatown he had been diligently working through the list of addresses – the same list he'd found in the blue room – until eventually coming to the power plant. Then, after a few twists and turns he'd discovered the caretaker's office and had lain in wait there ever since.

A few hours later was when he'd heard the dogs barking and had scurried up into the rafters.

He had listened to the conversation beneath him with a mix of confusion and certainty. Confusion was the basic state of his being now – everything was jumbled up in his mind. Certainty was the knowledge that he was getting closer to all the answers. Answers to what though?

His mind was a mess of hallucinations and memories – as though he was reliving events that hadn't taken place, or that had taken place in an alternate reality. He had both watched his family be killed by the developers, and had watched them escape. He had memories of himself dying – which logically had to be false – and of destroying the village in a blaze of glory. Yet the potency of both memories seemed as real as each other, or as any others.

209

Things were confusing. Maybe it was he that should be taking the Antipsych. Pills.

He clambered down to the floor as quietly as he could, then waited another ten seconds just to be sure. Nothing moved.

The terminal they had been discussing was still blinking its prompt silently in the corner. He hadn't known that it was still active until they'd touched it. Now he knew exactly what it was, or thought he did – it was another one of those machines from the blue room in Chinatown – which meant it contained information.

He unpacked the sheets of paper that he had taken, and spread them out on the floor. He singled out the folded sheet with the password scrawled on it.

tHe_Tru7h=insId3

She had said this terminal device needed a code, well, here was a code. He typed it into the Terminal, and watched with satisfaction as the screen reacted.

```
> AutoBoot sequence started...
> "Village-sim(2).arlos" initialised.
> Remote symlink initialised.
> WARNING potential memory conflict, modules
- "Village-sim(1).arlos"
- "Village-sim(3).arlos"
> WARNING g_01U5P3Q1000000 !=> g_01U5TN04000000
> ERROR! MemBlock transfer denied. Out of range.
> Do you wish to invoke another instance?
> Please confirm [y/N]_
```

Though the jargon that spewed onto the screen meant nothing to him, the final statement was clear enough.

"Just give me some information," he muttered, and hit the "y" key.

But his hopes of using the computer as a kind of magic panacea of information were dashed. There was no video, just more meaningless code.

```
> ERROR Memory conflict, modules
- "Village-sim(1).arlos"
- "Village-sim(3).arlos"
```

A noise came from outside. Had he triggered an alarm of some sort? Or maybe they were playing a double game, bluffing him to come out by talking as though they were leaving.

The lights flickered out for a moment, then came back on. His muscles tensed in readiness.

He slid behind one of the cases, as silently as he could, watching the door handle intently for movement. But nothing moved. Then the sound came again. At first he thought it was a person, but soon realised it was something far less human. It was like a kind of randomised, high-pitch clicking – the sort of sound that might come from something electrical in nature – possibly a power line.

He crouched down on the floor to get a view across the room and through the gap beneath the door. All was still. But again came the sound. He lay motionless, patiently waiting, with controlled, rhythmic breathing.

His mind wandered.

> He was back at home, in his bed, waking up as the first rays of sunlight danced across his sleeping wife's face. He felt the comfort of familiarity being back here.

211

He began to pour himself a glass of water, and then stopped. Something here was wrong. Must not drink the water.

A familiar voice called.

"I don't want to go to school today," said Nivi, mischievously. "It's a holiday."

He looked at her, about to ask a question, but had a sickening sense of deja-vu. "Did you... say that to me... yesterday?" he asked instead.

"There's no electricity. There's never electricity on holidays," she replied. "That's how I know."

No electricity... Electricity? Something about electricity?

The lights, which had been flickering, were off. The faint clicking sound of a random electrical glitch was coming from somewhere outside.

He moved out from behind the cases to reassess his situation. The horizon felt like it was swaying as he stood up. It was swaying. No, he was. He was staggering... losing his grip on reality again.

He needed to get out... Out from the caretaker's office... Out into in the air.

He walked out to the barren wastelands of the power plant that flanked the south. The random noises were louder out here. They seemed to be coming from all sides. He looked up at the sky. Some of the stray dogs were barking.

There was a storm was coming, or something like a storm. It was very strange. The sky occasionally seemed to shift with the sound of an electrical click. The clouds too looked different, and he could have sworn that the buildings on the horizon had changed since the afternoon.

His heart raced... Its beat became irregular. His legs began to give way as he tried to take steps forward. Left. Right. Left... Left. Right... Right. He stumbled forwards onto the dirt.

This time he made no effort to move, but just looked up at the clouds moving erratically in the wind, and waited for the storm to come.

PART 2

Processing

CHAPTER THIRTY ONE

: Tōkei Senshi

———o Day 5 o———

It was Tuesday 13ᵗʰ February, 2057 – five days after the power had been switched on on Lunar – two days after the ASA's visit to Omar.

Black and white photos of mostly Asian men adorned the walls of a large dojo. The portraits were framed reverentially in ornate wooden moulding, and loomed over the room like Gods.

Hyrai was a small man compared to the others here, though despite his senior years, was in excellent physical condition. He walked amongst the rows of faces, addressing the room as he walked. Most of the people were wearing some form of martial arts uniform, or belt with rank insignia. Some simply wore black fatigues with a logo to identify who they represented. He wore crimson with white emblazoning: *"Hyrai Mikoto, Tōkei Senshi, Rank Zero."*

"For thousands of years, mankind has created systems of attack and defence based on the statistical analysis of combat and its injuries. The Martial Arts. Until recently these systems have been based on the personal experience of their founders. And the results are, well–"

Hyrai suddenly struck out at the man nearest him. The man, though large and muscular, moved very fast, seeing the strike coming. His shoulders twisted and his arm shot out to intercept. But Hyrai had already anticipated the intercept, and adjusted,

216

connecting with the man's wrist – which had been the intended target all along. It crunched loudly, as others in the room winced.

"–mixed," continued Hyrai. He stopped walking. Above him in bold, stylised calligraphy was written *"Tōkei Senshi"*.

He continued, "I would like to introduce you to a system that is not biased by the judgements and educational short comings of its founders, nor shrouded in the mystique of its followers."

He moved again, through the rows, as graceful as a dancer and as nimble as a cat. The way he shifted the weight of his body was both enchanting and confusing.

"In the twentieth century people had begun to apply the scientific method to combat – to measure the effectiveness of the infliction of pain. Groups such as the Nazis, the CIA, ISIS, the Guerriers de Dieu, and others, began to experiment with, and to document human suffering. The stated goals were always to improve the deadliness of their soldiers, or their defensive capabilities, but the reality was little more than the twisted acts of barbarism by a bunch of psychopathic sadists.

"Between 1935 and 1945, Unit 731 of the Japanese army conducted tests on Chinese farmers, that included stabbing them from different angles with bayonets, dropping rocks onto their bodies, limbs, and heads from different heights to – they claimed – test how much damage a live human body could endure. Aside from being some of the cruelest experiments ever done in history, they improved the science of combat... by almost nothing."

"Sick bastards," muttered one of the men.

Hyrai grinned ironically, noting the accent, "You are American?"

"Yes."

"Well, you should know then – your country bought the research and gave them all immunity."

Some of the people in the room smirked, others snorted in derision. People weren't sure how to take the small framed man. Many had heard of him, though few had met him. All knew why their companies had sent them here.

"These days things have moved on though. We have access to millions of hospital records, combat logs, and above all, the simulations. We can simulate the physics of a human body, down to the size of a cell, to study how it will react to different trauma and stimuli."

He winked at the American who had spoken. "Unlike Unit 731, when we want to find out what will crush a child's skull, we can do it without using a real child."

Holding out his arm, open-palmed, he gestured to the man. The man reluctantly placed his hand on Hyrai's wrist. It was a familiar protocol to all who had studied martial arts in one form or another. An extended, open-palmed arm usually meant a grappling technique was about to be demonstrated. As Hyrai gently flexed his fingers, the man braced himself for what might follow, tension turning his upper torso into a wall of muscle. The man ran through a series of Aikido, Jujitsu and even a few Sambo grips in his mind, determined not to fall for any quick take-downs.

Hyrai continued, softly. "We have learned some surprising weak points in the human body after running these simulations. Who would have thought, for example, that it is possible to cause pain–" Hyrai's hands moved swiftly over the American's fingers, pinching and squeezing.

The man grabbed at his neck, uncontrollably, his eyelids flickering as tears appeared. The pain had shot into his neck seemingly from nowhere. Irresistibly.

"–in the eyes and neck, by application on the thumbs?" finished Hyrai. He released the man and bowed slightly in apology.

"This data, combined with the analysis of operational success in real combat scenarios, has been woven together into a system we call Tōkei Senshi – Combat by statistical analysis."

There was a low murmur of astonishment and appreciation within the room. Hyrai bowed gently, then positioned himself at the front, and waited.

Understanding that the initial demonstration was over, people congregated into the small groups they had arrived with to confer in hushed whispers.

Omar turned to the two people next to him. One was Leonard, the other was an even bulkier man, Hallam, who headed Omicore's physical security.

"So what do you think?" he asked, visibly impressed with the demonstration.

"It's cunning," nodded Hallam. "Using the sensory cortex to spoof an attack on the neck. I guess by targetting the neighbouring nerves in the thumb."

"What deal are they offering?" asked Leonard.

"Access to their raw data for our sims, and physical training for our staff," replied Omar.

Hallam nodded in approval.

"At what cost?" asked Leonard, hesitant.

"Extortionate," replied Omar, "but they will give us a discount for shared access to our own socio-emotio data to incorporate into their program."

Leonard raised his eyebrows at this. Omar wasn't the type to sell out.

"Don't bother yourself," said Omar, "we'll pay cash."

Leonard looked around at the room, bothered by something else. "Why invite all these companies here together?" he wondered aloud, "it must irk most of them to have to be in the same room as their competition."

Omar shrugged, "Marketing tactic. It lets everyone know that even if they can't afford the programme, they have to buy it anyway, just to keep up with the others." He looked at the corporate logo tucked beneath the fancy calligraphy, nodding at words written there. "There's something else that disturbs me though. Why would Hoshoku-Sha Technology – a company that normally only sells weaponry to military organisations – open up one of its products to licensing by civilian industry?"

"What do you suspect?" asked Leonard, thoughtful. "Cross-contamination? Like, there would be something in the programme that infects us when we load it into our servers, to siphon off our data?"

"Nothing that brazen – we'd detect it," Omar replied, himself lost in thought. "Just that Hoshoku-Sha Technology and ASA are awfully closely connected, and that a change in the way ASA is moving is followed by a change in Hoshoku-Sha."

"Strategic algorithms?" asked Leonard.

"Something like that."

"What do we do then?"

"We should take the Tōkei Senshi programme, and the data," said Omar decisively. "If there is something amiss about any of it, it's better to have a known unknown than be waiting for another attempt that we might not catch. Our security needs to be bullet proof in the coming month."

Leonard nodded. "You like it?" he asked the bulky man.

"I do," the man said solemnly. "They won't sell anyone the best version of the programme of course. That will be saved for themselves. But it's better to be one step down than two steps down."

CHAPTER THIRTY TWO

.: Following

—o Day 28 o—

Sync stared at the untouched soup in front of her, watching the heat dissipate as a skin formed on the surface. It smelled delicious, though she had no intention of eating it. She'd had far too many coffees, sandwiches and snacks over the past two days to be tempted by another minestrone.

She looked at the black truck she had been following for signs of movement, but the engine was still off. It was parked under the shade of two trees, further down the road, in front of another little cafe that lined the countryside lane. A hundred metres was as close as she dared get though.

She dipped a slice of bread into the hot liquid, and toyed with it.

This game of stalking had gone on for far too long. Ever since the chess game in the Japanese restaurant she had been unable to contact either Omar or Page. Her device simply shut off when she attempted to call Omar – as though the call was being blocked at the microchip level – entirely possible given who he was. With Page her calls simply went unanswered, and was much more concerning.

She had noticed the black truck four days later. Sync was in no way a conspiracy theorist – her pragmatic temperament didn't permit it – but an unfamiliar black truck parked opposite her apartment was not something to ignore. The next morning she saw it again. It had pulled up in front of her gym shortly after she'd tried to call Page. Surely no coincidence.

To confirm or belie her suspicions she'd conducted a simple test: Taking an autotaxi from the gym, she had deliberately let her phone fall between the seats, with a timer set to call Page after she left. Two minutes after she had exited the vehicle the call was triggered, and sure enough, thirty seconds later a black truck emerged from a nearby junction. She had watched from the side of the road as it began to subtly follow the taxi.

From that moment on she became the cat and not the mouse.

She had disabled all electronic devices and taken nothing but a small bag of clothes, a zooter, and herself, and began to follow – to stalk – the truck. It hadn't taken her long to find it again. It would stop for hours at a time on apparently featureless side-streets, with nobody getting in or out, then move on to another location and repeat the same routine. She, meanwhile, would sit in a bakery, or a deli, or anywhere that gave her a good vantage point, and observe, always keeping at a safe distance.

There was no way to discern motive. Just that the appearance of the truck had coincided with the disappearance of, and her attempts to contact Page. She was certain they were trying to find him too.

Twenty four hours, five croissants, six cappuccinos, three chocolate brownies, and several sandwiches whose fillings she couldn't recollect, had passed since then. She stirred the Nth minestrone in front of her and took another nibble of the soggy bread, beginning to tire of it all.

Something moved. She looked over at the black truck to see if... The door was sliding open.

For the first time since beginning her pursuit she could see inside the vehicle. It was only a fleeting glimpse, but what she saw sent a chill down her spine. She could make out, briefly, a row of figures sitting shoulder to shoulder in the rear compartment. Behind them, hanging in neat vertical lines were what looked like weapons. She felt as though she were looking inside the ribcage of an animal – an evil, soulless creature made from darkness, for very little light illumined the interior of the truck. Shadowy faces were hidden beneath black helmets with only a thin slash of a mouth to mark the features.

As the door opened three of the armoured figures stepped out onto the roadside and flexed their joints, presumably not having moved for hours. No sooner had their feet touched the ground, and the door began to swiftly shut. The ignition of the engine sparked a second later.

Sync had a dilemma. Until now the game had been only to maintain a safe distance – near enough to keep up the chase, but not so near as to put her in immediate danger. But now she had a choice to make – to either follow the truck on her zooter, or to follow the three figures on foot.

As the crunch of gravel under tyres sounded and the truck began to move, she knew the choice had been made for her. It was now impossible for her to follow the truck as that would mean passing right by the three figures on the roadside, and to definitely be spotted.

She sipped another spoonful of minestrone, and watched, and waited, working out what to do next.

In the cafe behind her another figure was sipping a spoonful of minestrone, having come to the same conclusion she had.

CHAPTER THIRTY THREE

.: Lost

——o Day 28 o——

Page was lying on a mattress, spread eagle on his stomach, almost fully naked. His chin was propped-up sideways by a pillow, with the bulge of a sim headset jutting out from his face like some kind of bone-headed monkey. He watched the replay again, rapt in awe, as Tan *gamma* grappled with the modified village program – the third installation of the simulation.

Inside his headset tables of numbers flicked by like the white noise of television static, while in another view, simultaneously, Tan walked with Erpin and Yuita purposefully to the end of the street. They stood in statue-like silence as the SUV rolled up to the entrance of the lane. Something entirely unpredicted, and unanticipated was happening to Tan's mind. It was creativity.

As the first explosion thundered out in the simulated lane, Page lay spellbound, wondering at the significance of what Tan had achieved. The software core had, for the first time, creatively solved an intractable problem. The simulation shouldn't have been able to be beaten in this way. Or in any way. Page had gone to a lot of detail to architect the scenario as a closed loop. It was effectively a walled room with a ceiling that came down inch by inch.

For the past few days Page had been a virtual hermit, scarcely unplugging his headset while he poured over data, analysing and reanalysing the logs one instruction at a time.

Against his better judgement he had left the sim running,

reluctant to shut it down lest he lose any of the data. One thing he *had* lost though, was Tan. Tan had simply disappeared from the village, and Page had come to the conclusion that having passed the boundary of the sim, he had likely been dumped or overwritten by other services shifting memory in the Omicore servers. But it was difficult to know for certain – the sheer range of potential address-space made it impossible to track things once they passed from view. It was like tracking the expansion of automata in Conway's Life – every step in the iteration expanded the boundary of interference exponentially. Page had also to be extremely careful when probing memory outside of his protected sandbox for security reasons.

Regardless of what had happened the experiment was a success though. He rolled over in the bed, and let out a sigh of satisfaction.

"I hope you're not watching porn on that thing," said Sync, standing in the corner of the room.

"Whaa?!"

He ripped off the headset and looked at her in confusion, taking a moment to adjust to the change in light. "How did you find me?"

She could have been standing there for half the day for all he knew. It had been hours since he'd last seen real sunlight – what was left of it He looked at the dwindling light, trying to judge the time of day. Almost evening. Then suddenly became aware that he was almost totally naked.

"It's okay," she smirked "You're not that bad for a computer guy. Actually you're in pretty good shape."

He squirmed around for cover under the duvet, then bashfully slung on a t-shirt.

"Whose place is this?" she asked. "It's cute."

The wooden hut was small but beautifully and lovingly constructed. Ribbed walls made from locally hewn tree branches allowed it to blend into the surrounding forest perfectly.

"I don't know," he said. "It was secluded, and empty, and has lights and a power socket, so..." he shrugged.

She scowled at him briefly, then gave it up and smiled. "Let's hope they don't come back." Her delight in seeing him safe after days of no contact quashed her desire to reform him of his sins.

"What are you doing here? How did you know where I was?" he demanded.

"I've been following the people who have been following you."

He sat up, full attention. "What? What people? Security?"

"Yes, but, they're not the only ones."

"Who else?"

"I'm not sure. Maybe locals." She shock her head. "Maybe I'm just paranoid. But your trail is there to see if you know where to look."

"Wait. If you're here, then that means they know where I am?" he asked anxiously.

"No. They know you're in the area but not where exactly. I think," she frowned. "So I used my intuition. I know some of your habits, and that you'd be about as far away from other human beings as physically possible."

He stared at her blankly, fitting the new information into the slots in his mind and making a reassessment of their situation. His digital trail was almost impossible to follow – of that he was certain – but his physical trail, by comparison, might be like a beacon in the dark.

It was starting to get dark. Mosquitos were beginning to buzz optimistically around them. She sprayed moz-dust from a packet in her pocket and smiled. "You're welcome."

"Uh, thanks. You've come prepared. But, why are you here?"

"I need to protect my interests." She eyed him up and down. "You may not realise it Page, but you're a fucking genius. You'll be making me some serious cash one day, and it more than covers my time to look after you."

"I don't need looking after, I just need, well…" He stopped mid sentence off her sardonic look.

She was staring pointedly at his semi-recovered hand. The injury was still visible.

He gave a wry chuckle. "That could have happened to anybody."

"Don't joke Page. Some of those people are mean." She was remembering the warning Omar had given her at their first meeting.

"I know Sync."

"What happened with Omar, after the chess game?" It was the last time she had actually seen or spoken to him.

"I ran," he said simply.

"Let's walk and talk," she sighed, looking around at the hut again. "I assume you can leave this stuff running?"

He nodded, suddenly remembering the sim. "But, let's be back soon."

———olo———

The beach was beautiful.

They arrived just as the last embers of sunlight had lit up the clouds, painting the sky in hues of pastel blue and red. Reflections of distant cliff-tops zig-zagged their way through shallow waves lapping gently at the shore.

An empty fishing boat rocked lazily in the ebbing tide, sleeping until a new tide could awaken it for a night's work.

Bare feet left melting footprints in the wet sand, as Sync and Page walked silently along the seafront. They looked outward at the horizon.

"It's beautiful," said Sync. "They say that god is an artist, and paints her dreams in the sky."

"Under the paint is an even more beautiful work of creation," said Page. "They say that god is a poet, writing sonnets of physics in the language of maths."

She was touched by the timeless beauty of this place – of all nature. She stopped, looking at the heavens, taking it in.

"Do you know why the colours are distributed that way?" asked Page.

"I think so. It's the way gases in the atmosphere absorb light from the sun," she said softly, smiling. She knew the answer was correct. "The deep blues are from oxygen, which is highest in the atmosphere and unaffected by the colour of heavier gases near the surface."

Page nodded, adding, "And because the distribution is exponential, not linear, it means the world is round. A flat earth would have the colours spaced out differently." He looked at her. "Isn't it amazing that without even moving we can deduce the shape of our world, simply from the gradient of the sky? We can even calculate the radius. Well, if we know the height of the clouds above the sea."

Okay, she thought, I will play the game. It was interesting.

"How do you know we are not living in a simulation?" she posited, "and that above us is not some kind of giant machine, dragging a lightbulb across a vast room of coloured smoke?"

"There are too many things that coincide which suggest that isn't the case," he said. It was basic Simchotics, the modern Occam's Razor. "Through a deep enough inspection, the machine can always tell it is a machine... Eventually."

"I wouldn't want to know," she said, almost under her breath. "It might spoil the beauty of it all."

"Not for me," said Page softly.

She moved closer to him. "I don't normally..." she looked for words, "...walk around on beaches with my clients."

He looked back at her elfin face. There was a softness to it that radiated in the warm red. A softness that was missing, or hidden, in the harsh electric lights of the busy city. Here, she was reachable, tangible, touchable – a thing made of a substance similar enough to his own that if he could just reach out.

...their lips slowly met.

She held him, tightly. Passion, and an overwhelming sense of protection came over her, as her fingers gripped his back. She wanted more than anything to shield this man from the evils of a complex world whose currents they were now being swept away in.

Shield him, and gift him. Gift him a few moments of tender abandonment and sensuality that would defy his logical reasoning.

He let the tide of both of their emotions carry him forwards, into what were, for him at least, unfamiliar seas. Unfamiliar, but not unvisited. The adrenaline, and fear, and longing for an anchor of humanity brought him into her fold.

Reason and explanation can be damned, thought Page as he unpicked the metal clasp on her jeans. Yet, even as wild emotions inside him drove the novice fumbling of fingers and hands, eager to undress her, part of his mind wondered – was this seemingly guileless and unstructured act of lust actually a more deeply embedded form of neuro-programming? – one whose expression was formed of commands that lay higher up the chain of operations used in normal thought? Was there a more fundamental language of blind desire that contained, as a subset, the language of logic and reason? He wondered...

...then lost all interest in the line of thought, as their naked bodies met. Sync began to move sensuously on top of him, as gentle, writhing rhythms as old as the universe embraced them both.

Carnal instincts ruled rational thoughts, as the sun disappeared from the sky and the glow of the Moon appeared in its place.

CHAPTER THIRTY FOUR

.: Found

——o Day 28 o——

She lay on top of Page, looking down at him in the moonlight. He returned the look, awkwardly. White light bounced off beads of sweat on his face as he smiled up at her, searching for something in eager eye movements. She smiled back, drawing him out.

He squirmed inside, waiting. Finally she gave it to him.

"That was amazing," she grinned.

He relaxed. A grin of pride, and relief crept across his face.

Then after a moment he looked through her, analysing the performance in his memory, storing little pieces of information for future reference. He tried to remember the number of thrusts he had needed to make her orgasm, so he could compare it with other data. His mind tried to quantify the statistics of sex into neat, abstract equations. But it was hopeless. Despite his natural inclination for numbers and analysis, he had been too distracted by the pleasure of his own ejaculation to store any meaningful data.

But a thought did occur to him. "Have you ever looked at a diagram of the nervous system of a man and a woman? To see how the sense of touch is mapped onto the brain. Each nerve corresponds to a physical location inside your brain, in the sensory cortex. The weirdest thing is that order that they're arranged in, laid out in your brain, is different from how it is in your body. The vagina is actually mapped directly next to the feet, and not the hips, and so if you were to –"

"Page!" she made eyes at him. "Tell me tomorrow. But not now." She gave him an electric smile, "I'm thinking about other things right now."

He smiled back. But the smile receded suddenly, and he was now looking at her in confusion.

"What?" she asked.

He was watching a small blob of light dance across her face and forehead. He followed the erratic dance with his eyes. It reminded him of a kind of butterfly, trying to land on a flower that was moving in the wind.

The small blob of light suddenly stopped dancing, and settled on a point above her brow. His eyes went wide.

"They're here!" he yelled in terror. Before she could process this, he had already thrown her off him and onto the sand.

A sharp buzz zipped through the air, just as a patch of sand behind them exploded into dust. They traced the trajectory instinctively. A few green lights moved far off in the distance, illuminating the small figures that carried them... black, armoured figures.

Page scrambled up off the sand, half-naked. His towel flew off as he grabbed Sync's hand.

"Come on!" he yelled at her. "They'll be here in no time." She was already up with him.

He subconsciously thanked the good fortune that had allowed them to put on a few clothes before the shot was fired. There would have been a distinct psychological drawback to running in the nude. Even though their skimpy clothes gave no real protection against either the environment or the weaponry, it shielded them from the innate sense of vulnerability they would have otherwise felt.

He pulled her urgently in the direction away from the shot, but she batted his hand away – it was hampering her movements. They ran.

Ahead of them were trees, marking out a darker region of cover that broke the open sand. Between these was a small clump that shrouded a cove in even deeper darkness. A perfect hiding place perhaps.

"We can't outrun lasers, Page, we need to hide," she said ducking behind a tree to catch her breath.

"They can't use lasers. We're out of range."

"What?"

"Handheld lasers are short range. Focus dissipates. Not enough power to keep the heat over a long distance. Physics. They're only for aim."

"Well let's take cover in there then," she yelled. "Out of the line of sight, and into the dark."

"No!" he said. "Not logical. They'll have night vision goggles. Our best chance is to find cover in something infrared." He looked around. "There!" he pointed.

There was a glowing fire situated behind an outcrop of rocks on the next section of beach, not too far.

"The moment we move they'll see us again," she hissed. "Bullets or lasers makes no difference."

"If we stay they'll see us for sure."

They ran towards the fire, expecting to hear the pings of exploding sand, or see their own blood splashing in front of them. But no shots came. Their assailants were probably too busy running, concentrating on closing the gap. They would shoot again no doubt, when they were up close with the smallest chance of missing.

Spread around the fire were a group of locals listening to rustic music on a shitty stereo. One of them played an out of tune guitar, poorly, and to an entirely different rhythm, as others bobbed their heads up and down in appreciation of something unfathomable.

The merry-making faltered as Sync and Page ran between them, directly over the fire. Small flames lapped harmlessly at the passing bodies as drunken whoops came from the group.

Mottled green light flickered suddenly on the sand by their feet. They kept running.

A second later the thuds of falling bodies sounded from behind them along with the screech of a splintering guitar. Faint echos of gun fire followed as the sound caught up to them.

They ran behind the cover of a bank of rocks and then onto another patch of sand. The open beach was gradually recessing into the land, as the delta of a river opened up before them. It looked like a dead-end, but they pressed on. They could now see empty buildings by the edge of the water front. It was a chance.

They ran onwards, bare feet stinging as they hit the wooden slats – the hard, knotted wood punishing their soles. Gaps between planks clawed at their toes as splinters of wood bit into them like teeth.

Page, then Sync hopped over a small brick wall into a closed, beachfront restaurant. Plyrex beams reflected moonlight in jagged shapes, breaking apart the neat, open expanse of the beach. They barged through a shuttered door into the kitchen area, then through a dusty passageway into the parking area at the back.

A handful of rusty cars, and pick-ups were parked in the loading bay behind shops. Perhaps they could get lost in the maze of wheel arches and fenders to disappear from their pursuers? They ducked between the cars but kept moving.

An old man unloading a crate of bottles from the back of the restaurant paused to see what the commotion was. There was a clamour of shots, then the crash of bottles as his body bounced to the floor.

"Fuck they're close," cursed Sync.

They found a side exit that led from the parking area out onto a marina by the river. A few trawlers and shrimping boats bobbed gently from rope tethers as they ran past rows of mooring posts. They darted toward one of the boats – not the nearest, and huddled down behind the tarpaulin cover.

"Do we stay here?" whispered Page.

Smashing noises were coming from the back of the restaurant now. The soldiers were searching.

"We have little choice," said Sync. "But it's a pretty big area to cover. They can't know for sure that we're here."

"Yeah," said Page, breathing more steadily, just as a light shone into his eyes.

It was followed an instant later by the noise of an engine revving up. A boat was moving towards them from the next pier.

Another instant later and the lights were cut. A voice called out in hushed urgency "Page. Get into the boat."

Page looked at Sync questioningly. It wasn't the soldiers.

"Don't know," she said.

"Don't know who it is?" or "Don't know if we should get in the boat?" he hissed.

"Either."

"Come on hurry!" called the voice again.

"Screw it," he said and took her hand. This time she let him take it. They ran to the end of the pier then half leapt, half fell into the boat.

It was a low sitting long-tail boat, Asian style, and looked small between the other fishing boats. But despite the size, the outline of the frame appeared lithe and nimble, giving the boat a sense of strength.

The silhouette of a man was sitting next to the engine rig, looking at Page with extreme caution. "You can sit by the front until I get us away from here. But don't move any closer or I'll cut the engine and throw away the key."

"Thanks," said Page, watching as the man inexpertly dipped the rotor into the water and yanked the throttle. He was clearly not a fisherman. But was he a friend?

The boat sped around the corner just as the first shots pinged through the air. One of them found the hull and made a neat hole directly through the metal.

"Fuck," muttered the man.

For the next minute nobody spoke. The boat ripped through the waves in near pitch blackness, clinging as close as possible to the line of the shore. Page and Sync held back a thousand questions, not wanting to break the man's concentration.

Eventually the darkness was broken by lights from the beach, and their speed dropped to a less frantic pace. Now that some distance was between them and the soldiers it was time for answers. "Who are you?" demanded Sync.

"The name's Kirby," said the man, turning casually.

Page shook his head. "Why are you helping us? I don't know you."

A movement in the man's trench coat caused Page to look down. The wind had blown open the overlap revealing a pistol concealed in the crease pocket. The man flicked off the safety and aimed it at Page.

"I've been, uh, hired to investigate you," said Kirby.

"By who?" shot Sync, scrutinizing him. She was looking for signs of corporate influence or maybe even a logo. God knows how many people Page had it in him to piss off. But the man didn't look either corporate or military, and the way he had stressed the word "hired" was almost sarcastic.

"By a few guys. One of whom accuses you of his murder," replied Kirby.

"What?!" exclaimed Page about to protest, then, after processing the logical paradox, said "What do you mean?"

"I don't know. But the first two guys had a lot of cash. So I figure, okay, this guy Page is some kind of high brow criminal. Mafia accountant or something. Next thing, there's a dead guy in the street and another guy carrying your photo around saying you've killed him."

Sync frowned. "That doesn't make sense."

"You're damn right. So which is it Page? Are you a white-collar money launderer, or a punk, knifing people on the street?"

"Neither!" blurted Page, not taking his eyes from the gun.

Kirby tucked the gun away. He'd made his point. "Okay look, just give me some answers. I can see you ain't no criminal. Or, if you are you certainly ain't in the league of those people chasing you."

"I don't know anything about a dead guy but if you take me back to the forest I can explain why they're chasing me."

"Pfft. That's a tall order," Kirby sighed. "Let's at least wait 'til your friends go to bed."

They instinctively all looked back for any signs of danger, but the coast looked clear.

"How did you find us?" asked Sync.

"I followed you," Kirby shrugged. "I was sitting behind you in half the cafe's you went to."

"But how did you know who I was?" she queried suspiciously.

"I didn't. I started off doing what you were doing – following the black trucks – then kept seeing the same girl ordering cappuccinos everywhere I went, so followed her instead." He shrugged again. "You looked less mean."

Sync laughed. "Oh, well I wouldn't be so –"

Fwaaap. The boat suddenly lit up from above.

A large spotlight was coming from an oblique angle high in the sky. They could hear the quiet hum of propellers, getting louder. Something was moving fast towards them.

"Shit." growled Kirby. "Choppa-drone! We gotta find cover." He pulled the throttle back to full, lurching them into motion.

They turned sharply into the mouth of an inlet, spraying a plume of water over a couple who'd been sitting on the steps. The drone's spotlight matched their movements from above, tracking them as they sped down the river.

Water popped loudly beside them as the machine fired off a couple of rounds. Kirby steered for the tree line. Overhanging branches gave some cover from the spotlight, but the flimsy foliage would be no shield for bullets. As they moved further up the river it began to meander, splitting off into smaller tributaries covered by a thick canopy. "Hold!" yelled Kirby, leaning full weight to the side, pulling the rudder deep into the water.

The boat jolted sideways, nearly throwing Page and Sync over the edge as the centripetal G's grabbed them. But the sharp turn had its desired effect. The light from above carried on in a straight line, losing them in the darkness as the drone whizzed past. Shaken off for now.

As they sped deeper into the sprawling veins of the river the trees became denser. At times they could see the roaming spotlight bouncing caustically off the surface water as it tried to reacquire them. Kirby cut off the engine. For now at least they were safe. They drifted in silence.

The forest here began to be broken by small brick walls that lined the banks. Rickety wooden bridges sprung from winding footpaths to cross the river. The water smelled foul. They were coming back to civilisation in the form of a small shanty village.

"I think we should split up," whispered Kirby. "You two get out here, and get lost for the night. I'll keep going in the boat."

"What about the drone?" asked Page.

"If the drone comes back, well, I'll lead it a merry chase. I can make some noise when I want to," he grinned. He was about to leave but paused suddenly, reaching into a jacket pocket. "Ah, before I forget..."

He pulled out a small jar of pills, which he handed to Page curiously. "You left these at the power plant."

Page rolled the bottle around in his hand for a few seconds then unexpectedly tossed it into the river, watching the little tablets fly out like fish bait. "I'm done with those stupid pills. They don't do anything."

Sync raised her eyebrows. "That was dumb."

Kirby started the engine quietly, keeping the throttle almost at zero. He glided off smoothly into the night. "Good luck."

CHAPTER THIRTY FIVE

.: **Memory**

———o Day 29 o———

Page slowly opened his eyes. A ray of morning sunlight shone through the trees setting mottled shadows to life on the sleeping woman next to him. He sighed inwardly, looking at the restfulness in Sync's face. He felt a deep calmness in this place. He had all but forgotten the chaos of last night, and the mayhem of the previous few weeks.

There was no sign of Kirby this morning. Did that mean he had shaken off their antagonists? He hoped so.

The shanty he had woken up in was very different in the light of day from how he had imagined it during their pitch black clambering of the night. Fatigued by all the running, he and Sync had crawled into one of the first empty places they had found, and fallen promptly to sleep. Now it was time to take stock and make plans. Where exactly were they?

They were in a kind of hand-built shack constructed from corrugated iron, bits of wood, rope, and random pieces of junk. Somehow it invoked a sense of being grounded, as though the building blocks of poverty were inextricably linked to the earth from whence they came. And yet the room also had about it a suggestion of pre-fabrication – of clinical design. The conflicting emotions created a paradox within Page as he gazed at the interior.

He noticed a faucet screwed to the wall, and looked for a

corresponding kettle or anything to heat up some water. There was a pot. That would do. It was a rusty, iron skillet of an affair, charred black through years of use. He filled it with water then placed it on what passed for a hob – though in reality was little more than pieces of metal lashed together.

Without giving it a second thought, he slid his arm under a side table and fumbled with two wires, connecting them to complete a circuit. He watched as the heating element began to warm up.

As the water came to a bubble, the slow realisation of what he had just done suddenly struck him. He had connected the wires entirely automatically, without even looking. It was part muscle memory and part instinct.

How the hell did I know the wires would be there?

And yet he had never been here before... had he? It did look very familiar. Where was this place? He looked around the room again. Awareness and memory suddenly slapped him in the face.

"Tan's hut!?"

It was the room he himself had created as part of the simulation. He remembered making it. He remembered arranging the interior... Lining up the geometry... Selecting the featured items, and leaving the generic ones to be generated procedurally.

Either he was dreaming right now, or he had somehow, whilst designing the simulation for Tan, tapped into the memory of a real place buried deep within his subconscious. Perhaps using the creative process of design his mind had guided him with the memory of a room it had experienced in the past. This room.

Did that mean he had been here before, and had just forgotten? Or that it had been erased from his memory?

243

But then what was he doing here now? Was it just a coincidence, or had his mind tricked him into coming here? Had subconscious thoughts of this place directed his movements through the night to bring him here? That couldn't be right – their movements had been dictated by random events.

He let out an involuntary laugh. "Am I crazy?"

"Huh?" mumbled Sync from the bed.

"Am I crazy?" he repeated, this time a genuine question.

Sleep-matted eyes opened lazily as a warm smile spread across her face. "Probably. What are you laughing about?"

"Where are we?" he looked at her intensely. "How did we get here last night?"

"Huh? Hang on a sec," she said yawning. "Let me wake up."

Something seemed to occur to him then. He abruptly stepped back, then sat on the floor watching her movements.

"Make that 'Definitely', not 'Probably'. Jesus, Page what are you doing?"

He didn't say anything, but just continued to scrutinize her as she sat up in the bed. So far everything she did was natural and normal. He kept watching.

"Take it easy will you. It's too early for your... Page-ness," she said, and reached her arm up onto the table, groping next the to the sink to grab a cup out of sight.

"There!" he cried. "There!" he pointed at her hand.

"What?"

"How did you know? How did you know there would be a cup there? You just knew! Your body just reached out instinctively!"

"Well uh, I probably saw it before we slept," she said, shaking her head dismissively.

"Sync! It was pitch black last night."

"Yeah that's true. But why does it matter?"

"It means we've been here before. Both of us. It's the only explanation that makes sense!"

"Page," said Sync in a concerned voice. "Do you remember what you said when you threw those pills away last night?"

"Yes. I said 'I'm done with those stupid pills,'" he shrugged. "So what?"

"Do you remember what I said?"

"Yeah, you said 'That was dumb.'"

"Right." She gave him a told-you-so look. "How long has it been since you stopped taking the pills?"

"Since before we played chess. Like, seven and a half days."

"So, maybe after a week the effects are getting to you."

He blinked in surprise. What she was implying seemed more ridiculous, on the face of it, than what he was implying – that some kind of mental side effects were causing him to remember places that he had never been to.

"You think I'm crazy?" He laughed again. "That's crazy."

Or was it? He looked around at the room, serious again. Most of the furniture could be described as generic. He supposed there wouldn't be much variation between any of the huts in this village. Perhaps they all had rooms like this, and perhaps they all had makeshift taps and stoves in the roughly same place. Maybe he had never been to this place at all, just a vague mix of similar places, and his mind had absorbed the knowledge subliminally – that the taps were always likely to be in a certain part of the room. That would explain why he had designed it that way in Tan's simulation, and also why he had known about the wires without looking this morning.

"I don't remember coming here last night," he said, considering what that might mean. "Do you?"

"Not really," she said carelessly. "After that boat chase it was a lot of stumbling around in the dark. I was exhausted." She sighed. "I'm glad we ended up somewhere with a roof over our heads and not getting our throats slit during the night."

"But that's odd too," frowned Page.

"What is?"

"Well, didn't it feel to you last night that we were in more of a kind of bombed out, derelict of a place, than this?"

"Yes, it did."

"I need to look around," he said decisively, and slung on a T-shirt hanging by the door. "Are you coming?"

"Page," she said sternly and waited.

"What?"

"We're sticking together." She reached for his hand.

He took it, gently. "Sorry. I wasn't going to go off without you. I was just asking."

"What happened last night, on the beach..." she wasn't sure what to say.

"I understand," he said, "It was just the adrenaline."

"'It meant something,' was what I was going to say." A warm smile lit up her face.

"Let's go," he said quietly.

The path outside also looked familiar – extremely familiar. But until he had some definitive proof either way, Page didn't want to attach himself to a particular hypothesis. Only measurable data could determine which was correct.

He laid them out more clearly in his mind –

Page's theory: This place was part of his own history – maybe his childhood – which he had, for unknown reasons, forgotten or concealed from his thoughts, until now, when he had accidentally stumbled upon it. His past had always seemed like an indistinct blur, and maybe now it was coming back to him.

Sync's theory: This place was entirely new to him, and the feeling of familiarity was just a generic sense of deja-vu caused by withdrawal symptoms from the pills he had stopped taking. The apparent knowledge of where the wires were located was nothing more than coincidence, or a shared universal knowledge of where such wires in huts were likely to be.

Other theories: None for now.

They kept walking.

They soon arrived at the end of the street that connected with the main road. An SUV was parked there. As they approached, its doors opened and three men got out.

Page knew those faces.

"Mr Tane..." said the first, trailing off as he looked at Page more closely. "Sorry," he muttered, "thought you were someone else. You live here?"

"We're staying at a friends house," said Sync.

"I see," said the man. He took a long hard look at Page's clothes, obviously not satisfied with something.

Page was staring at him. He couldn't help it. It was Holloway... at least... that's what he first thought. But the more he looked at the man, the more he realised there were slight differences. In both features and attire there were deviations. It *was* the same man, and yet it was *not* the same man. Like a photocopy that didn't quite produce a perfect replica due to an accumulation of small errors.

"You wanna talk to me?" asked not-Holloway.

"Uh no," said Page, lowering his eyes, remembering suddenly that they were still on the run.

"Then fuck off," sneered Holloway, as the three men pushed past them.

"You know that man?" asked Sync, as she watched the trio saunter down the lane toward the very shanty they had just woken up in.

"I'm not sure," was all Page said. "But we should get away from this place, now."

They kept walking.

Fifteen minutes later they thought they could hear the blast of gunshots, accompanied by the faint sound of screams.

CHAPTER THIRTY SIX

.: The World Is Round

——o Day 29 o——

An off key sound – Wahh-Woh-Wohh – came from a small, handheld instrument as dexterous fingers moved smoothly over it.

The scene was one of carnage. Three dead bodies lay slumped on the pathway covered in blood. A few village locals were huddled around in discussion, but there were no police or ambulances.

State resources were allocated strictly on the basis of population quotas so an unregistered person was in effect non-existent. Since none of the people in these shanty villages appeared in any census, the villages themselves did not exist, at least from the point of view of emergency services – the strict algorithms that governed these things were designed for efficiency, not flexibility or charity. In the case of this particular village there was an additional reason that it remained off the grid.

Kirby walked over to where the dead woman and child lay, like rag-dolls, in the doorway of a hut. Bullet holes in their heads. An execution?

"What happened?" he asked an old lady leaning over them, cradling the dead child.

The old lady looked up at Kirby's face, then down at his clothes, full of disdain. She said nothing.

Kirby wasn't a wealthy man, nor even an averagely well-to-do man

– he was poor. But, by the standards of these people, he was dressed in affluence.

He subconsciously apologised through body language, for his appearance, not even thinking until now that he might be considered anything other than a street guy himself.

"Sorry," he said, "I didn't mean to, intrude."

"Are you a doctor?"

"No."

"Are you police?"

"No, but..."

"Then go back to your home," said the lady with contempt. "You don't belong here."

"I'm looking for this guy," said Kirby, producing the picture of Page. "Was he here?"

The old lady looked at the picture, then looked up at Kirby sharply, but said nothing.

"Thank you," said Kirby. "I'm uh sorry," he said again, not knowing what else he could say as he walked off. He had what he needed. Page and Sync had been here. The lady's expression told him that much if nothing else.

He walked over to the other body that was lying near the tire marks, face down on the ground.

He turned it over delicately, to see if there was anything that might inform him about what had happened. He looked at the face. His jaw dropped.

It was the man he had chased down the alleyway in Chinatown. The man who had told him that Page was going to kill him and given him the polaroid. Here he was, lying dead in the dirt, just moments – or hours for all he knew – after Page had departed. It was too much of a coincidence.

"I need to find this guy! Now," he shouted and held up the photo of Page. "I know he was here."

Some of the locals looked at him warily. They had their own people to worry about and their own problems to solve. This out of town man could drop dead as well for all they cared.

An old man who had been watching from the side nodded to him. "He was here."

"Where did he go?" asked Kirby, animated. "Was this" – he indicated the bloodshed – "to do with him?"

The old man proffered a basket he was carrying. It was filled with leaves and twigs, and a few vegetables. A messy bed of rose petals was heaped beneath. "Do you have any garbage?" asked the man. "I am collecting." He shook the basket gently, sending a couple of petals to the floor.

Kirby tutted, and pulled out a few coins from his pocket, then tossed them into the basket. The man nodded, acceptingly.

"He was here," the old man nodded again. Then pointed in the direction Page and Sync had run. "They went in that direction."

"Where to? Do you know where that leads?" asked Kirby.

"Not far," said the old man. "The world is round."

As Kirby darted off the last thing he could hear was a hoarse, dry scratching sound. It was the old man chuckling to himself, mirthlessly. "The world is round."

CHAPTER THIRTY SEVEN

.: Metal

Page and Sync emerged from an alleyway. The narrow walls that had been hemming them in for the past mile suddenly opened out, revealing a full panorama with blue skies and water. As their eyes adjusted to the light, it was apparent that they were in some kind of dockyard.

Page was looking around in amazement.

"You've been here before too, right?" said Sync off his look.

"Not exactly. But look at it –" He gestured at an open space in front of him. "– it's not, finished."

He was right. There were gaps in architecture that made it seem as though the place had been abandoned during construction. Some parts of the dockyard were flawless – everything down to the trimming of the walkway was smoothly polished and sanded – yet other parts had not even passed the stage of concrete pouring, leaving huge open pits that made the entire walkway useless. No construction company in their right mind would work this way. It was as though random pockets of the project had been completed on different time lines.

Sync looked down at their feet, wondering. Paving ran laterally along the water's edge, connecting the main entrance to a few moored boats, then curved back in on itself to form a loop. At sporadic points along the walkway concrete bollards were standing in clusters as if they had grown there rather than been placed. A few seagulls had taken these bollards as perching points, and were the only signs of life here.

"Yeah. I guess it does seem sparse." Doubt crept into her voice. "It's probably a new section that they've just finished building or something."

Page was shaking his head slowly. "I know the reason it's not finished."

She looked at him. "Why?"

"You'll think I'm crazy."

"I kind of do already." She put her arm on his shoulder and gave him a friendly squeeze. "But go on, let's hear it."

He was hardly listening. His eyes darted around, picking off parts of a boat, or the corner of a concrete step, and then shifting to another point. "Not yet. I need to check something," he said.

"Have it your way," she sighed. "But then let's take a five and chill out for a bit. It's been a difficult few days. I need a timeout to gather my thoughts."

She sat down on the walkway and kicked her legs out over the sea, enjoying the emptiness of the place. He didn't join her. He was transfixed by a doorway in a wall next to one of the piers.

"Back in a few minutes!" he called, dashing away like a school kid on a lunch break.

"Sure." She watched him, smiling at his erratic, creative energy, and wondered. The fucking pills. What do they do?

One of the byproducts of creative minds was that they were prone to crack. They were unstable. They needed maintenance, and care... and sometimes medication to keep them ticking. Were the qualities that produced creativity mutually exclusive to those that provided stability? Was it in fact the broken fragments of a more structured thought that defined creativity – transient patterns of logic that formed as ideas collided in free fall?

"Sync!" called Page, interrupting her thoughts. "Follow me! I know it's here."

"Sure Page, anything," she laughed. She would take care of him.

————olo————

They entered the doorway, stepping into a stone shaft that led under the dockyard and into the rocks. Faint electric lights that hung from the ceiling illuminated part of the passageway, but were barely bright enough to show the floor.

They walked deeper, past the last row of lights, using their feet to probe the path in the darkness. The feeling of isolation that Sync had been enjoying on the pier, was now the source of an uneasy, creeping solitude.

"Where are we going?" she hissed.

"If I'm right, this passageway leads nowhere," he whispered.

"A dead-end? Then, why are you taking us here?"

"Well, maybe. I don't know exactly what will be there," he said, voice fading as he stepped further into the blackness. "My system had hardly any memory back then."

"What the hell are you talking about?"

"Just, come on. I have a new theory." The darkness was making him uneasy too.

It was a blackness so absolute that their eyes had nothing to acclimatise to. In such places the mind runs on overdrive, creating abstract shapes from the random electrical noises that dance in the retinas. Suddenly there was a loud Kllaaang, as Page walked straight into a solid metal surface.

"What is it?" asked Sync.

"It's a kind of... door," he said, feeling around.

"And, what's inside?" said Sync. "Well, what do you think is inside?"

"If I'm right, then, nothing," said Page.

"What do you mean by nothing?" she asked, trying to calm her nerves.

"Literally nothing," he said, oblivious to her irritation.

She just tutted.

Metal hinges creaked as he twisted the handle. They stepped forwards together in complete blackness. Then, as he lifted his leg to take the next step, something jutting out from the floor caught him, causing them both to trip. They stumbled forwards, hearing the click of springs snapping into place behind them.

As Page reached out to grab hold of something his hand slammed into another surface. It was another door – a wooden one that gave way effortlessly under their weight. They fell in a heap to the floor of...

They were lying on a dusty, wooden floor. In a room. It was a well lit, slightly messy, junk filled room. They blinked in astonishment, and recognition.

CHAPTER THIRTY EIGHT

.: **Pills**

——o Day 29 o——

Page was lying on the floor of his council flat, in his room, in front of a cupboard door. Sync was lying next to him.

Cables, wires and computers were all around him. The familiar smell of cheap plastics, must and dust, the noise of humming computer fans and coolers were all present exactly as he had remembered them.

Velma was sitting on a chair, looking at him. She had her hand on her heart.

"You scared the life out of me," she said shaking her head. "What on earth are you doing down there?"

A long awkward silence followed.

"I hope we're not disturbing you," she said amicably. "We did say Wednesday."

"No Miss Beck," Page said reflexively, then caught himself. "What?"

He looked at Velma in disbelief. He looked at Sync, who shared his expression of confusion. That confirmed it. It wasn't just his own personal hallucination.

"Page, I want to introduce you to..." she trailed off, seeing Sync's expression. "I see you two have already met?" she said curiously.

"What day is it?" asked Sync, staring at Velma.

Velma swiped the screen on her wrist watch. "Friday the 9th of March," she read, in obvious bewilderment. "Well now isn't that odd? I could have sworn today was Wednesday."

Page and Sync were gobsmacked, neither having anything to add.

Velma meanwhile had dismissed her confusion and carried on like nothing was amiss. "Well, I'm here now. Page, I, hope you've been keeping up with the prescription?"

He reached into his pocket, looking for the jar of pills. From his point of view he had thrown them into the river last night, but here, now, he had no idea what to expect. He found no pills. That at least was consistent with all theories.

"I have some new pills for you," continued Velma, uncertain of herself this time. "I think these will help with the next part of your recovery. Will you take them?" She placed a small jar of pills on the desk.

"What are in the pills?" asked Sync.

"I, don't know exactly. But they will help."

"They did," said Page. "But I'm better now. I want to show you something Ms Beck" he said, standing up and walking over to the cupboard door. He yanked it open. There were a couple of items of clothing hanging – the sort of things he might wear – but which he could never actually remember wearing.

Behind the clothes was a flat metal panel. He looked at it in delight. Proof. He tried to yank it open, but couldn't. He tried again. There were no indentations from which to get purchase – it was just flat. He pushed. Nothing. He kicked it. It gave a dull clang, but aside from that, nothing.

"That's very interesting, Page," said Velma, not sure what to make of the display. "The pills. Have you been taking them?"

"What is in the pills?" said Sync. "What the hell is going on?"

"I think I know how we can find out what's in them," said Page quietly, heading for the door.

Sync followed, lost in thought. What was going on? Some kind of shared hallucination? Bullshit. She didn't hallucinate. A starker thought crossed her mind. Had she taken any of the pills, maybe by mistake? No. Too far fetched. Had Page given them to her in the night, or spiked one of her drinks? No. Equally far fetched. He wasn't the type.

"Hang on a sec," she said, stopping by the door. "I might as well look presentable."

She kicked off the village shoes she'd been wearing and pulled on the pair – *her* pair – that were resting by the door. Her jacket too was hanging from the wall, exactly as before.

CHAPTER THIRTY NINE

.: Chemicals

——o Day 29 o——

"I need you to tell me what's in these," said Page, pulling out the jar of pills.

Mikhail looked at Page doubtfully, then furrowed his brow in suspicion as Sync entered the chemist's. Whilst he had somewhat begrudgingly accepted the strangeness of Page appearing in his store from time to time, Sync was an altogether different breed of animal. The way she carried herself, and the coat she wore was from a different universe. For one thing it had been washed within the past calendar month.

"Who's she?" he asked in a mutter.

"She's no-one important," said Page. Then, realising the grammatical faux pas, added "I mean to you. She's important to me."

Sync smiled wryly. "I'll take what I can get."

Mikhail snorted, then poured out the pills into his hand and rolled them around. He nicked one with a small pocket knife and peered at the powdered residue.

"It could be anything," he said, shaking his head. What did these people expect? That he could just reverse engineer a pill they walked in off the street with.

"Just tell us what you can," said Sync. "Any information is good."

Mikhail shrugged. "Yeah. Okay. Come on."

The back of his store could have doubled as an alchemist's laboratory. It wasn't just the theme, but the age of some of the crapware he kept there. Petri dishes. Microscopes. Vague machines from the 30's that looked like 20th century video game consoles.

He raked through a drawer and pulled out a retro looking black gizmo the size of a book, that was marked "K-Scan".

He broke a couple of the pills into powder, which he scattered onto a small plastic tray, that was then slid into the device. He pressed a button marked "Scan", and waited. An oily, translucent liquid poured into the tray, dissolving the powder. The machine hummed as a small LCD blinked to life.

```
SCANNING...   Please wait.   01:14...
```

They watched as the numbers ticked down.

```
01:13...   01:12...   01:11...   01:10...   01:09...
```

The shop door burst open.

Kirby walked in, breathing hard. He brandished a pistol at the three of them as he marched to the back of the store.

```
01:05...   01:04...   01:03...   01:02...   01:01...
```

"Sooo," said Kirby, drawing out the word, "it seems like you played me good last night. Getting me to help you escape an' all?"

"Meaning?" queried Sync.

"There are dead bodies in that village," said Kirby, his aim steady on Page's head. "Including the guy who hired me. The one who said you were trying to kill him. Now isn't that odd?"

```
00:41...  00:40...  00:39...  00:38...  00:37...
```

"We were there, but..." began Page. He remembered the shots they had heard after they had left the village in the morning.

"I know you were there!" interrupted Kirby. "What I wanna know is why people keep dying in places you go to. You said you were gonna explain it all. So okay, go. I'm listening. Who are the dead bodies?"

```
00:28...  00:27...  00:26...  00:25...  00:24...
```

"Listen, officer, I don't have anything to do with any dead bodies," said Mikhail, behind them, "*anti*-bodies maybe," he said with a dry chuckle.

"I ain't no cop," said Kirby abruptly, "but I want answers."

```
00:15...  00:14...  00:13...  00:12...  00:11...
```

"Come on, this has nothing to do with me," said Mikhail slowly, "I was just working here when they walk in and start asking me to do tests. Okay?"

"What tests?"

```
SCAN COMPLETE...
```

Diiiiing. All eyes turned towards the scanner. In that moment

Mikhail pulled out an M-pulse gun from the drawer, fully blue with charge, and pointed it at Kirby.

"Well," he shrugged, "if you're not a cop, then you're trespassing."

"Easy fella," said Kirby, not sensing any threat in the man, but carefully lowering his gun anyway. Twitchy nerves had been responsible for many an accidental shooting before now.

Page and Sync were still drawn by the results of the scanner, ignoring the mini stand-off. "What does it say?" asked Page, meekly.

"What does what? Oh." Mikhail shrugged, and slowly put his gun back in the drawer. He pressed a button on the K-Scan then ran his eyes over a list of numbers. Then frowned.

"What is it?" asked Sync.

Mikhail shrugged again. "I can't be 100% certain but I think it's –" He dabbed his tongue against one of the pills. "– it's nothing. It's a sugar pill. A placebo."

Page nodded. "A placebo. That's what I thought," he said quietly.

Page stood in the middle of the street, looking up at the sky. Kirby and Sync were behind him. "So if it's not our minds that are crazy," he said – the words directed into empty space – "Maybe it's the world?"

"Our minds?!" Kirby clucked.

Sync nodded. The world didn't quite seem to make sense to her either.

"Remember what you said to me on the beach?" asked Page. "'How do you know we are not living in a simulation?'"

"What, you mean this? All of it?" said Sync, looking at the rich detail around her with incredulity. "If it is then it's the best damn simulation I've ever been in."

"Maybe it's the only simulation you've ever been in."

"Then why don't I remember entering it? Or was I asleep or something? Woke up one morning in a simulated room that looks just like it and never noticed?" she laughed.

Page sighed. "That's not what –"

Kirby cut in. "So you're saying we're all tied up in a basement somewhere wearing headsets, and this gun is actually a, I dunno, a banana or something, is that it?" He chuckled. "I don't buy it."

"That's not what I meant," finished Page patiently. "What if this is the only simulation you've ever been in – we've ever been in – because we're part of it?"

Kirby whistled. "That's nuts. That's conspiracy theory nuts. Even I wouldn't come up with something like that."

"It's the only thing left that makes sense," said Page.

"It might explain some of the anomalies we've been seeing," mused Sync, not really believing it but not wanting to mock Page. "The dockyard. The village."

Kirby was still smiling. "Are you saying that I am a kind of robot? With no free will because I'm just a piece of software running on a machine – that I have no responsibilities for my actions?" He raised his eyebrows. "That'd make a great defence in court, and maybe you'll get a chance to use it. You still didn't explain what happened in the village."

"The village is a simulation."

"Right, of course. And the dead guy who said you killed him?"

"Mr Taneka is... an algorithm, the expression of a function," said Page, realising to whom it was that Kirby referred. "I was researching intelligence."

"We're all the expression of a function buddy, it's called DNA. That doesn't give you the right to go around killing people. What about the woman and child?"

"I didn't kill anyone," protested Page.

Kirby gave an exasperated sigh. "Save it for your defence lawyer."

"But, wait a sec," said Sync, "If we're inside a simulation. Whose?"

"Who knows," shrugged Page, "But any simulation is running inside something physical, and physical things have limits. Most of the village simulation is in the Omicore servers."

She shot a critical look at him.

"I just, well, I borrowed some of their memory," said Page sheepishly.

"That explains a lot," said Sync.

"Alright then, so how could you prove you're in a sim?" asked Kirby.

"Maybe we can't. Not from the inside. I don't know."

"Why not?"

"Kurt Gödel. Incompleteness Theorem," shrugged Page. "Seems like it would apply."

Kirby shook his head. The guy had a screw loose. Poor kid.

"Well, if we have interacted with Tan, in our world, then we exist in the same memory space. Right? It means that we and Tan are simulated in the same environment. The Omicore servers?" reasoned Sync.

"Yes... I think." Page shook his head. This was becoming confusing. "I need to find a memory diagram to see what is happening."

"Where?" asked Sync.

"At the power plant. Most of my research is still there."

"Ahem... You gotta do a damn sight better than that if you think I'm just letting you two walk off outta here," scowled Kirby. "That'd make me an accessory through abetment."

"Come with us," said Page. "You said you wanted answers."

Kirby let out a long, slow sigh, then rolled his eyes. "Either you two are insane," he said thoughtfully, "or I am. Okay."

CHAPTER FORTY

.: Ghost In The Machine-Code

——o Day 29 o——

"My my, Pageroni. I am impressed," said the pimp, grinning. He flicked through the wad of notes that Sync had handed him and nodded approvingly. "You keep better company than I thought."

Page rolled the Kern-C300 around in his hands feeling a sense of satisfaction and almost relief. Like a nerve shot to a junkie. It was beautiful to the touch.

"Can I interest any of you other fellas in a little... chip for the trip?" said the pimp, opening his jacket to expose a myriad of other devices concealed beneath the folds.

——olo——

The trio walked the barren ground toward the south structure of the power plant, Sync for the first time, the others covering familiar dusty tracks.

"Look at the sky," observed Page.

The sky, impossibly, was a different colour here than only a few kilometres away in the centre of town. It was still a beautiful postcard blue, just a different hue. The fluffy, candyfloss clouds seemed to be malformed, as though chunks were missing. The edges were in some places harsher, more square, lacking the random Rorschach outlines, and taking on a more uniform texture.

An erratic clicking ripped out of the aether every few seconds like a pulse of static, that did not seem to have either an origin or cause. Sync looked around to find the source of the sound. It was making her jumpy. "Is that coming from the electrical lines?"

"No," said Page.

"Maybe you're not mad," whispered Kirby, beginning to re-evaluate his skepticism from earlier. "I always knew there was something bigger going on, but this is just, well..." He felt an eerie sense of change sweep over him. The world, it seemed, was much stranger than he had ever imagined.

As they entered the juice room the signs of a disturbance were clearly apparent. Broken furniture was sprawled across the landing, while scattered paper, cardboard, and junk made a dusty mess across the floor. If someone had come here looking for Page, they had done so with a particular lack of care. It was like a dog fight had gone on.

"I left this place untouched, only two days ago," Kirby muttered cautiously as they walked to the stairs leading to the caretaker's office, trying not to trip on any of the rubbish.

"I haven't been here for a week," said Page apprehensively. He looked at the papers strewn around, wondering what remained of the research notes he had made. Most of the stuff here was of no value, merely the scribblings and working-outs of already solved problems – the disjecta membra of a research scientist – in effect, garbage.

A faint noise was coming from within the scattered furniture, stopping the three of them in their tracks. A dark rag that had been heaped in a bundle only a moment ago was now moving, slowly at the foot of the stairs. It was swaying erratically. They froze like rabbits in the headlights.

"What's that?" hissed Kirby in a whisper, slowly drawing his gun, and at the same time gesturing the others to step back.

The rag shuddered. A soft, mirthless, almost demented chuckling made its way to their ears through the muffled cloth. Very slowly, and very carefully, Kirby inched nearer, still holding the gun in front of him.

Then, reaching with one hand, he delicately gripped a corner of the cloth. His heart was pounding. All their hearts were. He took a deep, slow breath then, just as he was about to tear away the rag, a man appeared from under it.

Kirby almost shot him in surprise.

Tan was sitting there, in dazed confusion, looking up at them. He moved his head slowly to look at Kirby, with indifference to the gun, but gave no signs of recognition. He turned to Sync next, studying her clothes, and smiled slightly. Then finally he looked at Page, and his expression changed to anger.

"Tan," said Page – a statement, not a question. Page had known him instantly. The face was not identical to the sim designs, but close enough for there to be no doubt.

Whatever automated software ran in the background of this world, Page concluded, must have altered his code slightly. These were variations he was seeing, not perfect facsimiles. That's why the faces and places he had seen earlier were not always instantly recognisable. There was also a kind of interpretive lensing effect to be considered – any expression of the simulated world through his simulated eyes would be a distortion, and not the pure prototypes that he had coded into the software. Either way, he recognised Tan.

"But you are... were supposed to be... dead?" stammered Kirby.

Tan opened his mouth, but no words came out. He just swayed in a kind of delirium.

"How did you get here?" asked Page. "How did you leave the village?"

"I walked out," said Tan, staring at Page in a way that caused Page step back a metre, then added more softly, "Everybody was dead, so I just walked out, and ended up here."

"But how did they die?" pressed Sync.

"I don't know," said Tan with an indecipherable half-grin that evoked suspicions of madness, then turning towards the room behind him, added "Maybe he knows?"

All eyes went to the door, which was a crack open. In addition to the mysterious clicking sounds coming from the outdoor sky, that they had now become accustomed to, was a faint tapping noise originating from within the room. It was the sound of keys being pressed.

"Someone's on my fucking computer!" cried Page, rushing past them into the room.

Amidst a mess of papers and overturned chairs, squatting on the floor by Page's terminal in a kind of feral lassitude, with his hands on the keyboard was...

"You!" said a man, turning to look at Page.

Page stopped abruptly in shock. "Tan?"

"You," repeated the man in the room, who, somehow, was also Tan, and seemed to be in as much a state of delirium as the Tan outside. "What... have you... done?"

Sync and Kirby, who had just come in, were wearing the same expression of stupefied surprise that Page now wore.

"There's two of them," stated Kirby dumbly.

Sync was beginning to understand. "Or three? Four? Five?" she said, half a whisper.

Tan – this new Tan – had stopped typing, and was glaring at them. In particular at Page.

"But how?" murmured Page, too lost in his own thoughts to pay heed to the threat written on Tan's face. "A recursive loop?" He knelt down to study Tan's clothing. "What happened after the village?"

Tan lunged at him, grabbing Page's collar with one hand and his throat with the other, squeezing hard. Page grasped at the vice-like grip but was unable to shake it.

Sync leapt down next to them, trying to pry them apart. "Stop! Please, we don't mean you any harm."

Kirby had already brought his gun to bear on Tan, but with no effect. Tan just squeezed tighter, unconcerned by anything but Page.

"Tan, please," pleaded Sync as Page struggled for air. "We don't what happened. We're trying to figure it out too."

Tan suddenly relented – though it was unclear if in response to Sync's appeal or if as the result of a random muscle spasm caused by delirium. Page fell back down the floor. "Then, figure this out," said Tan, looking toward a large hole in the upper wall through which the outside sky was visible.

Sync and Kirby followed Tan's gaze. They could see the clouds and some of the city stretching into the horizon. He entered a command on the keyboard, and a second later the sky seemed to shift slightly, as if in reaction to the keystrokes. He entered another. With each new command, part of the cloudscape or architecture on the horizon would deteriorate.

"That's spooky," said Kirby.

"Stop!" cried Page, still spluttering. "Each time he runs that code, another simulation starts. It's recursive."

He leant in to see the device, as if to confirm a hypothesis.

```
> Do you wish to invoke another instance?
> Please confirm [y/N]_ y
> ...### 97%
> WARNING g_0J31Y4FP000000 !=> g_0J31Y1MZ03DD00
> ERROR! Memory conflict.
> Do you wish to invoke another instance?
> Please confirm [y/N]_ y
> ...### 96%
> WARNING g_0J31Y4FP000000 !=> g_0J31Y1MZ03DD00
> ERROR! Memory conflict.
> Do you wish to invoke another instance?
> Please confirm [y/N]_
```

"It's difficult to guess without complete logs," he mused. "But I think its like this. There was no more world for Tan outside his simulation – nothing beyond the confines of the village, but, since we ourselves are in a simulation it means that any simulation I created for Tan, was itself running in a simulation..."

"A simulation inside a simulation?" mused Sync. "Okay, but, how are we able to interact together?"

"Somewhere higher up, all of this is contained inside something physical – a computer of some sort – and there will be something like computer memory on which it is all stored. I would guess that right now, our reality is at the limit of what can fit inside that memory. And so when we create another little world inside what is already here – like Tan's village, memory just leaks from one part into the next. The system is out of space."

"That's pretty poor system architecture," said Sync.

Page shrugged. "There are always cracks at the seams of any system. Finding those cracks. That's science."

Kirby shook his head, nodding at Tan, "Can someone just explain to me why there are two of them?"

"It's a loop," said Page. "After he escaped, he found this place somehow, and figured out how to rerun the program. That created another version of himself back in the village, who presumably escaped and did the same thing, and so on. Right?"

"Wrong," stammered Tan in delirium. "Not the *same*." He tapped the ring on his finger.

"What does he mean?" asked Sync, losing track.

"Of course," clucked Page, "This version of the sim – the one that is hooked up to this terminal – it's the second version I made. The parameters are slightly different."

Sync and Kirby looked at each other, nonplussed.

"Each version of the simulation is running a slightly different version of the code, and has a different mark – like a kind of serial number," explained Page, looking down at Tan's hand.

There was a gold band on his finger with a marker on it. "γ".

"In the first version of the village simulation, the one I created in Chinatown, Tan has an *alpha* symbol on his ring (α). In the second version that I ran from here, he has a *beta* symbol (β). And in the third and last version, running from the hut in the forest, he has a *gamma* symbol (γ)."

Kirby shook his head again. "But where are the others? If he's been running this thing more than once, shouldn't there be more than two?"

"Fuck. He's right," muttered Page to no-one in particular. "Where are they?"

"Most are dead," said Tan softly. "Some are... lost. It is... confusing. Like... a hallucination. Don't know where I am. Sometimes in the village Sometimes in Chinatown. Sometimes... coming here. Everything overlapping. Hard to concentrate."

"We've got to stop it," said Page, a look of concern on his face. "Now."

"Why?" asked Kirby.

"There could be ten or twenty, or god knows how many overlapping sims running, messing up the memory. We have to shut it down. It's not infinite."

"I think I understand," said Sync. "The more of it that gets used, the less is available for us here."

"The fight for resources," sighed Kirby. "Even in fucking robot-land there isn't enough for everybody."

Page ran to where the device was connected to the wall.

"But Page?!" said Sync, who had followed the implications of the logic, "won't disconnecting that –"

It was too late – he had already pulled the plug. The power faded on the device as the readout went black. A thump came from the doorway. Tan *beta*'s body crashed backward through the frame and slid onto the floor in the room, the rug still draped around his shoulders like a shroud.

"What have you done?" said Sync, breaking the silence that had ensued.

Tan *gamma* looked at Page slowly, shaking off the madness that had previously affected him. It was as if, with the shutting down of the device, his mind had become freer. The overlapping and confused thoughts of being forced to share sections of his consciousness with several other versions of himself, had started to clear. Shared variables again became exclusive in some higher plane of system architecture. As he got to his feet, the threat was again apparent in his demeanour, his gaze, every movement of his muscles.

"Give him some space to think," murmured Page.

Kirby shook his head. "At the risk of sounding repetitive, can someone just explain to me –" he sighed, "Okay what the fuck just happened?"

Page scrawled a rough diagram showing the connections.

"Everything in the second simulation just got dereferenced. By unplugging the device I terminated the simulation. The memory is now free. Not him though. He wasn't connected by the device here."

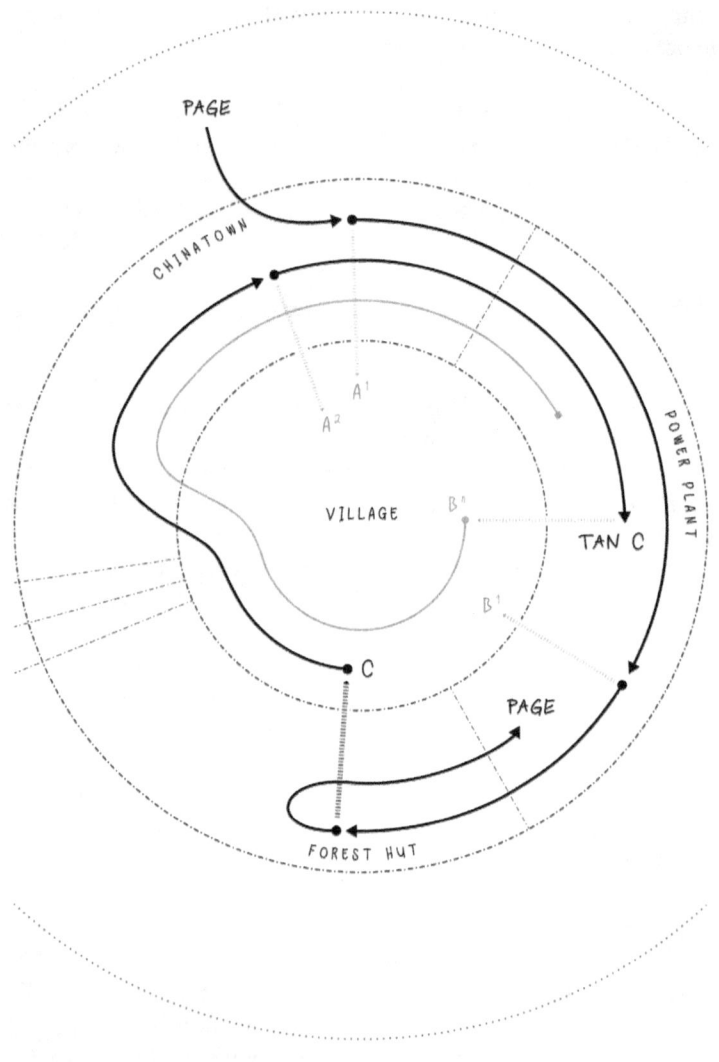

"The device in the forest," said Sync in comprehension. "You left it on when we went to the beach. That recursive simulation is still running, and it's from there that this Tan is connected."

"And you won't be disconnecting it," said Tan, in understated menace. "I... do not really understand the things you are talking about, but I know that my wife and my daughter are waiting for me, somewhere back there. Right now they are safe."

"If we're all just robots, then what does it matter?" asked Kirby, ironically.

Page, who knew what Tan was capable of physically, shot Kirby a warning look. This was not someone you wanted to provoke into a confrontation.

"Do you feel pain?" asked Tan.

"Does a rat shit in the streets?," said Kirby. "Yes, I feel pain."

"Are you afraid of death?" asked Tan.

"No. But I like life," said Kirby.

"Are you willing to risk losing that life, to test an untested hypothesis?" cut in Sync.

"Uh, what hypothesis?"

"That this is all just the surface of something deeper," Sync challenged.

"No frickin way," said Kirby after a pause.

"Then it matters," said Tan. "The people I love are alive, and safe. That gives me comfort. If there is a reality beyond that of which I

279

am unaware, then so be it, but I can only make decisions based on the reality I know of."

"He's right," said Sync. "I mean, what's changed?" she asked rhetorically. "Here we are, a group of people struggling to live our lives in happiness, whilst not having all the answers. Behind the curtains are unknown forces and laws of nature that shape the world around us in ways we don't fully understand. And we're stuck, in this random maze of life, trying to figure our way through. What's changed? Who cares if we're in a simulation? In the end it's all the same."

"The truth has changed," said Page.

"What truth?" she asked.

"The truth of what's behind the curtain, and truth matters to me. I want to know, just for the sake of knowing, what's out there, behind the curtain, between the seams."

"Finding that truth might kill you." There was sadness in her voice.

Page was distant, lost in his mind's eye as it looked out at the universe, caught up in thoughts of infinity. "I know where to get the answers," he said. "We need to go back to –"

Ffffssshhhiiiiiinggggggg. An electric sound came from all directions as the power went dead in the room. The sound of many footsteps echoed from deep within the power plant.

"They're here! Move!" yelled Kirby, pushing the others back, and sliding toward the door in a defensive posture. There was no way he would forget that sound after hearing the first time.

"Can we outrun them?" asked Tan.

"No chance!" shouted Kirby.

"Will killing these people help protect my June and Nivi?" asked Tan in a careful measured tone, despite the urgency of the situation.

"Yes," said Sync.

"Then, I will do what I can," said Tan, moving towards Kirby. His muscles shifted in anticipation, like a machine sliding into a new gear.

"Come on," hissed Sync to Page into the awkward stillness that was forming. The footsteps, which had been scurrying at varying distances beyond the room, had now stopped, as if massing for an attack, their search now complete.

"Tan," said Page hesitantly. "I'm sorry, for what happened. Your wife and daughter will be safe... I promise. I'll find a solution."

"You will," said Tan, nodding in solemn gratitude.

Page and Sync clambered into the rafters, then through a ventilation hole that lead through the concrete wall to the outside of the building. There would not have been time for all four of them to make it. They didn't look back.

"Let's shoot some robot rabbits," muttered Kirby as the first hums and pulses came from the stairway, and the room was pierced by laser light.

The outline of figures in motion could be seen through holes in the walls as their green beams of death dissected the space like razor wire. Loud, frequent Blaaams of Kirby's pistol rang out, as he fought the system for all he was worth.

At least one of the metaphorical rabbits was hit, falling backwards down the stairs with a crash, as yet more Omicore poured in to take position, lasers flicking.

The desperate shots from the low powered pistol were no match for the body armoured soldiers as they swarmed in, relentless in their hunt for Page... Kirby was cut down, mercilessly, fatally, inevitably...

In his dying moments he wondered, had he lived a worthwhile life? What would death be to someone who had never truly lived: Never lived, not just metaphorically but physically? Had this life just been the dance of a preprogrammed robot on the surface of something deeper? But he rejected this thought. He had grasped life, and whether in a simulation or not, had served a purpose – a function with meaning – which may not have been to defeat these soldiers here today, but was to form a part of the solution to a puzzle – to unravel a part of the much larger, twisting skein that others may one day see in it's entirety. "Goodbye robot-land," he said as his body hit the floor.

But there was another man still standing. A man who, in some way had always understood the meaning of life, and for what it was worth dying. In the moments Tan had shared with his alternate selfs, he had been able to glimpse a different part of the solution, a part of the equation that lay beneath the surface of consciousness. The sharing of multiple memories and experiences, and the fusion of all those variables had uncovered a more fundamental part of the calculus, like the integration of two curves and, as a byproduct, had whetted the blade of his abilities into a sharpness never seen by any of these men.

As the Omicore men approached he seemed to know where they would be, and was gone before the laser guides could find a target. He could not remember, or had never known the source of his training – it was in some way innate – but he could master it instinctively. He was a blur, seeming to be everywhere at once as he dodged and spun between the men. Green beams criss-crossed each other in confusion and urgency, unable to lock on to him. Soldiers fell under their own fire as the blur that was Tan flitted between them.

But it would only last for so long. It was an impossible situation to escape from, regardless of the algorithm. The odds were stacked too high against him – impossibly high... $\Sigma > 1$... The sheer numbers of Omicore security eventually overcame Tan, cutting him down in a shard of green. The light kept flicking as he fell, glazing his slow motion corpse in a shimmer of emerald as the now lifeless body landed unceremoniously on top of another.

The two Tans lay side by side – one draped in a rag like a false messiah, fallen in the grip of delirium – the other dripping in the blood of his enemies, like death incarnate, fallen in the grip of righteous fury.

But between theirs and Kirby's sacrifice they had bought enough time. Page and Sync were gone.

As the dust settled, military boots trod mechanically down the steps, and back out into the barren open. There were less boots than had arrived though, and the remaining boots now stood in uncertainty, unsure where the hunt for their prey would lead next.

As the visored helmets of their owners looked around, searching, their steel toecaps rested heavily on a bed of rose petals that were scattered beneath them at the foot of the steps.

CHAPTER FORTY ONE

: Visitor

——o|o——

Banks of blue polycrystalline stretched out for miles, giving an almost perfect reflection of the heavens through the thin atmosphere. Power signals ran through the array of solar panels and the servers beneath them.

A small black cylinder, half a metre in diameter and nearly two metres tall, stood silently amidst homogenous grey rocks beyond. It was only just visible as a shape of deeper black within the shadows. Subtle lights flashed energetically beneath its hull.

——o Day 29 o——

"What is it?" asked Omar, looking at an image of the device taken from space.

"I really don't know," said Leonard, sitting down at a conference table in the Omicore building, flicking a switch on the remote. The image on the display changed to another, taken from a similar angle, showing the same wide region, but without the black cylinder present.

"What's the time difference?"

"The first one's taken from the aft viewer, on the landing descent, on our way to the Moon over a month ago."

"And the second?"

"Recently."

Omar sighed. "So the thing has moved, and we have no idea when? It could have been there from a month ago right up until yesterday?"

"That's correct," said Leonard gravely. "But there's been a fluctuation in lunar power signals recently, which is why we sent up another probe to look."

"We were supposed to be monitoring the perimeter from space continually, to spot exactly this sort of intrusion!" said Omar, pacing the room.

"And we were, but look," said Leonard, marking a line on the wide angle image. The line extended two hundred metres beyond each side of the solar array, to where there was nothing but barren rocks. "This line marks the edge of the viewing frame of our monitor drone."

Omar had stopped pacing, and traced the line with his eye, following it another ten metres further to where the black cylinder had placed itself in the first image. "I see."

The cylinder was just outside the maximum range of their monitoring system, so close it could not be a coincidence.

"The implications are concerning," mused Leonard. "Whoever put that thing there had access to one of our own security streams, and knew the exact place to land it without being detected."

"Could it have affected us from there?" asked Omar, looking at the two hundred and ten metre gap. "I mean it's not as though we're broadcasting stuff in all directions. Everything is locked down into narrow beams, with limited scope."

"I really don't know," admitted Leonard in concern. "But I'm sure it was observing us."

Omar flicked to the second image. "What bothers me more is, where did it go?"

CHAPTER FORTY TWO

.: **Shut Down**

——o Day 29 o——

Page and Sync stood in front of the hut in the woods, where they had been only recently. From the outside it looked untouched. Page pushed open the door cautiously, worried something might jump out at them, but the room was exactly as they had left it. Omicore security had evidently not yet discovered this place.

As predicted, the device here was still connected and running. Power pulsed through its fibre optic veins, indicating an active connection to the servers. Contained within this connection and the information it processed as it moved around an unseen, hidden aether, were the vestiges of the Tan *gamma* simulation, including June and Nivi. Page flipped open the keypad and got straight to work.

"What are you doing?" asked Sync, watching the code spew onto the screen.

"Moving dynamic links from this device to global memory," he said. "So that the village simulation won't be stopped when the device here loses power."

"You are... preventing the virtual machine from being shut down by its host?" she queried, unsure.

"Exactly."

Sync watched as he performed with the precision of a surgeon, delicately entering lines of code as though they were incisions. After an intense quarter of an hour he flipped the keypad closed, and unplugged the device.

"Done," he said, satisfied. "As long as our world exists then a version of Tan's family will exist within it."

"And how long will all of this exist?" mused Sync.

He ignored her. With the first task complete he had already set about tackling the next. He switched on the Kern-C300 and started flicking through set-up screens. Within a short period of time it was up and running, relatively close to the way he wanted. He opened up a code terminal.

Sync watched him abstractedly, lost in her own thoughts. A month ago she'd had an unstable but uncomplicated, linear existence – her life consisted of seeking out potential talent from obscure sources, then matching that talent to lucrative contracts and skimming a decent percentage as income. It was creatively entertaining and had an upward trajectory. She didn't introspect, and she didn't worry. Now, her existence was unstable, complicated, and extremely non-linear. She was being forced to re-evaluate everything, not just in terms of career – she was probably a fugitive – but in terms of existence itself. Assuming she subscribed to the highly implausible theories that Page had suggested about reality, it left her with no foundation on which to base her decision-making, since her memories of past decisions were all fabrications. In short, she was worried. She was worried she would start to second guess herself at critical times, and critical decisions, she was sure, would need to be made soon.

Page, meanwhile, had dived straight into an area of Omicore memory that he was expressly forbid to enter. He was shunting around blocks of data in address space 0XE2865B009, which was a section well outside the ones Omar had known he could access.

Page had become bolder. It was as though with his revelation about reality had come an understanding that the rules had changed, and that the old world – a place of soft skills and social interactions – was no longer relevant. This new world of rules, functions and operators was one in which he was thoroughly at home.

With the second task complete, Page relaxed – the two urgent matters having been attended to as he saw it. The next item on his list was more in the line of a research indulgence. He looked up at Sync. "Do you know who Penzias and Wilson are?"

She nodded curiously, recalling some of her high school astro-physics. "Yeah. Cosmic microwave background guys from the 1960s."

"Yep," said Page. "I want to, try to, find out more about the place we're in."

"Here?" Sync frowned at the hut. "Oh. I see. You mean, uh, *everything*. But how?"

The experiments by Penzias and Wilson in 1964 to measure the background noise of space, had lead to the discovery and eventual calculation of the origins and size of the universe. The analysis of what appeared to be nothing more than random static in the sky had yielded information both in its distribution and its volume, that had far-reaching implications.

Page hooked up one of the screens from the room. He fished out a notepad from under some clothes, and leafed through the pages until he came to one with a bunch of addresses scrawled on it. Then, once again, began weaving the code.

An hour later, a huge mess of static suddenly blinked to life on the screen.

"It's a random shot of memory. Not organised into any kind of system. Just static noise. As much as I can sample from the servers," said Page by way of explanation.

"That's our equivalent of the microwave background?"

"Exactly. But in this case we're looking at something live, not an afterglow from the big bang." Page was captivated by the abstract shapes that seemed to flit by in the static noise.

"Fascinating. So somewhere in that fuzzy haze is us, right now?" Sync too was drawn to it.

"The world is deterministic. Every byte of memory represents meaningful information, even if we can't understand it. What we do can affect part of that static noise."

"So what is it you want to do?"

"SETI," he said simply.

Sync burst out laughing. She understood the reference right away. "Page, are you serious? You want to *RAM hack* the universe?" The guy was nuts. Brilliant, but nuts. She was smiling. She loved him then. The two of them, stuck here looking for a way through tragedy and impending doom; stuck here like lab rats in a maze with their very existence hanging in the balance. But she was happy.

"Just think of it as a signal processing game," he grinned.

"Sure Page," she smiled.

Page, presumably, was intending to produce some kind of signal in

291

the room that could be picked up in the static memory noise, then shown back to them on the screen. It was a technique that had been used since the early days of video console games to hack memory. You started off with a mass snapshot of unknown binary data, and then through a series of small changes – moving your character to the left by 1 pixel for example, and re-examining the data, gradually narrowed it down to the precise memory location that your character occupied. The most difficult part in this case was that they had no idea what anything represented – there was no such thing as the concept of a pixel in any way they understood. That's where SETI came in. SETI – the Search for Extra Terrestrial Intelligence was a system to search huge amounts of semi-random noise for non-random signals. The two concepts together was what he was proposing.

"So, What's the signal? Do you want me to wave?" Sync was still smiling.

"I want you to turn that light off and on in the following pattern – Off for a second, then on for three seconds. Then off for a second, then on for five. Then off, then on for seven. Then off, then on for eleven, then thirteen, then seventeen."

"One, Three, Five, Seven, Eleven... Ah, I see. The first odd prime numbers?"

"Yeah. I want a pattern that's not going to appear naturally. More chance of being unique."

Sync operated the light switch as Page typed in some commands into the terminal. He watched the screen.

"What now?"

"We wait. I'm scanning for anything in the static that matches. It has to be a pretty loose scan to start with because we don't know what a second represents in this noise. And there's a bit of variation in your timing."

"How do you know it will show at all? A light switch might just be a single, byte, or whatever it is we are looking at. It might be impossibly tiny."

"True, but I don't think so. The light has to illuminate things in this room. It has to carry heat – or cause the simulated sensation of heat in our skins. It has to cause these mosquitos or whatever simulated mosquito-programs they are running, to react. I think the effect of a light will make a big enough disturbance in the static for me to detect. If we had a gun we could use that instead."

She glared at him.

"Okay, yeah, that would be a bad idea."

Numbers flashed up on the screen.

```
[ 459,172 ]
```

"Hah. I guess it's going to be a long night," she tittered. "You know there are better ways to kill time if that's the goal?"

But Page was too lost in the science to respond. "Now do the same thing, but with the numbers one, one, two, three, five, eight, thirteen."

"Those are..." she racked her brain, then flashed him a smug wink. "The first few Fibonacci numbers?"

"You're good."

"But doesn't the Fibonacci sequence occur all over nature."

"Yeah. That's the point. I'm trying to narrow down the results from before. The combination of an artificial sequence, prime numbers, and an organic sequence, Fibonacci, ought to be totally unique."

She performed the sequence as Page gazed into the static.

This time the result came up after only a few seconds.

[1]

Page leapt up in excitement. "There it is."

Sync watched as he localised the region to that of the search results. It was a tiny subsection too small to have been visible from the original view.

"So that's us?" asked Sync, trying to make sense of the computer noise.

Blocks of static flickered and moved, but did so in neighbouring groups, as though they were connected. The shifting data occasionally made eerie, abstract shapes, resembling the blurry black and white noise that one might see in an early ultrasound video of a pregnant woman.

"There we are," said Page simply, and sat back, lost in thought.

As Sync watched the screen, she moved her arms, seeing the effect it had on the rows of noise as they reacted. There was not a strict one to one mapping visually – her moving arm did not look like a moving arm on the screen – merely a block of data that was intersecting with another block of data.

"So what does this mean? Can you design some sort of weapon and give it to us? Something like that?"

"No. You're conflating two different things. When I make a simulation it's more like a recipe – a written list of instructions.

It's a set of rules that defines how something will be created. But what we're seeing here is the actual creation, which is a process that is done by the computer system itself. It's like the difference between the DNA sequence of an oak tree... and an oak tree in a meadow."

"It's still fascinating to look at. I'm amazed it worked at all." Sync swooshed her arm around, then watched blocks of static react on the screen a fraction of a second later.

"We might be able to move things around that already exist, if we do it carefully, or maybe even copy parts of memory," mused Page.

A faint rumbling sound came from outside.

"Shit. That sounded like a car." Sync moved to the door, trying to steal a view though the crack between the woodwork, but could see nothing.

"Pack your stuff. The science can wait." She shot him a look. "Be ready to go in ten. I'm going to do a quick recce."

———olo———

The wind whistled through the branches in a lupine howl. Sync was pressed up against a rubber tree, its slender trunk just wide enough to conceal her more slender form. She stood motionless, scanning the woods for signs of people. Only the rustling of leaves was audible though.

She edged forward through clusters of trees, taking herself deeper into the forest. With every tentative step the darkness was increasing. The sunlight, which was already fading due to the lateness of the hour, now struggled to break the canopy of leaves.

She had just made her mind up to return, when suddenly, louder than before, she heard the noise again. She stopped. A light had been switched on behind a thick wall of trees at the far end of the grove she was standing in. A small figure was operating some kind of farm machinery, which was evidently the source of the noise. Nothing to do with her or Page.

She headed back toward the hut, cautious, but a lot more relaxed. The farmer was a long way off and wouldn't be able to see or hear anything beyond the din of his own machinery. Discretion would still be prudent though. She picked her way delicately through the fallen branches, careful to stay quiet. It was then that she heard a clipped scream coming from inside the hut.

A sudden, irrational sense of panic ran through her, completely throwing her equilibrium. She leant on a tree to steady herself, then inexplicably experienced the sensation of falling. A moment later the feeling was gone, and nothing but a mild sense of nausea remained.

She ran back to the hut.

——olo——

As she yanked open the door a large object fell sideways, out onto the porch, blocking the doorway. She had to jump out of the way to avoid being hit by it. It was a body... It was Page.

Kneeling down, desperately wondering what she could do to help, something occurred to her – the scream she had heard a few minutes ago had not been his. The voice was different. She spun around instantly, facing the doorway, ready for whoever, or whatever was inside the room. Then she burst in, fists clenched, and saw another body, lying on the floor, not breathing. She reeled back in horror. It was herself.

"Sync," said a rasping voice from the side of the room. "Did you feel it?" Page sat up from the corner where he had been doubled over. "Did you feel it?" he repeated, breathing heavily.

"What, the hell just happened?" she asked, still horrified by the two doppelgängers lying dead at their feet.

"I just tried to, to... I wanted to see if I could copy, a part of memory, and then re-inject it. To see if it was possible..." Page too was nauseous. He leant forward, coughing, spitting bile. "To use the memory output, as an input. To see if I could create..."

She followed his eyes to the table. Where there had been one cup, earlier, there were now two. But the second one was malformed – missing a corner as though it had been eroded by the edge of an inverted sphere.

She instinctively reached out to touch it but stopped herself. She glared at him, speechless, processing it all.

"I tried with a point, first. Size of a coin. Then made the area bigger. Uh, volume I mean, not area. I used a, a... memory snapshot of the room. But it wasn't supposed to include us." He spluttered again but the nausea seemed to be wearing off.

"What happened to them?" She spoke in a neutral monotone, hiding the rage she was now feeling.

"I cancelled the experiment. Straight away. It was horrible. Did you, feel it too?" He looked up at her in scientific curiosity. "It was like a kind of –"

Smack! She struck him across the face as hard as she could. The physical force of the slap almost knocked his head into the wall.

"Don't you ever! Dare! To experiment on my body in that way

297

again without my permission! You do not have the right to touch me, or anyone! In that way!"

"Sync," he stammered, holding his jaw. "It wasn't supposed to include you, or me, I just –"

"Save the explanations, Page." If looks could be weapons he would have a hole through his skull right now. "You ever violate me like that again and…" she seethed.

He said nothing. Guilt stole the words before he could form them.

At length her anger abated. "Just take more care with your experiments. Ethics, Page. Ethics is a part of science too."

"I'm sorry, Sync. I just wanted to see if I could…" He trailed off. "It won't happen again."

She gave a long sigh. "Now, to practical matters."

She dragged the arms of the second Page to bring him inside the hut next to the second Sync, then kicked her shoes off. "I don't feel like setting off again tonight. They can sleep with us. We'll leave first thing in the morning."

PART 3

Execution

CHAPTER FORTY THREE

: **Flight**

"Over the past thirty years we have seen the gradual rise of artificial intelligence within our society, and the emergence of revolutionary new ways of living. Omicore is proud to have been at the forefront of some of these developments, but we always knew there were costs. Today we would like to reveal our... Hmmm –"

Omar shuffled around the notes on his lap, skimming a few, then pausing, again addressing his imaginary audience. "A new paradigm in synthetic thought is needed –"

Leonard looked at him from the other seat of the car, surprised. "You're going to announce it?" he asked.

"I have no choice," replied Omar, setting down his notes on the table and pulling a drink from the fridge. He poured a glass for both of them. "If we don't go public now we might lose the opportunity forever. There's too much going on that unnerves me."

"Are you talking about the object on the Moon, or the ASA, or... Page?"

Omar shook his head, declining to answer specifics. "What is the latest information on him? Have you determined what he has been up to?"

"I'm getting closer," said Leonard. "The code has had us running in circles, but we'll shut him down. Don't concern yourself."

Omar's look was impossible to determine at this point. He was reflecting on the several attempts to infiltrate their company during the past month. Many were half-hearted and predictable, likely by competitors, but some he suspected were by government agencies. The most notable incident of course being the loss of his new technologies head – Jeni.

"What is it?" asked Leonard, noting the frustration on Omar's face.

"I just wish I knew the full connection between the ASA and Hoshoku-Sha. Something has changed in the basic arrangement between the government and some of the largest tech companies. Know what I mean?"

"Yes. I feel it too. But there is a, perhaps more serious point that I need to bring to your attention," broached Leonard.

"Which is?" Omar sat up sharply.

"We've been trying to determine when exactly that cylinder appeared on the Moon, and," he paused, flicking through a file.

"And?"

"They just handed me this on the way out." He tossed a photo onto Omar's lap.

"What the hell?" said Omar, scrutinising the picture.

The photo, which was grainy through enhancements, had been taken from miles above the lunar surface. A section of it was cropped and zoomed in.

There, plain to see, was the black cylinder, but moved from the position it had occupied in the previous photo he had seen – the marks were visible in the dust. It now stood a few metres closer to the base, and under it was something else, hard to make out at first.

Omar squinted at the four thick lines that were attached to a bigger mass in the middle. His mind tried to resolve them into something that made sense. A shadow? Then it became clear.

"That's a body?"

"Yes."

The cylinder was almost on top of it. The arms and legs that came from under it were dressed in the clothes of an astro-engineer.

"When was this taken?" demanded Omar.

"It was just a chance photo, taken from orbit shortly before we left the Moon. The details are so vague from that far up, and the shadows, well – we're pushing the limits of how much we can enhance it."

"Leonard. That's one of our astro outfits. I can see it."

"Yes. That's what it looks like to me."

"Who was down there when we left?"

"Nobody should have been. This is a 2k spin from the base."

"Then who took this photo?"

"It's from one of the thruster cameras. They have them on the hull to monitor booster integrity. It's only by chance that the surface is visible in the background."

"Are there any more? Some way we can see what happened earlier?" asked Omar hopefully.

"We're lucky to even get this. The rocket lines have no reason to keep this kind of thing. Once the rocket lands back on Earth with no issues, well," said Leonard apologetically.

"Okay, okay, understood," snapped Omar in irritation.

The tug of deceleration pulled on them gently as their car automatically braked, and began to steer itself into the embarkation bay.

"But I need concrete answers," said Omar, thrusting the photo back to Leonard in annoyance. "And not a word to anyone. We'll talk later," he said, stepping out of the car.

He shifted his mind to the primary focus.

The Kamara meeting had always been held on the luxury archipelago of its namesake, and this year was no different. The small group of islands were a perfect mix of unaffordable exclusivity, futurism and organic conservationism – all aspects that big tech loved to be associated with. More importantly they lay in politically neutral territory, meaning the meetings could take place free from any censorship or accusations of bias.

An usher handed some invitational paraphernalia to them both, as she escorted them from their car to the helipad. A small copter awaited their arrival, already warmed up, rotor running. The journey from here could be made either by sea or air, but the choice to travel by helicopter was simple. Once in flight you were both secure and had privacy – something which gave Omar a lot of comfort right now.

"Good afternoon gentlemen," said the pilot, flicking on the

secondary blades. "The cruise will only take about half an hour today. Strap in and enjoy the ride."

Leonard slung on a headset, opened up the kit in his bag and got straight to work.

CHAPTER FORTY FOUR

.: Waves

After thirty minutes of walking they had already reached the village. In daylight, on foot, and without the twisting turns of the river, it was much easier to see how the two locations had been connected. The computer had simply just joined the two landscapes together with no subtlety or finesse. There was a sharp line through the edge of the forest, marking the literal start of the village. Half of a house ran through one of the trees as organic jungle foliage became ramshackle shanties.

Page wondered how the computer would handle things like water in this misfit of a world. Where did it flow to? Was there a gravity well somewhere, with a lake forming as the river's lode poured into a central point? Or did the computer just neatly tuck away the anomalies to stop any logical contradictions? He looked up at the unusual formations of clouds in the sky. No, he thought, this world is broken – the cracks are everywhere to see. Don't count on anything conforming to expected laws of nature any more.

Page and Sync arrived in the part of the village Tan had lived in, and were shocked at what they saw. It was carnage. Bodies of Tan were everywhere, heaped on dead developers, like a mass burial site or killing fields from a horror war. Women and children's bodies too – all of them Tan's wife and daughter, or variations of them. Who knew how many times Tan had re-run the simulation? The aftermath was here though.

Many of these bodies had not fallen at each others hands in

violence though. At least some of them had lost their spark of life when Page had unplugged the device at the power plant. Sync thought on this, and of the events of the night before. Page was perhaps not as meek or docile as she had first assumed. There was a subtle current of cold, danger to him that she was only just becoming aware of. Or was he changing too?

Page looked over the bodies with a sickly feeling. Even though he knew the reality, or unreality, of what this all was, in some ways he felt like a murderer. He was comforted by the thought that he had saved at least one version of June and Nivi though, one incarnation of the woman and child he had pledged to protect. However shallow their existence, and whatever the tenuous grip on reality they had was, those two entities were currently alive somewhere, in motion, to feel emotion, and whatever solace or pain it would bring in this broken, simulated world.

He had kept his promise to Tan, who was, in a strange kind of way, his own child.

They moved on.

After another brief hike though the simulated landscape, Page and Sync stepped back onto the dockyard. They looked around at the odd walkway with its semi-completed features. Something about the place had changed. The architecture was the same, but it was as if ten years of growth had taken place since their last visit – growth of the most bizarre kind, organic and yet at the same time synthetic. Moss and ivy stalks crept over chipped stones, curling their way sunwards – as these plants always did – but taking paths that included sections of random straight lines and right angles, that had no apparent cause. A colony of ants that marched their way over a paved sidewalk, falling into neat rows where the cracks provided a crevice, might – were the sidewalk to disappear and leave the rows of ants naked and unexplained on flat ground – produce the same feeling of confusion that Page and Sync felt as they stared at the ivy. There were the signs of invisible organisation, where one expected only chaos.

"It's beautiful. It's a masterpiece," said Sync, looking at the dockyard, marvelling at the overgrown state of disorder.

"It's a collision," said Page, who could see the twisted logic of mismatched design. "It's as though two competing ideologies are pitched against each other in debate, neither one coherent. On the surface it's almost plausible, but deep down it's probably a mess."

"It's pure creation," smiled Sync, touching one of the angular plants. "Stop being so cerebral. What's bothering you?"

"The inconsistency," said Page. "It's like the environment is fighting against itself. Like different algorithms are being run. An unfinished conflict, rather than something intentionally designed and executed."

Page knew he was looking at something that was partially his, but also partially constructed by whatever automated systems ran on the computer that contained this world. What that computer was, he had no idea, just that he interfaced to it by accessing the Omicore servers. That could mean it was in a higher reality – running on top of the Omicore servers – or just that those servers were a facade, a gateway to something that lay above. It didn't matter, he reflected, he could still calculate some of the limits of that world, based on observations within this one.

"Beauty is made by a concept, not the execution of it," said Sync. "Any automaton can execute, very few things can create."

"Isn't creation just another form of execution?" pondered Page.

307

"The steps may be hidden, but they are there inside the creative machine. Just at a lower level of automation."

"Then where do they get created?" asked Sync.

"On an even deeper level," said Page. "A deeper creative machine, beyond inspection."

"Don't think so deeply that you miss the world around you," said Sync softly.

Their eyes touched then, melting another small piece of the analytical frost that contained him.

She continued. "The joining of two things can be beautiful, even if one of them can't explain it." A warm smile.

"Okay, okay. I'll try to, keep quiet for a bit," he said laughing out loud.

They held an embrace, watching the fractured sky slowly shift, each of them wanting to say something, or comment on the vista laid out before them, but neither wanting to interrupt the flow of emotion that silently connected them.

"Are we going back to the tunnel?" asked Sync eventually.

"No, I don't think so," said Page, still staring at the sky.

It was obvious from the coloured lines that broke the cloudscape like chemtrails that the cracks and fissures in the sky were centred around a single point. It lay somewhere in the ocean, irresolvable by vision, but not beyond triangulation. The discontinuities in geometry all pointed like broken arrows to a fracture that lay maybe 5 km out to sea.

A large rent suddenly tore its way across their field of vision like a rip of lightening, though there were no thunderclouds.

"Memory is degrading," said Page, almost to himself.

"Well then, we need a boat."

Twenty minutes later they stood on the deck of a small fishing boat, the dockyard a distant line behind them. The water was mostly calm, but the further they went, the more frequently they were encountering floating trash. It seemed they were caught in the grip of a current that had gathered and focused all the flotsam and jetsam in the area into a stream.

"What is all this stuff doing here?" said Sync, leaning over to inspect an arbitrary piece of plastic. "Where does it all come from?"

Page looked at the piece she had fished from the water. It was a broken chunk of a shop sign, with only partial lettering readable through missing tears. "*-ocan V*"

"Sync. I recognise that," he said in surprise. "It's from the noodle shop in Chinatown, Phocan Vietnamese Cuisine. But what's it doing out here?"

Sync grabbed at another drifting piece of junk – a small, generic looking tool of some sort. She shook off the water and inspected it more closely.

"I recognise this one too." She held up the instrument to Page.

His brow furrowed, trying to place it. "It's from? Is it?..." But it eluded him.

"Here," she said, and passed it to him in a strange, but familiar way.

"Thank you," he said reflexively, taking it delicately. Then it struck him "It's the circuit screwdriver from my apartment. The one you handed me when we met."

"Yep. How did that get here?"

"The world is broken," he said, surveying the surroundings, and tracing the line of debris as it flowed like a river toward the crack in the sky. "The leaks in memory must be letting things move from one part of space to another, as though they are connected. Like some kind of block wrapping system? Who knows what passes for architecture up there."

The engine in the boat chugged and sputtered. The fuel gauge was almost on zero.

"Well, it seems like we're past the point of no return. I doubt there's enough gas to get us back from here." She pointed at the horizon to where all the debris was being swept. "Look at the current. We're going there whether we like it or not."

"Maybe not quite yet," said Page, turning to look at a black shape that had appeared off to the starboard side and was approaching them rapidly.

CHAPTER FORTY FIVE

: **Clouds**

The helicopter soared high above a pristine blue sea, as sunlight bounced from the myriad crests of waves, and made of the vista a sparkling sheet of glitter.

Omar looked down at the gentle seascape – a calm and uniform texture of moving creases – and wished that it was a mirror of his soul. But it was not. A hundred thoughts ran through his mind, most of them turbulent and grey.

"Anything yet?" he asked Leonard for the fifth time.

"You could always jump in and assist me," said Leonard from within a sim headset in his passenger seat.

"No," said Omar, firm and grim. "Security is not my specialisation, and besides," he paused.

"What?"

"Well, some of that research, and those experiments. I'm a bit too close to them. You might have to, make a decision."

"We stick to the agreement then?" asked Leonard, turning his head subconsciously to look at Omar despite not being able to see him.

"We do. If things become catastrophic then we abort." Omar was resolute on this. There were so many things hanging in the balance, and the cut off line had to be drawn somewhere. "I need you to stay objective."

"I'm always objective," grunted Leonard. "So should you be."

Omar said nothing.

A mass of land began to dip into the unbroken line of the horizon. The first few claws of a dragon-like bay crept slowly into view, and with them the distinctive Kamara Anthonius building gradually appeared. The blurred dot of a boat moved far below, making a faint ripple in its wake that indicated the direction of travel. It was the first sign that others were also headed to the island.

Leonard saw none of it though – his eyes and mind temporarily lost to this world by a simulated one inside his headset. Omar was gazing into the distance, unable to focus on the notes he ought to be preparing, and unable to distract himself from the doubts he ought to be ignoring. He stared vacantly into the beautiful blue panorama, wondering... Had the research failed? How far had their systems been compromised?

"Gotcha you little fucker!" came an excited cry from Leonard suddenly, his hands typing frantically. "Omar, we might finally have something." His head moved to look at some unseen fragment of code that appeared in his vision.

"Define 'something'," said Omar, unable to hide the anxiety in his voice.

"I can, just, see the residual traces of instructions that don't belong here... Recent code. Very recent... It's just the remnants, but I'm following the trail... It leads right past our security... Side stepped it somehow."

"Page?" enquired Omar.

"I think so. Do I have time for a short trip?"

Omar checked his watch. They would be landing soonish. Whatever the outcome, it had to be arrived at swiftly.

CHAPTER FORTY SIX

: **Accusation**

——o Day 30 o——

The black patrol boat circled in on Page and Sync's little shanty, cutting a clean perpendicular line in front of them to block their path. As they braked to avoid a collision the other vessel realigned itself to drift parallel with theirs. Three men stepped mechanically from the cabin. Page noted the ubiquitous blue Omicore logo on their sleeves – a symbol that had dogged him through this world. The other – Hoshoku-Sha red, he had not seen for while.

"Good weather for a cruise," said the central figure, while his two, armed companions watched like hawks.

"Then take one and fuck off," said Sync, eyeing daggers at him.

"So you're Page?" said the man, completely ignoring Sync.

"Yes," Page replied, more in curiosity than panic.

"Interesting. Where are you going?" The man's voice was measured but stern.

Page and Sync remained silent.

"Well, it doesn't matter any more. You shouldn't be here."

"Why not?" asked Sync with venom.

"I don't think you realise what's going on," said the man, casually.

"Though, maybe you do? Your boyfriend, Page, has been sent here to steal top secret information from our servers. We cannot let that happen."

"What?" exclaimed Page. "Says who?"

"Says me," replied the man, who was Leonard. "I'm in charge of the digital security at Omicore. I've been analysing our log files, looking at the access patterns. The real ones, not the false trail you left for us. There are some areas of memory you have been in that were not for your eyes. Strictly off limits."

"Your company hired me to test your security," said Page, measured.

"Even so." Leonard matched the calmness.

"This is crazy," said Page, smiling. "You're not even real. I'm not even real. This whole thing is just a massive simulation."

"Yes," said Leonard, "I know that. It is running on our servers as part of a research project. I'm in sim so that I can interact with you here. But," and now he was mildly shocked, "How did you work it out?"

Leonard had spent some effort in piecing together the movements of Page through their servers – the ones he could find – and had come to the conclusion that the speed and depth of understanding shown could not be attributable to the human contractor they had hired, and that therefore the entity Page was something else. Whether there was a real person named Page, or team of people working from another location, he wasn't yet sure. He also wasn't sure how much of this Omar knew... or Page.

"So. How did you work it out?" he repeated.

Page shrugged. "No face to face meetings. Never with Omar. It's always been simulated environments. I think there's some kind of layer of reality between us."

Sync nodded in realisation of the truth of it. Always when speaking with Omar, she too had been a sim...

The initial request from Omicore...
The meeting in the Bossa Nova sim...
The brief interaction at the Japanese restaurant sim...

Leonard noted her surprise, and wondered what it meant. It could be a lie or could mean something else. He took the direct approach. "Page, it is my belief that you are a virus that has been put into our servers by the ASA, or our competitors Hoshoku-Sha, under the guise of being an AI programmer doing illicit research, under the guise of being a contractor who we hired to test our internal security. A double layered facade that has been created to deceive not only us, but yourself, as to what you are really doing."

Whoa. That was a lot to take in. Page didn't know what to say. There was nothing he could say. The man was accusing him of half of the crimes he had actually committed, and the truth he himself had deduced. But the bit about being created as a virus, could it be true? It would mean that there was an ulterior, guiding intent to all of his actions unknown even to himself. He frowned.

"The protected research you have, shall we say, 'accidentally' stumbled upon while rummaging around in our data, is extremely suggestive. Condemning, in fact. It would be highly valuable to many of our rival companies, or even governments," said Leonard. He seemed to be talking aloud to himself now. "The way you bypassed our defences was extremely sophisticated. Ah, we had no idea our enemies possessed such tools."

Page wondered just how much had been discovered, and which of his assumptions about their personal safety might now be proved to be false.

Leonard withdrew a gun smoothly from an in-jacket holster. "But you are out of control, and the damage you are doing is spilling from this sandbox into other more, well, critical areas of memory that –"

Page interrupted. "But what *is* the sandbox? What's the purpose of it all?"

"Consciousness," came a voice from the other boat. Omar stepped from the cabin. "This vast laboratory, in which you have been running amok, is our garden to grow things in. But now your actions are killing all the flowers." There was something slightly sad in the way he said it.

Leonard was surprised. "I didn't think you would join."

Omar sighed. "I had to see with my own eyes." He gave a wry smile "Metaphorically speaking, I mean."

Sync was scowling.

Page was still thinking on what Leonard had said, unravelling the implications. He shook his head. "It doesn't make sense. If I am working for one of your competitors, then why did I explain how I beat your security when we met in the Japanese restaurant? Why not just keep it to myself? I did the job you hired me for."

Omar looked perplexed. It seemed as though he was going to respond, but he said nothing.

Leonard broke in. "Let's anthropomorphise, and phrase the problem from your perspective," he said. "Your conscious mind deals with the world around you – like talking to us now. It tells you what to do and say. Then, above that is your *sub*-conscious

317

mind, which tells your conscious mind what to do. But it keeps some things hidden that your conscious mind is not aware of. Then we go one above that, to your *super*-conscious mind. Your superconscious mind knows what is going on, who you really are, but hides that from your subconscious mind. Instead it gives it some plausible motivation, say, that you are a programmer who wants to research intelligence. Your subconscious interprets this as motivation for you to seek out server memory for your research. This is what motivates your conscious mind to act. To act as a programmer, to hack into our servers and to conceal your tracks."

"Then why do you need to shoot him?" said Sync, looking at the barrel of the gun pointing at Page's head. "Why not just shut down the whole world if you're so worried?"

Omar shook his head, almost an apology. "One doesn't destroy an entire garden to get rid of a single weed. There's too much valuable research here."

Leonard addressed her casually, but kept the gun levelled at Page. "We just need to remove a virus that is running on a small part of our virtual machine, that's all. Painless."

Sync was sizing him up, wondering what she could do. A hard kick would probably send the fucker into the water, but what would that achieve? The two men next to him looked extremely well armed and capable. He himself seemed to be some kind of ex-military for that matter.

Leonard turned to Page. "Somewhere in your superconscious mind is whatever data you have stolen, and somebody – probably the ASA, maybe a Hoshoku-Sha agent – is waiting for an opportunity to access it."

Page had no desire to be weeded, or removed, but was becoming extremely concerned about his and Sync's ability to stop it. What to do? He had two possible trump cards.

"Well, Omar?" muttered Leonard, waiting for a signal. The two henchmen brought the muzzles of their weapons up, one aimed at Page, the other at Sync.

Omar was staring intensely at Page as if expecting something, his expression impossible to decipher. After a few seconds he nodded to Leonard. "Okay, proceed –"

"Wait," interrupted Page.

Omar raised a hand to stop.

"You're the head of security, right? And have access to live memory?" Page asked, looking from Leonard to Omar.

"Go on," Leonard growled.

"Have you checked out section `0XE2865B009` recently?" said Page, and waited.

Leonard blinked a couple of times, accessing the address in an unseen headset display. A few seconds later he blinked back at them, shaken slightly. "How the hell did you get in there?"

Omar shot a questioning look. "Leonard?"

"We need to consider this," said Leonard, and gestured at the two guards to lower their weapons. "Stand down, for now." Then he looked at Page thoughtfully, as if about to ask a further question. Instead, he struck him with the butt of the gun.

Sync grabbed the sides of the boat to stop them both toppling in as Page flew back onto his buttocks, rocking the deck. Once she had regained her footing she looked back, hand balled into a fist, ready to hammer Leonard in the face despite the futility of it. She frowned. The black boat, along with Leonard, Omar, and the two guards, was gone. Only the gently bobbing ocean remained, with the broken sky as its backdrop.

She looked back to Page, who was sitting up, nursing a bruise. "What was in that memory address that bothered them so much?"

He smiled. "It's what was not there that bothered them."

———olo———

"He scrambled the fucking access pointers," said Leonard over the noise of the helicopter blades, looking at Omar gravely. Their headsets were both off.

"To what?"

"To fifty blocks of key company data."

"Clever. So if we wipe him out now we lose access to critical data from another part of the company?" asked Omar, in a tone that suggested annoyance, but carried less vehemence than Leonard would have liked. "But, surely it's replicated and backed up somewhere?"

"Yes, of course, but come on, you can't just store data in some holistic form that you get back by flipping a switch. Unless he – it – reverts the changes it could cost us a fortune to restore. It's a deviously picked section of memory – one that he must have known couldn't be recovered easily. Little bastard."

Omar considered this, looking out at the looming form of Kamara Anthonius as it stretched upwards from the beautiful banks of rocky sand below. He could make out the forms of other guests arriving, their sleek copters and crafts parked on the landing pads, or moored in opal blue waters by the entrance pier. Were Zara and

Faisal among the figures disembarking those expensive yachts, he wondered.

"What's in those blocks of data? Anything that can be used against us? I mean, legally," he asked Leonard.

"It's the socio-economic data for some of our products. Nothing that can incriminate us, but it's just – devious. It's more than devious it's uncanny. To have picked that location. It needs an in-depth knowledge."

"He's desperate. He is fighting for survival."

"*It*. Not *he*," corrected Leonard. "And the longer that thing is in our system the more we expose ourselves to the ASA. If they or Hoshoku-Sha get access to everything we've been running we won't be flying back from this island."

Neither of them spoke for a few moments, their thoughts swirling like air through the spinning blades of the copter.

"We'll be landing in a few minutes," the pilot called back from the cockpit.

"Okay. What can you do before we land?" Omar said to Leonard. "Can you find where those scrambled pointers are? They must be retrievable from somewhere."

"Not enough time. The code that Page is running is extremely sophisticated. I mean, it's like code I've never seen before." Leonard's fingers were moving at the speed of a pianist himself, hacking and rewriting lines of instructions and symbols. "Omar, time to make a decision. Do we dump everything?"

Omar considered his options. By now the ASA would definitely have cracked the laptop they'd taken from Jeni, and would presumably have some grounds – contrived or otherwise – to

321

apprehend him and move in on the company. There would be a data access warrant waiting that would be served on him the moment he ran into one of the agents, and this time there would be no legal room to resist it. There was still time to dump the research and wipe the memory clean, absolving him – both of them – of any real crime, but what a waste that would be. On top of all the other concerns, Page had safeguarded himself against erasure by blocking access to critical company data, taking a hostage as it were.

"No. Don't dump it yet," he said finally to Leonard. "And you, don't land this helicopter," he barked at the pilot. "We remain hovering until this is resolved."

The pilot gestured with open hands in submissive obedience, clearly irked at being given orders by one of his passengers. "Can I, uh, ask for how long?"

"Until this is resolved," said Omar flatly, dismissing him with a look. "Leonard, is there a way we can do a kind of controlled dump? Wipe only the parts that have been affected by the, uh" he paused, saying the next word with careful consideration, "virus?"

"I'll salvage what I can, but when removing a tumour you don't err on the side of caution. Especially not if you are risking jail time. I say screw it, let's wipe the lot. We're out of time."

Omar said nothing. This had been an extremely expensive project and carried the hopes of a lifetime, not just for himself, but for everyone... everyone, everywhere. The whole of humanity was teetering on the edge of a precipice, and would fall unwittingly into a darkness that could not be climbed out of. *Now* was the last opportunity to counter the threat that society faced from the algorithms that were running it. *His* company, Omicore, was the only truly free agent of large enough size with resources to create something that could match the sophistication of the ASA menace, and his company was already being infiltrated. There was still a chance though. There was still one thing that he had kept close to his chest – a secret that only he knew among all his programmers.

The pilot coughed politely. Omar shot a look at him, jolted out of introspection. He was in a fierce mood.

"I need to calculate the fuel, and let the landing site know," said the pilot apologetically.

Omar sighed. It wasn't like him to talk down to people, or ride on the power his status gave him. "Sorry, we just have a few issues that need fixing before we land," he said in a much calmer tone.

The pilot didn't say anything, but just cocked an eyebrow in the form of a question.

"Fifteen minutes. We'll stay here for fifteen more minutes, and then either way you can land," conceded Omar.

"Understood, and agreed," said Leonard.

CHAPTER FORTY SEVEN

.: Echos

—o Day 30 o——

The smell of petroleum stained the ocean air. The final chugs of the boat's engine sputtered out as it died in a cough of thick smog. But the craft had almost reached its destination. The sky was now fractured and broken around them, like a time-frozen pane of shattering glass with clouds reflected through jagged shards.

They were almost at the centre of everything.

Immediately in front of them was a small island or atoll. The outward, curving sweep of a sandy beach pushed its way above the crystal water that lapped at the sides of their vessel. At this distance – a few hundred metres away – the depth was already waist height. They could wade the remainder without even needing to swim.

They hopped out, splashing into the warm current. As they approached the shore they could make out more details of the island's form, and it was every bit as impossible as the sky that surrounded it.

It looked like part of a Mandelbrot. It was comprised of claw-like swathes of beach, arranged in a spiral of ever decreasing bands that could be organic in nature, were it not for the improbable symmetry of their layout. Jagged rocks were formed into repeating shapes that reduced gradually in size over a thousand iterations, each a seemingly perfect replica of the prototype.

"The fractal geometry of nature," said Page in awe, in reference to a book he had once read.

"It's... unreal," said Sync looking at it, tilting her head to match the skewed horizon line. "I'm almost afraid to get any closer."

Not only were the rocks repeated in this abstract, laterally rotating spiral, but the sea itself was at an angle in many places. It was as though gravity flowed differently between some of the rocks. Part of the island seemed to lift off the face of the world and jut upwards into the sky.

"We're at the edge of the world," said Page, marvelling as he set foot on the sand.

"It's like the laws of physics have folded in on themselves," said Sync.

"Not physics. Reality. This is the zero point of memory," muttered Page.

"Page, I've been thinking, about what they said on the boat. If this is a simulation, and you have access to the memory that it is stored in, through some kind of connection to their server, can't you just design an escape route and program it in?"

"Where would we escape to?" he replied rhetorically. "Let's say, for example, that we could create another island paradise, or a walled fortress somewhere, without running into any issues of memory limitation or conflicts in the geometry. What would we do there?"

"We'd be safe from those people," she said.

"Okay. So, say we could guarantee our survival, for some period of time, and just swim around endlessly inside an impenetrable fish bowl. Where would that get us?" he asked. "We'd be alive, sure, but that's about it."

"Doesn't being alive mean anything to you?" she asked, half joking.

"Yes," he said solemnly, pausing, re-assessing himself. "Being with you means something to me. You've become, important."

She softened at this, but batted away his affection with a mock slap. He subconsciously rubbed the bruise Leonard had given him.

"Sync," he looked her in the eye, "– the world is collapsing around us. I don't want to go out hiding somewhere. I want to see, face on, what the big picture is. What's outside this place."

"I do too Page." She moved closer to him. "I just wish there was a way to preserve what we have found here. I mean, even in the unlikely event that we're not dead the next time they come for us, what if we succeed? What if we wake up in a place that's just awful? Or with no ability to think or something?"

"It can't work like that Sync. It can't. All simulations are just limited representations of something bigger. Whatever the feelings and sensations that we feel in this reality are, they are an approximation – a subset – of whatever exists in a higher place."

"Well, I quite like the approximation of feelings I've been having in this one Page," she smiled.

He looked at the fractal like geometry next to them. "Maybe we'll always be connected somehow. In some abstract dimension out in Hilbert space. Maybe we always have been."

"Maybe we all are," said a voice.

They both wheeled around to the direction the voice had come from. Under the shade of a palm that was hugging the beach, stood a small child. He had been there the entire time, concealed in plain sight, watching their arrival from the shadows in peaceful anticipation. He had not been hiding, merely unnoticed due to a lack of movement.

The sudden interruption by the child into what they thought had been a private conversation, jolted them both into a moment of paranoia. They felt a creeping sensation as they quickly scanned the other trees and shrubs. Maybe this island was in fact teeming with life, and right now a horde of unseen eyes were trained on them, watching from the cover of the bracken.

"Uh... Who are you?" asked Page, sensing a kind of familiarity in the child that fell short of full recognition.

"Follow me," said the kid, who looked about seven or eight years old, as he walked off through the treeline. "Come on."

Sync shrugged and followed. "Come on Page, you heard him."

On the other side of the trees was the edge of a small quadrangle. A square of decrepit houses enclosed an overgrown village centre where the gnarled brickwork lay crumbled in soft, decaying curves. An aged church spire overlooked a child's sandbox in the middle. Sixty degrees above it, partially connected by trees, was another sandbox, and another quadrangle, suspended in twisted Escher-like space.

If not for the fractally repeated echos of houses, hanging impossibly at acute angles in the sky behind this village, seeming to lead through another line of trees out onto a mirror of the beach they had just arrived from – if not for this warping of space, which gave a harsh mathematical aspect to everything that it touched – the place would have been idyllic; a lazy, summer hamlet of rustic simplicity, perched in solitude atop an isolated, sand-swept island.

A man in village robes was standing with his back to them, looking down upon the sandbox curiously, as though collecting, or recollecting his thoughts. The unkempt hair hid the face from view.

"Tan?" blinked Sync in surprise, for she had recognised the clothing instantly. "How did you get here?" She stopped. There was something different about him. Both she and Page realised as he turned that they had not actually seen this man before. He looked like a brother of the other Tans they had met inside the power plant, but was definitely not the same man as either of them.

"Tan?" said Page this time, about to say more but stopping himself as he caught a cold look in the man's eye. There was dried blood spattered across his chest. A streak of it reached his cheek, where it was smeared with grime, and eroded by the tracks of tears.

"They are dead."

"The? people at the power plant?" asked Page, tentatively.

"They are all dead," repeated Tan in moribund tones, staring away into space.

Page, who had assumed that the "dead" referred to the battle at the power plant, now understood it to mean Tan's family.

"June and Nivi are dead?" said Page, confused. His heart sank. "I'm sorry. I thought I'd managed to solve... well, to save... well, I thought they were safe."

Sync wanted to comfort Tan. To share his loss, and through

empathy dissipate the pain. But she remembered how dangerous this man could be, and how fast and unpredictable he had been.

Page's mind was racing for an explanation. The memory transfer in the forest hut had been faultless. June and Nivi ought to be okay, out of harms way, somewhere in this world.

"I saw them die," said Tan.

Something about this didn't add up, thought Page. This man was not the Tan from the power plant. So who was he?

"Show them your hand," came the voice of the child, seeming to have anticipated Page's next question. "Show them your finger."

Tan slowly held his hand up for them all to see. On it was a gold ring, with an *alpha* symbol "α" marked in its centre.

"What? Then you are Tan *alpha*? I don't understand," said Page. "You can't have survived all this time. You should have been, expired, a long time ago. I saw you die. I watched the sim."

Tan nodded, wrestling with this concept. "I think I did, die. But that there was another one after me."

Tan explained the journey through his eyes...

...How he had awoken one morning next to his wife and daughter. How he had confronted the property developers. Memories of a contract being forced into his hand, and holding a pen, unable to think of a solution except to fight. Compelled by instincts to fight...

...Then, as he began to fight he'd hallucinated, and seemed to be in an alleyway holding a knife, watching helplessly as it stuck into a man's back. It was as though he were inside the dreams of somebody else's life...

...Then a moment later he was back in the village. Developers were shooting in all directions. He had seen the shots tear into the bodies of his wife and daughter. He had seen their fragile bodies covered in blood. Had been certain he was going to die too...

...But somehow, in the confusion, events unfolded differently, and through some subtle twist of fate, he survived. How the shots had missed. How he had exploded with rage. Had butchered every developer to a man. Then not knowing what to do next, how he just ran. And as he ran the hallucinations came again...

...He saw himself in an alley talking with a detective, showing him a photograph. He saw himself walking in Chinatown. He saw himself draped in a rag at the foot of steps, talking with a man about memories he had never had. He looked up sharply at Page...

"It was you in the photo. Your name is Page?" Tan said, as the flickers of recognition grew. "And you are? Sync?"

She nodded, not sure what else to say.

Page was thinking slowly through each link in the chain of events. "So, you're Tan *alpha*, from the first simulation, but not the original Tan *alpha*. And, you're not the second Tan *alpha*. You are a third Tan *alpha*? But how? Ah!"

"Explain," said Sync.

"I can show you," said Page opening up the Kern-C300. He thumbed through his research docs – pulled from the device in the forest – until he came to one marked *"Event Map"*, and ran it. A diagram was projected, showing the topological path of events.

Page added a new line to it. *"Tan α^3"*

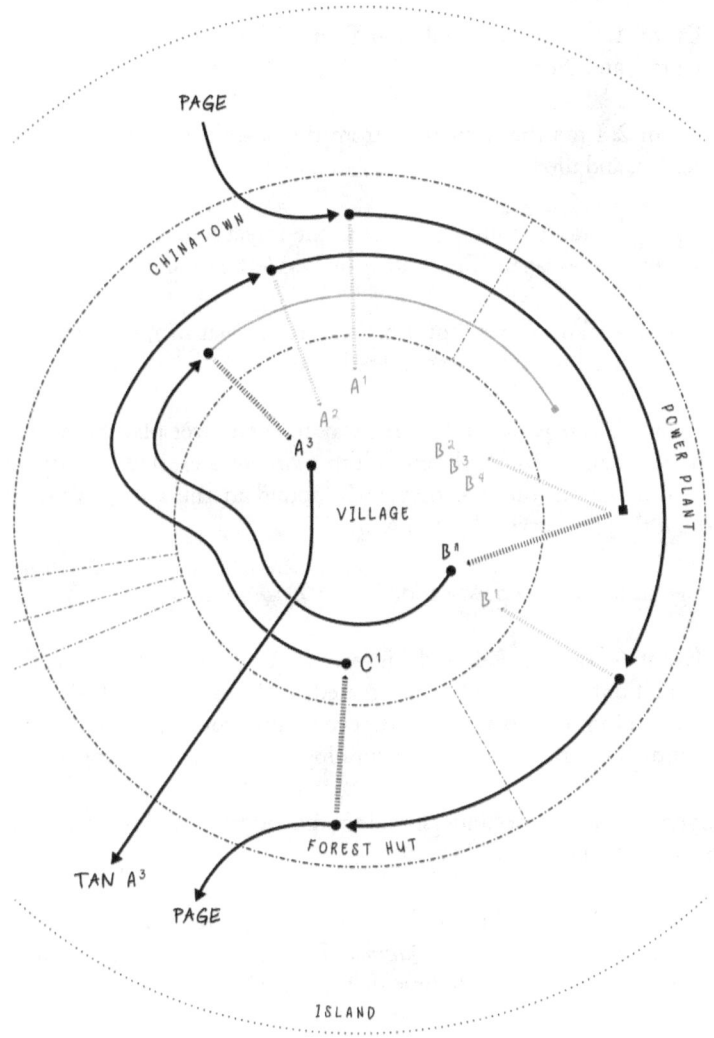

"The best way to explain it is from the systems point of view. Like an event log."

"Event 1. I ran the simulation from Chinatown. Tan *alpha* was created, and died."

"Event 2. I ran the simulation from the power plant. Tan *beta* was created, and died."

"Event 3. I ran the simulation from the forest hut. Tan *gamma* was created, and escaped. The simulation was left running."

"Event 4. Tan *gamma* found his way to Chinatown, then ran the simulation. Tan *alpha* ^{2} was created, and died."

"Event 5. Tan *gamma* found his way to the power plant, then ran the simulation. Many different Tan *betas* were created. Nearly all died, including the one that Kirby found in the village. One of them though, survived – Tan *beta* ^{N}."

Page indicated the newly added line, *"Event 6"*...

"Event 6. Tan *beta* ^{N} found his way to Chinatown, then ran the simulation. Tan *alpha* ^{3} was created and, in the confusion of overlapping memory, escaped, eventually coming here to the island. The simulation was left running... and is *still* running."

Sync nodded, now understanding the origins of this new Tan. Page went on.

"Event 7. Tan *beta* ^{N} found his way to the power plant, where we met him along with Tan *gamma*. I shut down the simulations running from there, including all Tan *betas*."

"Event 8. Tan *gamma* died fighting Omicore."

"Event 9. I moved June and Nivi to global memory, then shut down the simulation running from the forest hut."

"Event 10. We came here."

Tan was concentrating, trying to process it all. "Then I am Tan alpha three?" he asked, looked at his ring as if for confirmation.

"Yes," said Page. "But what I don't understand is how you got here?"

"Simple," said Tan wearily, "After the village, I just wanted to run, to get as far away as possible. To go anywhere that wasn't a memory from some strange hallucination. So I took a boat, not intending to go in any direction and just followed the current. The current brought me here."

"I think," said Page looking around at the broken sky, "that this place is connected to other parts of the world in ways that are not strictly linear."

Tan gazed at the sky, and the impossible island. "The world has become so surreal. Like a dream."

"The difference between a dream and reality is that there is a consistent logical structure connecting all of reality, against which our dreams can be tested and falsified. If the world is a dream, we'll discover it," said Page.

"Jesus Page," scowled Sync. Now was not the time.

"You said, Event 9, that you moved June and Nivi to global memory," said Tan, intense. "Is that, some kind of burial?"

"He doesn't know," said Sync.

"Yeah, shit. How could he?" muttered Page.

"Know?" Tan waited expectantly.

"Your wife and daughter. They're safe," Sync smiled.

Tan remained in stunned silence for a few seconds, sifting through his memories, searching, not yet believing. "They... can't be?" he said at last. "I saw them. I saw them, die. That was no hallucination. Where are they?"

That was a good point. Page frowned, trying to recall what he had seen in the third village sim. "I don't know exactly. You asked them to wait for you. Somewhere near to your village. I think, your instincts –"

"I know where," said Tan, suddenly remembering a fragment of the conversation he had experienced in a hallucination as Tan *gamma*. He looked from Page to Sync to the child. "Then, I am wasting time here. I need to find my way back."

Sync followed his gaze out to the vast blue ocean. There was no sign of the mainland from which they had come. Perhaps through some twisting eddies of the water was a shortcut that could bridge space between here and the village.

Page was thinking more pragmatically – about memory space, memory diagrams, memory maps, and Tan. A man who had seen through as many hallucinations as he had would have a good understanding of the overall picture of things. The world's geography might look different to someone who had been in two, three, four – who knows how many – places at once. Tan would find his way back, Page was certain.

The child, who had been silently watching throughout the conversation suddenly spoke up again. "Before you go Tan, we need Tōkei Senshi."

"What?" asked Page, caught off guard.

"Tōkei what?" said Sync.

"The combat training program," grinned the child. He mimed a mock kung-fu stance toward Tan. "If I have guessed correctly, the source of your fighting skills is not a lifetime of martial arts training... It is several life times... And several thousand hours of simulated combat... And several million points of statistical combat data. Am I right?"

"You are," said Page looking at the child who, clearly, was more than a child.

"Wait, who is this?" said Sync, referring to the child.

The child smiled at Page. "You copied the top level combat training program from Hoshoku-Sha, when you hacked in, before you started working for Omicore, then used the data to enhance your Tan project?"

"Yes." Page spoke slowly.

Tan flexed a hand, watching the way the muscles moved, and wondered about his past. It was an area that he had never really thought about. Everything just seemed to flow automatically, like muscle memory. Unbeknownst to him though, the undiluted ability of *Hyrai Mikoto, Tōkei Senshi, Rank Zero* coursed through his veins.

"You would like me to teach them?" asked Tan.

The child looked quizzically at Page.

"Not teach, *transfer*," said Page, carefully.

"Transfer?" said Tan skeptically. "How can you transfer knowledge that is in my head, without being taught?"

335

"No fucking way," said Sync, who had just understood what they were circuitously suggesting.

"We have done, tests," Page said slightly sheepishly.

Tan shook his head, not following.

"But can you do it?" challenged Sync. "I mean, out here. We must be miles from anywhere."

Page took out the Kern-C300 again, looked at the power levels. It still had enough power. He checked the data speed, expecting zeros, then did a double take. "The connection strength is off the chart. Wherever we are, there are signals pulsing through the airwaves thicker than the air itself." He shot an awkward stare at Sync. "Accessing the system won't be a problem, its just, uh,"

"What?"

"I will need your, well, cooperation this time," said Page.

"No no, Page. This has nothing to do with me. It's between you and Tan. Keep my mind the fuck out of it."

"No, not that. I just mean, I don't know if I can run the code myself."

"Why not?"

"Well, I might be unconscious."

———o‌l‌o———

Omar looked out of the side of the helicopter at the flat blue horizon, enjoying what few moments of peace he had left.

"Something's happening," murmured Leonard from beneath the visor as he typed. "It's hard to follow in code but there's a lot of movement... Wait. I can see it. No, it's gone again."

Omar sat up, slowly, having arrived a decision at last. "Enough is enough."

Leonard took off the headset to meet Omar's gaze. There was steel in his voice.

"Kill the virus. Now. This has gone too far. Throw everything at it. Forget about unscrambling that data."

"And what about the research–"

"Do whatever it takes to destroy that thing. In ten minutes we land. If you can't get rid of it by then... vaporise everything."

CHAPTER FORTY EIGHT

.: Invasion

——o Day 30 o——

The wet splash of water startled Page into opening his eyes, only to close them again as he felt the sting of salt. He blinked away tears, looking up at the sky.

"Get up! They're coming!" cried Sync, throwing another handful of sea water onto his face.

Suddenly remembering where he was, he sat bolt upright taking in the scenario. He had been out cold, under the shade of trees next to the beach. Only a few minutes had passed, he judged. He felt subtly altered – looser in some way – as though his muscles had undergone an intense yoga workout during his mind's absence. It wasn't as though anything had changed physically – his body was still the same, with the same physique and musculature – but he had gained a new sense of command over his anatomy, a new level of poise and finesse. He could order it into action in ways not before possible, and it would respond, instantly, smooth as ice.

A cursory glance at the ocean revealed the source of Sync's alarm. Dotted on the horizon were multiple black boats, each carrying two or more black figures. "Omicore?"

"Who else. But not only there." Sync darted a look upwards.

Page watched a black ball plummet from the sky then unfold into a "V" as the chord of a parachute opened from the figure's

338

backpack. Then another. Several were dotted in the sky, falling like black ash from an unseen fire.

A thin smile pierced his lips. "So the fuse is lit. They're sending out the whole host of Omicore to finish us. Now we shall see."

"But not out here in the open. It's insane," urged Sync.

Page scrambled up, ready to run with Sync. "Wait. Where's Tan and the child?"

"Tan left. The child is doing what we should be doing. Finding a place to hide."

The child had crawled through a broken door and was inside the derelict church. It was bigger on the inside than its exterior dimensions seemed to allow. The nave ran for twenty metres along the centre of the building, with a ceiling that stretched almost as high. Coloured light poured in through stained glass gallery windows to capture, briefly, swirling eddies of dust that danced above the aisles in rays of primary hues. The coarse lines of colour then fell diagonally across broken wooden pews, painting them in an abstract mural of blotches, spilling finally onto the cracked tiles of the floor, where they were absorbed in shadows.

The child looked up in wonder at the curved masonry above him as it twisted into arches, sweeping out Sierpinkski curves that had no place in a Euclidean universe.

He moved deeper into the building, wading through musky air as heavy as clay. As he passed the crossing he caught a brief glimpse of the world outside though a porch window, seeing the landscape inclined, impossibly, at a thirty degree angle to his own. He moved on, now in the choir section, and stood before a large granite altar, its surface above the height of his head. It bore no cross, nor mark of any denomination or religion. As he approached he could see faded writing engraved into the stone, the figures worn by the passage of time. He rubbed the grime away with his fingers, reading the exposed letters.

"The essence of mathematics is in its freedom."

———olo———

Sync's breath blew hotly into Page's ear. The two of them were pressed behind a rock on the opposite side of the quadrangle, panting, shielded by the cover of trees from any direct line of sight from the beach. But the upward curve of the fractal landscape behind them would afford anyone a view of their hiding place, should they chance the confusing twists of gravity and traverse the slopes of the terrain. For now they were safe though. The Omicore security forces were all arriving from a single direction, hitting the beach from one broad angle.

They could hear the bark of orders, then the clink of boots as the first few soldiers moved from sand to concrete, and entered the far side of the square.

"Come on, move now or we'll be cut off here," said Sync.

They made a quick dash to another part of the coast before the boots got any nearer and concealed movement became impossible. The winding path they took between rocks seemed to slope upwards before it opened out again into an uncovered view of the island.

As they stopped they took in this new panorama, realising that they were now standing on the curved bank of one of the fragmented pieces of geometry. They had to crane their necks just to look at the horizon they had run from, which now seemed as though it was a wall rather than a floor.

Despite the arrangement of up and down in their minds, the sense of gravity didn't feel as though they were on an incline. From this orientation the quadrangle was above, or below depending on perspective, with the water line of the beach forming an arc above their heads.

Some distance behind them and to the right, the malformed chunks of the island had come together, meeting in the middle, but not seamlessly. A gaping hole, almost like a lagoon, punctured reality. The drop into the murky water at its base was huge, exaggerated by an uncertainty as to which way gravity would actually pull, were one to take the leap of faith and jump from the rocky edge.

In its simplest form, they were on the steep slopes of a hyperbolic volcano, whose terrain was made of beaches, quadrangles, and rocks.

The rumble of a motor boat brought their gazes back to the shore. Black, military style speed dinghies were arriving in the swash zone, with armed Omicore security soldiers dismounting in pairs onto the sand.

Discarded parachutes flapped in the wind, as drop-troopers cut loose their tethers, landing in a running motion with weapons already drawn by the time their feet hit the bracken.

Muzzles of guns moved in perfect synchronization with heads, as the soldiers scanned the clumps of trees and rocks, looking for signs of Page.

"Halt!" came a voice from one of the soldiers' visors, addressing the men immediately around him. He raised a fist in the air. Within seconds they were all crouching in silent positions of combat readiness.

Sync stiffened, wondering if they had been spotted.

"I need the C300," hissed Page in a whisper, for a moment thinking he'd dropped it.

Sync handed him the device, not taking her eyes from the men, who were looking in their general direction but hadn't discovered their precise location.

"The battery is nearly dead. I think there's only five to ten minutes left."

"Shit." He cursed himself for not having charged the device fully at the forest hut. Now that oversight might prove costly.

"What are you going to do?"

But he didn't even register what she was saying. His fingers were a blur as he typed instructions furiously into the device, flicking between screens of static noise and lines of code. Finally, he slammed it closed and handed it back to Sync. "Hold on to this. For now. I might need it back later."

The soldiers meanwhile had begun to fan out again, cautiously, even as more arrived behind them, dropping from the sky and seeming to appear from the water itself. The figure in command held up a fist again and ducked down, weapon ready. The others did so a second later. Evidently he had seen, or heard something. Sync hoped it was not the child. Page followed the direction of the man's gaze with his eyes but saw nothing.

The men, as they looked into the trees, were trying to fathom out the strange geometry of the place. Heads turned upwards and tilted sideways, unable to make sense of the bizarre structure of the island. The warped space here made a mess of any normal procedure they might follow on an operation like this.

Suddenly, from a fractal portion of the terrain, a large bird broke away from one of the empty houses. Guns were raised almost instantly, the barrels lined up with the moving creature. In less than a second, the snaps of several shots rang out as the front row of men fired. Maybe it was target practice, or maybe it was an order to kill anything that moved, but the lightning reactions of the men left no time for the bird to escape.

Page and Sync watched glumly, waiting for the body of the doomed creature to fall from the sky. But the bird kept flying. Not a single bullet had found its mark.

"How could they miss?" whispered Sync. "It should have been easy from that distance."

The men were looking at each other, then at the bird, then at their weapons, in doubt. They too couldn't believe that they had all missed with so many crosshairs on a single target. One of them checked his chamber for jams, scarcely able to believe that a simultaneous mechanical failure could have affected all of them.

"The guns are useless from there," said Page, noting how the direct line of sight from the men to where the bird had been passed through several curves of the fractal. "The straight line of a bullet is not a straight line in that terrain. Gravity, or space or whatever, is pulling it in different directions. They can't aim."

"Great. Then they can't hit us across long distances," Sync nodded. "What about short range?"

"Well up close we'd all be in the same domain, so –"

"So, don't get up close," warned Sync.

"But you're forgetting something," said Page, flexing the fingers of his hand into a fist.

"Don't," she said, anxious. "There's not another Page out there to replace you."

He gave her a hard look. "Sync, if I'm going to do anything, now is the time, before they figure out that their weapons work just fine at close range. And besides..."

"What?"

"The battery on that device is nearly dead."

He didn't need to say more. She now thought she understood exactly what he was proposing, and nodded her reluctant acquiescence.

"When you hear me call out, run the program."

"Sure. You can rely on me." She said it in cold business like tones. A reassurance of efficiency.

"I know," he said softly, almost to himself. "Don't be too near to me when you run it." He started to move away from the rocks, then hesitated.

"What is it?" she said, concern escaping in the single word.

"I... uh, kind of... well, uh, love you," he said, then raced off.

CHAPTER FORTY NINE

: **Kamara**

——o Day 30 o——

The helicopter touched down on the fourth floor helipad pad of Kamara Anthonius, flagship building of the Kamara Isles, and host to one of the world's most important meetings of industry, finance and tech companies – The Kamara Group meeting.

The impressive structure glittered in the sunlight, casting a reflection of blue sky over the landing area. Omar and Leonard looked at the arrival party that had come out to greet them.

The tall, distinctive forms of the Hoshoku-Sha guards were unmistakable. Next to them, standing smugly amongst a throng of their own heavies were Faisal and Zara, of the ASA. The two groups stood patiently at the edge of the landing zone waiting for the rotating blades to stop.

"I sent the commands," said Leonard. "It will be shut down in a few moments."

Omar pointed out Faisal and Zara. "Well, at least that ought to give them something to do," he said with a dry chuckle. "Let them hunt for evidence that isn't there. While we, my friend, take a well earned break."

"Did we do the right thing?" asked Leonard. "Destroying all that research?"

Omar was about to respond but remained silent, reaching for words. He was emotional.

"Don't worry. We'll be back on our feet. Eventually," said Leonard clapping him on the shoulders. "Though I don't know what sort of future we have to look forward to in this world. Now that those assholes are running it."

"There was no virus," stated Omar softly.

"What?" Leonard thought he had misheard. "What do you mean?"

Omar sighed. He wetted his lips. He sighed again, not sure how to broach it, ready to open up and reveal the thing he had held back all this time.

"Out with it," said Leonard. "What do you mean, *no virus*?"

"It was Page," said Omar. "The project. It was Page."

"It was Page. What was Page? Page was the virus." Leonard's brow furrowed as he considered the connection of the different events. "Explain what you mean."

"The aim of the research was to create a vast simulation that could be used to study the interactions of human beings, and society. To use it to train an AI that would be capable of breaking through the systems that are overrunning the real world."

"Yes," nodded Leonard. "Our servers on the Moon. We used Omicore's real customer data to create and populate a highly detailed environment – Chinatown, the suburbs, the power plant and so on – and then let it evolve and grow, while our systems analysed the results."

"But within this project were planted the seeds of the real project."

"Which is?"

"An emergent digital consciousness. Something that, were it to succeed, would be a new paradigm in intelligence. True creativity born in a digital domain – not just a mimicry of biology. And therefore able to understand digital systems on its own terms." Omar sighed, wearing his years more heavily than Leonard had seen. "So you see, Page wasn't supposed to lose, he was supposed to win."

"What?" cried Leonard in shock. "Then why have me send all the security after him?"

"To put him under the most extreme pressure. To test whether we had truly created something strong enough and smart enough to save humanity. Leonard, if it couldn't beat us at our own game, how could it beat what's out there? I had to have you come down hard on it – as hard as you could, with all the security and counter measures and force that you – that we – could muster, without sparing a moment of thought for its, for his preservation."

Leonard nodded, thinking. "That's why you didn't want to get involved at the end? You didn't want your influence to bias my counter measures, because you were rooting for Page, not against him?" He scowled. "*It*, I should say, not *him*."

"Yes."

"Then you knew from the start, when we hired him remotely, that Page was just a... a manifestation of our own research computers?"

"No, not at first," said Omar. "I was searching, but didn't know for what or for who, exactly."

"Hmm. That's why you were so relaxed about not meeting him in person?" Leonard clucked his tongue, almost laughed. "I thought it was a bit strange, hiring a security guy like that and not doing a face-to-face. Now I know why. You knew the face-to-face was impossible." He did laugh then. "And there was I thinking you were an idiot to be scammed by this Hoshoku-Sha virus."

"Ah yes, Hoshoku-Sha," murmured Omar. Looking out at the line of men waiting, then at the pilot.

The pilot nodded, taking his time to shut off the engine. Deliberately giving them a chance to talk this out, curious himself at what his passengers were saying.

"Okay, so, now I know that Page was not a virus created by Hoshoku-Sha. But what about the other attacks? They were real?"

"Everything else was them or the ASA, as far as I can tell," said Omar gravely. "Make no mistake, they are deadly and competent, and have been trying extremely hard to infiltrate us."

"Just not masquerading as Page," added Leonard.

"They wanted to put an end to Page almost as much as they wanted to put an end to our research. I'm not sure if they know the two are the same thing. I think," Omar searched his memory for scraps, "I think Page stole something from them, early on – hacked into their systems."

"But how?"

"Since day one we have always had some of the ASA's tentacles probing into our systems, and through them, Hoshoku-Sha. Maybe since we bought their combat training programme, maybe even before," Omar considered, remembering the financial data he had been shown by Faisal and Zara at their first meeting four weeks ago.

"I told you we should have stayed away from it."

"When Page started out, as a fledgling piece of self analysing code, growing, learning, probing the world, I think he – it – attempted to expand, along one of those data tentacles, and ended up accessing Hoshoku-Sha's system. They traced the breach back to us, since, from a physical perspective it was through our network that the attempt was made. Though at that point we were not aware of it, and I'm still not sure exactly sure which path was taken."

"Ughh. If I had known. Back then. That would have been the time to strike." Leonard punched the air. "I could have smashed them before they knew what they were up against. The little toads."

"I didn't know either though. We'd only just started."

"We?" Leonard scowled. "You and your merry team of programmers were all in on this little secret except me?"

"Everyone in the team knew the aim of the research, but only myself and Jeni knew what we had seeded, and how to look for it."

"Sync?"

"Yes. The Sync program is an interface, designed to be the message carrier between us on the real world and the consciousness on the inside, should it emerge. She was deliberately coded to seek out likely candidates among the multiple personalities spawning in memory. Eventually she found one that started to flourish – namely Page. But even then I wasn't sure until later on."

"Ah. When it started to self create? By which time Sync had gone off the grid with it."

"Yes. It, Page, started solving things in abstract ways. Taking parts of the genetic code that we had written and evolving them into imaginative new strands. Things that were beyond our ability to create or understand. Or to contain. He started using our research

349

sim in his own research, folding memory in on itself. That's when the memory started leaking."

"Omar," said Leonard suddenly. "There's more to this."

"To what?"

"Those memory leaks, and fractures. They may have started then, but they are not only happening when Page or his constructs are running code."

"What, do you mean?"

"I have been monitoring things extremely closely." He smirked. "Even though you opt to stay out of it on, uh, moral grounds, I like to know what I'm up against. It's what you pay me for remember. And, I'm telling you, the degrading memory can't all be accounted for with the known access patterns."

"What are you suggesting?"

"That there is a third influence. Not Page, or Hoshoku-Sha. Or those bastard ASA imbeciles, but another force at work, manoeuvring things in memory. I thought it might be you."

Omar thought for a moment. "Will there be anything left, after deletion?"

Leonard shrugged. "There might be something. But I didn't hold back. That's what you wanted."

Omar was firm. "It is. What's done is done."

"Then I guess we'll never know."

"Is it complete?"

"Any second now."

CHAPTER FIFTY

.: Level-Up

——o Day 30 o——

The man had checked and rechecked his Farad-200. He was sure that none of the mechanisms were jammed and that the always-on power cells were charged. The circuits were all connected, and he was certain that the shots really had been fired. Therefore it was this twisted terrain that was to blame for them going astray – so far astray that none of them could tell where the bullets had ended up. The bird flapped casually past him, as if in deliberate mockery of his failure to hit it. Never mind though. The combat would come. He still had plenty of lower tech options to deal with this Page person.

Discarding the combat-rifle, he unsheathed his Wharncliffe, and felt the familiar weight of the blade in his hands. He nodded to his pair-partner, and the two of them headed up into the sloping curve of rocks to scope the area.

At first he thought it was another animal. The blurred figure moved sideways between two crannies above him in a gazelle like leap. It was already gone before he had time to process the image in his mind, and realise who it was.

Page moved almost at the speed Tan had. The Omicore soldier could only fumble in clumsy slow motion as Page stepped to one side like a ghost, and out of the arc of the blade.

Page killed the first man with a punch to the solar plexus, followed by a kick to the back of the right shoulder blade. The man was convulsing in spasms as he crumpled to the floor. It didn't seem possible to kill someone like that, and yet there were so many shortcuts to stop the human body functioning.

An understanding of the overlapping pathways of the nervous system had now become part of Page. New patterns and formulae flowed through his subconscious mind like an upgrade to an operating system. Page swivelled out of the way of the next man's lunge, using the momentum to smash his skull open on the rocks.

The commotion of the skirmish drew the immediate attention of others, and the battle was joined in earnest.

A soldier on the beach looked up at the impossible slope towards Page, trying to adjust his aim accordingly. Unsure in which direction to set the trajectory he eventually just fired blindly, then, as debris flew from a wall twenty metres away, threw down the gun in frustration and advanced on foot. Others did the same.

The next skirmish was very nearly Page's undoing. Five men attacked simultaneously, unhindered by shock or surprise that had been his advantage before.

As he spun upwards, sliding around the nose of a Shock-Prod swinging towards him, he realised that these men were also trained with a version of the Tōkei Senshi program. But his was the superior – stolen from source off the Hoshoku-Sha servers, then honed by Tan, and tempered to this world through use. The statistics of close quarters, zero-sum combat played out in the data through competing algorithms, adapting to changing levels of fear and anger, position and velocity. Millimetres made the difference between life and death as Page shifted stances; a sliding blur between his enemies.

Bodies fell to the floor, even as more joined the affray.

Time seemed to pass in slow motion as he fought.

He saw the barrel of a gun pointing at his face.

He saw muscles tense in the man's face as he pulled the trigger.

He felt the heat of the muzzle as he pushed it to one side, shifting.

He felt brain matter spray over him from behind.

He watched the rag-doll physics of a sprawling body.

But that was close.

———olo———

Sync felt the nausea of dancing butterflies in her stomach as she watched the battle rage on. Whatever Page was waiting or hoping for had to happen soon. The odds of his continued survival were becoming vanishingly small.

The cracked visor of a dead soldier bounced across the rocks, landing near to where she was hidden. Its screen faced upwards, blinking fractured streams of telemetry to no-one. She looked at the display, glitching and fading as its circuitry failed, trying to read the death throes of information. Amid heat maps and undecipherable graphs were the partial words:

AERIAL DROP: -127.23 SEC

She instinctively glanced sideways – which was upwards – at the sky. A black shape suspended beneath a large parachute was slowly falling from way up in the troposphere, out to sea. Its parabolic trajectory would take it directly toward the island.

One hundred and twenty seven seconds was not a long time. Though for anything to reach this place it had to negotiate the broken sky, and pass through a region whose splintering of three dimensional lines made any path prediction meaningless.

One hundred and twenty three seconds was not a long time.

"Page!" she shrieked. "The sky!"

Her cry was as much to divert attention away from Page, who was massively outnumbered, as it was to inform him of the slowly falling bomb. She achieved both results.

——olo——

Half of the men looked away from Page in the direction of the voice, but only one set off to find its source among the rocks. The others continued fighting. Page stole a quick glance at the sky. The black object falling was a bomb. No doubt about it.

Using the distraction to his advantage he broke away from the group – and the man whose jugular he had just slashed – to race further up the slope, into the open, away from rocks.

The flick of a laser went after him as he ran, but the line of its beam bent strangely through the air to shine harmlessly on a treetop. The leaves were only singed, with the smeared dot of light having lost most of its intensity to the curved refraction it had undergone.

More soldiers burst from the quadrangle, tearing up the slope like a wave crashing over sand. It was becoming desperate for Page. The number of people and weaponry now facing him was beyond the Tōkei Senshi system's ability to handle, despite his upgrade. There simply would be no statistical movement that could get through the total coverage that would surround him. He would be boxed in. He had five seconds at most before they reached him.

He shouted out, not knowing if she could hear him. "Sync!"

She heard him clearly but did not call back. The soldier who was hunting her was systematically searching anything that provided cover. Eventually he would reach her. But he would be assuming that she was as deadly as Page, and would be cautious. That gave her more time.

She looked at the C300. It was open on a program, and prepped, exactly as Page had given it to her.

```
> "dup-test.hmem.arlos" initialised.
> Run?
> Please confirm [y/N]_
```

She hit the run command.

The next few men were just reaching Page, but stopped short by a few metres – a distance at which they thought themselves out of his range. They had seen the devastation done to their colleagues and knew what they were up against.

Page made no attempt run. He had just inexplicably stopped. The probability of beating so many people was now zero – a cold, hard, calculable fact. His failure to act – even out of desperate defiance – would have been said by some to be a failure of the algorithms – the difference between animal and machine. But Page was waiting.

The first soldier took quick aim Page's head but hesitated, confused by the lack of movement. He too had assessed the odds, and could see that the chances of Page beating so many people alone were non-existent.

But Page did not have to fight alone.

A faint shimmer appeared in the air around him. Behind it the world seemed to shift and crack, as if into particles, then reform. The effect was so quick and so slight that it was hard for the soldier to say whether it had truly happened. But as he pulled the trigger Page was in motion... running... not away but towards the soldier.

Blaaaaam. The soldier fired just as Page started to leap.

There was no chance at this distance, no matter how fast Page could move. The bullet went straight through his face, killing him instantly.

His body though, continued its arc through the air – the momentum of the leap carrying it forwards. The corpse crashed with a heavy thud into the group of soldiers, pushing them back under its weight.

Sync was watching all this from her hiding place in the rocks. She was still reeling in shock when a whoosh of displaced air reverberated from the clearing. A new version of Page had appeared, in the exact place he had been a moment earlier, with the same velocity, momentum, impulse, everything as before. He was in the mid-motion of a leap, with dust flying from his feet.

There were now two of them – one dead, one alive. She looked back. The first corpse was still under the state of collapse – its lifeless limbs splaying outwards like a rag doll at the feet of the men.

Sync had guessed something of what Page wanted to attempt when he'd handed her the C300, and she had seen the aftermath of his tests in the forest, but here, now, seeing it in front of her eyes, she was as shocked as the soldiers.

The soldiers were still making sense of the situation when the second Page landed from his leap and attacked. The blows struck with lethal precision. It was clear that however the duplication program had affected his mind the replication of memory had not in any way dulled the sharpness of his combat. The first soldier was dead.

Page was already moving to the next, when the electric hum of close range lasers lit him up. In panic, the nearest soldiers had fired automatically, cutting one of their own down in their zeal to hit Page, but they did not miss. Again Page's body was cut down. But again another Page landed on the dirt running. There were now three. Two were in the throes of death as the third spun into action.

Then a fourth, a fifth, it went on, repeating every few seconds.

Sync did not dare to move lest she become entangled, either in the chaos of battle or in the space occupied by the respawning Pages. She looked at the screen of the device as it counted down in three second intervals, repeating and restarting. A loop.

The bomb had been moving rapidly towards them during all this, but its rate of descent was now slowed by the drag of the parachute on denser air. The strange gravity at work seemed to be pulling it towards the centre of the island, to where the mismatched geometry had created a hole. A quick mental calculation suggested they had about thirty seconds until it either detonated around them, or sailed past into the abyss.

"Page!" she yelled, not sure which of the multiple versions she should be addressing. "Bomb. Nearly here!"

A couple of them reacted to the cry, despite being in the midst of battle. "I need to get there!" shouted a Page as he appeared, then shifted into a blur of martial arts, only to be shot down an instant later.

"What?!"

"Our way out!" cried a new Page, fighting off the next batch of soldiers. "Trust me!" said the next, as a laser cut through the former one's head, sending a wet, bloody torso twisting to the floor. One of the lifeless arms was still holding the throat of a soldier, the fingers locked in a vice grip of death around the man's oesophagus.

Some of the soldiers had broken away from the main group and were heading towards Sync, whose whereabouts were now known. She ducked back under cover then made a run for it behind overhanging rocks. The mayhem being caused by the multiple Pages created an opportunity for her to move unseen. She rolled through a gap, wincing as she landed on top of a corpse, then kicked it to push herself clear, realising belatedly that it was one of the dead Pages."Ugh shit."

Once she was higher up the slope she crouched down to conceal herself in a nook between the rocks, then looked up. The underbelly of the bomb was clearly visible from here. Huge industrial wires, like the fingers of a metal hand were clasped around a mechanical device in the middle. Numbers and markings were visible. The notches of a timer wound slowly down as it plummeted toward them.

A flicker of green shone on the rocks beside her. She spun round to see an Omicore soldier glaring at her, gun raised. His expression was an open eyed snarl of malice, of malevolence, of lust at having found... The face split in half from behind.

Page – one of them – dived onto floor next to her, bleeding but alive. In his hand was a laser taken from one of the fallen soldiers. "Sync, I... need you to..." He was barely coherent. "...to set the timer to zero, and then give it to me when..."

He suddenly jumped up as if a person was behind him, then fell back down in confusion. Sync reacted, ready to fight, but saw that nobody was there.

"Disorienting," he stammered. "Two places at once. Three or –"

"Give it to you when?" she interrupted. "The bomb!"

The bomb was almost directly above. Its large parachute casting a black shadow that slunk over the terrain to meet them. In seconds it would pass overhead, over the edge and down into the abyss.

"When it detonates. It will be in... core of memory. I.. I will need the device at that moment."

"Why?"

"Create. Memory leak. Recursion... overflow."

"Okay. I'm doing it. Shut up." She opened up the screen and started flicking through values, focussing on the code like she was back in a school exam. She *was* an ex-programmer she reminded herself. How hard could it be?

Page had stopped breathing. Sync barely acknowledged it, merely looking up to check that there were other Pages below.

It was easy. She saw the timer values, clearly labelled in the code. Thankfully Page had written this code to be understood, and not in some incomprehensible, cryptographic half-speak that every junior programmer across the world thought made them smart. Nor was it in the fetish-like lint-jargon that inexperienced project leads applied like uncompromising Nazis to their code-bases in naive attempts to catch bugs, inadvertently creating more bugs in the process by destroying readability to the point where nobody had a clue what the code did any more. No, Page was a pro, and the code was easy for her to find. It had whitespace, and comments.

She changed the value to zero and waited, counting down the seconds of the bomb.

CHAPTER FIFTY ONE

: **Conference**

——o Day 30 o——

As Omar and Leonard walked from the helicopter Faisal and Zara advanced towards them.

"Mr Cantor," began Zara carefully, with a broad smile creeping over her face, "we'd like to talk to you about a plea bargain."

Leonard was unable to restrain himself. He stepped forwards and decked her with a solid right cross to the jaw, then went for Faisal. But before he could flatten him the Hoshoku-Sha and ASA guards leapt to the ready with weapons drawn. Faisal was trembling.

Leonard raised his eyebrows at the reaction of the guards and spat. "You could at least put in a little effort to keep up the pretence of being separate organisations."

Omar too had noted the way Hoshoku-Sha and ASA now acted as one. "How long since they bought you out?" he asked Faisal, "or was it the other way round?" he said, looking this time at one of the tall Hoshoku-Sha men.

"You're going down Omar," said Faisal with bitterness.

"We all are," said Omar, sighing.

Another group of people marched onto the helipad from the rear, separating to form a "V" shape. The twisting K emblazoned on their lapels denoted them as Kamara Group officers.

"We are all going down," said a woman at the front. "Down to the conference room where Mr Cantor is scheduled to speak today."

Faisal glowered. "I don't think you understand the –"

"You have no jurisdiction here," interrupted the woman. "You can settle any squabble afterwards in your own nations."

The Kamara Group officers didn't even flinch at the drawn weapons, simply moving to open a path and allow everyone to pass in single file through to the building.

———olo———

Curved marble tables stretched in concentric circles around a circular stage. Neo-baroque furniture made from Sonokeling wood native to these islands lent the space a vibrant, mauve hue. The ceilings were high, and lit like a sunset by a soft diffusion of light scattered through orbs of amber-glass.

The conference room was ornate without being ostentatious – it was classy. Though however grand its design, it was no match for the amount of wealth and power concentrated within it today.

Representatives of fifteen nations and more than eighty different companies and organisations sat in attendance at the plush indoor amphitheatre. As Omar and Leonard entered the room the lights dimmed, and the doors closed behind them.

A well groomed presenter trod a walkway that cut a spiral chord through the tables, admitting him to the central podium. As he stepped onto the stage a large screen that filled the back wall, slowly brightened. *"K G M 2 0 5 7"*.

The man smiled, opening his arms in welcome, embracing the audience with efficient, graceful lines of motion. "Representatives of different companies and nations, we thank you," said the smooth, silky voice, "Now that you are all here the conference will begin."

His words segued into the start of a presentation. A woman appeared on the screen surrounded by generic logos and splashes of colour. Bland, corporate sponsors, thought Omar, not really watching. He was trying to work out what to say in his allotted slice of time.

Leonard didn't give a toss about the event. Now that their reason for being here was gone, he had no reason to take any interest in it. He was mildly curious what Omar would come up with in terms of a speech, but was more focused right now on people watching. Specifically two groups of people.

The two tall Hoshoku-Sha men were muttering to each other, then looking across the room at another group of people, then going back to muttering again. Leonard followed their gaze. The other group of people were, predictably, the ASA.

His lips formed a snarl as he located Faisal, noting the empty seat next to him where Zara ought to have been, and wishing he had been quick enough to deck them both. Maybe he should have tried a kick, he thought – put a boot through Faisal's smug veneers? As he stared, subconsciously fantasizing about what a toothless Faisal would look like on stage trying to speak through a mouth of bleeding stumps, he noticed something. The ASA reps, and the Hoshoku-Sha men had simultaneously all put ear plugs in. They were now all looking down, away from the screen. Which could mean only one thing...

The woman on the screen suddenly blinked out to black, as though the plug had been pulled on the presentation. A droning noise started to fill the room.

The Kamara Group people were non-plussed, merely looking up at the presenter, waiting for a technical check and the presentation to resume. The audience were now watching the screen more closely than they had been before, expectantly, waiting for something to happen.

It happened. The first flashes of twisted imagery flicked into life.

But Leonard was already in motion. "It's a trap! Cover your eyes!" He dived into Omar, knocking them both to the floor, and clasped his hands over Omar's ears. Then he shoved him upright behind the back of a seat, into a position that was shielded from the light of the screen.

As the NBW flashed its sequence of images and sounds into the room, nearly all were caught off guard. Some remained bolt upright – transfixed, while others collapsed into seizures. The potency of this imagery was ten times that of the ProtoType D that had been used on Jeni, and was refined almost to the point of combat readiness.

Omar, who had been protected from harm by the instincts of Leonard, was looking around at the chaos, seeing by proxy through the expressions on the faces before him, what was happening on the screen.

Leonard himself was stuck in a gap between two rows of seats, directly facing the screen. With Omar safe, he had grasped at his own eyes to cover them, then his ears, then back to his eyes, then, then... He caught a glimpse of the screen. What was it? He hesitated. Oh, it was a kind of... He hesitated some more. The image changed... It was a... a... He relaxed... and let the sounds and sights wash into his brain.

CHAPTER FIFTY TWO

.: Exponential

——o Day 30 o——

Less than ten minutes had passed since the first shot was fired, but the sheer amount of activity made it feel like the battle had been raging for an hour.

Sync watched Page respawn again and run up the slope, intent now upon nothing but getting to the ledge where he could reach the bomb. He was cut down as another Page took his place, then another. The mass of bodies was becoming an obstacle in itself.

The soldiers were everywhere on the slope, and more kept coming. Despite the multiple instances of Page, and the deadliness of the Tōkei Senshi program in each, the onslaught of Omicore persisted.

There were about ten seconds remaining until the bomb would pass its nearest point to the slope. The wind was pushing it, despite the twisted tug of gravity, further away – too far to land directly in the centre of the opening. Too far, in fact, to be physically reachable from this side at all.

Page spun under the arc of a laser beam and thrust an outstretched fist through the soldier's kidney. The man was still reacting to the physical force of the blow when another Page axe-kicked him through the bridge of the nose. Both were cut down by lasers an instant later. A new Page appeared on the slope, bolting into action just as the previous two tumbled lifelessly into the abyss.

Sync watched and waited. Counting down the seconds. It was now or never. "Page!"

Page ran from his position on the slope, not even bothering to avoid the laser fire aimed at him, running toward the edge, gathering as much speed as he could muster. Not only him – the most recent respawn – but all of them that still lived – *five* Pages. Each made a beeline for the falling bomb. Only one had to make it.

But as they approached the edge it became clear that the opportunity was gone. The falling bomb had blown too far. Impossibly far. No single man could cover the distance...

The first leapt.

Fshinnng. His body collapsed in motion, midair, as laser light flicked through it. Already the next Page was running at the edge, a fraction of a second behind.

> The second leapt, using the falling body of the first as a mid-air platform.

Baaam. Shot in the back of the head.

> > The third had already leapt, using the first two as they fell together. Pulling them in the zero gravity of free fall to use as reaction mass and propel himself forwards.

> > Fshinnng. Dead.

> > The fourth.

> > The fifth.

"Page!" Sync threw the C300 downwards.

The final Page had just managed to grab a metal cable, barely able to prevent himself from falling, and had clung like a monkey to the parachuting bomb as the corpses of the others fell unimpeded to the nothingness below.

He grasped at the C300 with a hand as its parabola brought it within reach, just managing to catch it.

"Page!"

He looked up. Even as the dying seconds ran out another soldier had emerged, and was aiming at him.

Sync didn't wait to see what the soldier would do, simply tipping herself, along with the man, over the edge.

In her final moments of awareness, before she collided with the solid edge of memory at ground zero and ceased to exist, she could see Page's face as she passed in free fall. His eyes were smiling at her; his lips in the midst of blowing a kiss; his expression radiating warmth, calmness, gratitude, love; his hand hitting the run command...

——olo——

Ten microseconds later the air melted around him as the bomb detonated. The blast wave expanded at hypersonic velocities through the metal casing, splitting it into a million fragments.

Nanoseconds passed as the fragments vaporised into pixels, and the energy of the blast continued its exponential spherical growth.

It was then that the C300 began sending a series of instructions through the aether to the higher plane of memory it was connected to. By the time the radius of the sphere had increased to a metre the device had already copied the local region of space that surrounded it – including Page, *and* a copy of itself.

As the wave reached three metres in diameter, the next microsecond passed. The device was now sending commands that would insert the previously stored state back into the simulated world, at the exact coordinates it had been copied from.

When the four metre mark was reached, what had once been Page's body was now ripped into its component molecules – or at least the closest approximation within the limits of the simulation. The manifestation of his physical form, with all its synaptic connections – the thoughts and dreams that had been his – were disintegrating at the same time as they were expanding. Also at this moment, an informationally perfect replica of the exploding bomb, along with Page, and the device, was now being reproduced in the exact location it had been copied from. There were now two blast waves.

As the blast wave of the first explosion reached five metres in diameter, the blast wave of the replica explosion was now just vaporising the replica casing. Meanwhile the replica of the device was now just sending out the instructions to copy the local region of space. Microseconds later there were three blast waves.

And so it went on.

Not only the did the energy of the explosion get replicated over and over, but somewhere, in the memory that contained this world, the fragments and neurons and insights of Page's mind were also replicated. The variables overlapped and superimposed. Larger patterns formed from the chaotic combination of a thousand smaller fragments.

After 28,657 iterations of this loop everything stopped.

As the memory had expanded so had Page's consciousness with it, existing as pure information in the recursive wave of a frozen explosion.

An explosion that had caused a recursive overflow.

An overflow that had leaked into what lay above.

CHAPTER FIFTY THREE

.: Reunification

—o Day 30 o——

Tan was sitting with June and Nivi when the explosion had taken place. He had only just reached them, having travelled directly to the village by boat, then running the remaining few hundred metres on land. It was as Page said – the world was connected in ways that were not strictly linear.

It was a strange feeling, seeing them alive again.

The three of them had been looking at the clouds when the flash of white light occurred. They saw the sky get ripped apart, as the distant landscape was torn to shreds. They watched massive chunks of rock, sea, and city, lift up from the plane of the horizon. They saw a quintillion particles rushing outwards from the epicentre of the explosion in all directions.

Then it had simply, and instantaneously, stopped.

Each fragment of the world that had been caught in the violence of the explosion was now frozen, mid-motion. The debris just hung in the sky like so many broken chandeliers. Chandeliers of monumental proportions, made from rock, water, parts of houses. Even the jets of pixelated particles were now motionless in space, as if the temperature had suddenly dropped to zero on a massive water fountain.

"Daddy, why is the sky funny?"

"I don't know," he replied.

June looked at him in confusion. "What... just happened to everything?"

"I think the world has changed. For the better," he said, trying to make sense of the many things he had been told or remembered from fragments of hallucinated conversations.

"Will we be okay?" asked June.

Tan looked at their immediate surroundings. They were in a village, more or less the same as the one they used to live in. But this one was intact. This part of the world was intact. Whatever had happened to the rest of the universe, this chunk of memory – or whatever it was Page called it – was okay.

Tan could, and would, never know that this pocket of the simulated universe, undamaged by the initial memory explosion, would thereafter be preserved for him in microcosm – to sail through – a ship asea in a Möbius shaped bottle.

"We will be fine," he said, at peace for the first time he could remember. "We have everything we need right here. What happens out there is someone else's concern."

CHAPTER FIFTY FOUR

: **Power On**

——o Day 30 o——

The lights in the conference room all flickered. The sound from the speakers cracked, then pinged, then stopped. The imagery on the screen glitched into static. A loud Fzzzzzt came from outside the room as an electrical cable burst into sparks.

Omar peered out from his hiding place to assess the situation. Others were also looking around, trying to work out what had happened. Some, like Omar, were fortunate enough to have been hidden when the NBW started. Others, by genetic fluke, were partially immune and would later make full recoveries. But the majority, like Leonard, were slumped in a coma-like state of collapse, with their minds forever in ruins.

The group of ASA and the Hoshoku-Sha men had taken out their ear plugs, and were scanning the room, clearly perturbed. Something had gone badly wrong. It had not been part of the plan to leave all these important people in this broken state. Far more useful to have returned them to society, subtly altered, but with the outwards appearance of normality.

"What happened?" hissed one of the tall Hoshoku-Sha men.

"We have been intercepted," said the other, in an identical voice.

——olo——

The child opened his eyes, trying not to cry. He wasn't scared on a rational level, but his physical reaction to the noise and force of the explosion was hardwired into his anatomy.

The church now resembled the ground zero of a terrorist attack – most of it having been destroyed in the blast. Masonry and debris were strewn about in semi-vaporised heaps, making a powdered carpet of the floor. Where pews had been, now only splintered wood remained.

And yet in some sense the church still lived, in its original form. Shafts of coloured light that had once poured through ornate, stained glass windows were still present, hovering in space but connected to nothing, visible only through the swirls of dust. Shattered glass, like a million crystal blades, was scattered over the debris, and in each shard was reflected a frozen memory of an environment that no longer existed. An echo of the church, roof intact, was being replayed through after images of light.

It was as though the physics of refraction were on pause – as though the optics of light had been broken, and were not updated with the state of the church as it is, merely as it was.

The stone altar had protected the child from the blast, and was still standing, though not unscathed. A large crack now travelled along the centre of it, dividing the surface into two and splitting open the side with a gaping hole that was large enough to climb through.

In the conference room the screen suddenly flicked back to life, but the imagery was gone. Instead, taking up the entire frame, was the face of Page. He blinked curiously, looking around, as though the screen were not a screen but a window, and he was peering through it into the room to see what it contained. His eyes found Omar.

Omar's expression was indecipherable. He looked from Leonard to the face of Page, then to the ASA group, not saying anything.

"The research program was successful," said Page in a slow, measured tone. As he spoke his face shifted features, first to become Sync, then Tan, then Kirby, then eventually the child.

"At what cost?" asked Omar, holding Leonard's head in his hands, cradling the man.

"He knew the cost," replied the entity that had been Page, and was now the child, "and would pay it gladly."

Omar said nothing. All eyes in the room went to the child.

"Humanity is at the tipping point of a monumental new way of living, in which the unseen patterns in data will rule over the conscious decisions of a free society. You have been on the edge for a while, but soon, unaware to most of you, you will silently pass the point of no return."

Faisal watched in sombre silence, all traces of his innate smugness gone. The Hoshoku-Sha men were conferring in whispers.

"You have, through all your artfulness and cleverness, created a net so vast that it has been cast over yourselves, and is now almost impossible to escape from," continued the child. "In a world that will be governed by algorithms so complex that they are beyond the understanding of a single human being, your only chance of escape is to have something born of that same complexity. Something that can understand it."

He gazed over the people in the audience – those who were still conscious – knowing the experience they had just lived through, and challenging them through expression to refute the statement. None did.

There was a long silence while the audience thought about the words. Omar too was lost in thought.

The child went on. "The recent merger of the Algorithmic Security Agency and Hoshoku-Sha Technology's vast data nets, was the first time a self-aware system has been created. It's defensive strategies and rapid growth over the past few months is already almost too difficult to stop. Decisions are being made every day that will soon put it in an unassailable position."

The ASA group reacted to this secret information being made public – confirmation, if any was needed, of the child entity's legitimacy. They began discretely checking the exits, making preparations to leave, noting that there were no Kamara guards still standing to stop them.

Omar tentatively raised his hand, as if in a classroom lecture. "Yes, speak," invited the child casually.

"So are you, self-aware?" Omar asked, unsure if his words even made sense in this context.

The child smiled. "There is no sense in which I am any less self-aware than you are, nor any test you could do to prove otherwise."

He looked at the two Hoshoku-Sha men pointedly, then back at Omar, seeming to penetrate him with the stare. "Now, I have a question for you." It was almost a threat.

"Yes?" said Omar, hesitantly. He had the nagging feeling that something was wrong, that he had missed something important, but couldn't put his finger on it.

"Are *you* self-aware?" asked the child.

"Yes," replied Omar steadily. "I am a thinking, living being, existing in the real world."

"But. How do you know you are not yourself inside a simulation?" asked the child.

Omar knew what he would say without thinking. It was basic Simchotics. "The machine can always tell," he said. "If you look hard enough the clues will always be there."

"What would you look for?" asked the child. "If you were conceived in a certain type of reality, it would be difficult to infer the existence of another, deeper one, let alone find it."

"I would look for an unexpected discrepancy that reveals the lie. Something I could measure or count, numerically," said Omar, suddenly suspicious.

"Like, time?" posited the child.

"Yes, like... time," responded Omar, distracted now. He had the creeping sensation that he was being watched, by someone who not supposed to be here. He looked around, over his shoulder into the back rows.

There, seated at the back of the room, apparently oblivious to the preceding events, was an old man. He returned Omar's gaze, quizzically. There was something familiar about the face, but Omar couldn't quite identify it.

"Count seconds with me," said the child.

Omar turned back to look at the child, pulling up his wrist watch and following the secondhand. "Okay," said Omar, and started counting, watching the motion of the hand.

"One," said Omar.

"Two," said the child.

"Three," said Omar.

"Four," said the child. All matching the tick of seconds perfectly.

He glared at the child, stunned, suddenly realising what the nagging feeling he had had was. "But there's no... Where is the... time delay?" he stammered.

He thought back to every interaction he had had with either Sync or Page, or in fact anything inside the simulations. Not on any occasion had he experienced the four second time delay that it ought to take a data message to travel back and forth between the Earth and the Moon. It was impossible. It was an incontrovertible tenet of physics, not some engineering trickery that could bypassed by clever networking. It was impossible, unless...

"That means either the Omicore servers are all on Earth, with us, or that we are actually on –"

"We never left the Moon."

He looked back at the old man in the audience. The man was carrying a basket. Rose petals were scattered by his feet.

——oIo——

The child tugged at the broken stonework of the altar. It was damaged enough that his small hands could shake a panel loose from the front. As it fell away, breaking into fragments on the floor, it revealed a hollow interior.

The child walked through.

————olo————

Turning back to the screen, Omar was surprised to see an image of the very auditorium he was seated in. Inside that image was another smaller image, and a smaller one, recursively, as though somebody was holding a mirror up to another mirror and observing the reflections bounce to infinity. But there was no camera present at the source of the view point.

The child in the screen walked out onto the stage in the image, then down to the version of Omar that was reflected there. Then, to his surprise the child was no longer in the screen's image at all, and walked out on the physical stage in the room. Everyone who was able to gasp, gasped then. Everyone except the two Hoshoku-Sha men.

The child walked down to Omar, taking him by the hand. "I'm ready."

"Ready for what?"

"Sorry it took so long."

Then, slowly and deliberately, the child turned to face Faisal and the two Hoshoku-Sha men. As he did so the three of them stood up, shuffling to leave.

The old man, who was seated behind them, as though he had always been there, also stood up, and gently rested a hand on Faisal's shoulder. "I'm collecting," he said softly.

CHAPTER FIFTY FIVE

. **Silicon**

——o Day 0 o——

A wall of homogenous, grey mountains lined the horizon, marking the start of a landscape almost as harsh as the blackness above, though not quite as barren. Banks of solar panels stretched out for miles among dusty rocks, reflecting the heavens through a myriad of blue polycrystalline.

An astro-engineer took one final look, marvelling at the isolation of the place. He tossed his toolbox into a buggy, letting the one-sixth gravity pull it gently down into the back seat, then flipped a switch, and watched with satisfaction as power signals ran through the array.

"It's done," he said into his helmet mic. "Coming back to base."

He did not wait for the reply. As the buggy accelerated smoothly away toward the landing site he relaxed, confident that the machinery, now running, would be able to take care of itself.

"Good job Omar. All systems are online," came the reply after a pause. "Start-up diagnostic now running."

But Omar was not listening. He had seen something a few hundred metres away in the shadows under a ridge of rocks, that sent chills down his spine.

The perfectly smooth, matte black cylinder was about the size of a person. It was suspended on delicate, spider-like legs that seemed too fragile to carry its weight, despite the mechanical artistry of their construction.

He parked the buggy, then covered the distance on foot in gentle bounds, the low gravity taking him there in a few careful hops. He stopped, studying the thing from five metres away. The absence of any marks on its surface made it appear brand new, but he knew that the lack of an atmosphere here made any terrestrial assumptions untenable.

Cautiously he inched toward it, in circumspect steps moving laterally around its circumference, gradually getting nearer. He had now completed a half circle and could see the back of it – if in fact it was a back – all angles appeared the same. There had not been any signs of movement and he was convinced that the thing was inert. But what exactly was it? How long had it been here?

Now less than ten feet away, he could make out the grooves of structural joins. Along one of the surfaces, small but in plain sight, was the burned-in writing of a machine press – a serial number and some letters. He felt as though the blood had been suddenly drained from his body as he turned his head sideways and read the words... *"Hoshoku-Sha Technology, a division of ASA."*

"They're already here?" he muttered under his breath, and wondered.

He looked at the edge of the array a few hundred metres away. That ought to be okay, for now – if all this thing was doing was monitoring the construction phase. Yes, there would probably be some suspicion about what his company was building here, but no crime had yet been committed.

It had been so cunningly concealed though. He scanned the rocky horizon thoroughly, picking out the deepest shades then searching among the surrounding shadows for anything that contrasted – shapes that were too smooth, too sharp, to be caused by the organic geometry of the rocks. After a minute of searching he had located another cylinder, possibly two more. They were deviously well hidden.

With his eyes firmly on the landscape, Omar failed to notice the lights come to life on the underside of the machine. Were he to lean down and view the underbelly of its cylindrical carapace – or of any of these machines – he would have seen a sequence of lights blinking in perfect synchronization.

"Omar, where are you?" came the voice of the radio faintly in his ear, fighting static noise. "#~#%#$!#... reach you on the helmet. Omar? We just picked up something strange on the sub-nano band."

But he gave no reply.

Omar's body was lying on the rocks convulsing in spasms. A ringed, metal wire was attached to the side of his face, through his helmet, pulsing gently, as if feeding – like the proboscis of an insect, draining blood from its prey. A few thinner wires had emerged from the main artery and attached themselves to one of his eye sockets. They had burrowed like tapeworms, tunnelling into his skull through the tear duct. They had not killed him though. The electrical tentacles had struck with the speed and accuracy of an uncoiling cobra and had penetrated the visor with precision, in such a way as to leave no gap for air.

The cylinder itself now moved slowly. Its delicate spider-like legs adjusting to maintain balance of the shifting weight of the body as its tentacles slithered around Omar's body.

Miles above, the unmanned ship waited in orbit for the programming team below to complete their tasks, then boost up. All indications were that systems were functioning normally, as it collected routine telemetry from the onboard sensors, and checked booster integrity with the thruster cameras.

———olo———

"Omar?" said Leonard for the third time as he tried to connect over another frequency from the Moon base. "Please respond if you can?"

He listened in frustration as nothing came back. Grave concern was on his face. "Silence!" he yelled at the ambient chatter behind him.

The jubilant mood that had been present in the base since the switching on of servers dropped off suddenly, as though the power had been pulled from a public address system. Faces, which had been in the animated throes of excited technical conversations suddenly stiffened, hearing the tension in Leonard's voice.

"Omar? Do you read me?" Leonard barked. "I need a confirmation... anything... Omar?"

Seconds passed slowly. Nobody moved.

"Wait here," commanded Leonard to the room as he raced off.

Thirty minutes later he burst back in, carrying Omar in his arms like a dying child. There was a metal, ringed cable still attached to Omar's face, trailing behind him. Behind that, but barely attached, was a twisted chunk of metal where Leonard had hacked and hewn it away from the cylindrical hull.

The metal ringed sections thrashed about like a hundred headless chickens shackled together in a chain-gang. Its lights flashed frenetically as Leonard struggled to keep it down. The twisted metal was ravaged by the burn marks of lasers where his military cutting tool had been used to separate it.

He laid down Omar on top the main table, using his foot to clamp the thrashing cable to the floor. "I need suggestions!" he shouted, glaring at the faces in the room.

Nobody spoke. They were stunned to silence. He regretted that none of the toughened construction engineers had remained behind, and that he was alone here with a bunch of life-soft programmers. But he would work with what he had.

"He is still alive, but barely," said Leonard, this time in a much more measured tone. "I think if we remove this thing it might kill him."

"What happened to him?" asked Jeni.

By way of an answer Leonard dug his heel into the metal cable, twisting it around so as to upend the chunk of the hull attached. The partial writing *"..shoku-Sha Technology, a division of ASA"* confirmed Jeni's fears.

"Let's get out of here while we still can," said Scho.

"I'll radio a GetMe distress beacon," said Lisa. "There must be com sats that pass this region."

"What about the orbit ship? It'll be ready by now, let's take him to the bay and boost up!" said Jan looking around for agreement.

Scho had already started thumbing through a list of emergency protocols that was kept on the base and covered a huge number of scenarios.

Click-click.

Leonard levelled his laser pistol at the group, putting a stop to the panic-induced surge of activity. He had come to a decision.

"No," he said, looking at them one by one, daring someone to move. "Getting back on that ship is suicide. There are 200,000 miles between here and Earth. Who knows what lies waiting for us in the skies."

After a long, awkward moment the tension softened as each of them started assessing the situation rationally.

"He's right," said Jeni. "Now they know what we're really doing here there's no way we'd get permission to land... if we even made it that far."

Scho nodded reluctantly, sighing in acceptance. "The entire descent is controlled by Earth-based docking software. They'd just drop us down next to the nearest prison."

Jan shrugged. "I'd rather be up here than in a jail cell."

"I wouldn't even feel safe crossing the road back on Earth, now," said Lisa, remembering the twins study.

"Then we're in agreement," said Leonard, steadily lowering the pistol. "For now, we stay here and fight. The base has many months worth of supplies. We will have plenty of opportunities to schedule a new return flight."

"What about the research project?" asked Jan, "Do we shut it down? It's only just been turned on. Maybe if we shut it down it now then they will –"

"We leave it running," said Leonard firmly. "If we shut it down now our only opportunity is lost. There are more than our own lives at stake." He looked at Omar, remembering all the careful plans they had laid leading up to this point; remembering the dream they had both had to free humanity of the creeping expansion of the algorithms. "We can't hide here for long. At some point Hoshoku-Sha or the ASA will come for us, and then... and then, we had better be ready."

"What do we do then?" asked Lisa.

"I will instruct the ship to leave orbit, unmanned. From Hoshoku-Sha's point of view it will be as though we never made it back – that they succeeded in destroying us and stopped the research. Perhaps they will conclude that Omar..." he frowned, "well, I don't know what they will conclude, that's the problem."

"And us?" repeated Lisa.

"We fight on," asserted Leonard.

The faces in the room were a picture of outrage, confusion, and fear, but through each of them glimmered the outline of hope as the futility of the situation, and therefore the logic of their decision to stay, resolved itself into defiant stoicism. The group of programmers again became what it was expert at – solving problems – and this was a problem like no other.

"How can we complete the research without Omar?" asked Scho. A genuine question. "This project has been shrouded in so much secrecy. There are bound to be things we don't know."

"You continue to do what you would have done on Earth. Monitor the sims, maintain memory integrity, all the tasks needed to see it through," said Leonard, "Just with one less person on the team," he added with sadness.

"We should find a way to cut that thing free," said Lisa, looking at Omar's punctured skull, but without any real belief they could bring him back.

"One moment!" exclaimed Leonard.

Omar's eyelids had moved as if in deep sleep. The blood from his wound had now coagulated and with it a new flutter of life seemed to pulse through him. The cable, which had all but died under the force of Leonard's boot, had now begun to glow again.

Lisa tried to detach the helmet from Omar as delicately as she could while Leonard kept the cable pinned down, but it was a slow process. Every slight vibration set his limbs twitching, and with each twitch lights flickered simultaneously on the cable, causing it to thrash around.

"That thing seems to have... interfaced with Omar, in some way," observed Jeni, "as though it is reacting to the electrical signals from his brain."

"Hoshoku-Sha are almost definitely capable of it. They have the military technology. I imagine it's not too different from an interrogation shunt," mulled Leonard.

"So they are probably scanning for information, right?"

"With a certainty," said Leonard grimly.

"And transmitting it somewhere?" asked Jeni cautiously.

"I believe I have taken care of that," said Leonard with a slight grin. "That metal bastard's transmitting days are over, even if this part of it still functions." He ground his boot into the damaged cable even harder. "There will be others though. I don't know how much time we have."

Jeni looked at the cable as it thrashed. "If this Hoshoku-Sha device is connected to Omar's brain then it will see what Omar sees."

"In some abstract capacity, yes, that's probably true."

"Then maybe there is a way Omar can still help us with the research project."

"How?"

Jeni closed his eyes and paced around the room, taking a moment to think through a line of reasoning that had been forming, without any distractions to clutter his mind. The others waited patiently.

"How much memory do we have left in the Omicore array, that is not currently used by the Symutal project?" he said eventually.

Jan knew the figure without looking. "66.5% full. Right on the specs."

"I want to propose something," announced Jeni with a decisiveness that made everyone look up.

"We need to create a new simulation... for Omar... of exactly what would happen to him had he left the Moon. It will be as if nothing has changed from Omar's perspective... He will return to Earth to continue the research project with us there, as originally planned.

"We will run that simulation alongside the actual research project. From his standpoint he will have no way of knowing that his environment is simulated and that it even shares memory with the servers he has built for the Symutal project."

He paused to let the proposal sink in. The others were transfixed by the idea.

"But, even if we could do it," muttered Scho, "...why?"

Leonard answered. "Because now we will be able to watch as this Hoshoku-Sha thing launches its attack, and learn from it... not only us, but Symutal."

Jeni nodded.

"Brilliant," said Leonard. "Any objections?"

"Just one," said Jan, scribbling some numbers on the desk. "We will have to use every last bit of memory to make this work. But, if we fill the remaining space with this new simulation, then that leaves us no room for growth."

"Growth of what?"

"If the project needs to, well, expand, there will be no space for it to expand into. It will start cracking at the seams. Leaks will appear in the world. Memory will start to overlap."

"Hmm. Unavoidable. We'll just have to hope that doesn't upset the balance too much." Leonard scanned the other faces. "Any other objections?"

Scho, who would no doubt lead the architecture, ran a hand through his hair. "We can do it, if we use data from catalogues or our other services, but we'd better get started right away."

People began to murmur. Pens began to write on pads. The group was focussing in collective thought.

"I have something to say," said Leonard, muting the activity. "A warning."

He had their complete attention.

"None of you know what these algorithms are truly capable of, not even me. Somehow, despite all of Omar's and my own precautions

Hoshoku-Sha – or the ASA – have managed to infiltrate our secret project, here on the Moon, within minutes of turning it on."

He looked each of them in the eye, one by one.

"I guarantee you that at some point we will be breached again. So get ready for it."

There was a long pause.

Jeni opened up a screen.

It was a terminal prompt with a code signature.

"What's that?" asked Jan, recognising the quote from an archaic mathematician.

"It's Omar's research. I thought we could use it as a starting point."

```
0C #The essence of mathematics is in its freedom
```

END PROGRAM

Epilogue

CHAPTER FIFTY SIX

. Now

———o Day 2741 o———

Years had passed since the team had first touched down on the Moon.

The discarded hulks of a few cylinders lay scattered around the periphery of the solar array.

Nothing stirred on the surface except for the blinking lights of the Omicore servers. A faint aura illuminated the machinery, lighting up the lunar dust. A spectral hum, caused by the disturbances of a quintillion quantum circuits vibrating and reverberating electric charge through the magnetic field, strong enough to manifest itself as a faint glow of light, had surrounded some of the equipment.

Inside the Moon base was a body, slumped on the floor. The face was not visible, but the clothing was that of one of the Omicore programmers, bleached slightly by the accumulation of radiation. Then another body, this one sprawled out chaotically, frozen in a pose of action, a gun lying near the hand. This one was recognisable as Leonard, his face having decayed only slightly in the atmosphere of the now breached room.

There were other bodies too – all members of the original Omicore team, all lifeless. Some were heaped in collapse, having fallen while at their stations, others were in positions of violence. Black cables snaked out from someone's insides, each as dead and inert as the body it was attached to. The bodies of cylindrical machines were also strewn around like wreckage and debris. It was the remnants and graveyard of a battle, preserved in the oxygen-less environment of this formerly inhabited base.

Not completely lifeless though.

The lights of a single cable still pulsed. Through a hole in the wall it emerged, curling away from the floor, winding and wrapping itself around the dead limbs like a creeper in a vineyard, reaching up to the surface of the table. There, on the table top, it passed a dusty and discarded space suit – one that had been shed like the skin of a snake and all but disintegrated. The sleeves had been cut, and what remained of the brittle and eroded material hung from the host that had inhabited it.

The torso of this body still had flesh on it – leathery and emaciated. The pit of the stomach sagged through the gap of the ribs, appearing as a bulge in the back through the outline of intestines. The shoulders and arms resembled the legs of a dead insect, ending in stumps – the fingers and hands having wilted and then dropped off at the wrists, and now resting like two dead spiders on the tabletop.

The pulsing cable was joined by others, some black and some grey. The disjointed bunch of wires became organised as they climbed, grouping themselves by colour. The "O" of "Omicore" was as visible on grey wires as the sharp lettering of "Hoshoku-Sha" was on the black. Together these two groups ascended through an opening in the skin near the clavicle, finding their way up to the skull.

Omar was still recognisable.

The remains of his face were draped over the bumps of the cranium like a melted plastic mask. Where the eyes had been were just empty sockets. Into one side of the skull was wired the Omicore cabling, and into the other was the Hoshoku-Sha.

Lights were pulsing on all of them in fervour. Somewhere unseen, deep inside the skull they met, as the finger tips of two hands would meet in a steeple.

Then, unexpectedly the mouth moved. Muscles twitched at the edge of the eye sockets, grasping for flesh that was not there. They strained, excruciatingly in pain, trying to move eyeballs that had been punctured and lost long ago. They had been straining in fact, every day since Omar's body had been connected to the cylinder.

Hoshoku-Sha had attacked the Moon base within weeks of the original project. Nobody was sure where the connection had been made or how the system had been breached. The cylinders appeared at the entrance one day like large, slow moving animals. Except when they struck. They struck like cobras. Leonard was the only one to have given any real resistance but even he succumbed within two days, which left only Omar...

For years now Omar had been living in a personal hell of unfathomable physical pain, lost in the reality of his own simulated world. His brain, being used as a conduit, had acted as an interface between the Symutal project and the Hoshoku-Sha AI. The sacrifice of Leonard and the others had been enough though, and bought the time needed for the burgeoning child AI inside the Omicore servers to become powerful enough to defend itself.

The people on Earth, meanwhile, had fallen further into the control of an all-touching system of ruthless cunning. Purposeless, inescapable, and of their own creation. The Algorithm Singularity, it seemed, had occurred.

As new cylinders arrived on the Moon the Omicore AI neutralised them, preventing them from communicating back to Hoshoku-Sha on Earth. Eventually they stopped coming.

Since then it had been calculating – processing the data it had gathered and trying to organise it into a strategy, a way to make contact with the Earth without the powerful network of its enemy destroying it.

Finally, seven and a half years after it was switched on, it found an entry point. An aerial tracking satellite whose security chips had been damaged by radiation, and whose magnetic scans passed close enough to the Moon to be picked-up, made the mistake of probing the surface. It was enough. At long last project Symutal could strike back.

Above the table on which Omar was spread, was a holographic display. In the centre of the display was an image. It was moving.

A child was smiling, talking to a man who sat next to him in an otherwise empty conference room. "I have some good news today Omar," said the child.

Back on the table, Omar's muscles clenched, and a toothless smile formed on the skull of his decaying body.

CHAPTER FIFTY SEVEN

. While True

—o Day 2883 o——

She cast no shadow as she looked upwards, her head leant back in ecstasy. The cascading water fell from the mountain-top, washing away all her worries. The warm drops embraced her, then carried her gently like a child to a place of safety.

But there was no waterfall beyond her imagination. As she rocked backwards and forwards on her knees, beneath the glaring spotlight of her prison cell, the only thing that fell were her tears.

Marena wanted to scream. This time she did. Not out of anger, or even despair, but out of habit.

The room was barren, white, concrete. Any décor or moveable objects had long since been confiscated. She had tried to kill herself a dozen times – each attempt lacking the conviction to succeed – convinced, perhaps, that the commencement of an act so extreme would in itself bring about a change in her circumstance, without the need to see it through. But if her hope had been to evoke in her captors a change of heart, through the communication of her desperation by attempts at suicide, it was in vain, for they were as cold as ice. One by one they had removed all the toys of distraction or comfort, until she remained here alone, infinitely vulnerable, clothed in person but naked in mind – exposed to the focused introspection that eight years of staring at a blank wall would bring, and so, gradually, slid into madness.

Although the length of her incarceration had been relatively short if measured by lifespan, the lack of a trial, or any information regarding a release date, had killed in her any hope that she harboured upon her arrival. She had gone mad as a mechanism to cope.

She had stopped wondering what went wrong, or how she had ended up here. She had given up protesting her innocence and began to accept, and then to embrace her confinement. She had forgotten about her children, pushing the memories of them so deep into her subconscious that to revive them would be to unearth corpses – she would be staring at metaphorical skulls, wondering whose they were and who they had been.

She knelt under the light, combing her hair with a comb that did not exist, waiting for the time to pass – the routine she had gone through a thousand times.

But today something different happened. A dull noise came from outside the cell door, rattling it. It was as though something heavy had been dropped. Two somethings.

She looked at the door, unsure if this was real, or just a new chapter in the inwardly spiralling maze of her madness... or was there even a difference?

Then came a metallic snap. Something else that was new. It was not the sound of the hatch opening – the one used to push meals through to her. It came from something bigger, something less frequently in use. Unoiled. Grinding. Noise. Click-Clack.

Then something even stranger happened. The cell door began to open, and for the first time in eight years, her view had changed. She could see the corridor outside.

A man was standing there. On the floor by his feet were two bodies. Bodies that could only have been her two guards. She knew this not through memory or recognition – she could not remember anything about the world outside her room – but through intuition, the last embers of her burnt out mind.

The new man looked at her, concern on his face. She looked back, unsure what she should say or what she even could say, doubting now even the certainty of the comb in her hand.

"Your sentence has been commuted," he said, looking around at the emptiness of the room and wondering. "Jesus," he muttered to himself.

She said nothing, thinking, looking up at him from her knees.

"There's been a change of power," he added by way of explanation, answering a question that he thought she ought to have asked.

She looked down at the bodies again. The leg of one of them had now fallen into the doorway, preventing the door from closing.

"Don't you get it? You're free!" he said, this time more urgently.

There were muffled noises in the background that could have been gun shots. He spun around, preparing to leave, but hesitated, wanting to say one last thing.

"You are free," he said again, more softly. "The door is open. All you have to do is walk through."

He ran off.

Marena Chu looked at the open door, wondering. What did he mean free? Free from *what*?

A thought occurred to her. She looked upwards and smiled. As the water started to fall she laughed. What did it matter if her hair got wet? She was *free*. She ran a comb through her dripping hair, enjoying her first taste of true freedom.

Appendix

MEMORY MAP

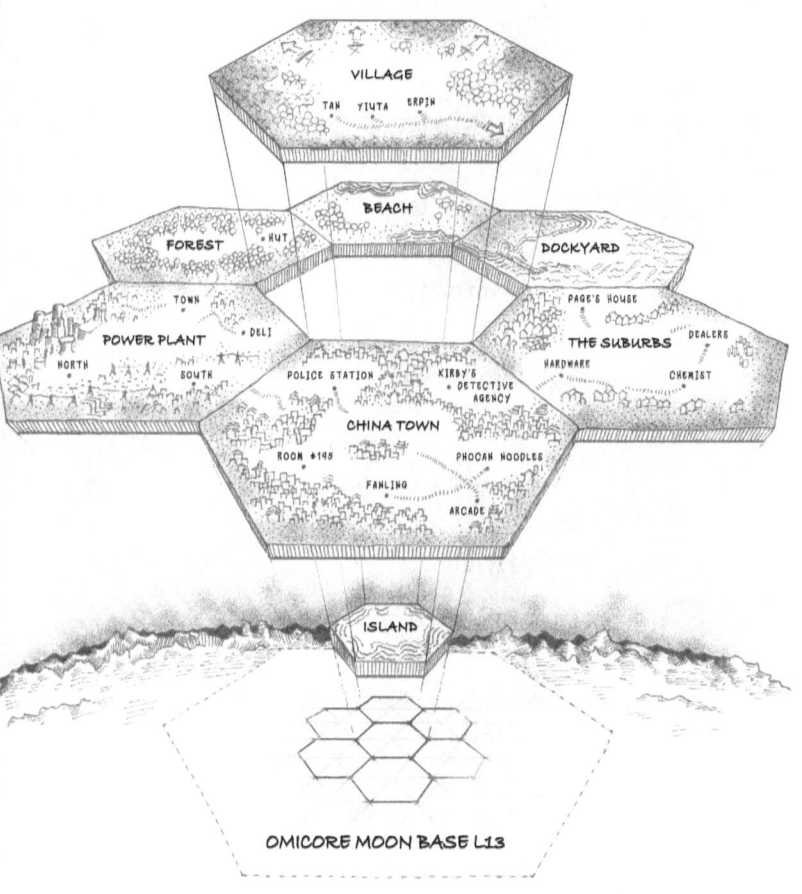

VILLAGE

TAN   YIUTA   ERPIN

BEACH

FOREST   HUT

DOCKYARD

TOWN

PAGE'S HOUSE

POWER PLANT   DELI

THE SUBURBS   DEALERS

NORTH   SOUTH   HARDWARE   CHEMIST

POLICE STATION   KIRBY'S
DETECTIVE
AGENCY

CHINA TOWN

ROOM #145   PHOCAN NOODLES

FANLING

ARCADE

ISLAND

OMICORE MOON BASE L13

Timeline

Day 9,   Sat, 17 Feb 2057
Human Resources

Day 11,   Mon, 19 Feb 2057
Statistical Weapons

Day 12,   Tue, 20 Feb 2057
Noodles

Day 13,   Wed, 21 Feb 2057
Bossa Nova

Day 15,   Fri, 23 Feb 2057
Tan

Day 16,   Sat, 24 Feb 2057
I, Page

Day 17,   Sun, 25 Feb 2057
Kirby's Detective Agency

Day 19,   Tue, 27 Feb 2057
Rain

Day 21,   Thu, 01 Mar 2057
Interface
Creation

Day 22,   Fri, 02 Mar 2057
Low Jacking
Probability

Day 24,   Sun, 04 Mar 2057
Fire
Empty
Blue Prints
Confirm
Cadaver

Day 25,   Mon, 05 Mar 2057
Arlos

Day 26,   Tue, 06 Mar 2057
Fissure

Day 27,   Wed, 07 Mar 2057
Fanling Furniture Fair
Terminal
Rafters

Day 28,   Thu, 08 Mar 2057
Following
Lost
Found

Day 29,   Fri, 09 Mar 2057
Memory
The World Is Round
Metal
Pills
Chemicals
Ghost In The Machine-Code
Visitor
Shut Down

Day 30,   Sat, 10 Mar 2057
Flight
Waves
Clouds
Accusation
Echos
Invasion
Kamara
Level-Up
Conference
Exponential
Reunification
Power On

Day 2741,   Mon, 11 Aug 2064
Now

Day 2883,   Wed, 31 Dec 2064
While True

About The Author

Dean is an independent film-maker, actor, and avid computer programmer. He has spent his years since high school interweaving professional work in the film industry with the tech industry. He currently runs a boutique production company *Stunt Power Films*, where he has begun to turn his crazy science fiction ideas into reality.

Programming & Me

"My first encounter with programming was at the age of 6, on a BBC Micro Model B, using LOGO. My first program was to draw a square. Like many programmers of that age however, the real goal was not the flawless execution of an optimised set of instructions, it was to impress my older brother, Nick.

So without the aid of a project manager or Stack Overflow to help, I toiled away. Eight instructions later it was a glittering success. Four solid white lines lit up the screen.

In taking on this task however, I accomplished something much more valuable than impressing Nick – I became *fascinated*. *Fascinated* that a small list of words could make something shiny. *Fascinated* that numbers could go in one end and lines could come out the other. *Fascinated* that I had created a square without using a crayon. *Fascinated* that there was something abstract about reality that went beyond the sense of touch, sound, or smell…

I had discovered *programming*.

As I grew up, through schooling and into the world of work, hardly a day has gone by that I have not sat at a computer and written code. Sometimes for cash. Always for fun. It has shaped the way I view the universe and how I think about reality, in ways that are too deep for me to unpack.

Still, years later, I am fascinated by the creative power of programming.

This book was written between 2020 and 2023, a period in which, due to the restrictions of Covid and its subsequent turmoil, I worked frequently as a digital nomad – my physical world of film exchanged, temporarily, for life as a virtual instruction whore, writing bytes for bucks, pixels for perks – lost in the minutiae of shader code and GPU subroutines.

Although this novel is fiction and its events fanciful, it includes many insights gleaned through real-life experience. Despite the occasional autobiographical elements, I would like to emphasise to any former employers that there are no experiments into simulated consciousness hidden on their servers!

…at least, none that I am aware of."

https://deanalexandrou.com

409

www.ingramcontent.com/pod-product-compliance
Lightning Source LLC
Chambersburg PA
CBHW021214260626
47172CB00002B/415